# DARK CREED

THE TORTURED ASTROPATH smiled in relief as the barrel of a bolt pistol was pressed to his temple. The shot was deafening in the holding cell. Blood splattered the walls.

'What is it, Coadjutor?' came the voice of Proconsul Ostorius over the grainy vox-unit. 'What did the astropath foresee?'

'Chaos,' was all that Aquilius said as he holstered his bolt pistol.

*In the same series*

Book 1: DARK APOSTLE

Book 2: DARK DISCIPLE


*Warhammer novels*

KNIGHT ERRANT
MARK OF CHAOS
EMPIRE IN CHAOS

A WARHAMMER 40,000 NOVEL

Word Bearers

# DARK CREED

## Anthony Reynolds

*To my friends and family, to Nick and Lindsey and everyone else at BL, and above all to Jacquie, thank you all for your patience and understanding.*

**A BLACK LIBRARY PUBLICATION**

First published in Great Britain in 2010 by
The Black Library,
Games Workshop Ltd.,
Willow Road, Nottingham,
NG7 2WS, UK.

10 9 8 7 6 5 4 3 2 1

Cover illustration by Klaus Sherwinski.

A CIP record for this book is available from the British Library.

ISBN13: 978 1 84416 787 6

Distributed in the US by Simon & Schuster
1230 Avenue of the Americas, New York, NY 10020, US.

See the Black Library on the Internet at
**www.blacklibrary.com**

Find out more about Games Workshop
and the world of Warhammer 40,000 at
**www.games-workshop.com**

Printed and bound in the US.

IT IS THE 41st millennium. For more than a hundred centuries the Emperor has sat immobile on the Golden Throne of Earth. He is the master of mankind by the will of the gods, and master of a million worlds by the might of his inexhaustible armies. He is a rotting carcass writhing invisibly with power from the Dark Age of Technology. He is the Carrion Lord of the Imperium for whom a thousand souls are sacrificed every day, so that he may never truly die.

YET EVEN IN his deathless state, the Emperor continues his eternal vigilance. Mighty battlefleets cross the daemon-infested miasma of the warp, the only route between distant stars, their way lit by the Astronomican, the psychic manifestation of the Emperor's will. Vast armies give battle in His name on uncounted worlds. Greatest amongst his soldiers are the Adeptus Astartes, the Space Marines, bio-engineered super warriors. Their comrades in arms are legion: the Imperial Guard and countless planetary defence forces, the ever-vigilant Inquisition and the tech-priests of the Adeptus Mechanicus to name only a few. But for all their multitudes, they are barely enough to hold off the ever-present threat from aliens, heretics, mutants – and worse.

TO BE A man in such times is to be one amongst untold billions. It is to live in the cruellest and most bloody regime imaginable. These are the tales of those times. Forget the power of technology and science, for so much has been forgotten, never to be re-learned. Forget the promise of progress and understanding, for in the grim dark future there is only war. There is no peace amongst the stars, only an eternity of carnage and slaughter, and the laughter of thirsting gods.

# PROLOGUE

THE ANIMAL STINK of humanity rose up the bladed sides of the Basilica of the Word, borne on hot updrafts, mingling with the heavy scent of incense and the metallic bite of freshly spilt blood. Behind it, the electric tang of Chaos hung in the air.

A balcony jutted from one of the basilica's great spires, five kilometres above the heaving masses below. The surface of the daemon world Sicarus was a honeycomb of mausoleums and temples, though from this height, it was partially obscured by blood-red clouds that whipped around the spires. Two holy warriors stood side by side upon the balcony, gazing across the skyline of their adopted home world.

Immense towers and shrines strained towards the burning heavens as far as the eye could see, and ten thousand mournful corpse-bells tolled. Moans of pain and rapture rose from the millions of proselytes

in the streets, the morbid sound carried on rising
thermals exhaled from the subterranean blood-
furnaces and daemonic forges.

Skinless daemons circled overhead. Others stripped
the flesh from the tens of thousands of living sacrifices impaled on the flanks of the basilica's spires.

The flayed skin curtain behind the pair of holy warriors rippled.

'Let them expose themselves,' said Erebus, First
Chaplain of the Word Bearers. His voice was low and
dangerous. 'Find out how deep the river of their corruption runs.'

The holy demagogue's head was shaved and oiled.
The skin across his scalp was inscribed with intricate
cuneiform, his flesh forming a living *Book of Lorgar*.
Erebus's eyes were cold and dead, giving away nothing. In their reflective darkness Marduk saw himself,
the lurid flames of the æther burning behind him.

'As you wish, my lord,' said Marduk.

'They will seek to deceive and to confuse. They will
undermine you, and try to sway your loyalty and the
loyalty of your captains. Trust only your own council
and judgement.'

'I understand, my lord,' said Marduk. 'I shall not fail
you.'

'See that you do not.'

Erebus's gaze remained fixed on a point beyond the
horizon, and Marduk followed it.

Though there was nothing to be seen bar the endless landscape of spires, domed cathedrals and
gehemehnet towers, Marduk knew where Erebus 's
thoughts lay.

It seemed an eternity had passed since blessed Lorgar had removed himself from his adoring Legion. It

had been thousands of years since the golden-skinned daemon-primarch had isolated himself within the Templum Inficio, forbidding any to disturb his meditations. Great had been the lamentation within the Hosts when the holy daemon-primarch had made his will known, for never had they been without the glorified one, the *Urizen* as he was known amongst the warrior brethren. Surrounded by a desert of bones, the Templum Inficio had been constructed by eight million slave-adepts, all of whom had given their lives upon its completion, staining the temple stones with their blood. As the voices of the Legion rose as one in mourning, the great doors of the templum were sealed, never to be opened until Lorgar's vigil was over.

Centuries rolled into millennia, yet every day hundreds of thousands of blood-candles were still lit in Lorgar's name. His name was whispered on the tortured lips of ten million penitents praying for his return.

In his absence, the Council of Sicarus continued to guide the flock, ensuring that the Legion maintained its adherence to Lorgar's teachings.

'He will return to us, my lord?' asked Marduk.

'In his own time,' assured Erebus. 'Have faith, Apostle.'

Marduk touched the glyph of Lorgar branded on his forehead, murmuring a prayer. He lifted his gaze, squinting into the burning atmosphere and the glory of the raw immaterium.

Thirteen immense battleships hung in low orbit overhead, motionless and menacing; five complete Hosts, ready to embark upon a dark crusade against the hated Imperium. His ship, the *Infidus Diabolus,* was amongst the deadly shoal, her flanks bristling with cannons and launch bays, steeples and shrine towers rising above her armoured hull.

'The crusade awaits you, Marduk,' said Erebus. 'May the blessing of Lorgar be upon you.'

'And you, my master,' said Marduk, bowing low. He turned and strode from the balcony, sweeping the flayed skin curtain aside.

Erebus watched him go then turned to face the distant horizon.

'Come then, my brothers,' he said. 'Make your play against me.'

# BOOK ONE: THE BOROS GATE

*'Five there shall be, by blood, sin and oath, five cardinals Colchis born, united in bonds of Brotherhood. Hearken! Rejoice! Harbingers of darkness they, augurs of the fall. And lo! With fury of hellfire, truth, and orb of ancient death, the gate shall be claimed. And so it shall come to pass; the beginning of the End. Glory be!'*

– Translation from the *Rubric Apocalyptica*

# CHAPTER ONE

FANGED MOUTHS OF a dozen grotesque misericords exhaled incense, filling the dimly lit shuttle interior. Seated shoulder to shoulder, their genetically enhanced bodies encased in thick plate the colour of congealed blood, the warriors of the Host sat in meditative silence, breathing the heavy smoke.

Hunched figures shuffled up the aisles, daubing the warriors' armour with sacred unguents. Their features were hidden beneath deep cowls. They hissed devotional prayers and blessings as they went about their work.

Kol Badar waved them away with a snarl, sending them scurrying.

Heavily scarred from thousands of years of bitter warfare, his face was lit from below by the ruby-red internal glow of his ancient Terminator armour. His head was dwarfed by the immensity of the armoured suit within which he was permanently sealed. Segmented cabling pierced the necrotised flesh at the base of his neck and at his temples.

'Initialising docking sequence,' croaked a mechanised voice. Kol Badar was jolted as the shuttle's retro-thrusters kicked in.

Uncoupling himself from the bracing restraints, Kol Badar rose and stalked down the darkened aisles of the Stormbird. Each heavy metallic step was accompanied by the whir of servo-motors and the hiss of venting steam. Seven holy warriors of the cult of the Anointed, the warrior elite of the Host, had been chosen to accompany the Dark Apostle and his entourage, and they bowed their heads low in respect as Kol Badar passed them.

The Anointed were the blood-soaked veterans of a thousand wars. Proud and zealous, each was a holy champion of Lorgar in his own right. They wore ancient suits of Terminator armour, their heavy gauge ceramite plates inscribed with scripture and hung with fetishes and icons. This armour had been in the service of the Legion since before the fall of Horus, lovingly maintained and repaired over the long millennia by the Legion's chirumeks.

Stabilising jets roared, and the Stormbird shuddered as docking maglocks clamped into place. Burning red blister lights flashed, and the scream of the engines began to subside. Reams of data scrolled before Kol Badar's eyes. He reviewed the information feed swiftly before blinking it away.

'Honour guard, at the ready.'

As one the Anointed brethren released their restraints and stood to attention as the shuttle lowered to the deck of the immense battleship.

Mechanical clicks and whines accompanied final diagnostic tests. Weapons were checked and loaded.

The pneumatic stabilisers of the shuttle settled. With a hiss of equalising pressure and a burst of super-heated steam, the assault ramp of the shuttle unfolded and slammed down on the deck. Kol Badar led the Anointed down the ramp. Tracking for targets, they stepped aboard the *Crucius Maledictus*.

An Infernus-class battleship, one of the largest vessels to have fought in the Great Crusade, the *Crucius Maledictus* was the flagship of the Dark Apostle Ekodas. The battleship had suffered calamitous damage fighting against the fleets of the Khan in the last days before Horus's fall, but had managed to limp to the safety of the Maelstrom. Extensively repaired, modified and re-armed upon the daemonic forge-world of Ghalmek, it now ranked amongst the most heavily armed and armoured battleships in the Word Bearers arsenal, rivalling even Kor Phaeron's *Infidus Imperator*.

The docking bay of the *Crucius Maledictus* was immense, with curved arches rising a hundred metres overhead. Ancient banners and kill-pennants hung down the length of giant pillars, recounting the victories of the 7th Company Host. Two other assault shuttles had already docked. They seemed small and insignificant within the vastness of the docking bay, which was far bigger than any aboard the *Infidus Diabolus*. Kol Badar merely scowled, unimpressed, and glared at the serried ranks of Astartes waiting for them.

There were more than two thousand Word Bearers, standing motionless, bolters clasped across deep red chest plates. The 7th was one of the largest and most decorated Hosts in the Word Bearers Legion, and their

Dark Apostle Ekodas was counted as close confidant of the Keeper of the Faith, Kor Phaeron. Ten ranks deep on either side, the warrior brothers of the 7th formed a grand corridor leading towards the titanic blastdoors at the far end of the docking bay, four hundred metres away. A blood-red carpet had been rolled out between them along its length.

There was no welcoming party, no fanfare to honour them as they came aboard the *Crucius Maledictus*. Annoyed, Kol Badar barked an order to his brethren. The Anointed fell into line at the foot of the Storm-bird's assault ramp, four warriors to a side. The sound of them slamming their fists against their chests echoed sharply. Kol Badar turned his back on the warriors of the 7th to wait for Marduk, his Dark Apostle and master, to emerge from the Stormbird.

His expression darkened. Master, he thought hatefully. The whelp should never have risen so far. He would have killed the whoreson that day on the moon of Calite long ago had Jarulek not restrained him.

Marduk appeared at the top of the ramp. Kol Badar's power talons twitched involuntarily.

Dark Apostle of the 34th Grand Host, the third leader to have borne such a title, Marduk wore a cold, disdainful expression as he gazed upon the might of the 7th. His deathly pale features were aristocratic and noble, the gene-lineage of blessed Lorgar blatantly apparent. His left eye was red and lidless, bisected by a narrow pupil. His jet-black hair was oiled, and he wore it long, hanging in an intricate braid down his back.

A thick fur cloak was draped over his shoulders and he wore a cream-coloured tabard secured around his waist with a heavy chain.

His red power armour was ornate and heavily artificed, a bastardised blend of plate from various eras,
ranging from his segmented MkII Crusade-pattern
greaves, to his reinforce-studded MkV-era left shoulder
plate. Every centimetre of it had been painstakingly
etched with ornate script. Hundreds of thousands of
words were carved around his vambraces and upon
his kneepads – litanies, scripture and extracts from the
*Book of Lorgar*. His left vambrace was engraved with the
third book of the Tenets of Hate in its entirety, and
dozens of sacred passages and psalms encircled his
pauldrons. Strips of cured skin bearing further epistles
and glyphs were affixed to his plate by rune-stamped
blood-wax.

In his hands, Marduk bore his sacred crozius
arcanum. A hallowed artefact consecrated in the blood
of Guilliman's lapdogs, the dark crozius was a master-
crafted weapon and holy symbol of awesome power.

Flicking his cloak imperiously over one shoulder,
Marduk began to descend the Stormbird's assault
ramp towards the floor of the docking bay. Following
a step behind him came two other power-armoured
figures.

The one on the left, Burias, moved with a swordsman's grace. Gene-born in the last days of the Great
War, Burias was a flamboyant, vicious warrior. His
black hair was combed straight and hung to his waist,
and he bore the sacred three-metre-tall icon of the
34th in both hands. There was not a scar or blemish
upon the Icon Bearer's cruelly handsome face; Burias
was one of the possessed, and his powers of regenera-
tion were impressive.

The other was more of an unknown to Kol Badar,
and was a stark contrast to the Icon Bearer. Shorter

and with a heavier build than most warriors of the
Legion, his broad face was a mess of scar tissue. His
downcast eyes were set beneath a protruding brow,
giving him a brutish appearance at odds with his
genetic heritage. His almost translucent skull was
shaved smooth and covered in jagged scars and
pierced with cables. A black beard bound into a single, tight braid hung half way down his barrel chest.
His armour was without ornamentation and he wore
an unadorned black robe. His hands were hidden
within heavy sleeves. A double-handed power maul
hung over his shoulders, and a chained and pad-
locked book dangled at his waist.

While Kol Badar had fought alongside Marduk,
Burias and every other member of the Host during the
Great War, First Acolyte Ashkanez had only joined the
34th recently. His combat record was impressive but
Kol Badar had yet to fight alongside him in battle,
and it was only in battle that true brotherhood was
forged.

Ashkanez had only been with the Host since they
had left the daemon-world of Sicarus, seven standard
weeks earlier. Deeming that the 34th lacked a suitable
candidate from amongst its own ranks, the Council of
Sicarus had appointed Ashkanez to the position of
First Acolyte to serve under Marduk.

'What a fine spectacle Ekodas has arranged for us,'
said Marduk, looking towards the silent ranks of
Word Bearers. 'Such an unsubtle reminder of his
strength.'

'Hardly necessary,' said Kol Badar. 'He is of the
Council, after all.'

Only eight individuals sat upon the Council of
Sicarus, the holy ruling body that guided the Word

Bearers in Lorgar's absence, and each was a dark cardinal of great authority and power.

'Intimidation is in his nature,' said Marduk.

With a roar of engines, another shuttle breached the shimmering integrity field of the docking bay. Banks of cannons bulged from beneath the snub nose of the heavily modified craft, and flickering remnants of warp-presence – semi-transparent, semi-sentient globs of immaterium that pulsed with inner light – clung to its hull.

'Cadaver-class,' said Kol Badar, assessing the arrival with a glance. '18th Host.'

'Sarabdal,' said Burias.

'*Dark Apostle* Sarabdal, Icon Bearer,' corrected Ashkanez.

Burias snarled and moved towards the newly appointed First Acolyte but Ashkanez remained motionless, offering no confrontation.

The debarkation ramp of the old Cadaver-class shuttle extended in four clunking sections and slammed onto the deck. A trio of corpse-like cherubs bearing smoking censers flew from the red-lit shadows of its interior, their pudgy childlike faces twisted into grotesque leers. Their eyes were sutured shut with criss-crossing stitches. Snarling, they exposed tiny barbed teeth. The cherubs began a circuit of looping dives and swoops, heralding the arrival of their master.

Dark Apostle Sarabdal stepped from his shuttle and took in the cavernous docking bay at a glance. He wore a heavy cloak of chainmail and his armour had been painstakingly sculptured to resembled flayed musculature. Every vein, tendon and sinew of it bulged in stark relief.

Sarabdal strode towards Marduk and his retinue fell in behind him. Marduk met him halfway, his own entourage moving with him.

The two Dark Apostles slowed as they approached, sizing each other up before stepping in close and embracing as equals and brothers. Sarabdal, the taller of the two, leant in to kiss Marduk on both cheeks. His skin tingled as the Dark Apostle's burning lips touched his flesh.

'Brother Erebus speaks highly of you, Marduk,' said Sarabdal, in a hoarse whisper.

Marduk inclined his head to accept the compliment.

'My lord,' murmured Ashkanez, and Marduk turned to see a skeletal figure making its way towards them.

Marduk's lip curled at the cyber-organic creature. Four mechanical, insectoid legs protruded from its bloated abdomen and propelled it forwards in a stop-start motion. Bone-thin arms were spread wide in an overly sincere gesture of welcome. The creature's lips had been hacked off, leaving its mouth set in a permanent rictus of teeth. Spine-like sensor arrays protruded from the back of its head, and the buzz of data-flow erupted from the emitters in its modified larynx.

Twitching, the vile creature came to a halt before the pair of Dark Apostles and performed an awkward bow, head flopping forwards. It righted itself and began to speak, though the words bubbling from its lipless mouth had no relation to the crazed articulation of its jaws.

'Welcome, brothers of the 34th and the 18th, to the *Crucius Maledictus*,' it slurred. 'Grand Apostle Ekodas, blessed be his name, regrets he could not welcome you himself, but he humbly requests that you follow this lowly mech-flesh unit to his audience chambers.'

'*Grand* Apostle Ekodas?' said Marduk.

'The arrogance!' fumed Sarabdal. He spat onto the deck floor in disgust. The thick wad of black phlegm began to eat through the metal, hissing and steaming.

The cyber-organic beckoned and twitched impatiently.

'Let me be the one to tear its head off,' said Kol Badar under his breath, and Marduk smiled.

'Depending on how this conclave goes, gladly,' said Marduk.

'Can't we do it now?' said Burias, as the insectoid-legged creature grinned inanely.

'Come,' said Sarabdal. 'Let us get this over with.'

# CHAPTER TWO

GARBED IN FULL parade regalia, Praefectus Verenus stood in the centre of Victory Square beneath the baking sun and awaited the arrival of the White Consul.

At his back, four thousand soldiers of the Boros 232nd stood to attention. Proud, royal blue banners hung limp in the still air. Alongside the Guardsmen were the ancillary support vehicles of the regiment: Chimera APCs, reconnaissance Sentinels, Trojan workhorses.

Rearing up behind the regiment, at the top of almost four thousand stairs, was the immense, white marble edifice that was the Temple of the Gloriatus. A golden statue of the Emperor looked resplendent at its soaring peak.

Verenus stood alongside his commanding officer and support staff in total silence.

With his mighty physique, Verenus was the epitome of Boros gene-stock, an imposing officer and soldier. His eyes were ice-blue and hard. His skin was deeply tanned. His nose had been broken a dozen times and poorly set, and his sandy blond hair was clipped short in a regulation cut.

Verenus swallowed heavily as the heat of the twin suns beat down upon him. He had forgotten how unforgiving Boros Prime's summers could be. It had been ten long years since he had been home. He indulged himself and let his eye wander over the majesty of the city before him.

Sirenus Principal was a gleaming bastion-city of white marble and manicured arboretums, and it stretched beyond the horizon in every direction. Home to more than eighty million citizens, all of whom willingly served at least a single five-year term in the Guard or PDF, it was one of the great cities of Boros Prime, and indeed of the entire Boros Gate sub-sector.

Perfectly symmetrical boulevards, a hundred metres wide and lined with towering statues of Imperial heroes and revered saints, ran past colossal architectural wonders, replete with columns, arches and gleaming alabaster sculptures. Tree-lined flyovers curled between soaring schola progenium collegiums and ecclesiastic shrine-wards, and tens of thousands of dutiful citizens could be seen coming and going, as they hurried to lectures and work. Mass-transits snaked soundlessly along curving aqueduct bridges, whizzing past mighty cathedrals that reached towards the heavens in praise of the God-Emperor. Each day millions of wreaths and aquila tokens were laid before hundreds of grand monuments scattered around the city that celebrated Imperial victories and honoured the valiant fallen.

Gleaming white fortress walls bisected the city. Far from being oppressive and domineering, they were sculptured masterpieces of classical design, with gently sweeping buttresses climbing their flanks.

Lush gardens fed by subterranean hydroponics butted up against the city walls, colonised with exotic flowering plants and broad-leafed shrubs. Fountains surrounded by grassy arboretums were located in each district, water spurting from the lips of cherubs.

Thousands of ordered PDF units marched across the tops of the walls, sunlight glinting off helmets and lascarbines. Their blue cloaks, the same as those worn by all members of the Boros PDF and Guard, were bright upon the pristine white stone. In all, Sirenus Principal boasted nearly fifteen million active soldiers; one in six inhabitants was a Guardsman, and it was the same all across Boros Prime. Few Imperial systems had such numbers.

The entire city was a blend of simple beauty and practicality, of form and function; an elegant and wondrously designed metropolis that was essentially a mighty and brilliantly conceived fortress, yet one that was aesthetic and pleasant for its populace to live within.

The city summed up all that it meant to be a citizen of Boros Prime: strong, determined, ordered, refined, noble.

Verenus's gaze was drawn heavenwards, towards the distant shadow of Kronos. As potent as all the ground defences of Boros Prime were, its true strength lay in the immense star fort orbiting overhead.

Bristling with weaponry and the size of a small moon, Kronos was the largest space station in Segmenta Obscurus. It was an ever-present sentinel that was both a comfort to the people of Boros Prime and a constant reminder of Imperial authority, for it was the seat of the system's governorship: the Consuls.

The White Consuls ruled with a benevolent hand, and the citizens of the Boros system – all eighteen inhabited planets and two-dozen colonised moons and asteroids – were afforded liberties and a quality of life undreamed of in many regions of the Imperium. Civil unrest was all but unheard of.

Two Consuls ruled Boros – the Proconsul Ostorius, and his Coadjutor, Aquilius. The highest authority in all matters military and political, they were regarded with awe bordering on worship by the bulk of the Boros citizenry. Such devotion was not officially encouraged, but neither was it discouraged – was it not true that the Consuls were formed in the image of the God-Emperor himself?

The Proconsul and his Coadjutor were responsible for somewhere in the realm of four hundred billion Imperial citizens, as well as the security of the vital Boros Gate subsector itself.

Verenus spied several shapes approaching from the star fort, gleaming like falling stars, and snapped to attention. He could hear them now, jet engines screaming as they penetrated the atmosphere, the sound rising from a distant drone to an ear-splitting roar.

Three strike aircraft streaked out from the glare of the suns, flying in tight formation, wingtip to wingtip. Verenus recognised them as agile Lightning fighters by their forward sweeping aerofoils and distinctive wail.

Slicing effortlessly through the air, they dived low and screamed over the heads of the Boros 232nd. Contrails of white vapour chased their progress like ribbons. Having shot overhead, the fighters peeled off sharply, turning in a wide sweeping motion. A blast of hot, displaced air struck the gathered soldiers of the 232nd a second later, sending their capes and banners fluttering.

As the scream of the Lightnings subsided, it was replaced with the resonant drone of bigger engines. A minute passed and a pair of Vulture gunships hove into view, their wings heavy with tubular rocket pods and autocannons. They were escorting a smaller Aquila lander. The Lightning strike fighters made another pass before pulling up and disappearing from sight.

The Aquila was resplendent gold, and Verenus was forced to squint against the glare reflected upon its gleaming metal skin. With vectored engines swivelled downwards, the lander and its gunship escort descended upon the gleaming white parade ground twenty metres in front of the Legatus and his officer cadre, landing gear unfolding beneath them.

They touched down smoothly, and even before their engines died, the golden-hulled Aquila was lowering its passenger compartment to the ground.

'*And behold, an Angel of Death walks among us,*' quoted the Legatus in a quiet voice. Verenus recognised the line from his years in the schola progenium, though he could not recall which scrivener had penned it.

All thoughts of ancient poets and their epics were forgotten as the blast door of the Aquila's passenger compartment slid open with a hiss of equalising air-pressure.

A huge figure appeared in the doorway, so big that it was forced to duck to exit the landing craft. Only as it stepped onto the parade ground did it rise to its full height, and Verenus's eyes widened.

The praefectus knew that the Consuls were big – he had seen countless holo-vids of their public appearances, and he had seen them commemorated in frescoes and sculptures his whole life – but nothing had prepared him for just *how* big. The warrior was a giant.

The Space Marine was encased in heavy plate armour as white and flawless as the marble of Sirenus Principal. He stood easily two heads taller than Verenus. His shoulders were immense, protected by huge pauldrons and the twin-headed eagle shone on his breastplate. He wore a royal blue tabard over his power armour, emblazoned with the eagle-head heraldry of the White Consuls Chapter. Its hems were stitched with delicate silver thread. Verenus recognised the Space Marine as Coadjutor Aquilius.

The Coadjutor's head was bare. He had a broad face that was solid and youthful. Carrying his helmet under one arm, he strode towards the Legatus of the 232nd. Verenus fought the urge to step back.

*'And fear incarnate is his name,'* Verenus heard his Legatus murmur.

The Coadjutor halted a few steps before the regimental commander and his entourage. He stared at the Legatus, his expression inscrutable and his colourless eyes hard.

'A quote from Sueton,' said the Space Marine. His voice, Verenus noted, was deeper than a man's. It seemed apt given his immensity. *'In Nominae Glorifidae.* Seventh act?'

'Ninth,' said the Legatus.

'Of course,' said the Coadjutor, bowing his head slightly in respect. A discussion on classical literature was the last thing that Verenus had expected.

At a barked order, the soldiers of the Boros 232nd saluted the Coadjutor with perfect synchronicity. The Space Marine returned the salute. Upon a second order the regiment snapped back to attention.

A robed adept of the Ministorum, the left half of his face hidden beneath a mass of augmetics, stepped to the White Consul's side. A servo-skull hovering at his shoulder beeped indecipherable date-code.

'Legatus Cato Merula, 232nd Regiment, Boros Prime Imperial Guard, rotated from battlefront Ixxus IX of the Thraxian campaign, under Lord Commander Tibult Horacio,' intoned the adept from a half-bow, gesturing towards the regimental commander with one outstretched arm. His fingers were needle-like mechanical digits, and they buzzed with exloading data. 'One month resupply, re-indoctrination and recruitment before return to frontline duties. Execution status XX.V.II.P.C.IX.'

The adept swung around to face the Coadjutor and abased himself, dropping to one knee and lowering his head towards the ground.

'Lord Gaius Aquilius, 5th Company White Consuls of the Adeptus Praeses, Dux Militari, Coadjutor of Boros Prime,' intoned the adept in his monotonous voice. 'Praise be to the God-Emperor.'

'Praise be,' murmured the Legatus.

'Praise be,' said Coadjutor Aquilius.

'It is an honour to address you, sons and daughters of Boros,' said the Coadjutor, his resounding voice easily reaching the ears of every soldier of the 232nd without the need of vox enhancement.

'The Proconsul was due to address you himself, but duties of state precluded him from being here,' said Coadjutor Aquilius. 'I pray my presence instead does not disappoint.'

Verenus knew that not one of the soldiers of the 232nd would have been even slightly disappointed. Only a few amongst them had ever laid eyes upon a Space Marine, and then only from afar.

'I am humbled to be in the presence of such noble soldiers as yourselves,' said the Coadjutor. 'You have given all that I could have asked of you, and more, and I have faith that you shall continue to do so. I salute you, men and women of the illustrious 232nd.'

An adjutant of the Coadjutor stepped forward bearing an exquisite, ornate regimental standard. A golden aquila gleamed atop the standard pole above the ornate crosspiece of carved bone. The banner itself was tightly furled and affixed with studs. The adjutant dropped to one knee and offered the standard to the commander of the 232nd, who gestured for one of his younger officers, the regiment's overawed aquilifer, to step forward and take the standard.

'It was with great sadness and regret that I learnt of the loss of the 232nd's standard during the Daxus Offensive on Thraxian Minor,' said the Coadjutor. 'I had my own personal artificers construct this replacement. May it serve your regiment faithfully.'

With a nod of encouragement from his Legatus, the regiment's young aquilifer began to release the studs of the standard with shaking hands. With a flourish, he lifted it high in the air, allowing the banner to unfurl. A tapestry of such beauty was unveiled that it brought a gasp from the regiment. The glorious image of a winged saint, the martyred Ameliana – the regiment's official patron – was emblazoned in gold and silver thread upon a field of blue. In the upper left corner was the unit's regimental insignia, along with the four-dozen campaign badges of the regiment's long history. The names of every Legatus that had led the regiment into battle since its founding – all three hundred and seventy-four of them – were picked out in silver thread on the back of the banner.

Verenus had not known exactly what to expect when meeting one of the revered Consuls face to face, but seeing such humility in one so far above the humble ranks of Guardsmen such as he was certainly not it.

The next few minutes passed in a blur as the Coadjutor was introduced by name to each of the 232nd's officers. Suddenly the White Consul was standing before Verenus. Few men were the equal of Verenus's height, but he felt like a child as he looked up into the broad face of the Space Marine.

The Coadjutor offered his hand, and Verenus clasped forearms with him. It was like gripping the arm of a statue. He could feel the terrifying strength in the Space Marine's grip.

Finally, the Space Marine saluted the 232nd, and made his way back to his shuttle. Awestruck, Verenus watched the golden Aquila lander ascend towards the Kronos star fort, like an angel returning to the heavens.

ABOARD THE AQUILA, Brother Aquilius drummed his fingers on his armrest.

'Where was the Proconsul?' he said.

'Regretfully, I am unable to say, Coadjutor,' said Aquilius's heavily augmented aide.

Aquilius took a deep breath.

'The banner was a nice touch,' he said a moment later.

'I thought that it would be appropriate, Coadjutor. It seemed to be appreciated.'

'It was. Thank you.'

The White Consul peered out through the narrow portal beside his seat. Kronos star fort filled his view.

Even several hundred kilometres out, the space station was immense. It rendered the tiny gold lander utterly insignificant. Aquilius could see a dozen Imperial Navy vessels of Destroyer-class and higher docked there. Even the two battlecruisers of Battlegroup Hexus, *Via Lucis* and *Via Crucis*, each more than three kilometres in length, were dwarfed by Kronos.

'Would you like me to run through the day's remaining commitments, Coadjutor?' said his aide.

Aquilius's gaze lingered on the massive launch-bays and banks of gun-batteries lining the space station's heavily shielded flanks.

'Coadjutor?' said his aide, offering the Space Marine a data-slate.

Aquilius turn away and nodded.

TWO HOURS LATER, his mind numb from meetings with bureaucrats and Ministorum adepts, Brother Aquilius walked the length of a brightly lit corridor, deep within the heart of the Kronos star fort. He came to a halt and pressed his palm against a matt-black sensorii tablet. Blast-doors opened with a hiss in response, and he went into the training chambers.

The stink of perspiration and ozone was heavy in the air.

Moving to the third and only occupied training cage, Aquilius stopped. He glanced down at the data-slate readout on the control pulpit, and pursed his lips.

From the cage came a high-pitched squeal of discharging energy as a training servitor was dispatched.

The warrior within moved with a subtle blend of power and grace. Every strike flowed into a parry or another blow, his every thrust precise and deadly. He displayed an astounding economy of movement, with no unnecessary flourish or extravagance. He fought with combat shield and sword, and his head was lathered in sweat. Four training servitors circled him, their blank-helmed heads and swift-moving bodies blurred by their humming shield-units. Bladed arms cut through the air as they sought to land a blow against the sublime swordsman. Programmed to complement each other, the training servitors attacked as one.

Far from being dim-witted protocol mech-organics, these training servitors were vicious combat models, their aggression heightened with stimms and Rage injectors.

Aquilius knew the damage they could inflict with those slashing blade-arms – he carried more than a few scars from their touch – and he watched the Proconsul with a mixture of respect, awe and frustration.

Until twenty-one months ago, Veteran Brother Cassius Ostorius had been Company Champion of 5th Company. He had held the post for forty-seven years, having been inducted into the White Consuls three hundred and thirty-four years earlier.

When Aquilius had first learned that he would be serving as Coadjutor to Veteran Brother Ostorius, he was overjoyed. Ultramar-born, and one of the White Consuls' most respected warriors – arguably its finest swordsmen – Ostorius had been Aquilius's idol as he rose from the neophyte Scout to fully fledged battle-brother.

That enthusiasm had waned significantly in the subsequent months.

With enviable skill, Ostorius turned aside a slashing blade with his combat shield. Spinning, he deflected a second and a third blow coming in at him from different angles and cut his sword across the face of one of the training servitors. Its shield registered the hit in a blaze of electricity and the servitor stepped backwards stiffly, powering down.

Ostorius kept moving, closing on another servitor. He executed a perfect kill with a thrust to its chest, before turning and dropping to one knee to perform a disembowelling thrust on another, a blade whipping just centimetres above his head. The last of the active servitors came at him and he rose to his feet. Sidestepping a vicious slash, he swung for its neck. His blow was turned aside and the servitor lunged, its reflexes and strength augmented with clusters of servo-muscles.

With a deft circular motion of his sword Ostorius turned aside both blades as they jabbed at his chest and braced himself, lowering his centre of gravity. Rising, he lifted his shoulder into the servitor's midsection. The weighty mech-organic lifted off the ground and was sent staggering backwards. Ostorius dispatched the machine with a brutal blow to the head.

'Pause combat,' said Ostorius before the combat servitors could come back online. He went to the side of the training cage and replaced his sword and combat shield on a weapons rack. Wiping a hand across his sweat-slick head, he glanced across the array of weapons before choosing a heavy double-ended polearm. It had an axe-blade at one end and a curving crescent-moon blade at the other. Ostorius swung it around him with deft flicks, gauging its weight and balance.

'You come to train, brother?' he said, though he paid Aquilius little attention, continuing to take practice swings with the polearm.

'No, Proconsul.'

'You come to watch *me* train?' Ostorius looked through the cage at Aquilius for the first time. His left eye was augmetic and he bore several long scars that distorted his lips into an ugly sneer. His left ear was missing, replaced with an internal augmetic. He was a brutal-looking warrior, intimidating in appearance and manner.

'No, Proconsul.' Aquilius always felt so young and inexperienced next to his senior Proconsul and fought against the heat rising in his cheeks. 'I came to check that all is well,' he said, diplomatically. 'You didn't make inspection this morning. I was concerned that something was the matter.'

'Recommence combat, threat level eight,' commanded Ostorius. The four training servitors jerked back into motion, circling him again. 'I had other matters to attend to,' he replied, raising his voice above the mechanical din of the servitors. Aquilius glanced down at the date-slate readout upon the command pulpit.

'You have been training for seven hours and twenty minutes.'

'A battle-brother can never train too much, Coadjutor,' growled Ostorius. The younger White Consul bristled at the implication.

'I train as many hours per day as the Codex stipulates,' he said. 'I would train more but for the duties and demands of my office.'

Ostorius spun, sweeping the legs from under one servitor before smashing another to the ground with an emphatic blow to the head.

'I judged that you were capable of conducting this morning's inspection without me,' said Ostorius, parrying a swift blow before kicking the servitor away from him with a heavy boot. 'Or was my belief in you misplaced?'

Aquilius bit his tongue, accepting the rebuke without complaint.

'Proconsul, there are matters that demand your attention,' he said, humbly, looking down at the data-slate in his hands. He was forced to raise his voice above the escalating clamour inside the training cage. 'Nine more regiments returning from the Thaxian Cluster are due in over the next two hours – six infantry, two armoured, one artillery. There are also military dispatches from the Assembly that require your attention, and depositions to be viewed from the Daxus moon conglomerate. Mechanicus emissaries from Gryphonhold that await...'

'Aquilius,' barked Ostorius, knocking the last of his opponents down with a series of stabbing thrusts.

'Yes, Proconsul?' said Aquilius, looking up from his slate.

'Not now.'

* * *

OSTORIUS EXHALED WHEN Aquilius had left. He knew his dark mood had nothing to do with his Coadjutor. Aquilius was merely doing his duty – he had no right to belittle him. Indeed, he had less than no right; as Proconsul, it was his place to mentor Aquilius.

Not for the first time, Ostorius questioned why he had been removed from his beloved 5th Company and dispatched to the Boros system. Every battle-brother served as a Coadjutor in the years after rising from the rank of neophyte, but only a selection of veterans were chosen to act as Proconsuls. To be chosen was a great honour, and a requirement of those harbouring ambitions to become a sergeant or captain within the Chapter. Nevertheless, it was not something that Ostorius had ever desired.

He had no wish to be a sergeant, let alone a captain. He was a warrior, and desired to be nothing more than that. He was Company Champion of the 5th, and that was all that he ever wanted to be. Protecting his captain in the midst of battle, that was his duty. That was what he had trained for and that was what he was good at, not governing some wealthy bastion system or trying to be a suitable role model for a young White Consuls Coadjutor.

Ostorius lifted a heavy, double-headed hammer from the weapons rack.

'Recommence combat, threat level nine.'

The training servitors powered up once more.

Thirty years, Ostorius thought. In the life of a Space Marine, thirty years was nothing.

To Ostorius, it felt like an eternity.

# CHAPTER THREE

Soaring almost fifty metres high, the observation portal of the Sanctum Corpus offered an unobstructed view up the length of the *Crucius Maledictus*. The castellated superstructure of the hulking battleship looked like a city, as if an entire quadrant of Sicarus had uprooted and taken flight. Scores of buttressed cathedrals rose above its hull, replete with spires, glittering domes and grotesque statuary. Multi-tiered banks of defence cannons and gun turrets, half-hidden within ten-storey alcoves, protruded like bristling spines along its flanks.

The battleship was forging through the roiling madness of the warp, parting the pure stuff of Chaos before its sweeping, skulled prow. A handful of the other ships of the redemptive crusade could be seen off to the port and starboard, though the immaterial realm through which they sailed blurred their ancient hulls. Daemons of all size and shape swam along in their slipstream, an ever-changing escort of the infernal.

Talons scraped against the outside of the observation portal, and sticky tongue-like protuberances slobbered against its surface. A flock of kathartes flew past on feathered white wings, angelic and glowing from within. Only in the æther did they appear in their true form. When they crossed into realspace, they appeared as skinless harpies, not these beautified creatures of elegance and deadly allure.

Even the majestic view of the warp in all its infernal glory could not appease Marduk's frustration and growing anger.

'This is an insult,' snapped Dark Apostle Belagosa from across the gaping Sanctum Corpus chamber, putting voice to Marduk's thoughts. 'He goes too far.'

Belagosa was a tall, gaunt figure. In an act of devout faith the Apostle of the 11th Host had clawed out his own eyes centuries ago. Nevertheless, he turned in Marduk's direction. Those empty eye sockets still were far from blind and bled red tears down his cheeks.

'Patience, brother,' said Dark Apostle Ankh-Heloth of the 11th Host. He spoke from behind the barbed lectern of his own pulpit, his voice a hoarse whisper. 'I'm sure that Grand Apostle Ekodas will not–'

'*Grand* Apostle,' spat Sarabdal. The holy leader of the 18th Host stood with his arms folded. 'Such hubris. It is a slight on our order than he affects such airs.'

'It was the Keeper of the Faith himself, revered Kor Phaeron, that bestowed the title, honoured brother,' said Ankh-Heloth.

A severe-looking warrior with a cruelly barbed, black metal star of Chaos Glorified hammered into his forehead, Dark Apostle Ankh-Heloth's flesh was a living canvas upon which he had performed his grisly, sacred arts. He bore numerous cuts and welts, the angry disfigurements evidence of ritual flagellation. Older scars lay beneath the fresher wounds. Marduk guessed that the Dark Apostle rubbed poisonous balms and linaments into his self-inflicted cuts in order to hamper the regenerative qualities of his Astartes physiology, for many of his wounds were open and raw. Such practices were not uncommon within the Legion.

'He can call himself what he likes,' said Belagosa. He gestured to Ekodas's empty pulpit. 'But when will the most honoured and revered Grand Apostle decide to grace us with his presence?'

Ekodas's rostrum was ringed with balustrades and spiked railings. It was far larger than those of the other Apostles, and occupied the central position of dominance in the Sanctum Corpus. Held aloft on skeletal arches, it extended thirty metres from the wall opposite the towering viewing portal, giving it an unobstructed view over and beyond the lesser rostrums. Clouds of incense billowed from the maws of hideous gargoyles carved into its underside.

The octagonal Sanctum Corpus chamber was a vertical shaft that dropped away into darkness. Over a kilometre from top to bottom, it bored right through the centre of the mighty battleship. The

Apostle pulpits were at its very top, just fifty metres beneath the glittering red-glass dome at its peak. They protruded over the seemingly bottomless chasm from vertebrae-like pillars set at the corners of the chamber.

Though the chamber was around eighty metres in diameter, the sheer height and depth of the Sanctum Corpus made it feel oppressive, even with the gaping viewing portal in its front wall. The walls were lined with books, codices and leather-bound holy writs.

Tens of millions of sacred works were crammed into alcoves and stacked upon shelves, with no apparent semblance of order or cohesion. Ancient, dusty tomes filled with Lorgar's teachings and scripture were piled in perilous heaps, and tens of thousands of annals and holy texts were stuffed into every crevice. They were all bound in human or xenos skin of various hue and texture. Many of these priceless books had been penned by the proselyte scribe-slaves of Colchis long before the launch of the Great Crusade, in time immemorial; before the blessed Primarch Lorgar had come to Colchis, before even the rise of the hypocritical and fraudulent False Emperor.

Fresh volumes were constantly added to this staggering conglomeration of the Legion's knowledge and wisdom, new tomes bearing more recent teachings and devotional scripture. Outside Sicarus, the scriptorium of the *Crucius Maledictus* was the greatest repository of the Word Bearers' holy teachings in the universe.

Loathsome archivist-servitors, wasted cadavers held aloft by humming suspensor impellers, floated up and down the endless rows of holy tomes, lovingly tending their allotted sections.

Huge, spider-web-like arches stretched up between the bookcases towards the domed ceiling above the conclave of Apostles. Ten thousand skeletons were fused into those arches, their contorted spines calcified with the marble structures. Their skulls were thrown back in voiceless agony, and they held their skeletal arms up in silent appeal to the gods. In their open palms was a thick candle of blood-wax. Twenty thousand glittering flames cast their light down upon the gathered Apostles.

'I'm sure Grand Apostle Ekodas has no wish to keep us waiting long,' said Ankh-Heloth.

'Just long enough to impress upon us that it is in his power to *make* us wait,' said Marduk.

'Barely elevated past First Acolyte and already he passes judgment on an honoured member of the Council,' hissed Ankh-Heloth, glaring at Marduk across the open space of the Sanctum Corpus.

'Better to see things as they are than to accept them blindly,' said Sarabdal.

'Speak your meaning,' said Ankh-Heloth.

'I mean,' said Sarabdal, 'that our newest brother Apostle speaks what we were all thinking. I grow tired of Ekodas's games.'

'I am sure that the honoured Grand Apostle has no intention of angering his devoted brother Apostles,' said Ankh-Heloth.

'Ever the sycophant,' said Belagosa. 'Your grovelling at Ekodas's feet is quite pathetic.'

'You cannot goad me into breaking the truce of Sanctus Corpus,' said Ankh-Heloth. 'You speak nothing but poison and bile.'

'Brother Belagosa has a point,' said Sarabdal, mildly.

'Oh? Please enlighten me,' said Ankh-Heloth.

'You are a puppet,' said Sarabdal. 'Nothing more than Ekodas's pet, and the 11th Host is nothing but an extension of his own. Like a dog, you grovel whenever your master deigns to throw you his scraps.'

The dull humming of the archivist-servitors' impellor motors reigned over the chamber. Belagosa was grinning broadly now, and Marduk too found it hard to hide his amusement as the blood drained from Ankh-Heloth's face. His entourage had gone very still.

'These are not *my* words, of course,' said Sarabdal mildly, pretending not to have noticed the effect on the incensed Dark Apostle of the 11th Host. 'Just… what I have heard said.'

'Who says such things?' hissed Ankh-Heloth.

'Everyone knows you are Ekodas's whipping boy,' said Belagosa, relishing Ankh-Heloth's incandescent rage.

Marduk had heard through Jarulek, his one-time master and the previous holy leader of the 34th Host, of the dubious manner in which Ankh-Heloth had come to power. Jarulek had told Marduk that while it was the Council of Sicarus that had instated Ankh-Heloth as the First Acolyte of the 11th Host, this was only at Ekodas's insistence. Less than a decade later Ankh-Heloth ascended to the position of Dark Apostle after his predecessor was killed under circumstances engineered, many believed, by Ekodas.

Marduk smirked, thinking of how he himself had come to power.

'Something amuses you, Apostle?' said Ankh-Heloth, staring venomously. His body was quivering with rage.

'Of course not, honoured brother,' said Marduk, his tone mocking. 'Such *obviously* slanderous rumours against one weaken us all.'

'We all know that the only reason we suffer your presence on this crusade,' spat Ankh-Heloth, 'is because you have in your possession the device that Jarulek unearthed. Let's hope it was worth the trouble.'

'That is the only thing that you've said here that has made any sense,' said Belagosa.

'Agreed,' said Sarabdal.

Marduk swallowed back his fury.

'I have fought and bled to attain and unlock the secrets of the Nexus Arrangement, dear brothers,' said Marduk, glaring at the other three Apostles. He clenched the barbed railing of his pulpit with such force that he threatened to tear it loose. 'Tens of millions have died in order that it came to me. Worlds have perished. It will win us this war, and when it does, it will be I who shall reap the rewards. In time, you will all bow your heads in deference to me, hearken to my words.'

Belagosa laughed, deep and rumbling. Sarabdal looked amused at the outburst.

'Tread warily, Marduk,' warned Ankh-Heloth. 'An Apostle can fall from grace very quickly if he does not learn to respect his betters.'

'His betters?' snarled Belagosa, quickly turning back on his favoured target. 'And you include yourself in that mix? Marduk may well be nothing more than a whelp, but remember it was not so long ago that you yourself were a lowly First Apostle, Ankh-Heloth. I can still remember when you were first inducted into the Legion. Even then you were a self-aggrandising worm.'

Ankh-Heloth turned his cold eyes on Belagosa. His entourage, standing in the shadowed alcove behind his pulpit, was tense. Ankh-Heloth's hulking Coryphaus clenched his hands into fists, the ex-loaders of his gauntlet-mounted bolters *chunking* as they came online. The warrior resembled a hulking primate, his back hunched and his augmented arms grossly oversized.

Belagosa's honour guard responded in kind, the daemons within their bodies straining to break from their bonds, just waiting for the trigger word from their master that would release them.

'You go too far, Belagosa,' hissed Ankh-Heloth. 'But I shall not be the one to break conclave peace, as much as you might wish it.'

'Still the coward,' said Belagosa.

'Enough!' snapped Sarabdal, forestalling Ankh-Heloth's reply. 'This bickering demeans us all.'

Of the four Apostles present, it was Sarabdal who had led his Host the longest, Sarabdal who had been groomed to become Dark Apostle of the 18th by none other than blessed Lorgar himself. Raised in the scriptorums of Colchis, Sarabdal had been little more than a child when he had taken part in the brutal Schism Wars that fractured the Covenant, the dominant religious order of the feudal planet. Impressed with the youngster's fanaticism and fiery demeanour, Lorgar had taken the boy under his wing and once reunited with his Legion, had personally chosen Sarabdal for indoctrination into the Word Bearers. Few Dark Apostles garnered more respect than Sarabdal, and Belagosa and Ankh-Heloth fell into sullen silence at his rebuke.

It was a formidable gathering of might here in this chamber, Marduk thought, and a slight smile touched his lips.

Between them, the four Dark Apostles commanded the loyalty of over five and a half thousand Astartes warriors. Together with the might of Ekodas's Grand Host, that number swelled to over nine thousand. Add onto that the battle-tanks, Dreadnoughts, daemon-engines and assault craft of the five Hosts and the number was swollen further.

Over a million fanatical cultists of the Word accompanied the Hosts, brainwashed men and women crammed together like cattle in hulking slave vessels. These pitiful wretches were subjected to an endless torrent of maddening warp-noise by floating Discords. After months and years of such unceasing abuse, their free will and resistance had long been broken, and they were now true devotees of Chaos. Of little tactical worth, they would be herded into the guns of the enemy, across minefields and sacrificed by their Astartes masters, and they would do it willingly.

Last of all, the fleet was accompanied by a single bulk-transporter of Legio Vulturus, a grim vessel twice the size of the *Crucius Maledictus*. Within its cavernous stasis hold resided a full demi-Legion of god-machines: twelve of the most potent war engines ever constructed on the forgeworlds of the Mechanicum. As part of the Ordo Militaris wing of the Collegia Titanica, they had fought in nigh on constant battle since the start of the Great Crusade. The Legio Vulturus had declared their allegiance with the Warmaster Horus, turning their guns against their brethren mid-battle, wreaking terrible havoc among the Legios Gryphonicus and Legio Victorum, destroying nigh on forty battle engines in that one unexpected engagement. This particular demi-Legion of Vulturus had fought alongside the Word Bearers since the start of the Crusade, and many within the XVII Legion credited Erebus himself with turning them to the cause of the Warmaster.

'This is outrageous,' snarled Belagosa. 'If I have to wait one more minute for Ekodas to grace us with his presence, I'll–'

His words were cut off as the blast-doors behind the domineering rostrum above them slammed open, venting steam and oily, incense-laden smoke. A procession of Terminator-armoured veterans stamped through the open portal. They stepped deferentially aide, and Ekodas walked forwards to take his place at his podium.

Ancient and heavily augmented, Ekodas's face bore the ravages of thousands of years of war; his features were cratered and cracked. There was nothing flamboyant or extravagant about his appearance. A simple black robe hung over the plain, austere plates of his armour. His only adornment was a handful of charms looped around his neck. These fetishes of bone and blood-matted hair were strung upon lengths of sinew, and Marduk recognised the characteristic style of the shamanistic priests of Davin. He carried no weapon or staff of office. It was said he preferred not to dirty his hands, preferring to let his underlings fight his battles.

'Don't let me interrupt,' said Ekodas. 'I am most interested to hear what you have to say.'

Ekodas looked down at Belagosa, his black eyes burning with contained fury. His sizeable entourage, vastly outnumbering those of the other Apostles, continued to file in behind him. It was an unsubtle display of military strength.

Belagosa's jaw twitched.

Ekodas's attention shifted and, as the full force of the Grand Apostle's gaze struck him, Marduk fought the urge to kneel. He was a Dark Apostle of Lorgar, he reminded himself angrily; he need bow to no one but the Urizen himself. He saw amusement written in Ekodas's burning orbs and his anger flared, hot and potent.

*There is great strength to be found in anger*, said Ekodas, jolting Marduk as the words stabbed painfully into his mind. Ekodas's lips didn't move, but Marduk heard the words as if they had spoken directly, and he knew instinctively that no one else had heard them.

An Apostle's mind was like a fortress. It had to be so that he would not be overwhelmed by the crushing power of the warp, nor his sanity ripped apart by any of the billions of deadly entities that dwelt beyond reality. With walls erected by centuries of mental training and conditioning, with ramparts constructed of unshakeable faith and utter belief, an Apostle's mind was virtually unassailable, yet Ekodas had torn straight through those defences as if they were nothing.

*Yet always be certain that your anger is directed at the real enemy, young Apostle*, continued Ekodas, his voice pounding. He continued to hold Marduk's gaze, his eyes burning with the fires of fanaticism, even as Marduk struggled to look away and reassert control.

Ekodas broke contact suddenly and painfully. Marduk clenched the pulpit railing as a wave of vertigo crashed over him. He felt physically drained, and a dull headache throbbed behind his eyes.

'Is everything well, my lord Apostle?' said Ashkanez, leaning forwards to whisper in Marduk's ear. Ignoring the First Acolyte, Marduk glared up at Ekodas. He was angry at being taken by surprise, that Ekodas had so easily breached his mental defences.

Had Ekodas gleaned anything of import? Had he learnt of Marduk's promise to Erebus, of the shocking suspicion that the First Chaplain had?

It was doubtful, for even the most talented psykers were generally only able to read those thoughts uppermost in an individual's mind with any consistency. Even then it was difficult to gain any coherency amidst the bewildering array of random images and emotions. Still, there was no way of truly knowing what Ekodas might have gleaned.

He realised then that he had misjudged the Apostle. He had always seen Ekodas as an unsubtle priest, a sledgehammer that overcame his opponents, both in war and in politics, through confrontation. Now, Marduk was forced to readdress his preconceptions.

'You have nothing to say then, Belagosa?' said Ekodas, his attention returned to the other Dark Apostle. Who knew what silent communication was being conducted between them. 'There is nothing that you wish to say to my face, *brother*?'

'No, my lord,' said Belagosa finally, lowering his gaze.

Ekodas flashed a glance at Marduk full of staggering, domineering force.

*I am not your enemy,* his voice boomed. A trickle of blood ran from Marduk's nostrils.

THE CONCLAVE WAS short and to the point. Ekodas's Coryphaus, Kol Harekh, ran through the final assault plans, his words spoken with the calm authority of one used to being obeyed.

In the open space between the Apostles' pulpits hung a three-dimensional hololithic projection of a binary solar system: the target of the crusade's wrath. The image flickered with intermittent static, and flashes of warp interference occasionally over-lapped the visual feed, showing screaming daemons and other horrific images.

Ignoring these anomalies, Marduk stared intently at the hololithic projection. As the details of the attack were laid out, he watched the tiny planets and moons of the binary system slowly orbiting each other, revolving lazily around the two suns at its heart. One was a massive red giant in its last few billion years of life and the other, its killer, a small parasite that burned with white-hot intensity.

Twenty-nine planets circled the two suns, as well as a handful of large moons. Streams of data scrolled down the screen of Marduk's lectern, relay-ing geography, population, defences and industry for each of the planets as he tapped its surface. Eighteen of the planets were inhabited. Three of those were naturally conducive to carbon-based life forms, while others had been terraformed to create atmospheres suitable for human habitation. The populations of the other inhabited moons and planets existed within domes large enough to have their own weather systems, within hermetically sealed stations pumped with recycled air or labyrinthine subterranean complexes.

An asteroid belt a thousand kilometres thick formed a ring within the solar system, dividing it into the inner core worlds and those beyond. The inner core worlds constituted the bulk of the inhabited planets, with only a few isolated mining and industrial facilities located on those celestial bodies in the cold outer reaches.

'The Boros Gate,' said Ekodas, 'staging ground of the End Times, according to the *Rubric Apocalyptica*. For ten thousand years Chaos has tried to take this system. For ten thousand years we have been denied. Until now.'

Throbbing red icons overlaid the hololithic system map, marking warp-routes to and from the system.

Streams of information bled across the data-slate of Marduk's lectern, and across the lesser terminals accessed by Kol Badar behind him. Desiccated servitors hardwired into the control feeds coralled this constant flood of data with serpentine tentacle fingers.

The information regarding the system and its defences was as accurate as could be obtained by the small, shielded drones that had been dropped out of warp-orbit into the outer reaches of the enemy system. Almost invisible to conventional scans and relay sweeps, they were currently hugging the system's thick asteroid belt and sending back steady streams of valuable information. It was a delicate process: too much data-flow and the enemy would register the feed and be ready for them; too little and they would be blindly entering one of the Imperium's best defended regions of space – only the Cadian Gate was more fiercely guarded.

The system was not particularly rich in mining deposits, nor was it an agri-hub that fed other systems. No sacred shrineworlds existed within it that needed defending, nor did it house any forges vital to the Imperium's ongoing existence. It was heavily populated and very rich, certainly, but that in itself was not enough to warrant such protection, nor the ferocity with which the XVII Legion desired it.

The key to the importance of the system was its wormholes. They were the sole reason it was so hotly defended and so jealously regarded by the Legions that had been loyal to the Warmaster.

Even for the Legions dedicated to Chaos, the warp-routes through the immaterium were often convoluted and difficult to navigate. Thousands of overlapping routes existed through the warp, twisting and turning in constant flux. There were fast moving streams that wound their way through the immaterium, allowing remarkably swift passage from one area of realspace to another, but also stagnant areas of null-time where a fleet could become becalmed for years or decades at a time. Skilful Navigators were able to predict and read the warp like a living map. The best of them were able to remain fluid, adapting to the changeable flow of the immaterium and making the most of its fluctuating ways. Often, a fleet would be forced to slip sidewards across several streams, being buffeted to and fro, pulled months off-course by the malign forces that dwelt there before slipping into the warp-route that would take them to their destination.

However, there were some rare warp-routes that remained stable and unchanging through all the passing centuries and millennia. Highly prized, and violently defended at their egress points, the most favoured of these stable wormholes allowed entire fleets to be shifted from warzone to warzone almost instantaneously, utilising the routes like mass transit highways that bridged the gaps between distant subsectors. The Imperial system that the crusade was soon to descend upon was the hub of one such cluster of wormholes.

In essence, the system was a transportation hub, a waypoint that allowed impossibly swift transference between almost two-dozen other, vastly distant locations. Anyone who controlled it would be capable of practically instantaneous travel to positions millions of light years away.

One such location was only a relatively short jump from Terra, the birthplace of mankind and the centre of the Imperium itself. The very thought of what it meant should they take the system made Marduk salivate.

Several Word Bearers crusades had tried to gain control of the region, but none had ever returned. In all, seventeen Hosts of the XVII Legion had been thrown against this system over the past centuries, and all had been wiped out. The Black Legion had lost double that number trying to find a way around the heavily guarded Cadian Gate. Other Legions too had suffered when attempting to strike at the region, most notably the Death Guard of Mortarion and the Iron Warriors of Perturabo.

A substantial fleet was docked at a devastatingly powerful space bastion orbiting the system's capital planet. That bastion alone had enough firepower to destroy half the Word Bearers crusade, but it was neither the fleet nor the bastion that was the system's most formidable defence. Nor were the standing armies that protected each of the inner core worlds, nor their fortress-like cities, warded by potent defence lasers, cannons and orbital battery arrays. Nor even were its Astartes protectors and stewards, the genetic descendants of those that Marduk and his kin had once called brother.

The true strength of its nigh-on impenetrable defences lay in the wormholes themselves.

Allowing practically instant transportation between a score of other systems, they also allowed the full might of the Imperium to marshal at a moment's notice. As soon as the system registered that an enemy fleet was attempting to breach from the warp, an alarm call would be sent out. Hours after an enemy fleet made realisation into the binary system's outer reaches, an Imperial armada of truly titanic size would emerge from the wormholes to combat the threat.

To go against this region was not merely to go against one system's defences and its Astartes guardians, but rather to go against the fleet of an entire subsector. It was to go against the entire force of the Astartes Praeses – an order of Space Marine Chapters that permanently patrolled the flanks of the Eye of Terror, ever vigilant for incursions from within. Utilising the wormholes of this region, the Adeptus Praeses were a thorn in the side of the Chaos Legions, able to quickly manoeuvre their companies to wherever they were needed.

However, with the Nexus Arrangement, the xenos device that Marduk had secured in his possession, that greatest strength would be completely undone.

'The Boros Gate is a staging ground,' Ekodas confirmed. 'As the gods will it, it will be *the* staging ground; the site where the fall of the Imperium begins.'

Marduk felt a shiver of anticipation.

'We, my brothers are the vanguard of the End Times, its heralds and harbingers. In consultation with the Warmaster Abaddon, the Council of Sicarus has appointed *us* to take the Boros Gate. Five cardinals of Colchis born, united in Brotherhood – such is the prophecy.'

None of the Dark Apostles spoke. All attention was locked onto Ekodas, all petty grievances and feuding temporarily forgotten.

'Others have believed that they were the chosen ones, that it was their destiny to fulfil the prophecy, blinded by greed and ambition. But where they failed, we shall succeed. For we have with us what the *Apocalyptica* foretold: the "*wondrys orb of ancynt death*".'

'The Nexus,' breathed Marduk.

With a gesture, Ekodas turned the revolving hololith of the Boros Gate system into images of war. Word Bearers marched through crumbling shells of bombed buildings, bolters barking soundlessly in their hands. 'And we know that the device works. The lifeless husk of Palantyr V is testament to that.'

'Palantyr V was a poorly defended backwater, my lord,' said Belagosa, his tone noticeably more deferential. 'The scale of what we attempt at the Boros Gate bears no comparison.'

'It doesn't matter,' said Ekodas. 'Once the device was activated, Palantyr V was doomed. The device shut the region down completely. The effect will be the same at Boros.'

Marduk nodded.

'And if it fails?' asked Belagosa.

'We'll be dead,' answered Sarabdal.

'It will work,' said Marduk. 'It is prophesied.'

'"With fury of hellfire, truth, and orb of ancient death, the gate shall be claimed",' quoted Ekodas.

'We are committed to this now,' he continued. 'The Warmaster Abaddon watches our progress closely. Already his envoys are gathering support, scouring the Eye and the Maelstrom for all who will fight under his banner. Rivalries and blood feuds are being put aside, for all can feel that the End Times draw near. Our triumph at the Boros Gate will herald the last Black Crusade. Because of us, the heavens shall burn and the Imperium of man will be dust.'

A heavy silence descended. Ekodas glared, as if daring any of his Dark Apostles to oppose him. After a moment, he nodded to his Coryphaus, Kol Harekh.

'We take these planets in turn,' Kol Harekh said, indicating the outlying planets of the system. 'Once they have fallen – it should not take longer than a month – then we converge here.'

He stabbed a finger towards one planet, five from the centre of the system.

'Boros Prime,' he said, 'is the lynchpin. It is the heart of the system. Take that, and we take the Boros Gate.'

Marduk peered at the sandy-coloured planet, rotating on its endless loop around the system's two suns. It appeared such a little thing. He need only reach out to grasp it. What looked like a silver moon orbited around the planet.

'The Kronos star fort?' he asked.

'A relic of the Dark Age of Technology,' said Kol Harekh with a nod. 'Its size and firepower is prodigious. It serves as the docking station for the system's battleships. It must be neutralised before planetfall can be achieved. We'll use Kol Badar's strategem for tackling it.'

'Prepare the way for Abaddon's Black Crusade,' said Ekodas, resuming his authority. 'Glorify the Legion and bring about the end of mankind. Warp transference commences within the hour. Ready your Hosts. That is all.'

DARK APOSTLE SARABDAL strode alongside Marduk as they marched back towards their shuttles. He spoke in a low voice so that only Marduk could hear.

'We must talk, but not here,' he said. 'Ekodas's influence even spreads into my Host. Doubtless it also grows within your own.'

'Impossible.'

'It is not,' said Sarabdal. 'Be wary. Things are moving beneath the surface.'

'Ekodas–' began Marduk.

'Ekodas is carving out an empire within the Legion,' said Sarabdal, interrupting him. 'He seeks to bend us to his cause.'

'"His cause?" I don't see–' said Marduk.

'Not here,' hissed Sarabdal. 'I fear this is bigger than any of us could have imagined, perhaps bigger than Ekodas himself. I am close to uncovering its secret, but–' said Sarabdal. He fell silent as Ekodas's veterans, providing an escort for the Apostles, closed in around them.

'Be wary. Be vigilant,' he said after a minute, before boarding his shuttle. 'We cannot act until we know. As soon as we make transference, we shall talk. Then you too shall understand what is at stake.'

'Lorgar's blessing upon you, brother,' said Marduk.

'And upon you, my friend,' said Sarabdal. 'We must speak, soon, you and I.'

'It shall be so.'

Turning away, Marduk strode up the embarkation ramp of his Stormbird.

BACK ABOARD HIS own battleship, the *Anarchus*, Ankh-Heloth knelt within his prayer cell. The doors were shut and sealed, and he had activated the null-sphere that would ensure that nothing that was spoken within could be heard from outside. He was alone in the room, and his eyes were tightly closed. A droplet of blood dripped from his nose onto the floor. His voice echoed off the bare cell walls.

'I believe that Belagosa will turn, given the right leverage, my lord,' said Ankh-Heloth.

*I agree*, pulsed Ekodas, his voice spearing through Ankh-Heloth's mind, making the Apostle wince.

'Marduk I am unsure of. Nevertheless, once the captains of the 34th are turned, the Host will belong to us.'

*How far along are we?*

'Our order grows steadily within his Host, my lord. Several officers within the 34th were most eager to turn. It seems that some of them harbour personal grudges against their Dark Apostle.'

*Good. That is something that can be exploited.*

'Which leaves us with Sarabdal,' said Ankh-Heloth. 'I fear that he will not be swayed. Already he has exposed several members of our cult within his ranks. Its growth stifles.'

*He knows,* pulsed Ekodas. *He is a danger to us.*

'What would you have me do, my lord?'

*I believe that we can solve the problem of Belagosa and Sarabdal in one. Be ready.*

'And Marduk?'

*Let the Brotherhood do its work.*

THE ASTROPATH SCREAMED and went into wild convulsions.

Hands held him down and the hilt of a knife was jammed between his teeth to stop him biting his own tongue. He registered them only dimly; his mind was filled with the horrific after-images of the searing vision that had brought on his fit.

It was more than an hour before his convulsions ceased, leaving him shivering and aching all over. He lay immobile on a pallet, his arms and legs strapped down.

A shape loomed over him and a voice intruded on his nightmare. It was insistent, and would not leave him in peace. He cried out for death, cried out for the Emperor to take him. He had seen too much, much too much, and he begged for release.

'You shall be granted the Emperor's mercy,' said a deep voice. 'Just tell me what you saw.'

The words tumbled from him in a torrent, and while only perhaps every tenth word was decipherable, they painted a clear picture: death was coming to Boros Prime. He spoke of eyes of fire, of a burning flame upon an open book, of living flesh inscribed with symbols that made his stomach clench painfully even to think of it. He babbled insanely, speaking of souls devoured by ravenous gods that dwelt in the dark beyond. He spoke of spinning silver rings that rotated within themselves, conjuring darkness, and how hell was coming to claim them all. Finally, sobbing, he begged for release.

The tortured astropath smiled in relief as the barrel of a bolt pistol was pressed to his temple. The shot was deafening in the holding cell. Blood splattered the walls.

'What is it, Coadjutor?' came the voice of Proconsul Ostorius over the grainy vox-unit. 'What did the astropath foresee?'

'Chaos,' was all that Aquilius said as he holstered his bolt pistol.

# CHAPTER FOUR

BURIAS HURRIED TO catch up with Marduk as he stormed through the corridors of the *Infidus Diabolus*.

He glanced at Marduk's face, which was a furious mask.

'Will it work?' he asked.

'It has to,' said Marduk, 'else we are all dead.'

Sirens blared, and Stormbirds and Thunderhawks were prepped for launch. The Host's Dreadclaws had been roused, their daemon essences stirred for the coming engagement in case of potential boarding actions. The Host's warrior brothers were undergoing final preparations, mournfully intoning catechisms of defilement and retribution.

'I don't trust Ashkanez,' said Burias.

Marduk's silence invited more.

'I do not understand why you allowed him into the Host. He is not one of us. It is bad enough that Kol Badar still lives, but Ashkanez?

'I don't need to explain myself to you, Burias.'

The Icon Bearer scowled. 'They will betray you. Mark my words. The First Acolyte covets power, and Kol Badar hates you enough to help him take it. Then, the 34th will become just another subservient Host under Ekodas. Let me deal with them.'

'I will deal with Kol Badar myself. For now, he serves a purpose. As for Ashkanez, he is First Acolyte. Of course he seeks to replace me, just as I sought to replace Jarulek, and he the Warmonger before him. It is our way.'

'Let them do it? You need warriors around you that you can trust! You need a Coryphaus–'

'I trust no one!'

'You trust me,' said Burias.

'You I trust less than most, Burias,' Marduk replied.

The possessed warrior looked affronted. 'I am your loyal comrade and friend. I always have been.'

'A Dark Apostle has no need of friends,' said Marduk.

'My loyalty has and ever will be to you,' said Burias, 'and as long–'

'Don't think me a fool, Burias,' snapped Marduk. 'You are loyal to me only as long as it benefits you. I know this. *You* know this. Let us not pretend.'

They glared at each other for a long moment before the Icon Bearer lowered his eyes.

'You are a warrior, Burias, a fantastically gifted one, and you serve well in that regard. The same can be said of Kol Badar. Ashkanez has yet to prove himself. If he does not, then I will dispose of him. Be my champion, Burias. Forget the rest. Now get out of my sight,' said Marduk. 'Go do something useful.'

'Whatever you wish, *blood-brother*,' said Burias, before stalking away.

THE CHAMBERS SET aside for Magos Darioq-Grendh'al's workshop were located deep within the stern of the *Infidus Diabolus*. They were crowded and claustrophobic, packed with salvaged mechanics, tech-implements, crippled servitors, discarded weaponry and engines of all kinds. Cylinders filled with bloody amniotic fluid stood in rows against the walls. The magos's experiments bobbed inside, vile blends of living flesh, metal and daemon. Further products of his enthusiastic tinkering crawled amongst the heaps of machinery, repulsive by-blows that moaned and twitched.

Once, Darioq had been a devotee of the Cult Mechanicus of Mars, a techno-magos worshipping the so-called Omnissiah, the God in the Machine. Now he was much more than that. Now he was Darioq-Grendh'al.

His body was concealed within a black robe, its edges hemmed with bronze wire. A single gleaming red eyepiece shone from within his deep cowl. As bulky as one of the Terminator-armoured Anointed, Darioq-Grendh'al moved with stilted, mechanised movements. Four immense, articulated arms extended from the servo-harness affixed to his frame, one pair curving over his shoulders like the stabbing tails of a desert arachnoid, the other extending around his sides like pincers. A pulsing cluster of umbilical cords and semi-organic cables trailed behind the tainted magos, hard-plugged into his spine.

Spread-eagled upon a table before the magos was a slave, arms and legs restrained. The magos was working on the figure, clinically cutting and dissecting flesh and organs. The tortured slave's skin had mostly been ripped from its body, exposing musculature, and it moaned in torment beneath the magos's ministrations.

Banks of brain-units sat in bell jars within refrigeration tanks, thin needles puncturing their lobes. The magos had up to five brains plugged into his mechanised body at any one time, picking and choosing which of the hemispheres would best suit his current pursuit. Many of them bore evidence of corruption.

Unfettered by petty moral constraints, the corrupted magos revelled in a universe of studies that had formerly been disallowed, and he now worked at a feverish, obsessive pace.

Thinking machines, xenos tech, mech/daemonic blends, experimental warp-based weaponry, engines utilising the immaterium itself as their power source; all these things had been deemed heretical and blasphemous, outlawed as deviant and fundamentally incompatible with the reverence of the Omnissiah. None of the strict and uncompromising edicts of Mars mattered to him any more.

Servo-arms, fleshy protuberances and mechadendrite tentacles worked independently of each other as the corrupted magos busied himself at his work. He needed no rest and gained what sustenance he required from the bodies of the slaves. Day and night the magos toiled. The Mechanicus code inhibitors implanted in his brain-stems had long been removed, and he found himself with a whole wealth of new areas of study now open to him – enough work for a thousand lifetimes.

None of this mattered to Inshabael Kharesh, sorcerer of the Black Legion. He was Warmaster Abaddon's personally appointed envoy, and all that interested him was the device.

The sorcerer's face was devoid of colour. Black tendrils pulsed within his flesh, runes of Chaos that were in constant flux. His hair was straight and long, as pale as spiders' silk. The colourless hue of the sorcerer's skin and hair made the glittering brilliance of his sapphire eyes all the more startling.

The sorcerer was staring at the device.

It hung motionless in mid-air, caught in a beam of red light. It was a perfect silver sphere roughly the size of an unaugmented human heart.

The Nexus Arrangement.

Three immense hoops of black metal surrounded the sphere. Each was carved with Chaos icons and runes of power. It was this construct that bound that device to the will of the Word Bearers. Those rings were currently motionless. Only when the device was activated would they begin to turn.

'It is remarkable,' said Inshabael Kharesh.

'The power the device harbours is like nothing recalled in any Mechanicus data record,' said Darioq-Grendh'al. 'Nothing stored in any of Darioq-Grendh'al's brain-units compares to this sublime construction. Darioq-Grendh'al is only able to tap into the smallest fraction of its power – no more than 8.304452349 per cent of its attainable output – and yet even so it can achieve much.'

'The Warmaster is very interested in the device,' said the Black Legion sorcerer. He had to raise his voice to be heard over the cries of the slave the magos was torturing.

'My lord will be interested in you as well, Darioq-Grendh'al,' Kharesh added.

'Lord Abaddon, Warmaster of the Black Legion and genetic descendant of Horus Lupercal, will be interested in the mech/flesh unit daemon symbiote Darioq-Grendh'al, formerly Tech Magos Darioq of the Adeptus Mechanicus?' said Darioq-Grendh'al, his emotionless voice overlaid with the growls and snarls of the daemon infused into every muscle, fibre and cell.

'Of course,' said Kharesh, smiling. 'You are a singular creature, a true blend of human, machine and daemon.'

The magos did not answer, intent on his plaything. The slave's cries had been stifled now, which pleased Kharesh. One of Darioq-Grendh'al's tentacles had pushed down its throat, and it pulsed with peristalsis as it bored through the slave's stomach lining, feasting upon organs.

'You have no ties to Marduk or his 34th Host,' said Kharesh, picking his words carefully.

'It was Marduk, Dark Apostle of the 34th Host of the Word Bearers Astartes Legion, genetic descendant of the glorified Primarch Lorgar, who brought Grendh'al forth from the empyrean,' said the corrupted magos. 'It was Marduk, Dark Apostle of the 34th Host of the Word Bearers Astartes Legion, genetic descendant of the glorified Primarch Lorgar, who released Darioq from the shackles imposed upon him by the Adeptus Mechanicus of Mars,' he added.

'True,' said Kharesh, smiling. 'But it is also true that the Warmaster Abaddon has a far greater access to archeotech caches and Dark Age technology than the XVII Legion.'

The magos paused. Only for a second, but it was enough to show the Black Legion sorcerer that he'd been heard.

'The Warmaster is benefactor to many Dark Mechanicus adepts,' he added, 'and many Obliterator cults. I think you would find much to your appreciation were the Warmaster to become your benefactor, Darioq-Grendh'al.'

'That is a most interesting notion, Inshabael Kharesh, sorcerer lord of the Black Legion, formerly of the Sons of Horus, formerly of the Lunar Wolves, genetic descendant of Warmaster Horus Lupercal.'

'Something to think about,' said the sorcerer, hearing the mag-locked doors hiss as they opened.

Marduk strode in, closely followed by his First Acolyte and Coryphaus.

'And how is Darioq-Grenhd'al today?' said Marduk.

'Darioq-Grenhd'al,' said Darioq-Grenhd'al, 'has been having an interesting conversation with Inshabael Kharesh, sorcerer lord of the Black Legion, formerly of the Sons of Horus, formerly of the Luna Wolves, genetic descendant of Warmaster Horus Lupercal.'

'Oh?' said Marduk. 'And what pray has the sorcerer got to say for himself?'

'The fallen magos was telling me how he has yet to access even ten per cent of the potential power of the Nexus Arrangement,' interposed Kharesh. 'Its potential is quite… staggering.'

'I see,' said Marduk.

'Inshabael Kharesh, sorcerer lord of the Black–' began the magos.

'I know who you mean,' interrupted Marduk.

'–has informed Darioq-Grendh'al that the Warmaster Abaddon is benefactor to many Dark Mechanicus adepts and many Obliterator cults,' said Darioq-Grendh'al. 'He thinks that Darioq-Grendh'al would find much to his appreciation were the Warmaster to become his benefactor.'

'Really,' said Marduk.

Inshabael Kharesh merely shrugged his shoulders, refusing to be cowed by the Dark Apostle.

'Would you deny the truth of the statement, Apostle?' he said.

'The device is *mine*, sorcerer,' said Marduk, 'Just as Darioq-Grendh'al is mine. I will not let either of them leave the 34th Host.'

'We shall see,' said the sorcerer, smiling.

'Yes, we shall,' said Marduk. Idly, he picked up something from one of the magos's workbenches. His eyes widened as he recognised the spherical device.

'A vortex grenade?' he said in wonder. The most powerful man-portable weapon ever conceived by the Imperium of Man, a vortex grenade was a priceless artefact capable of destroying anything – *anything* – that it touched.

'A gift,' said Inshabael Kharesh, reaching out to take it from Marduk's hands. 'For the magos.'

Marduk refused to relinquish his hold on the deadly artefact, and for a moment the Dark Apostle and the sorcerer were locked together, unwilling to back down. Finally, Inshabael shrugged and let go.

'A bribe,' growled Ashkanez.

'You would dare bring such an item aboard my ship without my knowledge?' said Marduk, holding the vortex grenade under the sorcerer's nose.

'It is a bauble, nothing more,' said the sorcerer. 'I thought the magos might like to study it.'

'Secure this,' said Marduk, handing the vortex grenade to Kol Badar. The Coryphaus took it gingerly.

'One cannot help but wonder why the creators of the Nexus Arrangement – the *necron* – had not used the device themselves,' said the sorcerer, changing the subject.

'It hardly matters,' said Marduk.

'Perhaps not,' said Inshabael Kharesh with an enigmatic half-smile. Marduk suppressed the urge to strike him.

For the millionth time in the last few months, Marduk cursed the day that the Council of Sicarus had agreed to allow the sorcerer to accompany Marduk's 34th Host.

While it was true that the Word Bearers and Black Legion had once been close, much of that good will and brotherly respect had evaporated upon the death of the Warmaster Horus. While Abaddon might have claimed the title of Warmaster for himself, it afforded him none of the respect that Horus had garnered from the XVII Legion. Of course, the Black Legion's strength was unparalleled – their ranks outnumbered those of the Word Bearers almost ten to one – yet many within the Word Bearers regarded it as but a pale shadow of its former glory, its self-proclaimed Warmaster worthy of contempt. Nevertheless, it was all but certain that it would be the Black Legion who would form the mainstay of the final crusade against the hated Imperium, and because of that, the Word Bearers held their peace.

Marduk begrudged Kharesh's presence upon his ship. He hated the self-satisfied, mocking gleam in the whoreson's crystalline eyes as he observed the daily rituals of the 34th Host and studied Darioq-Grendh'al's work on the xenos Nexus Arrangement device.

Perhaps more than anything else, he hated the fact that there was someone aboard the *Infidus Diabolus* whose life was not his to take.

He shifted his attention towards the twisted magos.

Darioq-Grendh'al's head was turned to the side, staring down in morbid curiosity as he prodded the now lifeless slave laid out before him. His tentacles continued to burrow through the corpse's innards, chewing and slurping. Part metal, part living tissue, part daemon, the mechadendrites were sinuous and writhing things, moving with a life of their own.

The stink of Chaos was strong on the corrupted magos, and though his heavily augmented body was fully swathed in heavy black cloth, Marduk could see it bulge and swell, writhing from within as Darioq-Grendh'al's body altered its form, in constant flux.

Marduk smiled to see the magos so changed, to see such a being of order, uniformity and structure released to become a true creature of Chaos.

'We make transference within the hour, Darioq-Grendh'al,' said Marduk. 'The device will be ready?'

'Yes, Marduk, Dark Apostle of the 34th Host of the Word Bearers Astartes Legion, genetic descendant of the glorified Primarch Lorgar,' said Darioq-Grendh'al. 'It will be ready.'

THE ROOM WAS dim and circular, with tiered steps around the edge. A two-headed eagle, the symbol of the Imperium marked the marble floor, but otherwise the room was bare of ornamentation. Marble columns supported the high domed ceiling. The walls of the room had been raised, hiding the view beyond from sight, and their photo-chromatic panels had been dimmed; in direct sunlight, the hololithic figures arranged around the room were difficult to see.

There were over forty figures standing on the circular steps, the higher-ranked individuals positioned on the lowest tiers. Only ten of those figures were physically in the room, including Aquilius himself and his Proconsul Ostorius, both fully garbed for war. The other six were officers of the Boros Imperial Guard and the Fleet Commanders of the Imperial Navy stationed at the Kronos star fort.

Aquilius recognised the Legatus and Praefectus of the Boros 232nd from his inspection of their ranks. Though neither was of the highest rank, and they stood on the upper tiers, the 232nd's combat record was faultless and the high legate of the Boros Guard had requested their presence personally. Ostorius had acquiesced to the appeal, and Aquilius had been pleased to see that Praefectus Verenus had accompanied his Legatus. He had seen something in the man, something akin to the pride of a White Consul. A shame that he was too old for indoctrination into the Chapter, for he believed he would have made a fine Space Marine.

The other thirty figures standing on various tiers around the room were all hololiths, the monochromatic projections of those that could not be present because of their distance. There were many gaps upon the tiers; those gathered were only the ones that were available at such short notice, and all were high-ranking individuals. There were admirals and lord high commanders, all positioned only a step or two from the floor, and high-grade officers of the commissariat and Ecclesiarchy positioned higher up.

Some of the images were clearer than others. At a glance, some appeared completely solid, excepting their monochrome colouring. Others were like ghosts, transparent and incorporeal, while others were thick with static and jerky with time-lapse, their mouths out of synch with their speech.

Upon the lowest tier were Adeptus Astartes, the Emperor's angels of death. All belonged to the Adeptus Praeses, the fraternity of Chapters that had been created for the sole purpose of guarding against incursions from within the Eye of Terror. They formed the first line of defence against the inhabitants of that hellish realm, responding to any threat with bolter, chainsword, unshakeable faith and the fury of the righteous.

Once there had been twenty Chapters of the Adeptus Praeses; now there were eighteen. The Archenemy had annihilated one Chapter and, more shocking still, another had been branded Excommunicatus Traitorus.

Aquilius's gaze strayed around the circle of these august Space Marines.

Chapter Masters, senior captains, Librarians, Chaplains; all were present here, members and representatives of the Adeptus Praeses. Never had he been in the presence of such prestigious individuals.

The Chapter Master of the Marines Exemplar, twin scars ritually carved down his cheeks, stood alongside captains of the Iron Talons, barbarous-looking in their skin-draped power armour, yet utterly devoted to the Imperium. The Chief Librarian of the insular Brothers Penitent stood alongside the captain of the

First Company of the Knights Unyielding, his ornamental armour plastered with purity seals and oath papers. A hooded member of the Crimson Scythes stood apart from the others, as was the way of his Chapter. Aquilius could not discern his rank.

Finally, Aquilius's gaze came to rest upon the last two Astartes warriors, the revered Chapter Masters of the White Consuls, Cymar Xydias and Titus Valens.

Unusually amongst the Adeptus Astartes, the White Consuls had not one but two Chapter Masters. While one patrolled the fringes of the Eye of Terror or partook in holy warfare, the other was located back at the Chapter's home world, Sabatine, governing the Chapter from its fortress-monastery high in the mountains. The Consuls were spread far and wide, battle-brothers and companies located across more than fifty systems at any one time, and it had served the Chapter well to have its pair of co-rulers, for the Chapter Master engaged in the theatre of war was able to concentrate his attentions fully upon the task at hand, confident that the Chapter was being run efficiently.

The Chapter Masters were a dramatic contrast in both appearance and demeanour.

Cymar Xydias, who had reigned as Chapter Master for almost twelve hundred years, and currently oversaw the Chapter's movements from Sabatine, was a severe warrior with an angular face. With a piercing gaze and cutting insight, Xydias was a strategic genius; his understanding of both the flow of battle and the politics of the systems the White Consuls oversaw was masterful and inspiring. He wore a long cloak and a metal wreath of ivy upon his balding head.

Xydias had won countless wars for the White Consuls over the centuries, glorious victories that had been forever documented in the annals of the Chapter. His perfectly executed stratagems were studied by White Consul neophytes and initiates, and he was renowned for his ability to outthink the enemy, always a dozen moves ahead. Weaving an intricate and often bewildering web of attack and counter-attack, of feint and rapid redeployment, his strategic ploys had achieved unlikely victory time and again. His strategic acumen was far beyond the ken of any regular battle-brother, and Aquilius had studied every battle that Xydias had overseen.

Where Cymar Xydias was lean and hawk-like, Chapter Master Titus Valens was a thick-necked warrior, his massive frame encased in an exoskeleton of Terminator armour that made his bulk even greater. His face was broad and blunt, his short-cropped hair sandy blond and speckled with grey where Xydias's was white and sharply receding. His left shoulder plate bore the Crux Terminatus, the holy icon that every suit of revered Terminator armour bore, each containing a tiny fragment of the golden armour worn by the God-Emperor himself ten thousand years earlier. The Chapter symbol, a resplendent blue eagle's head, was emblazoned upon his right, and a gleaming double-headed eagle was sculpted into his chest plate, every feather carved in immaculate detail.

Xydias's strategic brilliance came from a combination of natural talent, intense tutorage under the finest minds of the White Consuls and the Ultramarines in his youth, and a lifetime of study and experience. Valens's strength lay in his instinctive comprehension of the ebb and flow of battle.

While Chapter Master Titus Valens was as highly educated and classically trained as the most learned of the White Consuls, his true talents, as Aquilius understood it, lay in his innate understanding of warfare and its psychology. Valens always seemed to know the exact moment to press the assault in order to demoralise the enemy, the exact moment when a line was close to breaking and needed bolstering. He led the Chapter from the fore, an inspiring and prominent figure capable of turning defeat into a resounding victory with one well-timed charge.

Aquilius idolised Xydias, emulating his logical, strategic mind. Proconsul Ostorius was a fervent supporter of Titus Valens.

Aquilius had listened intently on the odd occasion that Ostorius spoke of the battles he had fought alongside the Chapter Master. Ostorius's eyes would shine with passion then, and Aquilius could picture the battle in his mind's eye as if he had been there himself. He felt the thrill that Ostorius had experienced as Valens had hurled himself into the breach at Delanok Pass time and again, heroically rallying the thirty White Consuls battle-brothers as they held for sixty-two days against a force of over ten thousand, desperately holding the line until reinforcements from the 6th and 9th Companies arrived and flanked the enemy, cutting them down mercilessly between their controlled lines of fire.

'Give your report, Proconsul Ostorius,' said Chapter Master Titus Valens.

The room descended into silence, every present member of the caucus listening to the Proconsul intently.

'Honoured brethren,' said Ostorius in a loud clear voice, addressing the gathered personages. 'Twenty-three minutes ago a considerable Chaos fleet was detected transferring from the warp. It is predicted that it will realise in thirty-five minutes' time, emerging on the dark side of the Trajan Belt. I request the aid of the Adeptus Praeses to defeat this threat.'

'From the incoming information, I see that this fleet consists of between eleven and fifteen warships of cruiser size or larger,' said Chapter Master Absalon of the Marines Exemplar. 'Do we have any ship recognition yet?'

'We do,' said Ostorius. 'Archive scouts have found two matches, with more pending. The first, the battlecruiser *Righteous Might*, which disappeared from Imperial records in M32.473. Its last transmission announced an attack from an unidentified raider fleet, attacking from the Maelstrom.'

'And the second?' said one of the captains of the Iron Talons, in a thick, guttural accent.

Ostorius nodded to the commodore of the Boros Naval Fleet, who cleared his throat before speaking.

'A positive match on an Infernus-class battleship,' said the commodore, which caused an outbreak of muttering and consternation. 'One of only seven ever launched from the forge docks of Balthasar XIX. An inefficient design. Monstrously powerful, though.

'We have matched the call-signature of this Infernus to that of the *Flame of Purity*. According to our records, the *Flame of Purity* turned traitor during the Heresy and suffered grievous structural damage during its aftermath care of the White Scars – your father Legion, noble captains,' said Ostorius, nodding towards the two Space Marines of the Iron Talons.

'We know this ship,' snarled the First Captain of the Iron Talons. 'We pledge our oath to support Boros Prime. We send six companies.'

Ostorius bowed to the Iron Talons before continuing.

'Since M33.089 the *Flame of Purity* has had confirmed sightings in eighty-four documented confrontations,' said Ostorius. 'It has since been redubbed the *Crucius Maledictus.*'

'The Word Bearers,' spat the warrior brother of the Crimson Scythes.

'So it would appear,' said Ostorius.

'Between eleven and fifteen battleships,' said the Chapter Master of the Knight Unyielding. 'A sizeable force.'

'The *Crucius Maledictus* was present during the destruction of the Black Consuls,' said Chapter Master Xydias. 'Undoubtedly, the Word Bearers know that Boros is under the control of the White Consuls.'

'The bastards have a taste for your bloodline,' growled one of the Iron Talons captains.

'It would seem so,' said Chapter Master Xydias.

'From the number of ships we are reading, I would hazard that there are around five or six Word Bearers Hosts bearing down on Boros,' said Ostorius.

'If that is true, we may be facing anywhere between five and fifteen thousand Word Brother zealots,' said Chapter Master Valens. 'Plus whatever foul allies they have brought with them.'

'Engines?' said a senior Imperial Guard warmaster.

'Highly likely,' said Chapter Master Xydias. 'The traitorous Legio Vulturus has been codified as fighting alongside the Word Bearers on dozens of occasions, often in the same systems in which the *Crucius Maledictus* has been sighted. It would be wise to expect to face Titans if the enemy was to make planetfall.'

'Pray it does not come to that, brother,' said Absalon of the Marines Exemplar.

'With the Emperor's grace, it will not,' said Chapter Master Valens. 'But we must be prepared for the eventuality.'

'I will notify Lord Commander Horacio and the Princeps Senioris engaged in the Thraxian campaign,' said the Chapter Master Absalon. 'I shall request that they spare some of the Princeps' Legios, upon the off-chance that the Archenemy makes planetfall. I am certain that the Legio Gryphonicus would relish the opportunity to exact their revenge upon the engines of their dark kin.'

'My thanks,' said Chapter Master Xydias, graciously. 'I need not remind you all of the importance of the Boros Gate. If the enemy were to claim it, then they would have an open path into Segmentum Solar and the heart of the Imperium. All available White Consuls battle-brothers will be marshalled to meet this threat head on. The only warriors of our Chapter who shall not answer this call are those officiating as Proconsuls and Coadjutors of our protectorate systems, and the Praetorian squads of Sabatine itself. The 8th and 9th reserve Companies are already mobilising here, for immediate transference. Brother Valens?'

'The war here in Bellasus VII is almost done,' said Co-Chapter Master Valens. 'Astartes presence is no longer required to complete the pacification. I shall disengage and lead the four battle companies with me to the Boros Gate immediately. The *Divine Splendour* shall lead my armada.'

Aquilius was impressed. The White Consuls were a fleet-heavy Chapter with three immense battle-barges and more than a dozen strike cruisers at their disposal. Fully two-thirds of the fleet was always scouring the fringes of the Eye of Terror, ever vigilant for incursion. That two of the Chapter's three hallowed battle-barges, the *Divine Splendour* and the *Righteous Fury*, were being re-routed to the Boros system, together with virtually the entirety of the White Consuls Chapter, spoke of the level of threat that the enemy posed.

'When can Boros expect the first of these reinforcements, noble lords?' said Ostorius. 'I have already mobilised the defence fleet, and it is closing on the expected warp translation location of the enemy fleet even now. If the enemy attempts to push through towards the core worlds, my fleet could engage as it emerges from the Trajan Belt, but it will not last long in a full engagement without support.'

'We are relatively close, Proconsul. With time adjustment, we will be there in approximately…' the co-Chapter Master's voice trailed off as he received information off-screen. He snorted and shook his head in wonderment. 'Truly the Boros Gate wormholes are a marvel. We will be there within the hour, Boros realtime. It will take us seven weeks of warp travel once we have mobilised, yet it will take less than an hour in realspace until seven full White Consuls companies make transference.'

'My thanks for the swift mobilisation, my lord,' said Ostorius with a bow of his head. 'And it pleases me that my brothers of 5th Company, aboard the *Implacable*, will be joining the armada.'

He wishes he were onboard the *Implacable*, realised Aquilius, hearing a note of bitterness in the Proconsul's voice. He would rather be out there with their brothers of 5th Company, taking the fight to the enemy, than standing here, impotent, watching the battle on the holo-deck of the Kronos Star fort.

'Why are they attacking here?' said Proconsul Ostorius. 'We know they covet the Boros Gate, and yet while the Word Bearers are many things, they are not stupid. They know of its defences. They know that even now we will be moving against them. They will be obliterated before they get within hours of the core planet, and yet still they come.'

'You overestimate them, White Consul,' snarled the Iron Talons 7th Company captain. 'The Word Bearers are fanatics. Perhaps their daemon-gods tell them to die. Who can predict them?'

Aquilius was not certain that he agreed, but he did not voice his concerns. The Word Bearers were known zealots, but they were not fools.

'You do not give them enough credit, captain,' said Chapter Master Harkonus of the Knights Unyielding. 'Don't let you hatred blind you. The Word Bearers would not sacrifice themselves needlessly. If they are attacking here, it is because they believe they can win.'

'I agree,' said Cymar Xydias. 'We must assume that they have a plan to bypass our defences. We must proceed with caution.'

A handful more hololiths had appeared during the conference, including more Astartes upon the lowest tier. Two of those were White Consuls, the captains of 5th and 2nd Companies. Aquilius stood straighter beneath the gaze of his direct superior, Captain Marcus Decimus of 5th Company.

The flickering holo-image of the Subjagators Chapter Master had materialised alongside the other brothers of the Adeptus Praeses. Blood was splattered across his face, and his armour bore evidence of recent battle.

Nevertheless, it was the last arrival that made Aquilius's breath catch in his throat.

'Throne,' he muttered, eyes widening.

The newcomer was bedecked in ornate Terminator armour of a style unique to his order, and this Grand-Master of the daemon-hunting Grey Knights bore an immense force halberd and appeared truly ancient. A devotional tattoo was plastered across his forehead and he introduced himself as Grand-Master Havashen. He spoke only briefly, informing the caucus that a full company of his brethren would rendezvous with the others in the Boros system forthwith to combat the Word Bearers threat. With that, his hololith promptly disappeared.

The Adeptus Praeses Chapters swore their oaths of support, pledging what companies they could. Battlefleet Gorgon was to be re-directed to bolster their strength, and the details of the defence were finalised.

The Boros Defence Fleet, bolstered now by the strike cruisers of the White Consuls 2nd and 5th Companies, was already ploughing at full speed towards the thick band of asteroids, the Trajan Belt, which divided the Boros Gate system. The enemy were expected to make translocation through a warp exit beyond the belt. If the enemy did not attempt to breach the Trajan Belt, then the Boros fleet would wait for the bulk of the Astartes Praeses fleets, and the devastating power of the Darkstar fortress that accompanied Battlefleet Gorgon, before pushing through to engage. If the Word Bearers attempted to breach the Trajan Belt, which was riddled with mines and defence installations, then the Boros Defence Fleet would engage, punishing them as they emerged piecemeal through the notoriously hazardous asteroid band.

With the stable wormholes, the exact moment of the supporting Fleet's arrival had been calculated, and so the Boros Defence Fleet could engage the enemy with confidence, knowing the precise moment when help would arrive. If all went to the meticulously detailed and coordinated plan that had been agreed upon by the caucus, then the enemy would engage the heavily outnumbered Boros Defence Fleet, confident of victory.

The full force of the Imperial reinforcements would hang back, massing just beyond the gate until the enemy was fully engaged. Then they would emerge from the warp and fall upon the flanks of the enemy.

It required perfect timing and was a dangerous ploy, placing the defence fleet of Boros Prime, and the accompanying White Consuls strike cruisers of the 2nd and 5th, in a precarious position.

It was deemed a worthy risk, however. By showing its full strength too early, they risked scaring the enemy fleet off, losing the chance to destroy a sizeable force of the hated Word Bearers.

'Good hunting, brothers,' said Chapter Master Titus Valens at the conclusion of the caucus, and Aquilius felt a thrill of excitement run through him at the prospect of the forthcoming battle, even though he would only be able to view it from afar.

It would be glorious.

# CHAPTER FIVE

LIKE A MONSTER rising from the depths, the *Infidus Diabolus* broke from the warp, its hull creaking and groaning as reality crashed in upon it. Phosphorescent waves of warp energy cascaded along its bow. Shimmering void shields blurred the edges of its outline as fragments of debris and wreckage battered against them.

'What in the name of the Urizen?' snarled Marduk from his command pulpit on the bridge as a chunk of twisted metal the size of a hab-block glanced off the prow of the ship with an unnerving squeal of the forward shields. 'Report.'

'Systems coming online,' drawled a servitor hardwired into the control hub of the ship. It was little more than the armless torso of a skeleton, with a thick bundle of pulsating tubes, wires and cables protruding from its ruptured skull, connecting its exposed brain to the cogitation units in front of it. It drooled yellow syrup as its blackened lips moved. 'Scanning in progress… scan complete at 10.342… 13.94…. 18.2343…'

'Plasma core at 85% and rising,' barked another servitor unit, a thrashing creature that jerked back and forth, pulling at the leaking plugs that connected its limbless torso to the humming banks of sensor arrays to either side of it.

'Internal comms established, external pulse ignition in five,' intoned another in a mechanised voice.

'Port battery cognition online.'

'Establishing fleet contact.'

Screens of data-flow filled with scrolling diagnostic reports and internal mechadialogue as the systems of the *Infidus Diabolus* slowly came online. A ship was always at its most vulnerable before its navigational and comms arrays were up and running.

Scanning the bewildering array of codeform and binaric data inloading across dozens of screens, Kol Badar frowned.

'Well?' said Marduk.

'I'm reading heat signatures and plasma bleed. Something is wrong,' growled Kol Badar.

'Is it us?' said Burias.

'No,' said Kol Badar. 'Our readings are fine.'

'Where did all this come from?' said Marduk in rising concern as the grating squeal of the shields continued. 'We were meant to realise two hundred thousand kilometres from the asteroid belt.'

'We did,' said Kol Badar, scanning the inloading data being transferred onto the console in front of him. 'This is something else.'

'Where is the *Mortisis Majesticatus*?' said First Acolyte Ashkanez, accessing the in-flood of data via a nerve-spike inserted into a plug in his left vambrace.

Marduk looked out through the viewing portal that dominated the bridge. The *Infidus Diabolus* was positioned towards the rear of the fleet, and he could see the shapes of the other Word Bearers ships beyond, flickering immaterium residue still clutching at their hulls. They had come through in battle formation, wary of potential attack, with the crude proselyte slave ships on the outside, and the hulking monstrosity that held the Legio Vulturus protectively in the centre.

Ekodas's immense Infernus-class battleship, the *Crucius Maledictus*, was located to the fore, but of the Dark Apostle Sarabdal's strike cruiser, the *Mortisis Majesticatus*, he could see nothing.

Kol Badar's brow furrowed, and he studied the data floods, eyes scanning quickly.

'Well?' snapped Marduk. 'Where is it?'

'It's not here,' said Kol Badar.

'It didn't make realisation?'

Kol Badar shook his head.

'It came through before us. It should be here.'

'Could it have veered off course?' said Burias. 'Made realisation elsewhere?'

'Not possible,' said Marduk. 'Well, my Coryphaus? Where in the name of the nine hells of Sicarus is Sarabdal and the 18th Host?'

'The *Moribundus Fatalis* is here,' said Kol Badar, stabbing a finger against a data-slate showing the positioning of the fleet. 'So half of Sarabdal's Host is with us. Wait…'

Kol Badar traced the flow of information with one ceramite-encased finger, before turning to face Marduk. His face was grim.

'Spit it out,' snapped Marduk.

'The *Mortisis Majesticatus* is all around us,' said Kol Badar finally.

'What?' said Burias.

Marduk leant backwards and licked his lips as more wreckage was repelled by the shields of the *Infidus Diabolus*.

His mind reeled. He had not thought that even Ekodas would go that far, at least not so blatantly. He realised how much he was relying on his alliance with Sarabdal. Without him, he felt exposed and vulnerable. Worse, whatever secret that Sarabdal had uncovered regarding Ekodas's plot had died with him.

'The murderous bastard,' he hissed.

'Surely you do not suspect one of our own being responsible, my Apostle?' said Ashkanez.

Marduk glanced over at his First Acolyte, but did not say anything.

'I'm reading heat discharge from the cannons and torpedo tubes of the *Crucius Maledictus* and the *Anarchus*,' said Kol Badar.

'Ekodas and his wretched toad, Ankh-Heloth,' murmured Marduk.

'No, First Acolyte,' he said, his voice thick with derision. 'I would never dream of suspecting one of my brothers.'

'The *Mortisis Majesticatus* had been destroyed?' said Burias.

'Very good, my Icon Bearer,' said Marduk. 'As you can see, Ashkanez, I keep Burias around for his cutting, fierce intellect. Nothing gets by him.'

Burias scowled, and Marduk felt the daemon within the Icon Bearer straining to be released.

'Is there such disunity within the XVII Legion that brother fires upon brother?' said a deeply resonant voice, and all hostility within the room was suddenly directed towards this newcomer. First Acolyte Ashkanez flexed his fingers, and Marduk knew that he longed to reach for his weapon; he felt much the same way.

Kol Badar, ignoring the sorcerer, continued to survey the incoming data.

'There is an Imperial fleet moving towards our position from co-ordinates X3.75 by 9 from the inside the asteroid belt. Advancing at engagement speed.'

'Warmaster Abaddon would be disturbed to learn that his favoured brother Legion was fractured,' continued the new arrival, the Black Legion Sorceror Inshabael Kharesh.

'If there was any disunity within the XVII Legion,' said Marduk coldly, 'then it would be the business of the XVII Legion, and no one else, sorcerer.'

Kharesh merely smiled in reply, a thin-lipped grimace exposing his bloodstained teeth.

'Incoming transmission,' said Kol Badar. 'From the *Crucius Maledictus*.'

'Bring it up,' said Marduk.

The crackling image of Ekodas filled the view-screen. The comm-link was dropping in and out, perhaps as a result of the shrapnel interference surrounding the *Infidus Diabolus*.

'…brothers… regret to inform you of the tragic loss… *Mortisis Majesticatus*… suffered catastrophic… destruction at the hands… enemy… mine-field… tricks, dishonourable and ignoble. Sarabdal and all hands… joined with Chaos almighty.'

'A minefield, of course,' said Marduk mockingly. He saw Ashkanez's frown deepen.

'...advocate that the remainder of...' continued Ekodas's broken transmission. '...Host be transferred under... Belagosa's wing, becoming... brothers of the 18th.'

'He's disbanded the 18th,' said Kol Badar. 'He's amalgamating them into Belagosa's Host.'

'A bribe?' said Burias.

Marduk did not answer. His mind was whirling. Ekodas must have learnt that Sarabdal was close to uncovering his plotting, and taken measures to silence him. The Brotherhood, Sarabdal had said. Marduk had believed that the Dark Apostle had been misled somehow, for the Brotherhood had not been in existence since the cleansing of the Word Bearers ranks, before Horus had turned. Why would it have been reformed? He realised now that Sarabdal knew something. Marduk had lost the support of that powerful Dark Apostle. He was alone.

'...arduk, the Nexus Arrangement... ready to be activated on my command?'

'Yes, Grand Apostle,' said Marduk, sending the vox to all receiving channels. His words would be broadcast to the bridge of each Dark Apostle within the fleet. Each *remaining* Dark Apostle.

'Good... Continue as planned...' came the crackling order from the *Maledictus Confutatis*. '...in attack formation, penetrating the... belt at co-ordinates FZ3.503.M... combat speed...'

'No turning back now,' murmured Burias.

The ships of the Word Bearers fleet began to advance, engines burning with the white-hot intensity as they moved towards the asteroid belt in the distance. The outer region of the binary solar system was in perpetual shadow, for such was the density of the asteroid belt that it virtually blocked out all light from the two suns at the system's epicentre.

'What is your order?' said Kol Badar, belligerently.

'You will refer to the Dark Apostle by his Council-ordained title at all times, Coryphaus,' rumbled Ashkanez.

'Or what, First Acolyte?' snapped Kol Badar, glaring down at Ashkanez.

'Or you will be duly chastened,' said Ashkanez, his gaze unwavering.

'By who?' snorted Kol Badar. 'You?'

'If such is the Dark Apostle's will,' said Ashkanez. Marduk could smell the adrenaline coming off the First Acolyte's skin as his body readied itself for combat.

'Enough,' snapped Marduk, conscious of the cynical smile that had appeared on the pale face of the Black Legion sorcerer as his underlings bickered. 'This is not the time. The *Infidus Diabolus* shall continue on course. Maintain formation. But re-route additional power to the shields. A precaution against... further *enemy* attack.'

'The disposition of the enemy defence fleet has been confirmed,' said Kol Badar, consulting his information feed. 'They have been bolstered by two Astartes strike cruisers. White Consuls.'

'Good,' said Marduk. 'It has been too long since I have killed any sons of Guilliman.'

'Those two cruisers will be just the start,' said Kol Badar. 'The defence fleet is heavily outnumbered – they will be hoping that we plough headlong through the asteroid belt like blood-crazed savages to engage them. As soon as we do, their reinforcements will drop in via the wormholes, coming through en masse. That is what I would do. There will be no chance of retreat. We will be annihilated.'

'Except it will not be us who are annihilated when their reinforcements fail to appear,' said Marduk.

'I shall believe that when I see it,' said Kol Badar.

'Have faith, my Coryphaus,' said Marduk.

'My faith in the gods is not in question,' said Kol Badar. 'It is my faith in the magos and that xenos device that is weak.'

'The engagement is beginning,' said the Black Legion sorcerer. He was staring through the viewing portal. Marduk followed his gaze.

A thousand kilometres in front, the lead elements of the Word Bearers fleet had reached the immense wall of asteroids. The hulking slave ships were expelling vast clouds of smaller craft, poorly armed shuttles and transports for the most part. Like a swarm of insects they entered the asteroid belt, urged on by the whim of their Word Bearers masters. The first explosions lit up the darkness.

From within the asteroid belt, scores of self-powered mines accelerated towards the intruders, drawn to their heat-signatures like flies to a corpse. Each was half the size of a Thunderhawk gunship and easily capable of inflicting catastrophic damage to even a well-armoured ship. They attached themselves to the hulls of the cult ships before detonating with catastrophic effect, coronas of red fire flaring across the battlefront. The larger slave hulks were ripped apart as dozens of mines clamped onto them.

Cannon batteries erupted, targeting incoming mines as the slave ships continued to plough ever deeper into the asteroid belt. Scores of mines detonated prematurely, their explosions prickling the darkness, but others weathered the storm of incoming fire, zoning in on the invading ships and blasting them into oblivion.

Lance batteries hidden within the hollowed out centre of the largest asteroids began to fire, concentrated beams searing through shields and cutting slave hulks in two. Asteroids exploded into dust and scores of ships were ripped apart as more white-hot beams of light speared through the mayhem, and more explosions deeper into the asteroid belt erupted as the ships pushing ahead drew more mines to them.

Thousands died in the first moments of the fusillade. Tens of thousands died in the next.

None of the ships of the Hosts had yet entered the asteroid belt – only the sacrificial slave vessels of the cultists had advanced into that deadly arena. Now, as they drew nearer, the Word Bearers unleashed the power of their battleships. An indiscriminate blanket of fire was directed into the asteroid belt. The weight of ordnance was staggering, destroying everything in its path: mines, asteroids, concealed lance batteries and slave ships alike were ripped apart.

The wretched slave-ships had done their duty. Singing praises to their XVII Legion benefactors and with prayers of thanks upon their tortured lips, their crews had gone to their deaths willingly, desperate to serve their infernal masters. Their deaths had cleared a path for their masters and revealed the hidden guns of the Imperials.

'We are being hailed,' said Kol Badar.

'Bring it up,' ordered Marduk.

The image of Ekodas reappeared, the five-metre-high vid-screen free of interference and filled with his glowering face. His jet-black eyes were filled with reflected hellfire.

Marduk began running through conditioning exercises and mantras, trying to seal his mind against intrusion. He didn't know if Ekodas were capable of penetrating his thoughts from afar, but he wanted to be prepared.

'Activate the device on my command,' ordered Ekodas.

'I know the plan, Apostle,' snapped Marduk. 'What happened to the *Mortisis Majesticatus*?'

'Transferral error,' said Ekodas. 'The *Mortisis Majesticatus* made realisation into a minefield. Sarabdal's death has not unnerved you, has it, Marduk?'

Ekodas's eyes were mocking, and Marduk seethed inside. Ekodas was barely making an effort to conceal the fact that he had been responsible for the death of Sarabdal.

'Not at all, Grand Apostle,' said Marduk. 'One must always be vigilant for attack. From any quarter.'

'Indeed,' said Ekodas. 'Sarabdal was a fool. He did not even realise the danger he found himself in until too late. I would hope that one such as yourself would not make such a mistake.'

'As would I,' said Marduk. He could feel the leech-like tendrils of Ekodas's mind worming their way into his thoughts, probing his defences.

'The enemy fleet advances, confident of their reinforcements,' said Ekodas. 'I want the device activated the moment we engage. Be ready for my word. I do not want any of them escaping.'

Marduk could feel the defences of his mind slowly crumbling. In seconds, they would be bypassed. Marduk was certain that Sarabdal had been killed to silence him. Doubtless Ekodas was seeking to learn what, if anything, Marduk already knew.

'I will await your order, my lord,' he said and slammed his fist down upon a glowing blister upon his console. The transmission feed was instantly severed, and Ekodas's glowering visage faded to black. The invasive tendrils of Ekodas's mind instantly receded, and Marduk clutched at his console in order not to stagger as they scraped at the inside of his skull, clawing to maintain their hold.

'My lord Apostle?' said Ashkanez, stepping forward to aid him.

Marduk shrugged off his First Acolyte's attentions. His mind was whirling. What was it that Sarabdal had stumbled across?

He snarled in frustration, knowing that whatever it was, it was now lost to him.

THE CHAOS FLEET contracted its width as it entered the asteroid belt, moving into the breach it had created with the force of its bombardment. Rock dust, spinning chunks of shattered asteroids and twisted metal hung in that gap, repelled by flickering void shields as the battleships of the dark crusade passed through the breach without slowing.

The flanks of the twelve remaining Word Bearers battleships were guarded by a second wave of smaller cult ships that had been ushered forward as sacrificial lambs into the mine-riddled field. They were poorly maintained, and their overcharged and unshielded reactor cores burnt fiercely, slowly irradiating their crew in order to maintain the speed of the battleships they guarded. These ships were mostly ex-transports, mining ships or rogue trader vessels that had been claimed by the Legion over centuries of raids, their crews slaughtered. Now they served the crusade as its ablative armour.

Occasionally, one of the sacrificial vessels that guarded the crusade's flanks was destroyed in a blazing corona of light and fire as isolated mines that had yet to be detonated latched on to their hulls. Sporadic fire stabbed from deeper in the asteroid belt, off to either side of the gateway the Word Bearers had created. Blazing white lance strikes took their toll on the cult vessels, but in doing so exposed their own position and were dutifully targeted by the Word Bearers battleships, immense cannon arrays blasting them apart.

The light of the system's twin suns could be seen now that the way before the fleet was all but clear of obstruction, making the dust of the destroyed asteroids glow a rich orange. Shafts of light speared through gaps in the asteroid belt, the light glinting off the spires and castellated fortifications of the Word Bearers battleships as they ploughed through the thick dust clouds. The sight was breathtaking in its beauty. It looked as if the light of the gods was shining upon the crusade fleet. A good omen, thought Marduk.

'The enemy is advancing at combat speed to engage,' said Kol Badar. 'Main cannons are running at full power, and boarding parties are ready.'

'Transfer power to the forward shields,' said Marduk.

'Clear of the belt in ninety seconds,' said Kol Badar. 'We'll have a better idea of the enemy positioning then.'

'No indication of Imperial warp transfer as yet?' said Inshabael Kharesh.

Kol Badar glared at the sorcerer, then glanced at Marduk who nodded.

'Nothing yet,' said Kol Badar. 'We're advancing right into the mouth of one of the wormhole exit points though. If and when they do appear, they will have us completely surrounded.'

'Encoded transmission inbound,' croaked a servitor.

Marduk tapped his console. A message appeared on screen.

<Be ready. Activate device on my mark.>

Marduk prayed that the magos would be ready.

THE ENEMY WAS emerging from the Trajan Belt and expanding its frontage to face the incoming Boros Defence Fleet, which looked pitifully small in comparison, despite the addition of the two White Consuls strike cruisers.

Proconsul Ostorius felt frustrated as he watched the three-dimensional hololith that showed the two fleets closing with each other. His brother Space Marines were out there preparing to face the brunt of the enemy's attack. Even now the company Chaplains would be conducting their blessings, readying the minds and spirits of the Chapter's warriors for battle.

Ostorius missed the rituals of pre-battle. He missed the surge of adrenaline as the moment of combat drew near. He should be standing with them.

Focussing on the flashing icon that represented the cruiser that held 5th Company in its entirety, Ostorius clenched his fist. He was Company Champion of the 5th – his place was by his captain's side. No, he corrected. He was Company Champion no longer;

that duty was now that of another. He was Proconsul of Boros Prime. This was his place now.

Still, he felt a sense of guilt that he was not standing alongside his brothers, regardless of the fact that he had never enjoyed fleet engagements. He disliked them for the same reason that he always felt a vague unease being carried into the thick of battle within the Rhinos, Land Raiders, Thunderhawks and droppods of the Chapter. He understood this unease. In the mayhem of the battlefield, amidst the roar of chainswords, the screams of the dying and the rumble of weapon fire he was master of his survival, but in a fleet engagement, or while being ferried into battle, he was at the mercy of dangers beyond his control.

He could sense Aquilius's excitement as the fleets closed with each other. He could understand his Coadjutor's emotions, for the enemy should be annihilated in the forthcoming battle. The trap was set. As soon as the enemy were engaged, the full force of the Adeptus Praeses would descend on them like a hammer.

'How long, do you think?' said Aquilius.

All contact with the incoming ships of the Adeptus Praeses, Battlefleet Gorgon and the battle-barge of the Grey Knights had been cut, so as to give the enemy as little forewarning as possible. Most of the reinforcements were ready for transference, anchored just beyond the veil of reality. They merely waited the order to come through, and fall upon the enemy.

Yet Ostorius could not help but feel a sliver of apprehension, as if there was something at play here that he, that all the members of the caucus, had missed. He prayed to the Emperor that he was wrong, but he could not shake the pervading sense of doom that was descending upon him.

'Not long,' said Ostorius.

ALONE, THE HULKING monstrosity that held the Titans of Legio Vulturus hung back within the protection of the asteroid field, guarded by a flotilla of smaller vessels as the bulk of the Word Bearers fleet advanced to meet the incoming Imperial fleet head on.

The *Maledictus Confutatis* was at the centre of the formation, with the other eleven battleships of the XVII Legion forming an arc to either side of it, reaching out to envelop the smaller defence fleet.

Hurtling towards the foe out in front were the last remnants of the cult ships, their reactors reaching dangerously critical levels as they expended the last of their energy reserves to close the distance. Not much was expected of them, but the enemy could not ignore them. Even unarmed they posed a threat; a ship could suffer serious damage if it were rammed by one of the slave vessels.

The Imperial fleet swung towards one of the advancing wings of the XVII Legion battleships so as not to advance into the centre of their formation, and the first shots of the engagement were fired. Massive torpedoes were launched from cavernous tubes sunk into the armoured prow of the Imperial vessels, the missiles speeding through the emptiness of space towards the *Crucius Maledictus*. The Chaos battleships responded in kind, launching torpedoes of their own as the right arm of its force swung around in a wide arc to engulf the enemy.

Hundreds of thousands of kilometres separated the fleets, yet prow-mounted laser batteries opened up, stabbing lances that shredded dozens of cult vessels. Several more exploded in blinding detonations as they advanced into the paths of incoming torpedoes.

The barrage of fire intensified as the Imperial fleet split into two and unleashed the power of its broadsides upon the slave vessels caught stranded between them. Within minutes of ferocious firing, immense cannon batteries laying down an impenetrable blanket of fire, the cult ships were gone.

Swivelling defence cannons mounted upon the battleships of both fleets swung around and began to rain fire upon incoming torpedoes. Fleets of fighters were exhaled from gaping launch bays like angry insects rising to protect their hive.

The fleets banked and turned, altering their trajectory as they reacted to the torpedoes and the movement of the enemy. Within minutes the symmetrical lines of the fleets were disrupted as the battleship commanders manoeuvred their ships into the best attack position.

Dozens of torpedoes were scythed down by the weight of fire from the *Crucius Maledictus* and the other Word Bearers ships. Others flew wide, exploding upon the walls of the Trajan Belt behind the Chaos fleet. A handful found their mark, exploding upon the monstrous battleship's forward shields.

The Imperial fleet came back together and swung around to form two fronts, turning their flanks into the face of the advancing Chaos fleet. The ships of XVII Legion ploughed on into the broadsides of their foes, and the battle began in earnest.

The Imperial fleet consisted of a single Retribution-class battleship, the *Dawn Eternal*, four Lunar-class cruisers and a host of escorts, and was bolstered by the two strike cruisers of the White Consuls. The enemy still heavily outgunned them. Regardless, it unleashed its fury into the face of the Chaos fleet, stripping void shields and crippling one battleship, the *Dominus Violatus* of Ekodas's Host.

Flights of Starhawk bombers hurtled from the yawning launch bays of the Imperial fleet, accompanied by Fury interceptors. The boxy shapes of Thunderhawks and larger, heavier armed Stormbirds spat forth from the Chaos ships to meet them.

A furious exchange erupted as the fighters and interceptors engaged. Thousands of las-beams stabbed through the mayhem of battle like needles of light, and bank upon bank of cannon unleashed their salvos, their firepower growing ever more destructive as the fleets closed.

The two strike cruisers of the White Consuls veered off from the Imperial line to target the *Dies Mortis*, Dark Apostle Belagosa's ship. They started stripping its void shields with concentrated bombardments. The powerful Chaos vessel began turning on its axis, attempting to bring them under its broadsides.

The nova cannon of the *Crucius Maledictus* roared like an angry god, and a massive blaze of light comparable to the output of a small sun surrounded its barrel as it fired. The beam of blinding light tore through the Imperial line, engulfing two cruisers and an escort, ripping them apart with seeming disdain.

'CONFIRMED KILL ON the starboard wing,' droned a servitor.

'Shields holding at eighty per cent stability,' said another.

A horrific wailing sounded within the bridge of the *Infidus Diabolus*.

'The enemy fleet is making transference,' growled Kol Badar.

'Lorgar's blood,' said Burias, looking over Kol Badar's shoulder. 'There are thirty-two vessels zoning in!'

An evil grin split Marduk's face. They had the Imperials by the throat. By the time they realised their reinforcements were not going to make the jump from warp space, they would have no chance of extracting themselves from the engagement. The slaughter would be glorious.

'Patch me a link through to the magos,' said Marduk.

'Link established,' gargled a servitor.

'Be ready, magos,' said Marduk.

'Darioq-Grendh'al is unable to comply,' came the reply.

'What!'

'Regretfully that action cannot currently be performed,' returned the corrupted magos's voice.

'Enemy fleet realisation in progress,' drawled a servitor on the bridge of the *Infidus Diabolus*.

Marduk swung around and slammed his fist into the servitor's face. Its skull collapsed like a moist shell, the Dark Apostle's fist pulping the rotting brain within.

'That was helpful,' commented Kharesh. Marduk glared at him.

'Darioq-Grendh'al,' said Marduk. 'Activate the device, now!'

'Re-calibration is required of the support brace X5.dfg4.234g enshrining the device designated "Nexus Arrangement" – recovered from xenos pyramidal structure classified c6.7.32.N98.t3, upon planet c6.7.32 "Tanakreg", suspect of mech-organism species NCT.p023423.2234.x, "Necron-tyr", origin incomplete – due to binaric system atmospheric inload frequency disparity–'

*Now!* came Ekodas's order.

Marduk took a deep breath

'*Darioq-Grendh'al,*' he snarled, exerting his power over the possessed magos. 'Activate the device now, or we are all dead.'

'Summary: Darioq-Grendh'al regrets to inform Marduk, Dark Apostle of the 34th Host of the Word Bearers Astartes Legion, genetic descendant of the glorified Primarch Lorgar that the xenos artifice device designated "Nexus Arrangement" will take longer to activate than previous estimation.'

'We do not have time to fire up the warp engines for transference,' hissed Kol Badar. 'We are committed to this engagement.'

'How long, Darioq-Grendh'al?' growled Marduk.

'Re-calculated estimate: the device will be active in 1.234937276091780 minutes. Clarification: this is an estimated supposition only, and has a variance of 0.00000234 seconds.'

'Too long,' said Kol Badar, shaking his head. 'The Imperial fleet could be ten times its size by then. We should never have put our trust in the cursed magos or that damned xenos device. This crusade is going to end in disaster.'

'No,' said Marduk forcefully. 'I have come too far.'

The Word Bearers within the bridge of the *Infidus Diabolus* waited in tense silence.

'Incoming transmission,' warned Kol Badar. 'It's Ekodas.'

'Block it,' said Marduk, foetid ichor dripping from his knuckles. 'Darioq-Grendh'al – get that damned thing operational, now!'

'Regretfully that action cannot currently be performed, Marduk, Dark Apostle of the 34th Host of the Word Bearers Astartes Legion, genetic descendant of the glorified Primarch Lorgar,' returned the corrupted magos's voice. 'There is a type XP3.251.te5 code error that requires calibration adjustment of the–'

'It will not end like this!' said Marduk. 'Magos, I am sending Burias down to you. If the device is not active by the time he gets there, he will tear you limb from limb. Get it working. *Now!*'

He swung towards Burias.

'Go,' he said.

The change came over the Icon Bearer in an instant, his features blurring with those of the daemon Drak'shal.

'Launching attack craft,' said Kol Badar as a wave of enemy Starhawks rose to greet to *Infidus Diabolus*. 'Defensive turrets engaging.'

Another incoming transmission from the *Crucius Maledictus* was rebuffed.

'How close are the enemy from making realisation?' said Marduk.

'Close,' replied Kol Badar, his eyes filled with accusation. *You have brought us to this precipice*, they said.

'The gods of Chaos shall deliver us,' said Ashkanez. Alone on the bridge, he seemed unaffected by the tension, as if resigned to whatever fate the gods decreed.

A pair of Imperial Cobra frigates were torn apart by concentrated broadsides, and the *Infidus Diabolus* shook as impacts from incoming Starhawks struck home.

'It shall not end like this,' snarled Marduk. 'This is not my fate.'

'Enemy fleet realisation commencing,' said Kol Badar.

Five new enemy blips appeared on the holo-screens. 'First realisation complete. Astartes vessels. Two battle-barges, three cruisers. More inbound.'

The Chaos fleet began to splinter, reacting to the sudden appearance of these new threats.

Marduk swore then dropped to his knees as pain blossomed in his mind.

*Activate the device now,* roared Ekodas.

'We have been target-acquired by the *Crucius Maledictus,*' said Kol Badar, his voice a warning growl. 'Its nova cannon is re-energising.'

*You dare defy me?* roared Ekodas, making blood ooze from Marduk's nose, ears and eye sockets.

'This... is... not... my... time,' gasped Marduk through clenched teeth.

BURIAS-DRAK'SHAL BOUNDED DOWN the corridor, skidding as he rounded a tight corner, his talons gouging deep wounds in the latticed floor. He burst through the doors of the workshop, shattering plate glass.

Magos Darioq-Grendh'al was standing before the spinning hoops rotating with increasing speed around the Nexus Arrangement, his four articulated servo arms spread wide. His mechadendrites waved languidly around him as the Nexus, hanging motionless in the air, began to vibrate and spin. Burias-Drak'shal hurled himself at the corrupted magos.

The red beams of light transfixing the Nexus in place expanded, filling the sphere formed by the spinning hoops of ensorcelled metal so that it looked like a globe of hellish light, a sun with a gleaming metallic centre.

The perfect silver orb of the xenos device shimmered, and glowing green hieroglyphs of alien design appeared upon its spinning surface. The speed of its rotation increased exponentially, so that the hieroglyphs were soon nothing more than a gleaming green blur, and then it seemed to melt and come apart, forming seven rapidly spinning rings.

Green light spilled from the device. As the Nexus spun faster and faster, it let off a keening wail that was at the upper echelon of augmented hearing. The noise was painful, and Burias-Drak'shal roared as it cut through him, Still, he came on. He leapt, bony talons extended to impale the corrupted magos.

In mid-leap, Burias-Drak'shal heard the corrupted magos say, 'Completion.'

Then everything changed.

Burias-Drak'shal was hurled against the far wall by the force of the blast from the Nexus Arrangement, blinding white light spilling from it in a sudden, devastating burst. Burias felt the daemon within him scream in agony as it retreated deep within him and his hyper-evolved and augmented physiology struggled to maintain consciousness.

Amid the blinding inferno of light and sound stood Darioq-Grendh'al, arms and tentacles spread wide, and he began to laugh, a horrible clucking sound akin to the grind of rusted pistons.

A ripple in realspace burst from the Nexus Arrangement and expanded outwards, gathering speed exponentially as it grew. It exploded outwards from the *Infidus Diabolus* and engulfed both warring fleets, knocking out communications and scanning relays aboard every vessel in an explosion of sparks and fire. All those with even a modicum of psychic ability fell to their knees, lesser minds bursting with aneurisms and clots, those of stronger stuff suffering intense pain and temporary blindness. Those who had been peering into the warp, notably the astropaths of the Imperial fleet, fell into sub-catatonic states, their minds wiped of all notable activity, collapsing at their posts.

The ripple continued to expand, engulfing nearby planets and moons. Within seconds it had spread across the entire solar system. Only when it reached neighbouring solar systems, over four light years away, did its strength waver.

'ENEMY REALISATION HAS failed,' said Kol Badar, blinking at the sensor array in front of him as it flickered and came back online.

A feral grin spread across Marduk's face, despite the lingering pain and emptiness that the ripple had caused him.

'It worked,' he said.

Kol Badar shook his head in wonder. 'The wormhole has been shut down. The whole of the Boros Gate has been shut down.'

'Open up a link with the *Crucius Maledictus*,' said Marduk.

'Warp-link down. Switching to conventional hail.'

'Ekodas,' said Marduk as the hail was received. 'I'd ask you remove that target lock on my ship now.'

'Marduk,' said Ekodas. 'A second later and–'

'You're most welcome, Grand Apostle,' said Marduk, cutting Ekodas off and severing the link.

The Imperials had no hope of further reinforcement now, and were committed to a battle in which the XVII Legion held the advantage, despite the additional White Consuls ships that had arrived before the Nexus had been activated.

Yet a lingering doubt hung over him like a cloud. In the moment of activation, something had happened. He'd felt a stabbing pain in the core of his being. It felt as if his link to the warp had diminished. But then, that was a minor thing when set alongside what the Nexus had achieved. He pushed his concerns aside.

Marduk smiled broadly. 'Let's get to killing, my brothers.'

'In the name of the Throne,' said Proconsul Ostorius as the hololith display and all the data-slates bearing incoming fleet transmissions went dead. With a strangled cry the astropath maintaining the link collapsed to the ground.

Coadjutor Aquilius went to his aid. As he rolled the astropath onto his side he saw that blood was leaking from the man's nose and ears. He felt for a pulse – it was weak. The astropath began to twitch and convulse.

'Repair the links now!' barked Ostorius.

'We're trying, my lord,' replied a robed tech-adept as he and a dozen others worked frantically over the dozens of consoles and cogitation units.

'Try harder! I need an astropath!'

'None are responding, my lord,' said an exasperated comms-technician.

Ostorius looked down at the twitching astropath on the floor of the chamber. 'Communications?'

'Sir, it… it is as if the entire system has been cut off.'

'What?'

'There are no transmission-links into or out of the Boros Gate, Proconsul,' said the man, paling. 'We are alone.'

*Alone.*

What had happened to the incoming Adeptus Praeses reinforcements? Battlefleet Gorgon? Had they made realisation?

With the astropaths down, communications were limited to standard transmissions – at a sluggish light speed. He cursed. Transmitting at that speed, he would not hear word from the fleet regarding the outcome of the battle out on the Trajan Belt for over three hours. The enemy may have annihilated the defence fleet and be ploughing towards Boros Prime by then.

'Alone,' he breathed grimly.

HALF A GALAXY away, an immense black ship suddenly altered its trajectory. It began to accelerate at an exponential rate, swiftly reaching, then surpassing, the speed of light. Impossibly, its momentum continued to increase.

It streaked through the cold darkness of the universe, guided by inhuman will. It passed through dazzling solar systems in the blink of eye and crossed vast empty tracts of space in seconds. On and on it hurtled, moving faster than any Imperial tracking station could follow.

As if responding to some distant siren's call, inexorably, it closed on the Boros Gate.

# BOOK TWO:
# THE BROTHERHOOD

*'Our fraternity represents divine change. On
ancient Colchis, a billion souls were released
from earthly flesh in the Brotherhood's purge of
the Covenant, and great was the rejoicing; and
stronger did Colchis become. The second
cleansing saw the Legion's ranks purified of
Terran taint; and stronger did the Legion
become, its chaff cast aside. Change is
inevitable; the Brotherhood's return is
inevitable. And so shall the Legion
be strengthened once more.'*

– The Arch-Prophet Baz-Ezael, recorded during his
torture/death-vigil after being condemned by the
Council of Sicarus for heresy and blasphemy

# CHAPTER SIX

THE BATTLE OF the Trajan Belt was short and brutal, the furious exchange seeing a dozen cruisers and battle-ships crippled within the space of ten minutes, yet to those involved it seemed to last an age.

The Boros Defence Fleet realised too late that rein-forcements were not coming, yet by then it was already fully committed. As they tried desperately to extricate themselves from the engagement, the Chaos battleships exacted a terrible toll.

Of the expected relief force, only the White Consuls battle-barges *Sword of Deliverance* and *Sword of the Truth* made realisation, four full companies of White Consuls borne within them, plus an attendant flotilla of Gladius- and Nova-class frigates. The Imperial allied fleet that had been ready to make the transition from the warp would have obliterated this Chaos fleet in the space of minutes, such was its size, but no other vessels had made it through before the entire region had been shrouded by the Nexus Arrangement, ensuring that no further warp-traffic was able to enter or exit the Boros Gate binary system. Within the bridge of the *Sword of Deliverance*, Chapter Master Valens, 5th Captain Marcus Decimus, and the captain of the 7th reserve company, Cato Paulinus, viewed the enemy fleet with dawning horror.

Outnumbered and outgunned, the reeling Imperial fleet sought to pull back. The White Consuls ships hurled themselves into the maelstrom of battle with guns blazing, attempting to buy the beleaguered defence fleet some relief. Powering into the middle of the Chaos battlefleet, the White Consuls ships brought their full battery arrays to bear, blasting away at close range.

The battleship *Sanctus Diabolica* was ripped apart between the concentrated fire of the two Space Marine battle-barges, and another Chaos ship, the *Dominus Violatus*, was rendered defenceless by the combined weight of fire of the Chapter's strike cruisers and frigates.

The monstrously powerful *Crucius Maledictus* annihilated the light cruiser *Scythe of Faith*, and a further four Boros Defence Fleet cruisers and frigates were destroyed as they tried to disengage. A desperate swathe of torpedoes, fired at extreme close range, critically damaged Dark Apostle Belagosa's *Dies Mortis*. Squadrons of Starhawk bombers riddled her hull with plasma detonations before themselves being obliterated by the battleship's cloud of daemon-infused fighters.

More manoeuvrable than the larger Chaos battleships, the White Consuls strike cruisers cut through the field of destruction like knives. They focussed their weapon batteries on the isolated and defenceless *Dominus Violatus*, pummelling it with bombardment cannons and las-batteries until it was a shattered wreck. The strike cruisers retreated as the heavier Chaos ships lurched around to bring their broadsides to bear, though the *Eternal Faith*, holding the entirety of the Chapter's 2nd Company, suffered grievous damage as she was caught at the edge of a nova cannon blast from the hulking *Crucius Maledictus*.

The *Pride of Redolus*, a truly ancient Avenger-class grand cruiser, was surrounded by three Chaos ships that circled it like sharks. They pounded it into submission as it attempted to disengage. Under the calm direction of its captain, it inflicted major structural damage upon Ankh-Heloth's flagship, the *Corruptus Maligniatus*, and stripped the shields of the *Infidus Diabolus* before it died, exploding in a series of catastrophic plasma-core detonations.

One of the White Consuls battle-barges, the *Sword of Deliverance*, caught a glancing blow from the *Crucius Maledictus*, knocking out almost half of its starboard cannon arrays and sending it keening off course as it came to a new heading. It collided with the *Dies Mortis*, and the powerful ships were locked together for some minutes before the *Sword* blasted its way free.

Now isolated from the Boros battlefleet, the *Sword of Deliverance* was rounded upon by the Chaos fleet, which battered it with ordnance and waves of heavy cannon fire. As powerfully armoured and shielded as the mighty battle-barge was, even it could not stand against such overwhelming hatred, and it reeled as its shields were torn apart and its hull hammered by the heavy incoming fire. Gleaming towers and castellated sensor arrays were ripped from its body, and its port-mounted lance batteries were shorn off, spinning into space.

Formations of Thunderhawks erupted from the launch bays of the *Sword of Deliverance*, but they were not enough to hold off the plague of fighters and Stormbirds that descended over her like a vicious swarm of predatory insects, tearing at the battle-barge's hide with plasma charges and cluster bombs. The proud vessel's core was approaching critical, and fuel and air bled from the gashes in its side. Still it continued to fight on, its active turrets and gun batteries blasting away at the enemy swarming around it.

The *Sword of Truth* and the surviving frigates of the White Consuls Chapter turned back into the face of the Chaos fleet. Desperate to save Chapter Master Valens and the mighty battle-barge, they launched a swift strike back into the fray. The desperate manoeuvre cut through the Chaos line, and while the White Consuls ships took heavy damage, the *Sword of Deliverance* managed to limp out of the danger zone under the protective fire of the Chapter's gunships.

As the survivors of the Boros Defence Fleet pulled away, finally extricating themselves from the slower vessels of the XVII Legion, the Chaos fleet vented its fury upon the White Consuls, enveloping them and pounding them with thousands of tonnes of ordnance. Having bought enough time for the *Sword of Deliverance* to extricate itself from the heaviest fighting, the heavily outnumbered Consuls vessels veered away sharply, attempting to pull back. The strike cruiser *Sacred Blade* was severely damaged in the firefight, and almost half the Chapter's frigates were destroyed in that one engagement as they attempted to fight their way free of the Chaos fleet surrounding them.

Slowest to turn and pull away was the retreating battle-barge *Sword of Truth*. Thanks to her guns, her sister-ship, the *Sword of Deliverance*, had managed to get away, bearing Chapter Master Valens to safety, but now the ship was suffering for its heroics.

A hugely powerful yet heavy vessel, the *Sword of Truth* did not have the speed or manoeuvrability of the smaller Astartes vessels. Pounded from all sides, its shields and armoured hull taking a hammering, the *Sword of Truth* nevertheless exacted a heavy toll on the Chaos ships, rotating turrets drilling its attackers with relentless fire. Diverting huge amounts of energy to its overloading shield-arrays, it could not pull away fast enough, and like circling predators, the Chaos ships moved to cut it off from its brethren.

Chapter Master Valens wanted to turn the *Sword of Deliverance* back around to aid its sister-ship, but the battle-barge was in no fit state, and he knew in his heart that if he did so both battle-barges would be lost.

Realising that he was cut off, Captain Augustus of 2nd Company, the most senior officer aboard the battle-barge, signalled his intentions to his Chapter Master and ordered the *Sword of Truth* to come about to a new heading, turning and ploughing straight towards the Trajan asteroid belt. The sudden move threw off most of its attackers, and Imperial battle platforms within the asteroid belt began to fire past the approaching battle-barge, zeroing in on its pursuers.

Alone amongst the Chaos fleet, Kol Badar had predicted the move, and the *Infidus Diabolus* had already been turning as the *Sword of Truth* swung for the safety of the asteroid belt.

Marduk's ship did not have the firepower to cripple the vessel before it was in amongst the asteroids, but the Dark Apostle had no intention of destroying it.

'Remember, Apostles, we need one of their ships left intact,' Ekodas had said in the conclave aboard the *Crucius Maledictus*. Marduk intended to be the one to claim the glory of achieving that goal.

The *Infidus Diabolus* turned on her side as she came astern of the mighty White Consuls battle-barge, raking her flanks with cannon fire. Then, as the roaring of the cannons died down, waves of Dreadclaws were launched from assault tubes, spat towards the battle-barge which could do little but brace for the inevitable impact, the vast majority of her Thunderhawks having already fallen and her defensive turrets now offline.

With pinpoint accuracy the Dreadclaws hurtled towards the battle-barge, their target locations designated by Kol Badar. The Coryphaus of the 34th knew the layout of the enemy battle-barge well, for he had orchestrated the destruction of its like in battle before, and the XVII Legion had several similar vessels in its flotillas. He knew precisely where to hit to inflict the most damage, precisely where to aim in order that the boarding parties secreted within the Dreadclaws would cause the most havoc. He knew where to strike to take control of the ship's engines, and the precise deck locales he needed to secure in order to bring the vessel to a halt.

A score of boarding pods screamed towards the neck of the battle-barge, while others dipped beneath its looming hull to strike in deep towards its belly. These would assault the shield generators and the engine-core respectively, while other waves hurtled towards other locations as identified and marked by Kol Badar – boarding parties designated to take control of gun decks, to cut off expected counter-attack routes, to knock out communications, and others to isolate the warp drives.

A last burst of Dreadclaws powered towards the towers atop the hulking stern. Rising over a kilometre above the rear of the battle-barge's superstructure, this tiered, crenulated location was not unlike a fortress-monastery in its own right. The warrior brothers packed into those assault pods readied themselves for combat, preparing to fight their way onto the bridge.

Leading the assault, Marduk roared the Catechisms of Defilement and Hate as his Dreadclaw screamed towards its target. Projected across all channels, his impassioned recitation drove his warriors into a fanatical blood-rage. Spouting psalms of debasement and vitriol, Marduk whipped them into a frenzied state of hyper-aggression, further heightened by the combat drugs pumping through their systems and the blaring roar of Chaos that thundered from the grilled vox-amplifiers of the Dreadclaws.

With colossal force the Dreadclaws struck the outer hull of the battle-barge, talon-like claws latching on tightly, gouging great rents in its metal skin. Phase-cutters hissed like monstrous serpents as they carved through the *Sword of Truth's* thick armour, metres of dense plating turning molten beneath the blinding arcs of energy. Blobs of liquid metal drifted off into space around the ships as the Dreadclaws burrowed through the outer shell, and unleashed their deadly cargo within.

In a tide of screaming hatred, the 34th Host boarded the *Sword of Truth*.

EXALTED CHAMPION KHALAXIS of the 17th Coterie was the first of the Word Bearers to step foot aboard the *Sword of Truth*. His cheeks were carved with fresh cuts inflicted by his own ritual *khantanka* blade, and his mane of thick dreadlocks swung wildly as he hurled himself into the enemy, roaring in hatred.

Always the first into any engagement, and invariably the last to be extracted, the 17th Coterie were brutal warriors all, savage berserkers who wore the grisly trophies of those they had defeated around their waists. Their shoulder pads were draped with skins ripped from the corpses of powerful enemies overcome in personal combat; it was an old Colchis belief that by donning the flesh of powerful defeated enemies, you were able to harness a portion of their strength.

While the Word Bearers as a Legion worshipped Chaos in all its glory, Khalaxis and his brood had a tendency to gravitate towards the sole worship of great Khorne, the Bloodied One, the Skull Taker, the brazen god of destruction and brutality. For the most part Marduk overlooked this failing, as had his predecessor Jarulek, merely for the fact that Khalaxis and his squad were such devastating shock troops, and that their pre-battle blood-rituals honouring Khorne lent them unmatched fury and savagery.

With an animalistic roar of pure rage, Khalaxis hacked his chainaxe into the chest of a White Consuls

Chapter serf, the screaming teeth of the weapon ripping apart carapace armour and hungrily shearing through his rib cage in a glorious explosion of viscera and bone. Hot blood splattered across Khalaxis's face, which was twisted into that of a monster by battle-lust, the heady, metallic scent of the man's lifeblood merely fuelling his frenzy further. He fired his bolt pistol at close range and another two serfs were slain, exploding from within as bolt rounds penetrated their bodies and detonated.

The Chapter serfs that served aboard the *Sword of Truth* were bigger, stronger and more disciplined than regular men, and had arms and armour equivalent to Imperial Guard storm-troopers. Even so, they were like children next to the fury of the power armoured juggernauts of muscle and rage that were the members of Khalaxis's 17th Coterie, who smashed into them with the force of a sledgehammer. Limbs were hacked from bodies and warrior serfs were tossed aside like rag-dolls, arms and spines shattering as the force of the 17th's charge hit home.

Automated defence turrets emerged from the battle-barge's decks and autocannons began to scream, shredding the armour of several Word Bearers, misting the air with blood. More Dreadclaws struck home, filling the air with acrid black smoke as they cut through the hull plating of the battle-barge to disgorge their Coteries upon the enemy.

Within moments, the silence of the lower deck corridors had erupted into roars and screams of pain, the deafening whine of autocannons and the deeper thump of bolters, as well as the painful grind of chainaxe and sword carving bone and armour. Word Bearers bellowed prayers and passages from their holy scripture. Khalaxis snarled as his enhanced hearing picked up the shouts of White Consuls sergeants as they barked their orders.

From the deck floor rose thick armoured barriers, angled shields of dense ceramite, adamantium and rockcrete designed to aid in repelling boarding actions. Through the smoke, Kol Badar saw armoured figures in white power armour taking up positions behind these barricades, dropping down behind them and hefting bolters up, bring them to bear on the invaders. In a microsecond he had noted their number and position, and as he hacked the head from the shoulders of another hapless Chapter serf, he registered an enemy Devastator squad moving up to join the defence, hauling their servo-balanced heavy weapons. Their sergeant ducked down behind a barricade and pointed in Khalaxis's direction as the last of the Chapter serfs were cut down, and the four heavy bolter-toting Space Marines accompanying him set their feet wide, bringing their immense weapons to bear.

With a snarl of hatred, Khalaxis threw himself into a roll as heavy bolter fire began to rake across the battle line, the deep percussive roar of the weapons deafening. Great chunks were gouged out of the walls and deck floor beneath the explosive barrage of heavy fire. Three of Khalaxis's Coterie were ripped apart, torn limb from limb by the annihilating rate of fire unleashed upon them.

Khalaxis slammed down behind a steel-plated storage crate, spitting in fury as bolter rounds screamed through the air around him. He thumbed a pair of grenades into his hand and rose from his position, hurling them towards the Devastator squad before ducking back behind cover. As quick as he was, a bolt round struck him in the neck, a glancing hit that passed through his flesh and out the other side. It penetrated one of the exhaust arms of his power plant backpack, which exploded in a shower of superheated shrapnel, peppering the back of his skull with razor shards.

The grenades detonated, and while none of the White Consuls dropped, they were forced to hunker down behind cover. It would be a second or two before they had set themselves again, and Khalaxis launched himself towards them, bellowing in blood-frenzy as he closed the distance, the last of his Coterie a step behind.

A bolt round whizzed past his ear, scant centimetres away, and one of his brethren was felled as a burst of plasma caught him in the head, turning his horned helmet molten. Khalaxis leapt a barricade, planting his foot upon its top and leaping towards the Devastators that were even now swinging their heavy weapons in his direction.

They began to fire a moment before he got there, taking down two more of his brethren before they were overrun.

Their sergeant, whose helmet was royal blue with a white laurel painted around its crown, rose to meet the charging Word Bearers, and Khalaxis threw himself forwards to meet the challenge.

Chainaxe met chainsword in a clatter of rapidly spinning ceramite teeth. The White Consul was Khalaxis's equal in height and strength, and he turned his blade expertly to the side, using the exalted champion's momentum to sidestep him. The White Consul fired a plasma pistol blast square into the chest of another of Khalaxis's Coterie as the blood-crazed champion staggered, sending the warrior brother flying backwards, his armour a molten ruin.

Snarling in anger, Khalaxis recovered quickly and slammed a kick into the sergeant's midsection, knocking him back into the barricade. His brethren were amongst the Devastators now, hacking them down without mercy, hot blood splattering across the White Consul's alabaster armour plates. The sergeant lifted his chainsword defensively, but the arm holding it was hacked off as Khalaxis struck downwards with his chainaxe, the biting teeth of the weapon grinding through power armour, flesh and bone.

Blood pumped from the wound and Khalaxis brought his knee up hard into the sergeant's groin, cracking ceramite. With a backhand slap he knocked the plasma pistol from the sergeant's hand, sending it spinning across the deck floor and planted the barrel of his bolt pistol against the White Consul's chest plate, right over his primary heart.

'See you in hell,' said Khalaxis, and he squeezed the trigger.

It took three shots to penetrate the thick power armour and the bonded ribcage of the White Consul, but the fourth detonated within the warrior's chest cavity, pulping the organs within. Still, the Consul was Astartes, and did not die. He continued to grapple with Khalaxis, who pounded his fist repeatedly into the White Consul's helmet, shattering one lens and caving in his rebreather.

With a wrench, Khalaxis tore the Space Marine's ruptured helmet from his head, so that he could see the face of the one he was about to kill.

The Consul's face was noble and proud, and three metal service studs protruded from his brow. His genetic lineage was readily apparent, for he had the same arrogant cast to his features as had the despised Primarch Roboute Guilliman, making Khalaxis's hatred surge all the more hotly.

'For Calth,' hissed Khalaxis, drawing his fist back.

'You did not win then, and you shall not win here, infidel,' said the White Consul, his voice defiant and haughty.

With a snarl of rage, Khalaxis drove his fist into the Astartes's face, killing him instantly.

Breathing hard, Khalaxis rose above the now unrecognisable White Consul. He spat upon the corpse and gave it one last kick.

There was a series of concentrated explosions as krak grenades were used to neutralise the automated turrets still peppering the warriors of the XVII Legion with heavy calibre fire, until the last of the guns were silenced.

'Deck secured,' growled one his warriors.

'We move,' said Khalaxis. 'We have our orders.'

With that, the warrior brothers of the XVII Legion advanced deeper into the hulking battle-barge, moving inexorably towards the main engine-core, their mission briefing explicit – bring the *Sword of Truth* to a halt.

IN THE UPPER collegia decks, the push towards the plasma core was faltering. The Word Bearers Coteries were pinned down between carefully staggered lines of White Consuls defence, their lines of fire overlapping.

Another Dreadclaw penetrated the hull, its talons piercing the inner skin of the ship and spitting the thick circular drilled core of the battle-barge's armour. The bladed arcs of the assault pod slid aside, belching smoke, but before the Coterie cloistered within could launch itself into the fray a missile was fired into its interior. It exploded inside, fire billowing forth in a rapidly expanding cloud, and the survivors staggered out, their armour blackened and peeling.

Concentrated bursts of bolter fire tore through the Word Bearers, cutting them down mercilessly as they fought to gain some cover. The last of them crawled across the deck, trailing blood in their wake, before carefully aimed shots took them in their heads.

'Assault group X5.3, requiring assistance,' said Sabtec, champion of the exalted 13th Coterie. His voice was calm and measured. 'We are at location P3954.23, facing heavy resistance. We are pinned down. Request heavy support.'

'Acknowledged, Sabtec,' came Kol Badar's voice, crackling through the vox-comms integrated into Sabtec's helmet. The sound of bolter fire could be heard accompanying Kol Badar's voice; the Coryphaus was currently marching his way towards the bridge of the *Sword of Truth*, accompanying the Dark Apostle himself with his Anointed brethren. 'Secondary Dreadclaw launch initiated. Heavy support inbound.'

'Received, my Corpyhaus,' said Sabtec.

With a quick glance around the barricade, he saw that the enemy were flanking them, moving into position that would catch the pinned-down warrior brothers in a brutal enfilade. Assessing the situation instantly, he passed his orders with short, concise commands relayed through his vox-comms, shifting the position of three of the pinned Coteries under his command to counter the threat.

'Brother Sabtec,' came the warning from one of his sub-champions.

'I see them,' he replied.

Moving up in support of the White Consuls were more Astartes, several of whom had heavy plasma cannons.

'Brother Sabtec,' hissed another champion, his voice tense as the destructive cannons were brought to bear.

Sabtec checked the flood of data being projected down the head-up display array of his helmet with a glance.

'Twelve seconds,' he said.

The plasma cannons hummed, powering up, but didn't fire.

They are waiting for more support, Sabtec assessed. Good. They were not the only ones.

The seconds passed with painful slowness, then the battle-barge shuddered as more Dreadclaws struck home.

As before, a missile speared into the yawning aperture of the first Dreadclaw that penetrated, but this time there were no warrior brothers stumbling from the flames to be cut down by bolter fire. No, this time there was a deep roar of outrage that reverberated deafeningly from the confines of the assault pod. As other Dreadclaws burrowed through the thick outer plating of the *Sword of Truth* to disgorge their lethal cargoes, Sabtec smiled in anticipation.

The deck shook as the immense armoured form of the Warmonger advanced out of the Dreadclaw, emerging unharmed through the inferno unleashed by the missile fired into the assault pod's interior, which had been modified to accommodate the hulking Dreadnought.

'For the Warmaster Horus!' blared the Warmonger, the booming, sepulchral sound projected from grilled vox-amplifiers to either side of the sarcophagus that forever held his shattered body. Bolts ricocheted off the Warmonger's armoured shell and the Dreadnought advanced through the weight of fire, seemingly oblivious.

With an ungodly wail, a plasma cannon fired. Sabtec's monochromatic auto-compensators reacted instantly to the painfully bright white/blue expulsion, dimming his vision momentarily so as not to blind him. The blast glanced off the Warmonger upon his armoured left shoulder, melting the outer casing of his thick plates but doing little substantial damage.

The blow rocked the Dreadnought back a step. With a bellow of fury, the Warmonger set its clawed feet wide and began firing. Heavy-calibre cannon slugs tore across the deck, shredding barricades and several White Consuls. The White Consuls' plasma cannon exploded with a sucking roar, spraying superheated plasma as its core was breached.

With a bellow the Warmonger broke into a loping charge, smashing barricades aside. A missile glanced off its angled armour plates and veered up into the ceiling before exploding harmlessly. The heavy flamer slung beneath the Warmonger's crackling power talons roared, pouring burning promethium. Pristine white plate blackened and peeled beneath the inferno.

Sabtec rose from his cover and charged forward, his bolter bucking in his hands as he fired it from the hip. His 13th Coterie were with him, moving swiftly from cover to cover while laying down a blanket of suppressing fire, and other squads moved up in support.

Several Word Bearers were cut down by bolter fire. One warrior brother screamed in anger when his left arm disappeared from the searing blast of a melta-gun. Sabtec slid his serrated power sabre from its scabbard and thumbed its activation rune, firing his bolter one-handed. Hot energy vibrated up the length of the blade, and the champion of the 13th Coterie closed the distance with the nearest White Consuls swiftly.

The potent weapon had been gifted to him person-ally by Erebus after the 13th's heroics upon the stinking deathworld of Jagata VII, when the Coterie had brought down the defences of a war shrine of the Adeptus Sororitas, ensuring a crushing victory against the hated sisters holed up there. Every last sis-ter had been stripped of their armour and their flesh ritually debased before being staked out around the outskirts of the defiled shrine, their bloodied forms affixed to crosses hammered into the earth. There they were left to perish, vast swarms of blood-sucking insects rising from the surrounding death-marshes and descending upon them. Their screams had been sweet music to Sabtec that night.

The humming blade passed effortlessly through the power armour of a White Consuls warrior as Sabtec brought it slicing down into his neck. The sabre cut down through the gorget and deep into the tactical squad member's flesh. Arterial blood pumped from the wound, an injury that would have been fatal to any but one of the Astartes. Sabtec planted a bolt in the White Consul's brainpan to fin-ish the job, and turned smoothly to deflect a stabbing combat knife aimed at his sternum. With a deft twist of the wrist Sabtec disarmed his attacker before running him through, sliding the blade of his power sabre through the Astartes' body all the way to the hilt.

Whipping the blade from the body of the White Consul, Sabtec turned and dropped to one knee. A pistol raised to blow his head apart fired over the top of his helmet harmlessly, and Sabtec swept his blade around in a low arc that sliced the legs of the warrior from under him.

The Warmonger was in the middle of the enemy now, and the mighty Dreadnought backhanded one Astartes warrior into a wall with a sweep of its crackling talons. The sheet plating of the wall buckled inwards and the White Consul was crushed to pulp, his armour wrenched out of shape by the force of the blow. Another warrior was snatched up in the Warmonger's grasp, lifted clear off his feet. His bolter barked as the warrior fired frantically, but it dropped from lifeless fingers a moment later as the Dreadnought clenched its bladed talons, the Space Marine falling to the deck in half a dozen separate pieces.

The Dreadnought fired into the other members of the tactical squad as they pulled back in the face of the rampaging behemoth, knocking several of them off their feet and bathing the others in flame.

More Coteries of Word Bearers emerged from Dreadclaws, heavy weapon toting Havoc squads bearing missile launchers and autocannons. Faced with the sudden reinforcements and seemingly unable to halt the enraged Warmonger, the White Consuls began to pull back, under the covering fire of Scout snipers located further back. It was no rout; the Consuls fell back in good order, moving from cover to cover and laying down fields of fire to allow their brethren to extricate themselves. Sabtec had to admire their coordination and discipline, even as he hated them with every fibre of his being.

A final Dreadclaw gnawed its way onto the deck before disgorging its sole occupant. Immense and shrouded in black robes, the corrupted Magos Darioq-Grendh'al stepped heavily aboard the White Consuls battle-barge, mechadendrites waving excitedly and four heavy servo-limbs curving around from his servo-harness as if ready to stab anything that came near him.

'Escort the magos to the central cogitation chamber, Sabtec,' said the Dark Apostle Marduk in his ear. 'Let no harm befall him.'

'Your will be done, Dark Apostle,' said Sabtec, motioning for a pair of Coteries to form an honour guard around the corrupted magos.

He needn't have bothered.

Darioq-Grendh'al strode straight towards the retreating enemy, eschewing any form of cover. Each step was heavy and mechanical, accompanied by the grind of motors and the whine of servo-bundles.

'My lord Sabtec?' questioned the champion of one of the Coteries he had designated to guard the magos.

'Leave him,' said Sabtec, shrugging.

A cough of a sniper rifle firing echoed through the deck, and a bubble of coruscating energy appeared around Darioq-Grendh'al, absorbing the force of the incoming shot and stopping it short of hitting home.

In response, the corrupted magos's four servo arms began to reform, the metal/flesh of his articulated limbs running like molten wax as they remoulded themselves. Oily, black blood dripped from the servo-arms as their skin split, but the magos seemed unaffected, continuing to stride with slow determination towards the enemy. The protective bubble of his refractor field flashed again as more fire was directed towards him.

Mechadendrites attached themselves to the gun-forms manifesting on the magos's four servo-arms, bulging and changing shape to become energy cables and power conduits. Gone were the grasping power clamps and las-cutters as four deadly weapons replaced them, their power drawn from the warp and the magos's own potent internal powerplant.

Darioq-Grendh'al began to fire, his servo-arms blasting in diagonal pairs, first one pair then the other. They fired blinding gouts of hellish energy drawn directly from the warp, and spitting red ichor dripped from the infernal barrels of his newly formed weapons, hissing and smoking as they struck the deck.

'Somehow I think it might be the magos that will be protecting us,' said Sabtec.

'Come, little brother,' growled the immense form of the Warmonger as he stalked by Sabtec, having slaughtered all the enemy within his grasp. 'We must gain the palace walls. The cursed betrayer of the Crusade, the self proclaimed Emperor of Mankind, will fall this day.'

Sabtec shook his head. With every passing century it seemed that the Warmonger's grip on reality slipped further. Often in the midst of battle the ancient warrior believed he was refighting the battle for the False Emperor's palace, ten thousand years ago. The Warmonger had been amongst those within the palace when the battle had commenced in earnest, the fools unaware that there was an enemy within.

Sometimes Sabtec wished that he too could lose himself in the dreams and delusion of battles long past. Perhaps in them the outcome would be different, and the False Emperor thrown down. It would be the Legions loyal to the Emperor that were hunted to the galaxy's fringes, and the Great Crusade would be re-launched, deviants and xenos exterminated in glorious warfare that would set the universe ablaze. All of humanity would be united behind the teachings of his master Lorgar, and a new era of unity and rapturous praise of the Gods of Chaos would emerge. All who spurned the teaching of the primarch of the XVII Legion would be sacrificed. There would be war, of course, but without war humanity would become weak.

Sabtec bitterly dispelled such thoughts, and ordered his Coteries on, plunging deeper into the belly of the *Sword of Truth*.

HATE-FUELLED BATTLE ERUPTED all across the *Sword of Truth*. Resistance was heavy, and equal numbers of XVII Legion warrior brothers and White Consuls fell in the brutal, close-quarter fighting. Nowhere was the fighting more fierce than upon the corridors leading to the bridge. Here, the loyalist Astartes were dug in, determined to defend the bridge until the last. Through them marched Kol Badar's Anointed, carving a bloody path for their Dark Apostle.

Wrenching his unholy crozius arcanum from the shattered skull of a White Consuls Scout, Marduk urged his brethren on with roared quotations from the *Book of Lorgar*.

'We have reports that the *Corruptus Maligniatus* is advancing into close range,' said Kol Badar, speaking of the Dark Apostle Ankh-Heloth's personal warship. Marduk alone heard his voice across the closed channel.

The Dark Apostle activated his holy weapon, and the blood and brain matter that had gathered upon its spikes was burned off by the surge of power.

Was this how it was to end then? Had Ekodas chosen to dispose of him and his Host while they were aboard the enemy battle-barge, ensuring that the Nexus Arrangement remained unharmed, safely ensconced aboard the *Infidus Diabolus*?

'Does she target the *Sword of Truth*?' he said in reply, also using the closed channel.

'Negative,' reported Kol Badar. 'The *Corruptus Maligniatus* is opening her Dreadclaw tubes. Assault pods are being launched.'

'Where?' snarled Marduk.

'They are targeting the corridors higher up the command spire,' said Kol Badar.

'The bastard is seeking to take the bridge from under our nose,' said Marduk. 'We draw the ship's defenders, and he takes the glory of claiming the ship.'

'Your orders?' asked Kol Badar.

'We advance on the bridge, double speed.'

You will not steal my glory, Ankh-Heloth, he thought.

'It shall be so,' intoned the Coryphaus.

'Come, sorcerer,' said Marduk.

The Black Legion sorcerer, Inshabael Kharesh, looked up from where he was kneeling over a fallen enemy. He had his hands clasped around the Space Marine's head. The sorcerer released the warrior, his hands still smoking with infernal power, and the

Space Marine fell face first to the floor, dead, his liquefied brain oozing from his nose and ears.

Marduk had wanted the sorcerer to stay aboard the *Infidus Diabolus*, yet he had little real power over him, and when he had expressed his desire to accompany the strike force he had agreed, albeit somewhat reluctantly.

The sorcerer rose with a cynical smile on his lips.

'Your wish, Dark Apostle,' said the Black Legion sorcerer, his tone mocking.

Remembering Erebus's words to ensure no harm befell the sorcerer, Marduk swung away, his First Acolyte at his side.

He would take his anger out on the Space Marine captain.

# CHAPTER SEVEN

KOL BADAR SNARLED as the blast of a combat shotgun fired at close range struck him, peppering his armour. The powerful kick of the weapon was unable to knock him back even a step, and he continued on through the hail of fire, combi-bolter roaring.

Another White Consuls Scout moved up from behind the barricade, combat shotgun booming. They were lightly armoured, their bodies not yet fully ready to bond completely with power armour. Doubtless most had only begun their indoctrination a decade or so past. To Kol Badar they were children, inexperienced and worthy only of contempt. His combi-bolter barked, taking the Scout's head off.

From further up the heavily defended corridor – one of three that the Word Bearers were advancing up towards the bridge – a blinding lascannon beam struck, punching a cauterised hole straight through one of his Anointed brethren. Even mighty Terminator armour afforded little protection against such a weapon.

Waves of bolter fire struck the advancing Terminators, and though few of his warriors fell to the unrelenting swathe of fire, it was slowing their progress. The enemy fell back before them, taking cover behind barricades that rose from the corridor floor. As the Word Bearers advanced, the barriers retracted, denying the XVII Legion their cover. Kol Badar cared not. The thick ceramite and adamantium plating of the Anointed's Terminator armour could withstand easily as much incoming fire as the barricades themselves.

Behind the enemy squads up ahead, towards the four-way junction roughly forty metres in front of the advancing Terminators, Kol Badar could see a White Consuls Techmarine at work, setting up a series of Tarantula sentry guns.

A stabbing lascannon beam struck down one of his warriors, and another lost an arm to a plasma gun. Kol Badar snarled in frustration. A dozen target markers were blinking red before his eyes as the head-up targeting display of his quad-tusked helmet identified threats, and he selected the lascannon-wielding enemy Space Marine with a blink.

'Suppressing fire,' ordered the Coryphaus, allocating the target to one of his Anointed squads.

'Target confirmed,' came the growled reply from the squad's champion.

A second later a Reaper autocannon began to scream, the heavy underslung cannon swinging towards the allocated target. The twin barrels of the devastating weapon spat a torrent of high-calibre fire towards the enemy squad, and the deck floor around the Terminator was showered with countless hundreds of spent shell casings in seconds.

A grenade rolled to Kol Badar's feet but he ignored it and continued his advance. It detonated in a blinding fireball, spraying the area with super-heated shrapnel. He marched on through the fiery conflagration without concern, ignoring the fact that his armour was now alight and riddled with debris. He didn't even feel the heat of the blaze through the thick insulated layers of his exo-armour.

Emerging from the flames, he gunned down two Scouts as they ducked back to the next barricade before switching his attention as his auto-senses flashed him a warning. He turned to see a combat squad of power-armoured Astartes advancing up to flank him, using a dimly-lit side-passage filled with cables and pipes. The two enemies in the lead both carried melta guns, potent weapons easily capable of liquefying even Terminator armour. Kol Badar activated the flame unit of his combi-bolter, sending burning promethium down the corridor to meet them. The rolling fire filled the narrow service tunnel, engulfing the enemy Space Marines. The Coryphaus pumped bolts through the inferno. His targeting array revealed that the flamer had only incapacitated two of his enemies.

With a clipped order to his Anointed to advance, Kol Badar stomped into the service tunnel and unleashed another burst from his flamer. He came upon the first White Consul within the blaze. The Space Marine's armour was blackened and smoking. Kol Badar's crackling power talons clenched into a fist and he smashed the warrior backwards, crumpling his thick power-armoured chestplate like foil.

A melta gun seared a glancing blow across his shoulder, making Kol Badar hiss in sudden pain, and he launched himself forward as the enemy squad frantically back-pedalled. His combi-bolter created gaping craters in the armour of two of the White Consuls, not penetrating but knocking them off-balance, and he grabbed the arm of one of them as the melta gun was turned again in his direction.

With a sharp twist, Kol Badar ripped the White Consul's arm off at the shoulder. He kicked the warrior square in the face, shattering the front of his helmet before planting a fatal bolt through the ruptured rebreather grille.

A chainsword hit him on the arm, its teeth screaming as they sought to shear through his thick armour amid a spray of ceramite chips. Kol Badar backhanded the warrior into the wall and gunned down the last White Consul in the corridor.

Angry at having been slowed, Kol Badar turned around awkwardly, snarling in frustration as his massive shoulder plates ground against the service tunnel walls. He stormed back out into the main thoroughfare, crushing the corpses of his bested enemies beneath his tread.

The Tarantula sentry guns had been deployed and were now online, and the White Consuls were falling back towards the bridge under the cover of the automated turrets. They fired at an incredible rate before falling silent momentarily, turning with mechanised precision to pick a new target as one fell and they unleashed their fury once more. Huge drums of ammunition spooled, and smoke rose from the spinning barrels of the guns as they raked the Terminators of the Anointed with heavy weapon fire.

One of the turrets was destroyed as Reaper autocannon fire shredded its armour and ignited its ammunition store, sending it catapulting backwards as it exploded. The Anointed's advance ground to a halt as the White Consuls, having taken up new positions further up the corridor, just outside the armoured entrance to the bridge, began to add their weight of fire to those of the remaining sentry guns. The corridor was filled with tracer fire, gouts of plasma and the contrails of missiles that screamed down its length to explode amongst the warrior brothers of the XVII Legion, and Kol Badar ground his teeth in frustration.

'We are too slow,' came Marduk's unnecessary assessment from further back, conveyed in Kol Badar's earpiece via vox-link. His talons clenched in anger at the implicit rebuke in the Dark Apostle's voice. 'I will not let Ankh-Heloth take the bridge before us.'

'I am well aware of the situation,' snarled Kol Badar as a line of assault cannon fire stitched across his breastplate.

A wealth of information bombarded the Coryphaus, scrolling down his irises as reports from elsewhere within the *Sword of Truth* flooded in. He expertly sent his orders through to all the champions serving under him, coordinating their efforts to achieve the swift control of the enemy vessel, while still advancing and engaging the enemy. His ability to maintain a strategic overview and continue directing the elements of the Host even when engaged in the fiercest conflict was part of what made him such an effective Coryphaus. From the data updates and visual feeds he was receiving from the other members of the Anointed, he could see that the advance up the other corridors too had stalled.

Another Tarantula sentry gun was silenced, and Kol Badar once again began to stride forward, ordering his Anointed on. A missile spiralled past his shoulder, exploding just metres behind him but he ignored it, pumping bolt shells towards the dug-in White Consuls up ahead. The twin-linked assault cannons of a spider-legged turret ripped across the Anointed, felling one of them and forcing another to his knees, but the remainder came on, combi-bolters bucking in their hands.

The turret began to walk backwards, its movements stilted and jerky, and Kol Badar knew that it was being remotely operated by the White Consuls Techmarine, who was undoubtedly back with his brethren at the bridge doors. The Tarantula turned and unleashed its cannons into one Anointed brethren who was within metres of it now, the powerful weapon tearing his armour apart at such close range.

Still, the Terminator-armoured cult-warrior had not died purposelessly, and Kol Badar broke into a heavy run as the turret spun towards another warrior of the Anointed bearing down on it, power axe crackling with energy.

Kol Badar reached the turret as its smoking assault cannons began firing once again, and he smashed it backwards with a sweep of his talons, knocking the field cannon off its mechanised feet. The turret weighed well over a tonne, yet Kol Badar tossed it aside as if it were nothing, his prodigious strength augmented by the thick servo-bundles and hydraulic amplifiers of his Terminator suit.

Thirty metres ahead he saw the heavy blast-doors leading to the bridge, and bellowed his orders as he began striding through the enemy fire towards them. Missiles belched from behind barricades, and the intensity of the incoming bolter fire was considerable, even to his heavily armoured brethren. Taking the bridge was going to be costly.

In addition to the enemy foot troops, there was a pair of vehicles parked in front of the thick blast-doors. He knew that service elevators ran from this wide corridor down through the ship. Clearly, these vehicles been raised from the ship's armoury depot in the lower decks to guard the wide corridor's approach.

Kol Badar recognised them as Razorbacks, Rhino APC variants that had come into production in the millennia since the end of the Great War. Atop the boxy white Rhino chassis, replete with blue eagle-head Chapter designs and campaign markers, were twin-linked heavy-bolter turrets. They began to roar, adding to the heavy weight of fire directed towards the Anointed.

'Burias,' Kol Badar growled into his vox-comm. 'I am target-marking a location. I want you there now.'

No reply was forthcoming, but that did not concern the Coryphaus. He could see from his trackers that Burias and his possessed kindred were responding to his order, and the Icon Bearer clearly did not wish to risk giving away his position by sending a vox response.

Kol Badar fired towards one of the enemy squads, his shots blowing chunks out of the barricades, forcing them to duck. A red target-laser appeared on his chest plate and he saw the White Consuls Techmarine with his ornate bolter a fraction of a second before he fired. Kol Badar snarled as he was knocked back a step, warning signals announcing a breach in his exo-skeleton's integrity. The Techmarine was using non-standard anti-armour shells, their explosive tips replaced with melta-charges.

He fired in return, grimacing in pain, but his shots went wide, missing their target.

'Anytime, Burias…'

IN THE WAKE of the Anointed vanguard, Marduk moved up more cautiously. Ducking behind cover, he slammed a fresh sickle clip into his Mars-pattern bolt pistol. The White Consuls had wrapped around behind the advancing strike force, threatening them from the rear as they plunged deeper into the battle-barge. A sniper round impacted with the wall scant centimetres from his head, gouging a heart-sized crater out of the smooth plascrete surface.

'Get down, you fool,' he snapped at the Black Legion sorcerer accompanying him.

Inshabael Kharesh strolled calmly through the mayhem. Trailing white smoke, a missile screamed towards the sorcerer but he merely flicked a hand dismissively as it neared him and it was deflected into the ceiling.

Marduk scowled and broke cover, snapping off a shot and taking down a White Consul who was dashing towards a better firing position.

The Coteries accompanying Marduk fell in around him, bolters roaring as they kept the White Consuls dogging their progress at bay.

Behind them a combat squad with a pair of heavy bolters hustled into position under the covering fire of their brethren, falling in behind a barricade to bring the heavy weapons to bear up the corridor.

Inshabael Kharesh turned towards them, mouthing his infernal magicks, and Marduk saw his eyes flickering with violet electricity. The Dark Apostle could feel the power growing within the sorcerer, the sensation tingling at the base of his neck. The sorcerer continued mouthing his incantation, flexing the fingers of his hands. Marduk shook his head, but then Kharesh took a step forwards, bracing his legs as the power surging within him was unleashed.

It leapt from his fingertips in a crackling violet arc that struck one of the distant heavy bolter-armed Space Marines as he readied his weapon, cooking his flesh within his power armour. More arcs leapt from the White Consul's convulsing form to strike his companions, and Kharesh sent a further purple lightning bolt slamming into them as he thrust his other hand towards them, lifting one of them off his feet and slamming him back against the wall behind. The sorcerer hurled three more bolts into the enemy, relishing their pain as they collapsed to the ground, twitching and jerking as the last vestiges of warp energy sparked across their bodies. The sorcerer then turned away, flashing Marduk an arrogant glance.

'Cheap tricks,' muttered First Acolyte Ashkanez.

Marduk grunted.

Turning, he saw the Anointed's advance slowed by the weight of fire they were drawing, and he snarled in impatience.

'Kol Badar,' he growled, opening a vox-link to his Coryphaus.

'I know,' came the snarled reply before he could say any more.

BURIAS SLITHERED ALONG the vent, worming his way forward. His arms were by his sides and he squirmed through the tight confines by relaxing and flexing his genetically enhanced muscles. He came to a junction and turned to the right, continuing another hundred metres through the lightless pipe before coming to a halt. He could hear his kindred coming up behind him. The sound seemed deafeningly loud to his ears. Still, the enemy was unlikely to hear a thing over the gunfire.

Burias exhaled a long breath as he released the shackles that bound the ravaging daemon Drak'shal, and the change came over him. His modified power armour expanded as his musculature bulged and swelled, his arms thickening and his fingers fusing into broad talons. The air-recycling pipe groaned in protest as his body expanded, the metal wrenching out of shape. Curving horns extended up from his now bestial face, and drool ran from lips that were pulled back to expose a maw heavy with fangs and tusks.

He sniffed, hatred growing, as he tasted the unmistakeable scent of loyalist Astartes on the air. His talons extended and he punched them through the constricting embrace of the pipe. With a wrench, he tore the pipe apart and launched himself down onto the grilled sheeting below. He crashed down through the metal roofing as his brethren emerged behind him, dropping down into the midst of the enemy position.

Burias-Drak'shal landed on all fours atop the armoured hull of a Razorback, and he let out a blood-curdling roar, throwing his head back like an unfettered beast howling at the moon.

The White Consuls spun, turning their bolters towards this new threat without panic or fear, and bolts sliced through the air around Burias-Drak'shal. One took him in the side, gouging a deep wound in his daemonic flesh, but he ignored the injury. Bounding across the top of the armoured vehicle, talons ripping into its hull plating, he tore the twin-linked heavy bolter turret from its housing with a surge of warp-fuelled strength. He hurled the sparking turret aside and leapt from the tank.

He landed amongst the White Consuls, roaring his hatred, and bore one of them to the ground beneath his talons. His jaw distending unnaturally, Burias-Drak'shal clamped his teeth around the warrior's helmet. With a wrench, he tore helmet and head from the warrior's shoulders. Blood spurted like a fountain.

His possessed kindred dropped down among the enemy, their forms altering as they allowed the daemons lurking within them to surge to the fore, inviting them to sate their hatred upon the foe. Astartes were ripped apart, torn limb from limb by the brute force exhibited by these monsters.

One of the possessed was lifted into the air by the clamping jaws of the White Consuls Techmarine's servo arm, kicking and screaming in rabid fury, before the Techmarine tore it in two with a burst of fire from his master-crafted bolter. Its lower body continued to kick as it dropped to the deck in a shower of blood, while its upper half was hurled away.

Marduk broke into a run as the weight of fire dropped. First Acolyte Ashkanez ran at his side, immense power maul clasped in both hands. The

rest of the Coterie members accompanying the Dark
Apostle were only a step behind, quickly overtaking
the slower Anointed brethren. While Terminator
armour turned an Astartes into a living tank, able to
shrug off incoming fire and march staunchly on
enemy positions, it slowed a warrior down consid-
erably – an acceptable compromise in situations
such as boarding actions and close-quarter fire-
fights.

The possessed carved a bloody swathe through the
White Consuls, and their roars and bellows echoed
sharply up the corridor. Still, there were only a
handful of the daemonically infused warriors, and
the Consuls were reacting quickly to their presence,
squads falling back into disciplined fire channels
that hammered them with bolter fire. Another two
possessed were torn to shreds by the concentrated
weight of fire. Their forms mutated wildly as they
perished, the daemons within seeking desperately
to maintain control over their dying host-bodies.

Nevertheless, the possessed had done their job
and cracked the enemy formation, allowing the
Word Bearers to close the distance.

Marduk holstered his pistol and drew his
chainsword. Barbed thorns set into the daemon
weapon's hilt pushed through the perforations
drilled into the palm of his gauntlets, and a tingle
ran though him as they pierced his flesh. His blood
mingled with the daemon-blade, and he felt a surge
of fury and power as he and the daemon Borhg'ash
bound within the roaring blade became one.
Borhg'ash's anger and desire to feed flooded
through him, and he revelled in the sensation, more
powerful than any hyper-stimm or combat drug.

'Death to the False Emperor!' Marduk roared, and wielding the daemon weapon in one hand and his humming crozius in the other, he leapt a barricade, hurling himself amongst the White Consuls. His chainsword roared, carving power armour and flesh, and his blessed crozius was wreathed in dark energy as he laid about him with it.

Ashkanez was only a step behind, and a powerful blow of his power maul took a White Consul under the chin, lifting the Space Marine off his feet and sending him flying backwards. The weapon's power source surged on impact with a sharp crack of discharging energy, splitting the warrior's power armour and shattering his jaw.

A White Consul deflected Marduk's next strike with his bolter, the teeth of his daemon-blade ripping chunks out of the gun's casing. The Dark Apostle slammed his crozius into the warrior's side, puncturing power armour and lungs with its spikes and hurling the Consul into the wall. Before he could finish the warrior, a bolt pistol wielded by another Consul boomed, the shot taking Marduk in his shoulder, spinning him half around. His own blood sprayed out around him for a moment before the potent hyper-coagulants of his bloodstream sealed the wound, and he growled in pain and outrage.

The bolt pistol was raised for another shot, but the White Consul's arm was shattered by a heavy double-handed blow of Ashkanez's power maul, splinters of broken bone gleaming brightly within the messy wreckage of power armour and flesh. The First Acolyte's return blow crunched down upon the Consul's white helmet, killing him in a splatter of gore.

'Apostle!' growled Ashkanez in warning, and Marduk turned, hissing at the pain in his shoulder, but managed to lift his crozius up to deflect a buzzing chainsword that was aimed towards his neck. He smashed his own chainblade up into his attacker's groin, and blood sprayed as the hungry teeth of his daemon weapon ripped through power armour.

The White Consul fell to the deck, his plate armour covered in blood, and Marduk spun away from him, deflecting the thrust of a combat knife before stepping in close and ramming his elbow into the Consul's face.

'Guilliman's weakness resides within you, *brother*,' sneered Marduk. Still, the warrior was Astartes, even if he was descended from the False Emperor's bastard lapdog primarch, and he recovered quickly, spitting teeth and blood from his mouth. With a roar he hurled himself at Marduk, lunging for the Dark Apostle's neck with his combat knife.

Marduk battered him aside with his crozius and struck out with his chainblade in a blow intended to rip his enemy's neck apart. The Astartes warrior felt Marduk's intent a fraction of a second before the attack was launched, and lifted an arm into the path of the daemon weapon. The weapon screamed as it tore through ceramite and flesh, biting deep into bone. The White Consul grimaced in pain, but dragged the chainsword away from his neck and lashed out with his knife. Marduk threw his head back, avoiding the worst of the blow, though a deep slash was carved across his face just under his left eye.

'Heathen filth,' snarled Marduk as hot blood ran from the wound, and he brought his crozius crashing down upon the White Consul's shoulder, pummelling him to the ground. Before the warrior could rise, he stepped forwards and brought his weapons together, catching the warrior's head between them.

Behind him, Burias-Drak'shal grabbed hold of the Techmarine's servo-arm and lifted the Space Marine off the ground, smashing him into a wall. The red-armoured adept lost his grip on his weapon and fell to the floor, the sheet plating of the wall behind him a crumpled ruin. He reached for his gun, but before he could lift it Burias was on him, snarling and spitting. He grabbed the Techmarine's head in one hand and rammed the talons of his other into his face, transfixing him to the wall for a moment before the possessed warrior ripped his talons free with a tortured wrench of metal.

One of the Razorbacks was thrown into reverse, its engines roaring, but Kol Badar held it in place, his power talons digging deeply into its fore armour. Tracks squealed as they spun, and smoke rose from the vehicle's engines, but Kol Badar held it firmly in place, allowing his chainfist-wielding Anointed brethren to close in, carving a gaping hole in its side. Heavy flamers roared, filling the interior and cooking the driver and gunner inside.

Smoke was pouring from the other tank from grenades that had been hurled into wrenched open hatches.

Anointed brethren with roaring chainfists had moved on to the blast-doors and begun to carve through its thick layers, but their progress was slow, and Marduk snarled in frustration. In the time it would take to breach the doors their position might have been overrun or, perhaps worse, the bridge might have fallen to Ankh-Heloth's boarding party, coming at it from a different angle.

'Quickly now!' snarled Marduk.

He cast another glance down the corridor, seeing the White Consuls inching their way forwards there. The enemy were gathering for a counter-attack from the rear, but they were holding back as they waited for more reinforcements.

'What are you waiting for, you whoresons?' he roared. 'Come to us and die!'

He was answered almost immediately. Red light began to strobe from a pair of warning beacons mounted in sconces thirty metres back down the corridor. Grinding gears announced the arrival of two service elevators, and steam and smoke belched from within them as their doors clattered open. The deck shook beneath heavy, reverberant footsteps, and Marduk swore under his breath.

From out of the steam and smoke, a pair of immense shapes emerged.

'I think they may have heard you,' said the Black Legion sorcerer dryly, and Marduk cast him a dark look.

'Dreadnoughts,' snarled Kol Badar.

These were clearly the reinforcements that the White Consuls had been waiting for, and the battle-brothers of the hated Chapter began to advance behind the two behemoths, bolters roaring.

One of the Dreadnoughts was armed with an assault cannon that whined as it began to spin, muzzle-flare spitting from its barrels. Its exhaust stacks belched fumes as it heaved itself forward with titanic steps, its massive power claw clacking open and shut in eagerness. Its sepulchre was carved in the likeness of a stylised winged Astartes warrior, bolter clasped in its hands.

The other Dreadnought was draped in regal blue banners depicting scenes of victory. It planted its heavy feet and stabilising maglocks slammed down, rooting it in place. A second later it began to lay down a withering barrage, missiles streaming from launchers and superheated blasts screaming from the scorched double barrels of its multi-melta.

Marduk threw himself into a roll as the newcomers' fire tore across the breadth of the corridor.

Bolters roared in response, spraying the enemy Dreadnoughts, and Reaper autocannons tore chunks out of their hull plating, yet they were barely scratched. The floor shook as the advancing Dreadnought's momentum increased, while the screaming of its assault cannon reached a deafening pitch.

Melta guns integrated into combi-bolters fired, blurring the air with waves of heat, causing blistered welts to appear upon the Dreadnought's ceramite plates. Cables and servos melted, dripping steaming gulps of liquefied metal onto the deck floor, but the Dreadnought did not slow.

Still firing its assault cannon, it grabbed the first Anointed brother it reached, its massive paw closing around his Terminator-armoured body and lifting him into the air. The warrior slammed his power axe into the mechanical beast's armoured forearm, embedding it deep, before he was hurled away.

The Dreadnought smashed another cult warrior aside with a sweep of its massive arm, knocking the Terminator into a pillar. Even such a blow was not enough to finish the heavily armoured Chaos Marine, and he rose to one knee and blasted white-hot plasma from his combi-bolter into the Dreadnought's sarcophagus. It was merely a last-ditch act of defiance and the damage it caused was negligible. The Dreadnought's assault cannon roared and the warrior was torn apart. The mechanised behemoth's armoured bulk rotated towards Marduk, and it began to advance upon him, stitching the corridor with lines of fire.

Krak missiles streamed up the corridor, obliterating all they touched in devastating explosions. Ignoring the danger, XVII Legion warriors moved to interpose themselves between the advancing Dreadnought and their hallowed Dark Apostle, but they were swatted aside like children and cut down by the torrent of fire spitting from the whirling barrels of its assault cannon. The torso of one warrior, a battle-scared veteran who had fought as part of the Host since its inception, simply disappeared in a cloud of bloody vapour as a multi-melta blast struck him square on. The super-heated mist of blood splattered across Marduk, who stood snarling up at the Dreadnought as it bore down upon him.

Ashkanez leapt past him with a defiant roar, smashing at the Dreadnought with his power maul. He scarcely dented its armoured plates, and the Dreadnought swept him aside with a heavy blow. He crashed into an exposed girder, which buckled beneath his weight, and fell heavily to the deck floor.

Servos and pneumatics wheezing, the White Consuls Dreadnought drew back its massive power fist. If it struck, it would crush Marduk utterly. The Dreadnought struck with a speed that belied its bulk, and Marduk only barely avoiding the blow, throwing himself into a roll that took him beneath the strike. There was a mighty crash and the sound of wrenching metal, and as Marduk came to his feet, he saw the Dreadnought's fist embedded deep in the buckled metal of the blastdoors.

It struggled to pull itself free, and with one arm still embedded in the metal door, it dragged its assault cannon around, tearing up everything in its path as it sought to bring the heavy weapon to bear on Marduk.

With a curse, Marduk threw himself flat as thousands of rounds ripped across the corridor, leaving a smoking line of impacts where they struck.

Another warrior was melted beneath the intense heat of the other Dreadnought's multi-melta, fusing him to the thick armoured blast-doors. Missiles roared from the launch tubes, engulfing a Coterie in a series of explosions that tore them to pieces.

Marduk heard Kol Badar's coldly detached and calm orders to the Host, the Coryphaus confident of victory even when faced with such odds. He was directing the other assault parties, advising them and passing on fresh orders as enemy dispositions came to light.

Burias-Drak'shal and his possessed kindred were leaping towards the advancing White Consuls, tongues lolling from distended jaws and claws gouging deep furrows in the deck in their eagerness to close with them. Bolters tore great chunks out of their armour and flesh, and more than one was cut in half by concentrated fire, but only killing shots dropped them. They shrugged off lesser injuries and tore into the hated descendants of Guilliman.

The Icon Bearer himself closed the distance with the enemy Dreadnought with bounding leaps. The hulking construct fired a trio of krak missiles at Burias-Drak'shal. With unholy speed, Burias ducked beneath the first two missiles, and swung his horned head to the side to avoid the last, which missed him by less than half a hand's breadth.

Maglocked stabilisers unhooked themselves from the deck and the Dreadnought began to back up, attempting to put more space between it and the possessed warrior bounding towards it. Its multi-melta screamed, but Burias-Drak'shal swayed to the side to avoid the blast and launched himself into the air.

He landed on the Dreadnought's chassis, claws digging in deep. With a bestial roar, he drew back one fist and smashed it into the armoured sarcophagus. The blow did not breach the thick armour, but he clung on as the Dreadnought swung from side to side, trying to shake him loose. Nor did his second or third blow penetrate the Dreadnought's armour, but his fourth produced a crack.

More possessed warriors, their hulking bodies rippling with mutation, closed in around the Dreadnought. Like a rabid pack, they snarled and roared as they leapt upon its massive form, tearing armour plates loose, ripping at cables and wiring.

Marduk grinned as his chainsword carved through the midsection of a charging White Consul, relishing the rich taste of Astartes blood as it sprayed onto his lips. Blood was eagerly sucked up into the innards of his daemon blade, the beast within gorging on this feast and roaring its pleasure in the revving motor of the chainsword. He could feel the daemon pulling at his hand, urging him to kill again.

Burias-Drak'shal punched a talon into the widening crack of the Dreadnought's sarcophagus, still clutching on to the front of the immense war machine like a horrid gargoyle. He hooked the claws of both hands into the crack and heaved at it, his entire body straining. Muscles mutated and swelled to twice their size as Burias-Drak'shal sought to rip open the sarcophagus.

More White Consuls were moving up steadily now, and a flamer was brought to bear on the Icon Bearer, liquid promethium spraying across the front of the Dreadnought. Even as his armour and flesh caught fire, Burias Drak'shal continued straining, using all his warp-enhanced strength to tear the Dreadnought's armoured shell apart.

With a series of violent yanks, the possessed warrior tore off a cracked section of the sarcophagus, sending it clattering to the deck floor. With a roar of victory, he reached inside, grabbing the shattered form of the White Consul within and kicked off backwards, tearing the pitiful semi-living corpse from its protective housing.

He landed five metres away, patches of his skin still on fire, and looked down at the thing clutched in his talons. It was pathetic to think that once it had been an Astartes warrior.

It had no arms or legs, and its head was that of a cadaver, flopping limply over its wasted, skeletal chest. Its troglodytic skin was pulled taut across its bones, pallid and lifeless. Its eyes were sutured closed, though Burias-Drak'shal could see them moving spasmodically behind the eyelids, like a man trapped in a nightmare. A wealth of cables and wires protruded from its body, emerging from plugs inserted along its spinal column and seemingly at random all over its torso and head. Torn from the life-support and internal controls of the Dreadnought, they leaked stinking milky paste and oily fluid.

Burias-Drak'shal snarled in disgust as the thing twitched in his hands. With a powerful wrench he corkscrewed its head from its shoulders and tossed it aside.

The Dreadnought was lifeless now, as if waiting for the shattered master that made it whole to return. Marduk saw Burias-Drak'shal grin in feral satisfaction.

A bolt took Burias-Drak'shal in the thigh half a second later, and he snarled in anger and pain as he dropped to one knee.

Marduk gunned down a White Consul and ducked back behind a pillar as carefully laid down bolter fire pushed him and the Coterie members around him back.

They were taking heavy casualties now. From the reports flooding in from the other areas of the ship it was the same story: Word Bearers and White Consuls selling their lives dearly, with an XVII Legion warrior falling for each loyalist scum that was killed.

The assault cannon-armed Dreadnought was still struggling to free its fist, allowing a Coterie to approach its exposed rear. Arming melta bombs one-handed, they closed in and affixed the potent grenades to the Dreadnought as it strained to turn to face them, almost tearing its arm off at the shoulder.

Finally it freed itself with a sickening sound of protesting metal, and staggered around, assault cannon screaming as it raked its attackers with fire. Then the melta bombs detonated. The Dreadnought stood for a moment, half its engine and drive mechanics melting down its legs onto the floor, before it tipped forwards and collapsed, belching black smoke.

The deck shuddered as the monster fell, and as if this were a signal, the locking mechanisms of the immense blastdoors were suddenly released, mag-locks grinding. Interlocking serrated teeth unclamped, and like the jaws of a yawning beast the doors parted, retracting into the floor and ceiling to reveal the bridge of the *Sword of Truth*.

There in the doorway stood the figure of a White Consul. A tall white crest rose above his gold-edged helmet. His pristine white armour was heavily artificed, and a rich blue cloak with gold thread was thrown back over his shoulders. Gleaming claws slid from the sheaths of his power gauntlets, energy dancing along the elongated, gently curved blades. Behind this defiant warrior stood a semi-circle of veterans, their helmets regal blue and their spotless white armour swathed in blue tabards. One held aloft their company standard, and all were bedecked with purity seals and military decorations.

Marduk licked his lips in relish.

'For Guilliman!' the captain of the White Consuls bellowed, a cry echoed by his bodyguard before he broke into a charge, leading his warriors into the ranks of the Word Bearers. The other Consuls pressed in behind them shouting war cries of their own.

The warrior brothers of the 34th Host welcomed this test. It had been too long since they had met foes their equal. The prospect of killing the enemy Chapter's captain was intoxicating. With verses of hatred upon their lips, the brethren of the XVII Legion surged forwards to meet their foe head on.

Ashkanez smashed one of the charging veterans from his feet with his double-handed power maul, and Marduk brought his crozius crashing down on a White Consul's arm with a sickening crunch. The warrior's arm flopped uselessly, blood leaking from his ruptured power armour, and Marduk ripped his chainsword across his warrior's throat as he staggered. The eager revving of the chainsword rose to a fever-pitched squeal as adamantium teeth shore first through armour and flesh, then vertebrae.

Marduk was battered sideways as a charging veteran slammed a crackling storm shield into him. Recovering quickly, Marduk parried the warrior's follow-up thrust, batting a power blade away with his crozius, and he swayed aside to avoid a hissing burst from the bulbous barrel of a plasma pistol.

A Word Bearer nearby spat a curse as he was impaled upon a humming falchion blade, and another died as the back of his head exploded, a bolt fired at close range detonating inside his helmet.

Another warrior brother staggered back, clutching at the thick ropes of innards spilling from his abdomen. The captain of the White Consuls came after him, energy dancing across the tips of his lightning claws. Cradling his intestines in one arm, the Word Bearer lifted his bolter towards the captain. With a blinding slash, the arm was severed, falling to the ground, and in a heartbeat the warrior brother was dead. The captain's fist smashed up under the Word Bearer's chin in a brutal uppercut; the blades of his lightning claws penetrated his brain and speared out through the top of his helmet.

Marduk blocked another stabbing blow and launched a lightning riposte, which his enemy took on his crackling storm shield. The percussive shock of the impact jolted Marduk's arm, numbing it to his shoulder. At his side, First Acolyte Ashkanez flattened a veteran with a heavy overhead blow of his flanged power-maul and turned on Marduk's opponent. A two-handed blow clubbed the storm shield-wielding Consul to his knees, and Marduk dispatched him with a heavy blow to the side of his head that splintered his helm.

The captain of the White Consuls took down two more Word Bearers. The first fell heavily, half his head sliced away. The second died as the Space Marine captain's lightning claws sank deep into his chest. The Word Bearer was lifted off his feet and hurled contemptuously away. Marduk snarled in rage and moved towards the enemy captain.

Kol Badar was bleeding from several wounds, but continued to fight with a cold-burning fury, destroying every White Consul that came within his reach. A humming power sword slashed towards him, but he caught the blade in his talons, halting it mid-strike. With a wrench he ripped the blade from his opponent's hand, and as the White Consul staggered back, raising his pistol, hurled the power sword after him. It spun once, end over end, before embedding deep in the warrior's chest, sinking to the hilt. Bringing his combi-bolter up, Kol Badar finished off the White Consul with a concentrated burst of fire.

Marduk could not close with the enemy captain, whose bodyguard were holding tight rank around him. The Dark Apostle gave vent to his frustration, his fury giving him strength. Swinging up his crozius, he knocked aside a bolter aimed at his head and brought his chainsword around in a bloody arc that struck his enemy in the shoulder. The daemon entity residing within the blade was raging, adamantine teeth whirring madly as they sought to tear through the warrior's power armour.

The White Consuls captain killed another Word Bearer, tearing him to shreds with his slashing claws before kicking him away to find another victim.

'The enemy press in behind us,' said Ashkanez, as bolter fire peppered off one of his shoulder plates. 'We are caught between them. Our position is untenable.'

'Where are our damned reinforcements, Kol Badar?' replied Marduk through gritted teeth, glancing behind him. His First Acolyte was correct – the enemy were moving up solidly, pressuring their position, and it would not be long before they were overrun. 'Shouldn't they be here by now?'

'They are delayed,' replied Kol Badar. 'They have encountered higher enemy concentrations than expected.'

'A flaw in your plan? I'm shocked.'

'They will be here.'

'Not fast enough,' said Marduk, battering a sword aside with his crozius.

The Black Legion sorcerer released the helm of a White Consul, his hands glowing with warp energy. Coiling blue-grey smoke whispered from the Space Marine's ruptured lenses as he fell to the ground, a lifeless, burnt-out husk. The stink of burning flesh rose from the corpse, mingling with the electric tang of Kharesh's warp-sorcery.

'If I may?' the sorcerer ventured.

Marduk flicked a glance towards the sorcerer. It was impossible to gauge his facial expression, hidden as it was behind his sickeningly ornate battle-helm, but he was sure it would be mocking.

'I may be able to slow them,' the sorcerer said.

'Do what you will,' said Marduk, his attention diverted as he was forced to sway to the side to avoid a falchion blow.

He heard the sorcerer begin to incant, speaking in the infernal tongue of daemons. It felt as though skeletal fingers were clawing at the back of Marduk's mind, but the sensation was not unpleasant. He struck a heavy overhand blow towards his foe, who blocked the strike with a standard overhead parry, as he knew he would. He slammed a kick into the warrior's chest, knocking him back into one of his comrades, unbalancing them both. Kol Badar, talons balled into a fist, punched the head off the shoulders of one, and the other was downed by a sweep of Ashkanez's power maul. Marduk finished him off, planting a kick into the side of the fallen warrior's head. The sound of his neck cracking was audible even over the battle's din.

Marduk felt the hairs across his flesh stand rigidly to attention as the Black Legion sorcerer completed his spell, and he glanced back to see what the invocation heralded. A rippling wall of black mist was stretching out to block the corridor behind them. It moved like a living entity, tendrils reaching out like wriggling worms to bridge the expanse. Forms could be vaguely discerned amongst the smoke, swirling within it in a seething mass. Marduk saw sinuous bodies writhing around each other before disappearing once more, fanged mouths opening and closing and eyes glinting like stars within the thickening darkness.

He could still see the enemy advancing beyond the veil of warp-spawned mist, but no gunfire seemed able to penetrate it. A feral grin cracked Marduk's face as he realised that the sorcerer had brought forth a minor warp-rift into existence, a link to the holy æther itself. Bolts and plasma fire disappeared in small puffs of smoke as they struck the ethereal wall, transported to the gods only knew where.

One of the White Consuls attempted to push through the insubstantial barrier, and his body was instantly the focus of frantic movement within the mist. Smoky claws and tentacles latched onto the warrior's armour, which began to run like melted wax. The warrior's battle-brothers tried to drag him back, but this merely ensnared them as well, and they were all dragged into the hellish warp-rift. In the blink of an eye, they were gone.

Marduk nodded appreciatively towards the sorcerer, who inclined his head in acknowledgement. With the threat from the rear at least temporarily held at bay, the Word Bearers spread out, encircling the enemy captain and the last of his veteran battle-brothers.

One by one, the blue-helmeted warriors were cut down, dragged to the ground and butchered. Held aloft by one of the few remaining veterans, their Chapter banner burst into flames at a word from Inshabael Kharesh. In a heartbeat, nothing remained of it but its skeletal standard pole, the ancient design rendered to ash. The banner bearer was dropped a second later, Marduk's crozius buried in his skull.

The captain's champion was next to die, ripped limb from limb by Burias-Drak'shal. The possessed warrior's wounds, deep cuts sustained from the champion's slender power blade, began to heal instantly. His long, forked tongue lapped at the blood on the side of his face and he looked towards the lone figure of the White Consuls captain with undisguised hunger.

The captain stood alone, the bodies of his comrades piled around him. Even facing certain death, he showed no fear. Sparking energy danced across his bared lightning claws.

'Now you die, like the dog you are,' said Marduk, relishing the moment. The enemy captain tensed himself, dropping into a crouch.

'Face me, heretic,' said the captain. 'One on one.'

'No,' Marduk said. The enemy captain seemed momentarily taken aback by the unexpected answer.

'Have you no honour?' said the White Consul. 'Do you fear to face me, to be humbled before your brethren?'

Sheathing his chainsword, Marduk reached up and removed his skull-faced helmet. His face, an ugly mess of scar tissue, regrafts and augmentation, was amused. He cleared his throat and spat a thick wad of black phlegm at the captain's feet. The floor plating began to sizzle and melt beneath the impact.

'Coward,' taunted the White Consuls captain.

'You are the bastard get of the thrice-cursed Guilliman,' said Marduk. 'You do not deserve an honourable death.'

'Let me take him,' growled Burias-Drak'shal.

'No,' said Marduk.

'Let me face your warp-spawned pet,' said the White Consul. 'In the Emperor's holy name, I shall cut it down and spit upon its corpse.'

Burias-Drak'shal snarled and stepped forward. Marduk halted him with a word.

'No,' he said. 'He wishes to die a noble death. Therefore, he shall not have it. Gun him down.'

Marduk smiled as he saw the shock and outrage written in the eyes of the enemy captain. The White Consul made to leap at Marduk, but he was cut down before he could move, struck from all sides by gunfire.

The bridge belonged to Marduk, and he grinned in savage pleasure as a second blast door exploded inward less than a minute later.

'Too slow, Ankh-Heloth,' he said with relish as the rival Dark Apostle and his warriors stormed through the breach, weapons raised. 'I have already informed Ekodas that the 34th has taken control of the vessel.'

ANKH-HELOTH HAD DEPARTED the *Sword of Truth* in a rage, and the last White Consuls still holding out against the Word Bearers were isolated, bulkheads locking down around their positions as the dark magos Darioq-Grendh'al linked with the ship's controls. Marduk had felt the unspoken question from his warriors that these last survivors were not killed, but the Dark Apostle felt no need to explain his actions. The ship's communications had been severed before the bridge had fallen, ensuring that the enemy had not learnt its fate. For all they knew, the battle-barge had made it to the safety of the asteroid belt, escaping the wrath of the Chaos fleet.

The Dark Apostle was standing upon the bridge of a White Consuls battle-barge, gazing upon its cogitator banks and data-screens in distaste. He spied a shrine to the Emperor, a small statue surrounded by candles and papers of devotion, and his lip curled in loathing.

'First Acolyte?' said Marduk, nodding his head in the direction of the shrine.

In response, Ashkanez stepped forwards and smashed the statue to dust with his power maul, intoning the psalms of desecration. A second sweep saw the candles and papers scattered.

'Kol Badar,' said Marduk through his vox. The Coryphaus was located half a kilometre distant, assessing the weapon-caches of the White Consuls vessel.

'Yes, Apostle,' came the reply.

'Where is the sorcerer? I wish to speak with him.'

'I believe he has already returned to the *Infidus Diabolus*, Apostle,' said Kol Badar. 'He returned on one of the first shuttles.'

'Find him,' said Marduk.

'It will be done,' said Kol Badar.

Marduk cut the communication, irritated that he had no real authority over the Black Legion sorcerer's movements. He felt a presence behind him and turned to see his Icon Bearer, still in the thrall of his daemonic possession.

'Yes?'

'I am your champion,' snarled Burias-Drak'shal, forming the words with difficulty. He shook his head and his face returned to his own regular, slender, handsome features as he pushed the daemon back within. 'That was my kill.'

'Do not question my decisions, Burias.'

'And as for your precious Coryphaus... His plan to take the bridge almost saw us killed. So much for his being a master strategist.'

Burias once more held the heavy Host icon in his hands, having snatched it from the Anointed brother who had borne it in his absence. The heavy base of the tall, dark metal icon thumped into the floor repeatedly as Burias paced back and forth alongside Marduk, his free hand clenching and unclenching into a fist. His face was flushed and his cruel mouth set in a deep scowl.

'We just took a fully manned Astartes battle-barge in under thirty minutes,' said Marduk. 'That is hardly the result of an incompetent Coryphaus.'

'I don't know why you show the whoreson such favours,' snapped Burias. 'Be rid of him! You know he will betray you.'

With a single word, Marduk dismissed all the warriors of the Host from the bridge.

'You too, First Acolyte,' said Marduk.

With a bow, Ashkanez left the room, leaving Marduk alone with the Host's Icon Bearer.

'I see I am going to have to spell this out to you, Burias,' said Marduk. 'You are my blood-brother, and for this reason I have given you much leniency, but I'm not prepared to take any more.'

'You are making a mistake,' said Burias, his voice tinged with bitterness. 'Be rid of Kol Badar, before he turns on you.'

'You think there is someone more suitable to be Coryphaus within the Host than Kol Badar, Burias?' said Marduk.

The Dark Apostle had considered the option long and hard. Sabtec was the obvious candidate, but Marduk did not believe that even he, the exalted champion of the glorified 13th Coterie, was anywhere approaching Kol Badar's equal, at least not yet. There was no one that came close. The taking of the *Sword of Truth* confirmed Kol Badar's pre-eminence, had Marduk harboured any doubt.

'We are brothers, sworn in blood,' said Burias. 'I am the only one you can trust.'

'You honestly thought that *you* would become Coryphaus upon my ascension? Is that really what all this is about?' said Marduk.

He had always known that Burias was a devious and ambitious warrior who hungered for power and prestige, and that he had always planned to rise up the ranks of the Host, buoyed by his close relationship with Marduk, but... Coryphaus? He turned back towards his Icon Bearer, a look of exasperation on his face.

'You are important to the Host, Burias, and you have a role to play. But Coryphaus? Really?' said Marduk.

Burias's jaw jutted forward stubbornly, and though he did not speak, his silence was confirmation enough to Marduk.

The Dark Apostle shook his head and chuckled. He placed a hand upon Burias's shoulder.

'Ah, my brother, you do so amuse me,' he said.

Burias shrugged off his hand.

'I do not see what is so amusing,' Burias said, his voice heavy with bitterness. 'We are blood brothers. You owe me—'

The Icon Bearer silenced himself, perhaps hearing the words spilling from his own lips, perhaps seeing the murderous light that was flaring in the Dark Apostle's eyes.

'I owe you?' said Marduk in a quiet, deadly voice.

'What I meant—'

Burias didn't see the blow coming. Marduk slammed his fist into Burias's face, snapping the Icon Bearer's head back sharply, breaking his nose. He staggered, and touched his fingers to the blood dripping down his face.

'You dare—' he began, but Marduk struck again, the blow catching him on the temple as he tried to turn away from it.

'*I* dare?' snarled Marduk. '*I* dare? I am your Dark Apostle, you insolent wretch. You dare question *me*? You dare suggest that I *owe you* somehow?'

'I felt that–' began Burias, but Marduk did not let him finish. His face was a mask of fury. He stepped in close to Burias and raised his hand to strike him. The Icon Bearer stepped back instinctively.

'Do not recoil,' snarled Marduk, and Burias froze, waiting for the blow to fall.

Marduk unclenched his fist, and sighed. 'Burias, you are my champion, and the Host's finest warrior. Is that not enough?'

The anger simmering in Burias's eyes said that it was not.

'I had hoped that we would not need to have this conversation, Burias,' said Marduk. 'I had hoped that you would come to accept your place in the Host, but I see now that I will have to speak even more plainly. Accept what you are, Burias, and stop trying to become something you will never be. Let me make this perfectly clear: you will never be Coryphaus, Burias. Kol Badar is Coryphaus, and your superior, and that is not changing.'

Burias stood glowering at him.

'You are my champion, and the Host's Icon Bearer, but you a warrior, Burias, just a warrior. You will never be more than that. Never.'

Marduk let these words sink in, holding the Icon Bearer's gaze, before he added, 'Now get out of my sight. Six hours on the pain deck. Perhaps that will help you learn to accept your place.'

Without a word, Burias turned and marched from the bridge. Marduk stood there silently for a moment, before slamming his fist down onto a console.

Standing unseen in the shadows outside the bridge, having overheard the entire exchange, First Acolyte Ashkanez smiled.

A BLINKING VOX-BEAD interrupted Marduk's brooding. It was Kol Badar.

'What?' he said.

'I have just received word from Sabtec. The Black Legion sorcerer has been found.'

'Have him wait for me in my quarters. I am returning to the *Infidus Diabolus* now.'

'There is a problem,' said Kol Badar.

ANGER RADIATED OFF Marduk in waves. Together with Sabtec and Kol Badar, he stood inside a little-used, dimly lit storage space located on one of the lower decks of the *Infidus Diabolus*. Humming fan units spun overhead. All three of the Word Bearers were focussed on the body strung up in the centre of the room. It hung there like a martyred saint, arms wide, wrapped in razor wire that cut deep into its armoured wrists and ankles.

It was the body of Inshabael Kharesh, Warmaster Abaddon's personal envoy within the Host. Blood had pooled and congealed upon the deck floor beneath him.

Kol Badar made a warding gesture. The killing of a sorcerer was a blasphemy said to bring down the ire of the gods.

'It is a bad omen,' said Sabtec.

'You think?' said Marduk.

He lifted the sorcerer's head. His neck had been slashed open, a cut so deep that it had reached the spine. The sorcerer's eyes had been put out, and there was a runic icon carved into his alabaster forehead. It was Colchisite cuneiform in origin, he knew that, but the symbol meant nothing to him.

'Abaddon will have our heads for this,' said Kol Badar.

Marduk's mind was reeling – first his only ally, Sarabdal; now the Black Legion sorcerer.

'Why would anyone want him dead?' said Kol Badar.

'To dishonour the 34th? To spread disharmony and doubt?' said Sabtec.

'Or to ignite antagonism between us and the Black Legion,' said Marduk.

'What is this symbol?' said Kol Badar.

'I don't know,' said Marduk.

'There were more than two hundred warrior brothers onboard the *Infidus Diabolus* at the time when this took place,' said Sabtec. 'I will begin verifying the whereabouts of each of them.'

'We do not have the time,' said Marduk, shaking his head. 'This is what they want – to sow confusion and dissent.'

'Ashkanez,' said Kol Badar. 'He's the only one of us who is not of the 34th.'

'The First Acolyte was aboard the White Consuls ship,' said Marduk.

'If not him, then we must face the fact that there is one – or more than one – working against us from within the Host,' said Kol Badar.

The thought was not a comforting one.

BURIAS WAS LYING upon his spike-rimmed pallet, his flesh awash with agony, when there came a knock on his cell door.

'Wait,' he said, and dragged himself to his feet. His pain receptors were still burning with residual agony from the ministrations of the black-clad wraiths of the pain deck. Serums had been injected into his spinal column that retarded the accelerated healing of his body, ensuring that he felt every nuance of his punishment. It was not the physical pain that bothered him – in truth, its purity was a welcome – but rather the fact that his blood-brother had humiliated him so. Anger seethed within him, coiling around his twin hearts like a serpent.

Rising to his feet, nerve endings searing, he pulled a robe around his body.

'Come' he said, his voice raw, as he tied the black rope of his robe around his waist. First Acolyte Ashkanez entered.

He gazed around the cell, taking in its few details. A MkII bolter and twin bolt pistol hung upon one black iron wall, and a heavy chest was at the foot of the Icon Bearer's austere pallet. A small bookshelf holding scripture and texts hung upon one wall, and a myriad of sacred symbols of Chaos and assorted severed body parts dangled from chains overhead. A buzzing red blister shone its dim light down upon the cell. The tanned flesh of a human being was splayed out across another wall, the skin covered in tiny scripture. There was a scent of blood and meat in the air, detectible even above the incense.

'What do you want?' snarled Burias.

'You are the Host's champion. It was a slight on your honour not to face the enemy captain. The Dark Apostle shamed you.'

The First Acolyte kept his eyes upon Burias, studying the reaction to his words.

Burias felt the serpent of hate tighten its grip around his heart.

'And you have come here why? To gloat?'

'Not at all,' said Ashkanez. 'I feel that the Dark Apostle erred in his judgement. You have fought together for a long time, have you not?'

'A long time,' agreed Burias.

'He's holding you back,' said Ashkanez.

Burias said nothing, eyeing the First Acolyte warily.

'We understand each other, you and I, I think,' said Ashkanez.

Burias opened his mouth to rebuke the First Acolyte, but he held his tongue. His eyes narrowed. Was this some trick? Had Marduk sent his First Acolyte down here to test him, to see if he needed more time in the pain deck?

'There is something that I would like to show you, Burias.'

The First Acolyte opened the door to Burias's cell and stepped outside, looking up and down the corridor beyond. He turned back towards Burias, who had remained motionless, eyeing him suspiciously.

'If you wish your eyes opened, to see the true face of things to come, then come with me. If you wish to remain blind in ignorance, stay here,' said Ashkanez, shrugging his shoulders. 'The choice is yours.'

The First Acolyte turned on his heel and walked out of Burias's cell. He paused outside.

'Well?' he said.

Moving warily, Burias stepped out of his cell. Its gate clattered shut behind him, and the First Acolyte smiled.

He led Burias deep into the bowels of the *Infidus Diabolus*. The Icon Bearer tried to ask Ashkanez several times where he was leading him, but his questions were answered with silence.

Their route was circuitous and indirect, backtracking on itself a dozen times as if the First Acolyte was wary of being followed. Finally, in the lowest of the ship's dimly lit sub-decks, Ashkanez drew them to a halt.

'We are here,' he said.

'Where?' said Burias.

Ashkanez pointed at a small symbol scratched into a rusted wall-panel besides a narrow side-passage. He would never have noticed it had it not been pointed out.

'What does it mean?' said Burias.

'A meeting place,' said Ashkanez. 'For like-minded souls.'

Without further explanation, Ashkanez pulled his hood over his head, hiding his features in the gloom. He gestured for Burias to do the same, and stepped into the dimly lit side-passage.

From the shadows, a voice challenged them. Burias could easily make him out in the darkness, though a deep hood obscured his face too.

'Who goes there?'

'Warriors of Lorgar, seeking the communion of brotherhood,' answered Ashkanez.

'Welcome, brothers,' came the voice. The figure backed away, and Ashkanez swept past.

'What the–' began Burias, but Ashkanez gestured for silence.

Burias was led into a dark cave-like room. Immense pistons rose and fell within the gloom above, filling the air with their hissing and venting steam, and Burias realised that they were located beneath the fore-engine drive shafts. Withered fingers protruded from beneath the grilled decking, desperately seeking the attention of the Word Bearers walking above them, and their pitiful cries ghosted up from below.

As his eyes adjusted to the gloom, Burias came to a halt as he saw that there were other figures located here in the dim confines, hugging the shadows, their faces obscured by hoods. There must have been several hundred gathered, and more were filing in from side-entrances and service tunnels; a sizeable chunk of the Host was arrayed here, warriors that Burias had fought alongside for thousands of years.

'What is this?' he growled.

'This,' said Ashkanez, spreading his arms wide and speaking at last, 'is the Brotherhood.'

# BOOK THREE:
# THE CLEANSING

*'Faith, hate, vengeance and truth; these are our tenets. Embrace them.'*

– Keeper of the Faith, Kor Phaeron

# CHAPTER EIGHT

'I PRAY THAT Boros Prime will pose more of a challenge,' said Kol Badar. 'Taking this backwater was beneath us.'

The Coryphaus stood alongside the Dark Apostle Marduk upon the world known locally as Balerius II, the ninth planet of the Boros Gate. A tall, gleaming hab-spire could be seen in the distance, breaching the jungle canopy. Smoke was billowing from its ruptured sides.

'I yearn for the challenge,' said Kol Badar. 'Not one of the White Consuls cowards dared face us here.'

'We will face them again soon enough,' said Marduk.

Having defeated the Imperial armada at the battle of Trajan Belt, the XVII Legion pushed deep into the Boros system, spreading like a malignant cancer, and the process of subjugation and indoctrination was begun in earnest. Each Host struck out for a different quarter of the system, and world after world fell before them. Spouting catechisms of revilement and hate, the Dark Apostles had led their Hosts against the PDF and Imperial Guard regiments, butchering tens of millions – a grand sacrifice to the insatiable gods of the æther.

In less than a month, over half the Boros system's inhabited worlds had fallen to the advancing Word Bearers, as planned. On worlds where the Astartes of the White Consuls stood side by side with the PDF the battles were fierce and bloody, but the loyalist Space Marines were but few and scattered, isolated beacons of hope trying to hold back a ravening tide of destruction. All they had achieved was merely to forestall the inevitable.

One by one the core worlds of the Boros Gate binary system fell. The enemy fell back before them, towards Boros Prime, the core planet in the system. A steady stream of escape pods, mass transits and shuttles ferried Imperial Guard regiments and citizens towards the fortress world. Of those left behind, the millions who died in the fierce bombardments and firestorms were the lucky ones; those that survived to see their planets overwhelmed by the Word Bearers were either sacrificed in mass killings dedicated to the Dark Gods, or were enslaved, chained together in endless lines and subjected to horrors unspeakable.

The XVII Legion had already taken millions and once pristine core worlds were being steadily reduced to hellish realms of madness and despair. Hives, cities and entire continents were levelled, their remains used to construct immense towers and monuments of unholy significance, and the ritual debasement and insidious corruption of Imperial citizens advanced steadily. The minds, bodies and will of the slaves were slowly broken down, all hope and faith ground out of them, their souls as tortured as their flesh by the horrors unleashed upon them.

Discords drifted amongst them, horrific floating constructs trailing tentacle-like limbs blaring a barrage of noise from their speaker-grilles, a maddening cacophony of deafening roars, screams and pounding heartbeats – the sound of Chaos itself. Voices within this insane din whispered into the hearts and minds of the slaves, corrupting their souls even as their bodies were corrupted. In time they would come to understand the truth of the Word that the XVII Legion bore, giving in gladly to Chaos.

A dozen naval engagements had been fought as the ships of the White Consuls launched lightning attacks upon the Chaos fleets, but these were little more than skirmishes. The Imperialist Astartes were unwilling to stand and fight in a full-blown engagement, preferring to strike hard and fast before pulling back when the enemy fleets turned to engage. They were irritating, and the Consuls managed to destroy and cripple a handful of Chaos vessels in their hit-and-run strikes, but these skirmishes had little bearing on the overall outcome of the war.

The Boros Defence Fleet and the ships of the White Consuls had drawn back to the protection of the star fort orbiting Boros Prime. The stage was being set for a grand confrontation.

The time drew close for the Hosts of the Dark Apostles to come back together, to converge on Boros Prime. There, the final battle for the Boros Gate would take place.

*Anthony Reynolds*

From out of the jungle, a Land Raider rolled towards Marduk and Kol Badar. It growled like an angry beast as its massive tracks crushed a path through the thick undergrowth. Its armoured hull bristled with rotating sensor arrays and antennae, and its assault ramp opened like a gaping maw as it came to a halt before them, belching blood-incense.

First Acolyte Ashkanez stepped from the red-lit interior, Icon Bearer Burias, sullen and brooding, behind him.

'Well?' said Marduk.

Ashkanez held a data-sheaf out to Marduk, the bone-coloured parchment punched with holes. The Dark Apostle gestured to Kol Badar, who stepped forwards and took it. The Coryphaus fed the data-sheaf into the reader unit inbuilt into his left forearm, and the information was relayed across his irises.

'Finally,' said Kol Badar.

Marduk raised an eyebrow.

'We move on Boros Prime,' said Kol Badar. 'The 34th has been chosen to act as vanguard. It is our role to achieve planetfall.'

'Ekodas honours us,' said Ashkanez.

Marduk grunted in response, certain that there was more to it than that.

'What of the other Hosts?' asked Ashkanez. Marduk scrutinised him, certain that his First Acolyte had already read the dispatch. Indeed, it's what *he* would have done in his place, when he were First Acolyte. The heavy-set warrior-priest gave away nothing, his expression a blank.

'Ankh-Heloth and Belagosa will make planetfall once we have established a landing zone. The 11th Host will assault the frozen polar north, the 30th will land on the dark side of the mega-continent and push towards the equator. Ekodas will take the star fort itself.'

'*Grand Apostle* Ekodas,' said Ashkanez in a low voice, making Burias scowl.

'He gets the glory, while we bleed,' observed Kol Badar.

'Fine,' said Marduk. 'The 34th will not shirk from this challenge. Ready the Host.'

ALMOST FOUR HUNDRED warriors were gathered within a long unused underdeck slave pen deep within the bowels of the *Infidus Diabolus*. All were cloaked and hooded. In the time since Burias had been embraced into the Brotherhood, its numbers had swollen, and more brothers of the 34th Host were being sworn into the sacrosanct, secretive ranks of the cult with each passing week. It had become a close-knit community, a brotherhood within a brotherhood.

'We are the legacy of Colchis,' said First Acolyte Ashkanez to the hooded gathering of Astartes brethren. 'The blood of our home world flows in the veins of each and every one of us. We are brothers in faith, and brothers in blood. Twice before has the Brotherhood been needed. Twice has it performed its duty.'

Burias was in the front row, his hood pulled low and his eyes filled with fanaticism as he listened to the First Acolyte's sermon.

'The Great Purge,' growled Ashkanez, 'was a time of blood and faith, a grand cleansing that saw one in three men, women and children of Colchis burn. In their arrogance, there had been those amongst the holy Covenant that had sought to defame our blessed primarch, blinded by jealousy. They led their devoted, ignorant flock against Lorgar, who wept as he was forced into conflict with those who ought to have been his brothers. With great reluctance he empowered the Brotherhood, warrior-monks handpicked and indoctrinated by our lord himself, to act as his foot soldiers, and thus began the first great cleansing. Over a billion souls perished in that grand conflict, but it only made us stronger. Our faith became as iron.'

Ashkanez stalked back and forth as he addressed the gathered supplicants, his hands balled into fists at his sides.

'The Second Purge came a century later, after our blessed lord, the Urizen, had been reunited with his Legion; after our glorified primarch's eyes were opened to the lies of the golden-tongued so-called Emperor of Mankind,' said Ashkanez. He spat in loathing, as if expelling a foul taste from his mouth, before continuing.

'With realisation came the understanding that the old beliefs of Colchis were the only truth in the universe; that the old gods were the only powers worthy of our faith and worship. There were those amongst our blessed Legion that would not have understood these things, brainwashed and conditioned as they had been in their formative years. Our lord Lorgar once more reformed the Brotherhood, again with great mourning and remorse. Thus were the Legion's ranks cleansed and unified. In one week, thus were all warrior brothers of Terran birth eradicated, leaving only those of Colchis blood behind.'

Ashkanez licked his lips and glared around at his audience, his eyes blazing with passion.

'Great was the Urizen's lamentation, for those warriors slain were his sons, his flesh and blood, children of his own gene-code. And yet, through no fault of their own and as a direct result of being raised in isolation from him, they had to be removed. Their will had been utterly corrupted by the lies of the False Emperor. Their souls had been closed off to the great truth.'

Burias leant forward, absorbing every word. For millennia, such knowledge had been denied him, denied all those who had not themselves taken part in the great cleansing. He himself had been born and raised in the monastery-prisons of Colchis but only indoctrinated into the Legion during the first great influx, once the old beliefs had been re-embraced wholeheartedly. He had only ever known of the Great Purge – of the second, he had only ever heard insinuations. Now that this knowledge was being freely given, he was soaking it all in like a sponge. Truly, he could not understand why the Council had forbidden it.

Even Marduk, his oldest comrade and *faithful* friend – who had, he had learnt, been an active part of the Brotherhood itself during the Second Purge – had kept these secrets from him, holding him back with ignorance.

'Ignorance is control. Ignorance is slavery,' Ashkanez had said to him when he had broached the subject with the First Acolyte, and Burias had long pondered the words.

'We move towards a grim time in our Legion's history, my brethren,' said Ashkanez. 'Once more, the Brotherhood has been reformed, at the will of Lorgar himself. The third purging of our ranks approaches, brothers, and it us, you and I, who have been chosen to enact it.'

FLANKED BY WARRIORS of the Anointed, Marduk stood on one of the cavernous launch decks of the *Infidus Diabolus,* his arms folded across his chest.

An ancient Stormbird was crouched before him like an immense, predatory beast. Its assault ramps were lowered, and a score of warheads were being carefully emptied from its hold on tracked crawlers, under the supervision of Kol Badar. Just one of those warheads would have crippled the *Infidus Diabolus.* Dozens more had already been stowed away within the ship, delivered to them by a score of separate shuttle runs.

However, Marduk's attention was elsewhere: his focus was on the Nexus Arrangement. The xenos device and its weighty housing unit had been loaded onto a similar tracked crawler unit, and it was slowly being led towards the now empty hold of the waiting shuttle. The hulking form of Darioq-Grendh'al moved ponderously alongside it, physically attached to the crawler unit by a swathe of cables and fleshy pipes.

'I am not happy about this,' said Marduk.

'And your opinion has been noted,' replied Kol Harekh, Ekodas's Coryphaus. 'Nevertheless, the Grand Apostle has decreed that the device will be taken aboard the *Crucius Maledictus,* for safekeeping.'

'Safekeeping,' sneered Marduk. 'Ekodas wants the device for himself, so that he can claim its success as his own.'

'Think what you will, Apostle,' said Kol Harekh. 'The device is being requisitioned. He is Grand Apostle, and has a seat on the Council. You have no authority to refuse him.'

'It is *mine*,' said Marduk. 'My Host has bled for it. *I* have bled for it.'

'The Grand Apostle thanks you for your loyal service. You do your Host proud. However, the device belongs to the Legion, not to you. And the Grand Apostle feels that it will be safer aboard the *Crucius Maledictus*. The death of the Black Legion envoy, Inshabael Kharesh, has made the Grand Apostle doubt your ability to keep the device secure.'

'I did not know that Ekodas was already aware of the sorcerer's death,' said Marduk.

Kol Harekh smiled coldly.

'I am merely here to supervise the safe passage of the device,' he said. 'Is there going to be a problem here, Apostle?'

Kol Harekh appeared unconcerned that he was standing upon the deck of Marduk's own ship and heavily outnumbered. On Marduk's word, Kol Harekh and his entourage would be butchered where they stood.

Marduk did not answer Ekodas's Coryphaus. Kol Harekh shrugged his shoulders and broke eye contact, turning and ordering his warriors to ready the Stormbird's engines.

Marduk watched in silence as the Nexus Arrangement was loaded aboard Kol Harekh's Stormbird. Sitting atop the slowly moving crawler unit, the Nexus Arrangement continued to spin smoothly, its silver rings revolving in mesmerising arcs. The air vibrated with each turn, like the huffing of some immense infernal beast. Where they crossed they blurred together like quicksilver, only to reform themselves instantly on the other side. The green light exuded by the alien device was held in thrall by the harsh red light projected into it from the daemon-machine that the fallen magos had constructed, creating a malignant, diffuse glow.

The corrupted magos stepped onto the Stormbird's ramp. It groaned under his weight.

'Darioq-Grendh'al…' said Marduk.

'That is the last of the warheads,' said Kol Harekh. 'You have established the teleportation link?'

'Of course,' said Marduk.

'Kol Badar's plan is a good one. See that it is enacted successfully.'

Marduk glared at Ekodas's Coryphaus.

'You have what you came for,' he said. 'Now get off my ship.'

Coadjutor Gaius Aquilius of 5th Company looked back and forth between the gathered White Consuls, reading the tension upon their faces. While he knew rationally that, as Coadjutor of Boros Prime, it was only right for him to be involved in the discussions of its defence, he still felt out of his depth amongst the senior battle-brothers and captains, let alone in the presence of one of the Chapter Masters and a high-ranked Librarian.

The discussion was taking place high within a three-kilometre-tall spire that protruded above the Kronos star fort, orbiting Boros Prime. Floor-to-ceiling observation portals granted a panoramic view across the orbital bastion. From here it resembled an immense cathedral city, bristling with defences. More than twenty-five kilometres from side to side and octagonal in shape, it was the largest construction of its kind in the entire sector. Hundreds of shuttles and transports darted over its superstructure like tiny bees around their hive. Docking arms extended outwards around the orbital fortress, coupled to more than a score of battlecruisers and heavily armoured mass transports. For all the majesty of the view, none of the White Consuls paid it any mind, intent as they were upon the holograph. The tension in the room was palpable.

'Relays confirm it,' said Chapter Master Titus Valens. 'It is the *Sword of Truth*. It is approaching at combat speed, bearing directly upon us.'

'The *Sword of Truth* was lost. This is clearly a ploy,' said Ostorius, his arms folded across his chest. 'We should target it and bring it down as soon as it comes into range.'

'It is one of our own,' protested Aquilius, 'One of the three battle-barges of our noble Chapter. We cannot destroy it out of hand.'

Ostorius threw him a glance.

'You have much to learn, Coadjutor,' he said. 'The enemy are cunning. This is a trick.'

Aquilius bristled to be spoken to in such a manner in front of the senior Consuls.

'We must be wary, but I will not authorise its destruction out of hand,' said Chapter Master Titus Valens. 'We have had no confirmation of its loss to the enemy, and it is one of ours. Marcus? Your view?'

'I agree with Ostorius,' said Marcus Decimus, Captain of 5th Company, stroking his grey beard thoughtfully. 'We have to suspect this is a ploy. Our hubris has already lost us too many battle-brothers.'

'Agreed,' said Titus Valens. 'We underestimated the foe. I do not intend to do so again. The Trajan Belt massacre shall forever tarnish my honour. And yet, we feared the *Sword of Truth* lost. Now, it appears before us. If there is a chance that there are battle-brothers aboard, I dare not destroy it out of hand.'

'The last we saw, Brother-Captain Augustus was attempting to disengage by manoeuvring the *Sword of Truth* into the Trajan Belt,' said Sulinus, Captain of 3rd Company. 'As unlikely as it seems, there is a chance that he managed it.'

'And successfully evaded destruction in the last month?' said Captain Decimus. 'Without making any contact with us in the intervening time? I cannot see that happening.'

'Perhaps her communications were knocked out in the engagement,' suggested Sulinus. 'I know it is unlikely, but it is possible. Do we take that risk?'

'It's a fool's hope, Sulinus,' said Captain Decimus.

'For all we know, Captain Augustus is still onboard and alive, along with Throne-knows how many battle-brothers. Can we in all faith destroy the ship if there is even the slimmest chance of that?'

'Epistolary Liventius?' said Chapter Master Valens, turning towards the blue-armoured Librarian stood alongside him. 'Can you confirm that for us?'

Liventius nodded, and closed his eyes, touching the fingertips of one hand to his temple. Aquilius felt a disconcerting prickling sensation at the base of his neck, and he shivered involuntarily.

Aquilius held all Librarians in awe and reverence, for they were masters of powers the like of which he could barely conceive. Liventius's face was heavily lined and drawn, as if all the moisture had been drained from his flesh. He leant upon a tall force-halberd, a weapon charged with a portion of his awesome psychic mastery. His hairless scalp was pierced with diodes and wires connecting him directly to his psychic hood.

Holding the rank of Epistolary, the highest attainable for an Astartes Librarian barring Chief Librarian, Liventius was held in high regard amongst the Chapter, both for his fearlessness and skills in battle and his potent psychic abilities. His wise council was greatly respected by battle-brother and Chapter Master alike.

The Librarian opened his eyes a moment later, and Aquilius felt the prickling sensation dissipate.

'There are battle-brothers alive onboard,' he confirmed.

'Captain Augustus?' said the Chapter Master.

'I am not sure,' said the Librarian. 'Maybe. Something clouds my vision.'

'More proof that this is nothing but a ploy of the enemy, surely,' said Ostorius.

'Perhaps,' said Liventius, 'but there are White Consuls alive onboard the *Sword of Truth*. Of that there can be no doubt.'

'How many?' asked Chapter Master Valens.

'More than thirty,' said Liventius.

'Are they in control of the *Sword of Truth*, or are they imprisoned upon it? Has the enemy kept them alive merely to use them as living shields?'

'I cannot say,' said the Librarian.

Aquilius looked out of the towering observation window, but the *Sword of Truth* and the ships closing in behind her were still well beyond even his enhanced vision. In his mind's eye he imagined the White Consuls battle-barge ploughing towards the Kronos star fort, explosions and coronas of light flashing upon her flank as the enemy targeted her. Even considering firing upon the noble vessel felt like sacrilege, let alone doing so if there were any White Consuls still alive on board.

'*Sword of Truth* closing at eleven hundred kilometres,' blurted a mechanised servitor hardwired into the operational panel of the Kronos deck.

Aquilius's gaze took in the expanse of the Kronos star fort, bristling with laser batteries, cannons and torpedo tubes. Its architecture was studiously practical, yet still pleasing to the eye with its militaristic, classical aesthetic. Protected as it was with immense armour and copious layers of void shields, Kronos was virtually impenetrable, and with such potent defences, nothing short of an entire battlefleet would pose a threat.

The curve of Boros Prime could be seen out of the observation window, and its beauty briefly distracted Aquilius. Blue atmosphere gave way to the sprawling continents below, which the Kronos station watched over like a benign god, ready to unleash its fury upon any who wished the planet harm.

It was unfathomable to Aquilius that the enemy would dare attempt a frontal assault upon the planet or the star fort itself – Kronos would obliterate any such attempt, surely.

Aquilius's gaze moved back towards the holoscreens. They showed the *Sword of Truth* being pursued by one massive battleship – the *Crucius Maledictus* – three strike cruiser-sized vessels and a handful of smaller craft. The enemy were harrying the valiant White Consuls battle-barge, and he saw flashes of colour that indicated the Word Bearers ships firing upon the *Sword of Truth*.

One of the smaller enemy ships disappeared from the screen.

'Look!' said Aquilius. 'The *Sword of Truth* retaliates! One of the enemy ships has been brought down!'

'Sacrificial,' said Ostorius. 'They seek to fool us.'

'Even if that is the case, I do not believe that we can risk it,' said Brother-Captain Sulinus.

'White Consuls battle-barge is in range of orbital cannons,' said one of the grey-uniformed Kronos personnel. 'Do we take it down, sir?'

Chapter Master Titus Valens balled one of his hands into a fist in frustration.

'Damn them,' he said. 'They know that we cannot gun down one of our own, not with battle-brothers still living on board.'

'They know that, and use it to their advantage,' said Ostorius. 'They are banking on us having just this dilemma. If we shoot it down now, then we take back the advantage. It is what the enemy would do were they in our situation,' said Ostorius.

'And that is what sets us apart from them,' said Epistolary Liventius severely.

'I do not believe that Augustus would want us to compromise Kronos for his wellbeing, nor those of any of his brothers,' said Decimus.

The Chapter Master sighed, the weight of responsibility falling to him. While Ostorius was the Proconsul of the Boros Gate system, in the presence of his captain and one of the White Consuls Chapter Masters, his authority naturally deferred to them.

'Let it get closer,' said Chapter Master Valens after a moment, 'Lock gun batteries on the ship. One false move, and we destroy it. But I will not order its destruction until we know, not with battle-brothers on board.'

'The closer the *Sword of Truth* gets, the more damage it could potentially achieve,' said Ostorius.

'Our shields can absorb anything that she could unleash,' said Sulinus.

'What damage could the *Sword of Truth* do to this installation if it rammed it?' said Decimus. 'That would bypass our shields, wouldn't it?'

'The damage would be negligible,' said one of the Kronos officers.

'Scan the *Sword of Truth* for evidence of atomic warheads,' said Chapter Master Valens.

'The scan reads negative,' said the officer a moment later.

'Are you sure?' said Ostorius.

'One hundred per cent accuracy, sir,' said the officer.

'Thank you,' said Ostorius. 'At least that is something.'

'Send a flight wing out to meet the *Sword of Truth*,' said Titus Valens. 'Order them to cripple her engines if she does not slow her advance.'

'Incoming transmission,' announced another of the Kronos personnel.

'Bring it up,' said Ostorius.

The screen crackled with static before the bloody face of Captain Augustus of 2nd Company flashed up. The linkup was rough with interference, but it was irrefutably the captain.

'…under heavy fire… immediate assistance…' came the accompanying vox-stream, as patchy and unclear as the visual feed. '…immediate assistance, repeat… half company still live… transmissions failure…'

'Well, that settles it, then,' said Sulinus as the link dropped.

'With respect, brother-captain, I think you are mistaken,' said Ostorius.

Aquilius could scarce believe that Ostorius was so bold as to speak in such a way to a captain. Ostorius was an honoured veteran, true, but he was far down the line of command from a company captain.

'That was Captain Augustus, Proconsul,' said Sulinus hotly. 'We were inducted into the Chapter from the same sub-hive. I've known him since childhood. I'd recognise him anywhere.'

'The *Sword of Truth* is within firing range,' came a warning report.

'Continue to hold, but keep scanning her for any evidence of weapons powering up,' said Chapter Master Titus Valens. 'I will not fire upon our own until it is beyond doubt that this is an enemy trick.'

'The Word Bearers continue to fire upon the *Sword of Truth*, but their ships are holding back,' Sulinus noted, nodding at the vid-screens. 'They are wary of our weapon systems, as they should be.'

'Nor are they attempting to descend towards Boros Prime,' said Decimus.

'They are not stupid,' said Ostorius. 'As soon as they attempted that, we would obliterate them. Nothing can descend on Boros Prime without coming into range of Kronos.'

The *Sword of Truth* was looming ever larger, ploughing towards the star fort at speed. Explosions detonated upon her bow as the Word Bearers continued to direct their fire towards the ship.

'Distance five hundred kilometres,' came a servitor's voice.

'Get that link with the *Sword of Truth* back up,' said Valens. 'I want contact with 2nd Company.'

'Trying, sir,' came the reply. 'We are having trouble establishing a link. There might be a communications malfunction at their end.'

'Keep trying,' said Valens.

'She is not slowing down,' warned Ostorius.

'Order the flight wing to target her engines on my mark,' ordered Titus Valens.

'In doing so, my lord, we leave her at the mercy of the enemy,' said Sulinus. 'It's as good as a death sentence.'

'Two hundred kilometres.'

'What is Augustus doing?' said Chapter Master Valens. 'Control malfunction?'

'The *Sword of Truth's* shields are still up.'

'She is too close,' said Valens. 'Take out her engines.'

'Sir! The enemy ships are accelerating en masse! They are within range and coming fast!'

'Fire upon them,' said Chapter Masters Titus Valens. 'Bring them down. All guns.'

'Torpedoes have been launched towards Kronos.'

'They'll not get anywhere near us,' said Sulinus dismissively.

'Sir, the flight wing is taking casualties. Do we continue to cripple the *Sword of Truth*?'

'Keep at it,' said Valens.

'One hundred kilometres.'

'Any readings of heat build-up in her weapons?'

'No, sir,' came the reply from an officer sat before one of the scanner arrays.

'Another of our escorts is down! The *Sword of Truth's* engines are at fifty per cent, but it will not be enough! Fifty kilometres, and closing! She is going to hit us!'

Warning klaxons blared through the star fort, warning of immanent impact.

'We have to take it down,' said Ostorius, urgently. 'It poses too much of a risk!'

'No!' shouted Captain Sulinus. 'We cannot! Our brothers are aboard that ship!'

'We cannot risk Kronos!' said Captain Decimus.

'Twenty seconds to impact!'

'May the Emperor forgive us if we are wrong,' said Chapter Master Valens. 'Take it down.'

Hundreds of cannon turrets, each the size of a Titan, rotated towards the incoming battle-barge, but the Chapter Master held off from giving the order. The utter wrongness of killing a brother Astartes was ingrained in them all.

'Transmission! It's the *Sword of Truth*!'

'Hold your fire!' shouted Valens as the blurred image of Captain Augustus of 2nd Company again flashed up.

'...lacking reverse thrusters... malfunction... not fire, attempting emergency...'. the captain was saying.

'Torpedoes closing. Commencing defensive barrage.'

'Lance batteries locked and ready to fire upon encroaching enemy fleet, sir!'

The dark void of space lit up as the first incandescent beams of energy stabbed towards the incoming Word Bearers ships.

'Ten kilometres! Five!'

Aquilius's eyes widened as he stared out of the deck window, watching the rapidly approaching battle-barge.

'Sir?' called one of the deck officers suddenly.

'What is it?' said Ostorius.

'Teleport signature!'

'What? Where? Onto Kronos? Our jammers are operational, aren't they?'

'Not onto Kronos, sir! The signature is locking onto the *Sword of Truth*!'

'What are they doing?' asked Decimus, his eyes narrowing.

'I don't know,' said Ostorius. 'Scan the *Sword of Truth* again, officer.'

'In progress, sir!'

'One kilometre!'

'Sir! We are reading… Throne! Sir! Massive readings of atomic warheads aboard the *Sword of Truth*!'

'Guilliman's blood, they've teleported them across,' said Ostorius, the colour draining from his face.

'Is such a thing even possible?'

'Apparently so.'

'Five hundred metres and closing!

'Bring it down!' shouted the Chapter Master.

Aquilius looked out of the observation window towards the battle-barge, looming large and coming in fast. Turrets began to fire upon it, but it was already too close…

'Throne above,' he breathed.

Half torn apart from close-range cannon fire, but still coming, the *Sword of Truth* ploughed into the side of the Kronos star fort. The timed warheads that had been teleported across into her holds detonated and the battle-barge's plasma core exploded in a blinding corona.

MARDUK SMILED FROM within the dead flesh of the White Consuls captain. As the *Sword of Truth* ploughed into the side of the immense orbital bastion, mere seconds before the atomic warheads that had been teleported across were detonated, Marduk retreated from the corpse. Without his spirit animating it, the dead body collapsed to the floor moments before being consumed in the immense explosion.

The Dark Apostle slammed back into his body aboard the *Infidus Diabolus*, and he felt a moment of dislocation before full control and feeling returned. He stood, and moved forward to observe the destruction.

Through the forward bridge observation portal he witnessed the massive explosion upon the enemy star fort, engulfing several enemy battleships that had been sluggish in disengaging from their docked positions. Secondary detonations rippled outwards from the point of impact, rolling flames bursting into space briefly as oxygen vented before being sucked inwards, hungering for more air to feed upon. Bulkheads would be crashing down within that massive orbital fortress, isolating shattered decks.

The weight of incoming fire directed towards the Word Bearers ships dropped markedly, the overwhelming destructive barrage reduced to a trickle of sporadic fire as explosions continued to ripple along cannon arrays and laser batteries.

Marduk narrowed his eyes against the brightness as another detonation exploded in the heart of the star fort, larger than any other so far.

'Plasma reactor,' said Kol Badar.

When the flame cleared, Marduk could see a massive gaping wound in the flank of the mighty star fort, exposing a mess of twisted metal and exposed sub-decks. A thick cloud of debris and wreckage spiralled outwards from the blast, and Marduk saw with amusement the tiny figures of people blasting out into the emptiness of space alongside twisted metal scrap and ruptured gun turrets. The orbital bastion was still operational, but it had been dealt a terrible, near fatal blow, and it would be long minutes before it would be able to rotate to bring its undamaged weapons to bear on the advancing Chaos fleet.

'Commence planetfall,' said Marduk, savouring the words.

# CHAPTER NINE

AQUILIUS PICKED HIMSELF up from the deck floor, using the command podium to haul himself back to his feet. The air was thick with smoke, and flames were all around. His white armour was scorched and peppered with shards of scrap metal. He was bleeding from the temple, but the blood flow halted within seconds thanks to the hyper-coagulants in his bloodstream.

The Coadjutor's eyes were watering from the smoke, but he could see the carnage around him well enough. White Consuls were picking themselves up from the floor, surrounded by flames and twisted girders. He saw Chapter Master Valens still standing, scowling darkly as he hauled Captain Decimus to his feet.

Aquilius's augmented senses picked up the unmistakeable odours of blood and burnt flesh before he saw the bodies or registered the agonised screams. The officers of the Kronos star fort who had been within the room were scattered across the deck floor, their flesh torn to bloody ribbons. Protected by their battle plate, the White Consuls had merely suffered scratches and abrasions, but these men and women had no such aegis. The Coadjutor began moving around the room, checking for life-signs. Three of the seven officers were still alive, at least for now, and he echoed Ostorius's cry. One of them had, miraculously, escaped all but unscathed. Dutiful even in the face of such destruction, the man climbed unsteadily to his feet and moved back to the consoles, checking to see if any of them were still operational.

'Apothecary!' Aquilius shouted, doing what he could to staunch the bleeding of one officer, a woman in her middling years.

A still form, garbed in white power armour caught his attention, and Aquilius rose to his feet, moving swiftly towards the sprawled figure and dropping to his knees beside him.

A heavy girder had fallen atop the figure, pinning the warrior brother to the ground. He saw it was the captain of 3rd Company.

'Help me,' Aquilius shouted as he strained fruitlessly to budge the heavy weight.

Chapter Master Valens was at his side a moment later. The Chapter Master grasped the girder one-handed and heaved it aside as if it were made of balsa.

'God-Emperor, no,' said Aquilius as he rolled the motionless figure of Captain Sulinus onto his back and looked into staring, dead eyes. A shard of metal thirty centimetres long was embedded deep in his left eye.

'Damn,' said Chapter Master Valens.

Tracked servitors trundled into the room, bathing the flames with foam.

'Status update!' shouted Ostorius.

'Aft shields at twenty-five per cent!' shouted the sole standing officer on deck, having found a working cogitator unit. 'Re-routing power from the subsidiary banks!'

'Torpedoes incoming, contact in thirty seconds!' called the captain of 5th Company, Decimus, having taken the place of one of the fallen officers.

'Emperor damn them!' said Chapter Master Titus Valens.

'Kronos rotation underway. Sixteen per cent completion.'

'Too slow!' said Ostorius, standing and looking out through the cracked observation portal. 'The traitors are already descending towards the surface.'

Aquilius glanced out into space, and saw that several of the Word Bearers vessels had taken the opportunity in the sudden cessation of fire to cut away from the other incoming traitor vessels and drop towards Boros Prime.

The coadjutor knew as well as any White Consul the procedure for an Astartes strike force launching an attack upon a hostile planet, and though the enemy were vile and corrupted, an abasement of the Adeptus Astartes, he suspected that their modus operandi would be sickeningly close to how such an engagement was dictated in the *Codex Astartes*.

Within minutes, streaming fire would be launched from bombardment cannons, targeted at key lance batteries upon the planet's surface, softening the way for the drop. On the back of this bombardment, the first wave of drop-pods would be launched, striking hard and fast, their mission to gain a foothold upon the surface and take out anti-air and flak emplacements. Further drop-pod waves would help establish this goal and eliminate prime enemy targets, before Thunderhawks descended towards designated landing zones, deploying more troops, support and armour in preparation for a counterattack.

In all, a well-coordinated attack could be launched in minutes, giving the beleaguered ground forces little time to react. It was part of the reason why the Astartes were so devastating – they might be outnumbered a million to one, but the sheer force that could be brought to bear on one location, and the speed of its deployment, was almost impossible to counter. There was little in the universe that could resist against a determined Astartes spearhead. Still, if any world could hold, it was Boros Prime.

Alarms sounded, preceding the stream of incoming enemy torpedoes. Unable to do anything, the White Consuls looked out over the star fort from their spire in horror as they struck home. Less than a third of the torpedoes were taken down by the severely depleted defensive fire, the rest slamming into already straining void shields, overwhelming and tearing rents through them. A score passed through and impacted upon the tiered, castellated sides of the Kronos star fort already ripped asunder by the explosion of the *Sword of Truth*.

'Ground fire will not be enough to stop the Word Bearers drop,' said Captain Decimus. 'Not without the firepower of this installation.'

'I want 5th Company down there on the ground, captain,' said the Chapter Master. Decimus slammed his fist against his chest in salute.

'I believe Pollo Dardanius is the most senior of 3rd Company's sergeants?' said the Chapter Master.

'Yes, my lord,' replied Captain Decimus.

'Inform him that he is now acting captain of 3rd Company. Get him here, now, for briefing.'

'It will be done,' said Decimus.

'I want 3rd Company stationed here. The enemy will attempt to take Kronos. It is 3rd Company's duty to ensure that does not happen. I will accompany 5th Company planetward.'

'You will stay here as well,' said Proconsul Ostorius, addressing his Coadjutor. Aquilius nodded his head solemnly. 'You will be in charge of coordinating the station's defence, deferring to brother Captain Sulinus's original tactics.'

'No,' said the Chapter Master. 'Aquilius will accompany us down onto the planet's surface. You will remain here to oversee the Kronos's defence, Proconsul.'

'My lord?' said Ostorius. His face remained stoic, but Aquilius could see the tension around his eyes.

'You will remain here, Proconsul.'

'My lord, I must protest,' said Ostorius. Aquilius could see that he was struggling to maintain his composure. 'I am the Proconsul of Boros Prime. It is my place to fight on the front line, and to be seen doing so.'

'How many soldiers of your world do you know by name, Proconsul?' said the Chapter Master.

'What?' said Ostorius. 'I do not see–'

'How many?'

Ostorius fell silent.

'I have read the reports,' said the Chapter Master, his voice softening. 'The men of Boros know Aquilius.

They will follow him. I am not saying that they would not follow you, but he knows them better. It will do the defenders of this world good to know that the star fort is being held by their Proconsul. As long as Kronos holds, so too will their morale. Your Coadjutor will descend to the surface, and will marshal the Imperial Guard and PDF regiments there. He will do you proud.'

Ostorius was silent for a moment, glaring at the Chapter Master. Then, as if remembering himself, his lowered his gaze.

'I am a soldier, not an administrator,' he said at last. 'I have never had any desire to be more than that. I understand Astartes, but of these unaugmented men of Boros, its Guardsmen, its officials, I know little. I cannot relate to their short lives, nor their fears and mundane concerns. I know that once I was the same as them, but I can remember little of that time. It is as if they are a breed apart.' He snorted. 'Whereas in truth it is we who are the breed apart, are we not?'

'Did you never think that perhaps it was to learn empathy for these people that I posted you here? They share our blood,' said the Chapter Master. 'They are as important, nay, more important than we. We exist merely to protect them. *They* are our reason for being. We are warriors, yes, but we must be more than that, Ostorius.'

The Proconsul hung his head.

'Aquilius understands them better than I,' he said, finally. 'It is right for him to lead them upon Boros Prime. Forgive me, Chapter Master, I realise that I have performed my duties here poorly.'

Aquilius stared at Ostorius in surprise. Never would he have expected the taciturn veteran to speak so openly of his own shortcomings, and despite himself he felt a sudden devotion to him.

'There is nothing to forgive, Proconsul,' said the Chapter Master. 'Hold Kronos. Make the enemy bleed as they try to take it.'

'On my honour, my lord,' said Ostorius, dropping to one knee before his Chapter Master.

'They've bypassed Kronos, and will be hitting the planet in minutes,' said Chapter Master Valens. 'Once they are established on the ground, we will not beat them. All we will be able to do is stall them.'

'There are close to five billion trained Guardsmen on Boros Prime, my lord,' said Aquilius. 'We will grind them into the dust.'

'They are Chaos Space Marines, Aquilius,' said the Chapter Master. 'And there might be as many as fifteen thousand of them. Even by conservative estimates, there will be at least five, six thousand. Imagine it. That is the same as five or six loyal Chapters descending in their entirety upon one world. Nothing could stand against that – not five billion Guardsmen, not even ten. We need Astartes to fight them, and we ourselves number less than three hundred.'

Aquilius dropped his gaze, accepting the truth in the Chapter Master's words.

'Our only hope is in identifying and nullifying whatever it is that has shut down the Boros Gate,' said the Chapter Master. 'With that veil removed, the Adeptus Praeses could make transference instantly, and we would crush these traitors. Ensuring that comes to pass is our only hope here now. We hold until such a time as that goal is achieved.'

'Are you any closer to identifying the source that shrouds the Boros Gate, Epistolary Liventius?' said Ostorius.

'My attempts are being thwarted, Proconsul,' said Liventius, shaking his head. 'There is a powerful warp presence working actively against me. One of the traitorous Apostates, I would presume. His psychic defences are staggeringly powerful.'

'What help do you need?' said Chapter Master Valens.

'Were I to have a circle of psykers at my disposal, working together, it might help me breach the Apostate's defences.'

'Do it,' said the Chapter Master. 'Gather whoever you need – Navigators, astropaths, sanctioned psykers. Find the source, Liventius. The future of the Boros Gate depends upon it. Now come, my brothers. Let us take the fight to the enemy.'

MARDUK RECITED PASSAGES from the *Canticles of Mortification* as the Dreadclaw reached terminal velocity, his voice barking out over the deafening roar of turbine engines and the groaning of its superheated, armoured sides. The assault pod screamed down through the upper atmosphere, hurtling towards the planet's surface, bringing death to Boros Prime. G-forces pulled at the ten warriors ensconced within the armoured shell; any unaugmented human would have long succumbed to them and blacked out. Opposite Marduk, Burias grinned with savage pleasure and howled like a beast, his face hellishly lit by the red light emitted by the pulsing blisters above.

'Impact thirty seconds,' croaked the infernal, mechanised voice of the Dreadclaw through vox-grilles.

Marduk roared his hate-filled sermon at the top of his lungs, his voice further enhanced by the vox-amps within the grille of his gleaming skull helmet. Down through the intensifying barrage being directed up at them from the ground the Dreadclaw screamed, shuddering and shaking violently, yet Marduk's sermon never once missed a beat. He spat out his words with passion, hatred and vitriol, fuelling the fury of his warriors. Combat stimms and adrenal glands sent their serums surging through the augmented warriors' systems, further preparing them for the glorious worship of battle.

The Dreadclaw was struck a glancing blow from below, sending it careening off course for a moment, before righting itself and accelerating downwards once more. A further impact ripped one of the side-panels completely off the assault pod, filling the interior with glaring sunlight and roaring wind. One of the warrior brothers within was ripped away with the panel, the scream of shearing metal sounding for a moment before both disappeared.

Scores of other Dreadclaws hurtled planetwards like meteors, their undersides glowing with heat and burning contrails streaking behind them. Tracer fire stitched across the skies, strafing up from below, thousands of kilotonnes of ammunition being fired indiscriminately heavenwards in a desperate attempt to destroy the Dreadclaws before they struck home. Retina-searing defence laser beams stabbed upwards, and a Dreadclaw no more than ten metres away simply evaporated as it was engulfed in one of these beams, every devoted warrior brother within perishing instantly.

Still Marduk continued his fiery exhortation, the death of his brothers merely adding fuel to his sermon, his voice heard over the roar of engines and the deafening wind.

The Dreadclaw tilted its trajectory slightly, its guidance controls struggling to keep it on target, and as it rotated its occupants were afforded a view across the sprawling city below them.

Bathed in sunlight, the city below was a gleaming expanse of white marble and parapets, and streaming defensive fire scythed up at them from hundreds of castellated towers, fortified bastions and rotating turrets set atop domed cathedrals and spires. Like industrious ants, people could be seen moving purposefully through tree-lined streets and along colonnaded boulevards and arched bridgeways, though whether they were soldiers or mere civilians, Marduk neither knew nor cared – they would all die.

The ground was approaching with alarming swiftness as the Dreadclaw screamed downwards, and even as he bellowed his hateful catechisms and psalms of defilement, Marduk prepared himself for disembarkation. With a glance he assessed the combat readiness of his comrades, and ran a swift diagnostic check of his weapons and armour, information feeds scrolling across his irises.

His heart was pounding with anticipation, and he could detect the scent of eagerness being exuded by his gene-brothers. Cannon fire screamed by them, missing the Dreadclaw by scant metres, and then the view outside was obscured by marble and sculpture. Retro burners kicked in, filling the air with flame and screaming engines, and their rapid acceleration was reduced, slowing the descent just before the moment of impact.

A fraction of a second later the Dreadclaw hit the ground with spine-compacting force, its talons embedding deep into marble.

Restraint harnesses were retracted instantly and the Word Bearers piled out of the assault pod behind Marduk, roaring with fury and hatred.

Enemy soldiers were falling back away from them, and Marduk's pupils contracted as he focused on this prey.

'Come, my brethren!' he bellowed. 'Let us murder them!'

The Dark Apostle hurled himself into the fray, hacking and cutting like a berserker. Bolters bucked like angry beasts in the hands of the Word Bearers, and chainswords revved furiously as their hunger was sated on the blood of these pathetic specimens of humanity. Only after these first soldiers were slaughtered did Marduk take in his location.

They had landed in the middle of a large column-edged square, overlooked by towering arched bastions and profane temples. Soaring arched bridges and flyways crossed far overhead, and huge weighted royal blue banners stitched with Imperialist propaganda and symbols were draped down their sides. Statues stood atop the massive columns, and Marduk snarled in hatred as he saw that they were depictions of White Consuls and Ultramarines, standing sentinel in heroic poses, bolters clasped in hands and heads wreathed in ivy.

Other Dreadclaws were streaming down from the heavens. Several crashed nearby, causing the ground to crack beneath them. One of them brought a towering statue of a Space Marine captain plummeting to the ground as it hit it with the force of a falling meteor, smashing it to splinters. Another struck one of the high arched bridges and broke straight through, leaving a gaping hole before slamming down into the middle of an ostentatious fountain. A great spume of water and steam was sent up as the glowing red assault pod hit home.

One drop-pod was shredded by flak as it descended, and came apart in mid-air, trailing black smoke, flames and debris. Astartes figures could be seen silhouetted against the fire as they tumbled from the shattered Dreadclaw.

It took Marduk a moment to assess his location, estimating that they had been driven several hundred metres off course. He saw their target up ahead and with a roar led his warriors in its direction, sprinting across the square as the sky overhead was torn apart by gunfire, streaming missiles and rapidly descending drop-pods.

Their objective loomed up ahead of them, and Marduk stared up at it hatefully. The gigantic, broad-based tower squatted at the north end of the square, replete with statuary and bas-relief of famous White Consuls battles. Fifty-metre-high lance battery barrels protruded from its gleaming, golden dome, and dozens of flak-cannon turrets and missile racks bristled down its sides. The weight of fire from this tower was immense, and Marduk saw several Dreadclaws ripped apart. There were a dozen such towers within the landing zone, and each of them was marked as priority targets for the assaulting Chaos Legion.

The air tingled with electricity and there was a sudden influx of air before the lance battery fired. Were it not for the autosensors of his helmet dimming his vision at the sudden burst of light, Marduk would have been blinded temporarily as it fired. A beam of pure light stabbed upwards towards the distant Word Bearers fleet in high orbit. Concentrated fire from lance batteries could cripple even the largest battleships; neutralising them was of paramount importance.

Even without the immense firepower of the enemy star fort, Boros Prime's ground defences were more than enough to see off the most determined orbital assault. As such, merely bombarding the world into submission was not an option. The *Infidus Diabolus* would unleash its payload and launch the warriors of the 34th Host from its hangar bays and Dreadclaw tubes, but once done, it would pull away and join Ekodas's attack upon the star fort.

Lasfire stabbed from the buildings overlooking the square, fired from behind crenulations and through vision slits. Marduk hissed in anger as one of the shots struck him, scorching his shoulder plate black and causing several of the devotional oath papers nailed there to burst into flame, the scripture reduced to ash.

He could see figures running to take up position above them, lining up along the fortified rooftops overlooking the square, but Marduk ignored them, focussing on his target. One of his brethren stumbled and fell as he was struck by a dozen white-hot lasbeams, penetrating and igniting the external cabling and tubing of his power armour. None of the Word Bearers deigned to stop to help their fallen brother; the Gods of Chaos had clearly seen weakness in his soul, and had thus failed to protect him. Further beams struck Marduk on his shoulders and back,

making him grit his teeth in fury. Burias was struck a
glancing blow across the side of his skull, taking off
his left ear and leaving a cauterised burn down the
side of his head. He snarled in anger and the change
came over him in an instant as the daemon Drak'shal
surged to the surface.

Autocannon fire from armoured turrets upon the
immense defence tower began to rip across the square,
tearing up chunks of marble and smashing XVII Legion
warriors from their feet. The sacred power armour of
the Word Bearers caught in the enfilades was torn to
shreds and their flesh riddled with bullets, but most
battled on, the pain merely adding to their hate. A
spray of autocannon fire struck Burias-Drak'shal in the
shoulder and side, and he roared in defiance, lifting the
34th's holy icon high over his head as his daemon-
infused bellow echoed out across the square.

'Incoming!' came the shout from one of Marduk's
warriors.

A moment later, a modified Dreadclaw smashed
down in front of Marduk and his Coterie, striking with
colossal force, cracking the marble slabs beneath it. Its
sides, blistered and charred from atmospheric entry,
exploded outwards, slamming heavily down onto the
ground. Marduk dropped down to one knee behind it,
taking cover from the intensifying fire.

'Greetings, young one,' boomed the Warmonger,
stepping heavily from the modified drop-pod. 'The
Emperor's Palace will fall this day. I feel it in my bones.'

The holy Dreadnought had been rearmed for this
mission, heavy bolters replaced with an immense
breaching drill, studded with adamantine teeth capable of tearing through even the most heavily fortified
bastion. The apex of the fearsome weapon was formed

of a dozen separate, rotating adamantine cones, studded with coral-like teeth. Designed by the warsmiths of the Iron Warriors to crack the defences of the Emperor's Palace long ago, Marduk was not surprised to discover that armed in such a manner, the Warmonger was again locked in one of his delusions of times past.

Anything struck by the breaching drill, be it a reinforced rockcrete bunker, a front-line battle tank or the leg of a Titan, would be torn apart. Underslung beneath the potent weapon, a twin-linked meltagun protruded.

'The gateway, revered one!' shouted Marduk, pointing towards the golden doorway leading into the defence tower. 'It must be opened!'

'If such is Lorgar's will,' boomed the Dreadnought, turning towards the gateway. Lurching into motion, the war machine began to walk steadily forwards, cracking paving stones underfoot with every step, ignoring the autocannon rounds and stabbing las-rounds that stung its immense armoured form. Marduk and his warriors broke into a loping run, using the Dreadnought as mobile cover.

The golden doors were wide enough for a super-heavy tank, and over thirty metres in height. A twin-headed eagle had been sculptured in bas-relief upon its surface, and Marduk felt the rage build within him as he stared at the hateful icon, the symbol of the Imperium and the cursed False Emperor, the Great Betrayer.

The Warmonger struck the doors like a battering ram, lowering one shoulder and driving its full weight into the golden surface, which buckled – but held – under the impact. With a mechanical roar, the Dreadnought slammed its madly whirring breaching drill into the slim fissure where the two doors came together. There was a hideous sound of screeching metal, and sparks and glowing splinters of gold plating and the underlying bonded ceramite and adamantium spat out around the Dreadnought. Lascutters and meltashears built into the drill carved through the door. Lasbeams stabbed ineffectually at the Warmonger from narrow slits either side of the gateway's alcove. Marduk hurled a grenade through one of those slits high overhead and grinned in satisfaction as he heard the panicked shouts within, followed by the muffled explosion.

Then a breach the size of the Warmonger was carved in the gateway, and Marduk and his brethren followed the Dreadnought through, roaring their fury.

Soldiers wearing blue tabards over grey carapace armour were waiting for them, arrayed in overlapping serried ranks, lasguns lowered, and they unleashed a barrage that saw several Word Bearers fall. Another one dropped, his chest plate melted beneath a searing plasma blast.

'For Lorgar!' bellowed Marduk, and led the charge.

The enemy began to fall back. They maintained good discipline but were unprepared for the sheer ferocity of the Word Bearers, who raced headlong into their fire, bolters and flamers roaring.

Marduk snapped off a trio of bolts, each a killing shot, before he reached the enemy lines and the blood began to flow in earnest. None of the soldiers stood even to his shoulder, and he smashed two of them aside with one sweep of his crozius, bones turned to powder beneath the force of his first blow. He smashed his bolt pistol into the face of another, the man's features disintegrating as his bone structure crumpled inwards, before knocking aside a lasgun pointed at his head and planting a foot squarely into the chest of another, shattering the soldier's ribs and pulping the organs within.

It was amazing that they had ever achieved anything at all, Marduk thought as he slaughtered the hapless soldiers. He and his brethren were so far beyond these wretched, redundant, pathetic creatures. The only possible purpose of their meaningless lives was as slaves and sacrifices.

The Word Bearers tore through the tower guards without mercy. With curt orders, Marduk sent them spreading throughout the enemy structure. The entire tower was constructed around the immense defence laser protruding up through its middle, and the air was electric as the mass energy capacitors buried beneath the structure powered up to fire once more.

'I want this place silenced and secured!' he roared, stamping towards a spiralling stairwell. 'Every moment it remains operational more noble sons of Lorgar perish!'

FIVE KILOMETRES TO the north-east, Kol Badar broke the spine of a Guardsman with a twist of his power talons before tossing the broken body aside as if it weighed nothing at all. He stalked forwards, glass crunching beneath his footfalls. He ignored the butchered enemy soldiers and adepts strewn across the floor and slumped at their machinery, and looked out of the control room window.

The control room was positioned atop another of the defence laser towers, and he stared out across the wartorn city. In the space of ten minutes it had been turned into hell, but Kol Badar felt no particular satisfaction. After millennia of constant warfare, after organising the deaths of a thousand worlds, he felt nothing. The sky was still being torn apart by missiles and tracer fire and he grimaced as defence lasers continued to send their searing blasts heavenward.

'Target secured and silenced,' he growled. 'Strike groups, report.'

One by one, the reports came filtering in. The attack was going well. Each of the defence lasers designated as the prime targets should fall silent within the next five minutes, creating a safe corridor for the heavier mass transports to descend. Still, they should have been silenced already.

A report from high orbit was relayed to him, the information scrolling before his eyes, and he swore.

'Objective update,' Kol Badar growled, re-opening the vox-channel to all the champions leading the various strike forces. 'The enemy star fort has almost completed its rotation, faster than predicted. Our ships in high orbit will be coming under heavy fire within five minutes, and must pull back. Mass transporters en route. The window for their safe deployment has been reduced dramatically. Silence those damn guns! Silence them now!'

MARDUK SWORE AS he received Kol Badar's update, and he grunted with effort as he slammed his foot into the heavy-gauge door, half tearing it off its hinges. Sparks spurted from damaged cabling, and the door crashed inwards as Marduk kicked it again.

A pair of robed acolytes, their shaven heads tattooed with binary code, rose in alarm, and Marduk gunned them both down, his bolt pistol kicking in his hand. Their chests exploded, blood and bone spraying across the walls as the mass-reactive tips of the bolts detonated.

The interior was dark and filled with the mechanical whine of gyro-stabilisers and grind of ammunition feeds. This was one of the dozens of flak turrets on the exterior of the defence tower, and as the powerful weapon began firing again the room was lit up harshly. The sound was deafening. Two gunners were strapped into the rotating turret. Their control harness was a framework capable of swivelling up and down and through one hundred and eighty degrees, powered by wheezing servos. Flickering green screens hung before them, showing targeting matrices and data streams, and they gripped the pistol-grip controls of the flak-turret tightly, thumbs depressed upon triggers.

Intent upon their targeting monitors and with their ears muffled from the roar of their guns, the gunners had no clue that their pitiful lives were about to end.

One of the men gave a whoop as he brought down a target, and Marduk growled. Stepping forward onto the turret, he grabbed one of the gunners by the front of his flak-vest and ripped him from his seat, snapping his restraint buckles. He pounded the man headfirst into the turret's framework, and tossed the lifeless corpse aside. The other gunner, seeing the fate of his comrade, struggled to release himself from his restraint. Marduk punched his hand through the soldier's chest, fingers straight as a blade. Closing his hand around the man's heart, he ripped it free with a yank. The man stared incomprehendingly at his own beating heart in his moments before death.

Marduk dropped off the turret, which fell silent as its one remaining, lifeless gunner slumped backwards in his seat.

Marduk strode back into the corridor. Adepts were being dragged from side rooms and butchered. Conserving ammunition, warrior brothers broke necks and shattered skulls with clubbing blows from bolters and fists. Others had their throats torn out or were cut from groin to neck with knives the length of a human's thigh. Others were merely slung into walls, their skulls caving in from the force, or tossed over the gantry banisters, falling to the distant floor below.

More doors were kicked in as one by one the turrets of the tower were silenced and the occupants butchered or beaten to death.

The entire structure shuddered as the defence laser fired, and Marduk swore once more.

'Khalaxis,' he growled. 'Why is the defence laser still active?'

KHALAXIS STOOD AMID a scene of absolute destruction, blood covering every surface of the room deep below the defence tower. The bodies and limbs of over a dozen adepts and soldiers were strewn around him. His chest was rising and falling heavily, and he was crouched over one of the bodies, his hands and forearms glistening with gore. His lower face was caked in blood.

Licking the blood coating his lips, the towering champion moved towards the humming power array.

He looked it up and down for a moment then swung his chainaxe around in an arc, smashing it into the controls with a satisfying crunch. He pounded his madly whirring axe into the panels again and again, smashing and ripping them apart amid a burst of sparks and electrical smoke, and the strip lighting overhead flickered and died.

Even in darkness, Khalaxis could see quite comfortably.

'Better?' said Khalaxis, establishing a link with his Dark Apostle.

'Better,' agreed Marduk. 'Now get yourself topside. The enemy gather for a counterattack.'

Khalaxis slammed his chainaxe into the control panel one more time for good measure. With a nod to his Coterie, he led them loping out of the room, on the search for fresh prey.

Kol Badar watched as the Hosts' assault screamed towards the surface of the planet, coordinating their deployment from his position atop the defence tower he had just conquered. Cannons fired as they descended, targeting the gathering enemy ground forces, and hunter-killer missiles were launched from beneath wings, along with hellfire bombs and streams of missiles.

Armoured columns of enemy Guard were moving swiftly through the city towards them, but Kol Badar was unconcerned. With all of the defence towers silenced within the fifty-kilometre radius he had designated as the landing zone, few of the Host's shuttles were shot down on the descent. Those that had made the drop unscathed were barely touching down upon the boulevards, flyovers and colonnaded squares of the enemy city before releasing their deadly cargo.

Hundreds of the Legion's warrior brothers streamed from embarkation ramps, taking up defensive positions in the face of incoming enemy ground forces. Rhinos and Land Raiders were dropped in, tracks skidding on marble when they ripped free of their couplings. Daemon-engines and Dreadnoughts stalked from transports as their binding chains and wards were loosened, roaring in fury and hatred.

And high above them, just visible in the upper atmosphere, were the immense mass transports housing the potent engines of Legio Vulturus.

Movement out of the corner of his eye attracted his attention, and he glimpsed boxy white shapes moving at high speed through the city streets towards the Word Bearers position.

'Enemy contact,' he warned. 'Moving at speed towards the north-western cordon.'

'Acknowledged,' came the reply from Sabtec, the battle-brother in command of the strike teams controlling the location.

'Coryphaus, we have additional inbound contacts sighted, approaching from the west,' said a warrior brother nearby, an auspex held in his left hand. He was splattered with blood, and one of the horns had been shorn from his helmet in the recent gun battle. 'They are coming down from the orbital bastion in force.'

'Show me,' said Kol Badar, and the Word Bearer passed the auspex to the hulking warlord.

'It is hard to lock onto them,' said the warrior. 'They are coming in fast, below our scans, and they are actively jamming our signal, but you can see their ghost presence sporadically… there.'

'I see them,' said Kol Badar. 'Look at the heat distortion. Thunderhawks.'

Kol Badar glanced up at the immense mass transporters slowly making planetfall. He gauged that it would be at least another twenty minutes before they were down safely. The Host's warriors had to hold the towers until then.

'White Consuls counter-attack inbound,' said Kol Badar, patching through to all the Host's champions and commanders. 'Prepare yourselves. Dark Apostle, Sabtec, Ashkanez; they are converging on your locations. Re-routing reinforcements in your direction.'

'Let them come,' replied Marduk, his voice tinny over the vox-channel.

'This location is our foothold in taking this cursed planet,' said Kol Badar. 'It is our beachhead. If we fail to hold it, then our entire attack will stall. We will not get another chance.'

'Then we had better hold,' replied Marduk.

Kol Badar grunted. Leaving a skeleton defence to guard the defence laser he had claimed, he descended the wide stairs onto the square below, barking orders as he went and coordinating the deployment of the Host's warriors. His personal Land Raider rumbled forwards to meet him. It was adorned with spikes, chains and crucified Imperial citizens. Some of the poor wretches were still alive. The huge machine rolled to a stop, its red headlights burning with fury before they dimmed in bestial servitude, the way a beaten dog would cower before its master. Kol Badar had no doubt that the daemon inhabiting the mighty war engine – it had had no need for a driver or gunner for over four thousand years – would turn on him the moment he let his guard down, but that day had not yet come.

With a submissive growl, the Land Raider lowered its assault ramp. Accompanied by his Anointed brethren, Kol Badar ducked as he embarked. The assault ramp slammed shut, cutting off the painfully bright light outside, and the immense war machine began advancing towards the location of the enemy attack.

In the red-tinged darkness within, Kol Badar smiled. The taking of the *Sword of Truth* had merely whetted his appetite. Killing pathetic mortals did little to raise his interest. Astartes, on the other hand, now *there* was a foe worthy of his attention.

# CHAPTER TEN

THE AIR WAS filled with the whine of incoming artillery, followed by the reverberating thump of explosions as they tore their way across squares and boulevards, demolishing statues, turning arboretums to muddy ruin and toppling gold-veined pillars. From his position on the crenulated battlements of the captured defence tower, Marduk could see the warriors of the XVII Legion in the streets below taking cover behind their Rhinos and in the lee of buildings as the Imperial artillery barrage began. He knew it would be a constant presence in the war from here on in.

Few of his brothers would fall in these attacks, but that was not the point: the barrage was chiefly designed to ensure the Word Bearers were pinned down, taking cover rather than concentrating on targeting the incoming enemy forces.

Marduk was unconcerned, confident that whatever the White Consuls could throw at his Host, they would emerge victorious.

'There,' said Burias, pointing.

The Icon Bearer had joined Marduk a moment before, his face and arms caked in drying blood, and he stood alongside his Dark Apostle, staring westward across the gleaming marble city. Marduk looked where Burias indicated, and the targeting matrices built into his helmet flashed momentarily as they locked onto fast-moving shapes, flying low and jinking around columns and statues, before he lost them again within the maze of streets.

'Land Speeders sighted,' relayed Marduk.

The anti-grav vehicles were moving at great speed as they roared through the city, closing the distance swiftly. They had split into two groups, one gunning their engines towards Sabtec's position and the other moving towards Marduk's.

Through the thick artillery smoke, larger shapes could be seen flying low over the rooftops, approaching fast – Thunderhawks, gleaming white and adorned with the blue eagle head motif of the White Consuls. Missiles streaked from beneath their stubby wings, and heavy battle cannons roared.

Marduk glanced up at the mass transports and heavy shuttles descending through the upper atmosphere. They were coming down painfully slowly, retros burning fiercely to control their momentum, and he knew that they were at their most vulnerable now. The contents of those transports were incalculably valuable; ensuring their unmolested arrival was of paramount importance for the success of this war.

The enemy's intention was obvious – take these towers back and blast those mass transports to pieces before they landed. They were not fools, clearly; they understood how much of an impact the precious engines held within those transports would have in the forthcoming ground war.

The Land Speeders appeared again suddenly, only a few hundred metres away, banking sharply around the corner of a domed cathedral and roaring towards the defence tower, heavy bolters barking. They were about twenty metres off the ground, and as soon as they appeared, dozens of bolters and heavier weapons began to target them. They jinked from side to side, avoiding the worst of the incoming fire, and Marduk was forced to duck as heavy bolter rounds stitched across the battlements of the tower, ripping out chunks of marble.

One of the enemy vehicles was struck by a lascannon, taking the driver's head off and ripping a hole through its engines. The Land Speeder veered sharply and spun out of control, trailing black smoke, before smashing into a towering Space Marine statue atop a pillar, shattering like glass as it struck the stone figure at full speed.

The remainder kept coming, and split smoothly into three distinct groups.

One group, using the buildings opposite the defence tower to protect them from ground fire, rose to be level with Marduk's position and hovered in place, raking the walls with assault cannons and heavy bolters. Under this cover, a handful of speeders – their chassis longer than the others – rose and banked sharply, heading westward over the rooftops before lingering over a heavily defensible building nearby. As the sights in his helmet zoomed in, Marduk saw lightly armoured Scouts rappelling from them onto the building's roof, sniper rifles slung across their backs.

The third group dipped low, and disappeared from sight.

'Enemy snipers moving into position,' Marduk said. 'I have target-marked their last sighted location.'

'Acknowledged,' came Kol Badar's reply. 'Sabtec, be wary; that is near your position.'

'Understood,' said the exalted champion of the decorated 13th Coterie.

Marduk rose and snapped off a shot with his bolt pistol, which glanced off the armoured screen in front of an enemy gunner. One of his brethren nearby rose and fired a missile from his launcher that ripped apart a Land Speeder in a blinding explosion.

As if that had been a signal, the others dropped sharply, engines roaring and they disappeared from sight.

Marduk glanced over the parapet and saw White Consuls vehicles moving swiftly up the streets, having been dropped in by Thunderhawks. He also saw Rhino APCs, Predators and other vehicles that he had no name for, variations of the Rhino pattern that he had not encountered before.

'Enemy armour, moving on my position,' said Marduk.

'Received and moving to intercept,' replied Kol Badar.

Further communication was forestalled as hissing static interference suddenly washed the comms-network across all channels.

'Curse them,' snarled Marduk. 'We are being jammed.'

There was a roar of engines close by, and a strong downdraft struck Marduk. He looked up to see a Land Speeder hovering directly overhead. White Consuls Scouts were rappelling from it onto the roof of the tower.

"Ware the sky!' roared Marduk, as he began to fire. He caught one of the Scouts in the back of the head, killing him instantly, before the remainder ducked out of sight. He saw four Land Speeders veering away, just a fraction of a second before a hail of small projectiles were lobbed towards his position.

'Grenades!' roared Marduk, throwing himself back inside the tower. The concussive explosions of the frag grenades picked him up and hurled him inside, razor-tipped shards of shrapnel embedding in his power armour.

He crashed down, red warning lights flashing before his eyes. One of his brothers was nearby, armour blackened and filled with fragmentation shards. Marduk barked a warning as the warrior rose to his feet. Before the warrior could respond, his head was pulped by a shotgun blast fired at close range.

Burias was picking himself up off the floor nearby, snarling. The left side of his face was a blackened ruin of charred flesh, and he was about to hurl himself back out onto the battlements when there was a crash behind them, and a shower of plasglass.

Marduk spun to see a white-armoured Astartes figure on one knee behind him, smoke billowing from its bulky jump pack, plasglass surrounding it. Before he could fire, Marduk saw looming shadows appear outside, and more Space Marines suddenly crashed through the plasglass, jump packs and chainswords roaring.

Acrid exhaust fumes filled the interior of the control room, and Marduk rose to his feet, firing. He hit one of the Assault Marines in the chest, but the bolt was unable to penetrate the thick ceramite armour, merely knocking the warrior back half a step.

Marduk felt a surge of warp energy as Drak'shal rose to power within Burias's flesh. Roaring in infernal fury, the possessed warrior leapt past him, bowling one of the Assault Marines to the ground, talons digging through power armour. A bolt hit Marduk in the shoulder, half spinning him, and he snarled, firing a pair of shots in retaliation.

Holstering the sidearm, Marduk took hold of his crozius in two hands and leapt forwards to meet the advancing Assault Marines head-on, bellowing his hatred. He ducked beneath a buzzing chainsword and slammed his crozius into the side of his attacker, the spiked head of the holy weapon penetrating ceramite and crackling with energy as it knocked the White Consul aside.

Marduk swayed backwards and a chainsword, roaring furiously, tore through the air where his head had been a fraction of a second earlier. He only just managed to get his weapon into the path of the return blow, his muscles straining against the strength of his opponent. The teeth of the madly whirring chainsword ripped at his crozius, threatening to tear it from his grip. Marduk kicked the White Consuls Assault Marine away from him, straight into the path of Burias-Drak'shal, who impaled the warrior upon the Host's icon, lifting the spitted enemy warrior off his feet before hurling him aside.

A chainsword tore into Burias-Drak'shal's neck, ripping at power armour and flesh, and blood sprayed out. He roared in fury and pain and spun, dropping to one knee and smashing the legs from under his attacker with a sweep of his bladed icon. Before he could leap upon the downed warrior and finish him, a bolt hit him in the back, making him stumble forwards, and he lost his grip on the icon.

A bolt pistol was levelled at the possessed Icon Bearer's head, but with preternatural speed he swayed to the side, avoiding the shot, and as another chainsword roared in at him, Burias-Drak'shal merely grabbed the whirring blade in one hand, blood splattering as he pulled the wielder towards him. With the palm of his other hand he struck the White Consul under the chin, snapping his head back sharply and exposing his neck. Still holding the chainsword tightly in one hand, blood continuing to splatter out as its mechanisms strained to rip the flesh from his bones, Burias-Drak'shal lunged forwards and tore the White Consul's throat.

A shotgun blast took one of Marduk's companions in the back, knocking him forwards and into the path of the blue helmeted veteran sergeant of the Assault Marines, who used his full body weight to deliver a powerful punch with a massive power gauntlet. The blow sundered the Word Bearer's chest plate and the fused ribcage within, pulping his twin hearts and sending him crashing to his back, flickers of electrical energy dancing across his exposed chest cavity.

Marduk deflected a swinging blow aimed at his head and risked a glance onto the battlements, seeing several squads of Scouts dropping down onto the area he had recently vacated, combat shotguns held in their hands. More Assault Marines crashed through the tinted plasglass, and another of his brethren went down, impaled on a chainsword that ripped and tore at his flesh, splattering hot blood across the room.

'Back!' shouted Marduk, swallowing down his bitterness. 'Pull back!'

WITH SMOKE SPEWING from its daemon-headed exhausts, the Land Raider smashed through the wall, rockcrete and marble crumbling around it. It came down hard, powering onto a quad-laned road, and with a sickening crunch ploughed straight into the side of a White Consuls Rhino. The smaller APC was slammed sidewards, tracks skidding on the rockcrete roadway before it was rammed at speed into the corner of a building and came to shocking halt.

Dust and rock crumbled from the building, crashing down upon the vehicle's armoured roof. The Rhino's engines spluttered and died, and smoke rose from its buckled chassis. The Land Raider roared, tracks spinning into reverse, kicking up rocks and dust as it spun around to face the other enemy vehicles in the convoy.

Two Rhinos had slewed to the side and ground to a halt, their occupants spilling from within. The White Consuls dropped into cover on either side of the road, bolters bucking in their hands. The Word Bearers Land Raider fired and its twin-linked lascannon struck one of the Rhinos as it started to reverse, punching a pair of gaping holes through its armour and engine block. Its heavy bolters chased the White Consuls as they ducked into cover.

The Land Raider's assault hatch slammed down on the rubble strewn across the road. Kol Badar was first out, his combi-bolter blazing. He ordered his Anointed forward, while he strode towards the Rhino that his Land Raider had just rammed.

Smoke was rising from the wreck, and as Kol Badar reached the vehicle its side hatch slammed open. He grabbed the first White Consul to emerge by the head, his power talons closing around the Astartes's helmet. With a wrench, Kol Badar dragged the warrior out and lifted his combi-bolter, spraying bolts into the crowded interior. Kol Badar twisted his power talons, ripping the head off the White Consul held in his clutches, and continued firing. When he had exhausted a full clip he switched to the flamer affixed to his combi-bolter and filled the inside of the APC with burning promethium.

Satisfied, Kol Badar turned away, and began stalking towards the other enemy warriors, who were engaged in a brutal, close range firefight with his advancing Anointed brethren. Four lascannon beams hit the second Rhino, and it exploded in a blinding fireball, flipping end over end ten metres into the air before smashing back to the ground as a blackened, twisted heap of metal.

Targeting icons flashed as they identified heavily armoured tanks further up the roadway, turning southward.

'Tanks moving on your position, Sabtec,' he said, reloading.

'UNDERSTOOD,' SAID SABTEC, his hand held to his ear. He had formed a perimeter around the outside of the silenced defence laser turret that he had been assigned to secure, his warriors hunkered down behind makeshift barricades.

'13th!' he shouted. 'Incoming armour!'

'The attack on my position was a feint,' came the crackling voice of First Acolyte Ashkanez across the vox. 'Moving to support you.'

Seeing the enemy tanks hove into view, Sabtec gritted his teeth.

'You had better hurry, First Acolyte,' he replied. 'The 13th will hold as long as able.'

Half a dozen enemy vehicles had rounded a bend three hundred metres from his position, and were rumbling towards his cordon. At the forefront was a pair of Predators, Destructor-pattern: heavily armoured frontline battle tanks with rotating autocannon turrets and heavy bolter side sponsons. The autocannon turrets began to fire towards his position, tearing huge chunks out of the tower behind him, and Sabtec grimaced.

With clipped orders he organised his defence, redeploying the two Havoc squads accompanying him into enfilading fire positions and picking out the prime targets. With a nod, he ordered the lascannon-wielding heavy weapon specialist within his own 13th Coterie to fire, but just as the warrior's finger squeezed the trigger he jerked backwards, the back of his head blown out.

'Sniper!' roared Sabtec, throwing himself towards his fallen brother to commandeer the heavy weapon. '27th Coterie, do you see them?'

A burst of heavy bolter fire from atop the defence tower roared in answer.

'Three confirmed kills, Exalted Champion Sabtec,' replied the squad champion of 27th.

'Be vigilant,' said Sabtec. 'There will be more of them up there.'

He hefted the lascannon onto his shoulder and flicked out its optical sight. He did not unhook the heavy power generator from his fallen brother's back – he did not have time – and the insulated cables connecting the bulky weapon hummed as he linked to its targeting systems.

The enemy tanks had fired smoke and blind grenades; broad-spectrum electro-magnetic radiation blinding both sensors and scans as well as blocking conventional sight. Sabtec swore.

He aimed the lascannon into the thick smoke that confused his auto-sensors. The edge of the smoke was no more than a hundred metres off, and he panned left and right as he sought a target.

Abruptly, he saw headlights appear through the smoke and his target icons flashed red. He swung the lascannon around towards them and fired

The shot glanced off the Predator's angled fore-armour. Sabtec gritted his teeth in frustration as the weapon began to power up again, venting steam.

'Come on,' he said as more enemy vehicles materialised out of the blinding fog, moving at speed towards him.

Missiles streamed from the Havoc team on his left, and an enemy Rhino ground to a halt as its tracks were torn clear. Autocannons ripped across armoured plates and tore a barking heavy bolter sponson loose from a Predator. The turret of the battle tank turned molten, dripping down over its hull like wax as a plasma cannon found its mark.

The heavy vehicles gunned their engines and accelerated.

The Predator unleashed a torrent from its weapon systems, raking fire across the Word Bearers line, and bolters began to roar as White Consuls disembarked from their Rhinos. A melta blast seared a burning hole through the marble balustrade that Sabtec knelt behind, but he remained unfazed as he calmly waited for his weapon to reach full power.

Bolts ricocheted off the marble around him, and as a blinking red icon turned green, he took careful aim and squeezed the lascannon's trigger.

The shot hit a Predator in its armoured vision slit, burning straight through the high-compound rein-forced plasglass and killing the tank's driver instantly. The Predator slewed to the side and struck a Rhino, half spinning it, before ploughing up a bank of marble stairs and ramming into a wall. The tank's turret started to turn, but a well-aimed missile hit the Predator's exposed rear. There was a muted explosion and smoke and flames began pouring from inside, and the turret froze.

No more than two metres from Sabtec, a warrior dropped without a sound as a result of sniper fire, half his helmet blowing out in a blossoming cloud of blood. Sabtec ditched the lascannon and threw himself to the side as a Rhino, an immense dozer blade painted in yel-low and black chevrons affixed to its front, ploughed towards him. Bolts and autocannon rounds pinged off the thick protective dozer blade, and the APC drove straight through the balustrade, debris, chunks of masonry and fallen statues smashed out of its path.

Side hatches slammed open and enemy Astartes leapt out, bolters barking. A shot took Sabtec in the side of the head, obscuring his vision as sparks and smoke filled his helmet. Firing his bolter one-handed, he ripped his hel-met off, and the full sound and scent of battle crashed in on him.

Blood was dripping down his face as Sabtec ordered the 13th to reform and fall back now that their defen-sive position had been compromised. He saw two of his brothers torn to shreds by concentrated bursts of close-range fire, but continued to issue his orders with cool detachment.

'I could really do with that support, First Acolyte,' said Sabtec, calmly.

'Hold on, brother,' came Ashkanez's voice across the vox. 'Closing on your position. One minute.'

Sabtec drew his power sword. Its hilt resembled bones blackened in fire. It hummed into life as he thumbed its activation rune. He dropped to one knee as a burst of bolter fire tore through the air above him, and fired his bolter one-handed, the shot taking a White Consul in the head, then rose to his feet again, slashing upwards with his power sword.

The humming blade caught another White Consul under the chin, slicing up through his power armour like a lascutter and carving his jaw in two.

Flamers roared, bathing the assaulting White Consuls in burning promethium, scorching battle plate black. A roaring chainaxe hacked the head from a loyalist, but the victorious Word Bearer was then himself slain, a plasma pistol fired up close slamming him backwards.

Another enemy vehicle was halted, a missile impacting into its side and slewing it sideways. The enemy attack was faltering, Sabtec realised, and he ordered his warriors to converge. He emerged from cover and began to advance upon the enemy, who had taken up position behind the same cover that the 13th had been using moments before.

The concealing smoke fired by the enemy vehicles was drifting down the avenue, becoming patchy, but it suddenly cleared as the huge shape of a White Consuls Thunderhawk came screaming low over the rooftops and descended sharply. The downdraft of its powerful engines sent eddies of dust and smoke fleeing before it, and multiple heavy bolters opened up, their heavy thuds barely heard over the deafening Thunderhawk's engines.

Before the Thunderhawk's landing gear touched the ground, the Land Raider held tight to the gunship's belly was released, couplings unlocked, and it dropped the last few metres to the ground, where it bounced once before settling.

More heavy weapon fire stabbed into the Thunderhawk's hull, shattering one of the windows of its cockpit and damaging one of its engine turbines, and it lifted off again, engines roaring. It banked violently as it rose, and was gone.

The massive Land Raider's flanks were gleaming white and adorned with gold, and royal blue banners hung from its side. It was rumbling forwards, and unleashed a heavy fusillade that ripped one of his Havoc squads to pieces.

'Enemy Land Raider has dropped in at my position,' said Sabtec coolly, raising his voice to be heard over the roaring gun battle.

Backing away towards cover, snapping off shots with his ornate bolter one-handed, Sabtec gave clipped orders to target the heavy battle tank.

A squad of Word Bearers was almost completely annihilated as the Land Raider unleashed its fury. It had a weapon outfit that Sabtec was not familiar with. Ranks of bolters had replaced the standard lascannon side-sponsons – six bolters per side – and twin-linked assault cannons were built into its front turret. Clearly, it was a pattern designed for frontal assault, and it performed that role admirably.

Missiles and lascannons struck the Land Raider as it powered forwards, but they had little effect. It came through the heavy barrage like an enraged beast, shaking off everything that the Word Bearers threw at it. It smashed the smoking chassis of an immobilised Rhino out of its path. Sabtec gunned down another White Consul, then grunted in pain as a bolt hit him in the wrist. The explosive round took his hand clear off. It landed some metres away, still clutching his ornate bolter, and he frowned in irritation at having been disarmed.

The hulking behemoth smashed a path towards the 13th Coterie, crushing a low wall beneath its tread. Sabtec registered that there were explosive charges set to either side of the Land Raider's assault ramp a fraction of a second before they were fired, and he threw himself down behind a fallen statue. Above him, the air was suddenly filled with shrapnel as the assault launchers detonated, unleashing a swathe of destruction that tore one of his 13th brothers to shreds.

Then the assault ramp of the Land Raider slammed down, and Sabtec glimpsed a massive warrior striding from within, bedecked in gleaming Terminator armour, a billowing blue tabard across his body. A golden metal halo framed his head. In his right hand he held a thunder hammer. Across his left arm was strapped a crackling storm shield shaped like an over-sized crux terminatus. A Chapter Master, Sabtec realised.

A Librarian emerged alongside the heavily armoured commander, a nimbus of shimmering light emitting from his psychic hood. A command squad followed them. Caught between these newcomers and the other White Consuls closing in to either side, there was nowhere for Sabtec to fall back to, no room for manoeuvre. For all his tactical savvy and strategic brilliance, all the experience garnered from thousands of years of constant warfare, he had few options.

Nevertheless, death held no fear for him.

'Thirteen!' he roared, rising from his cover, one side of which was pockmarked with shrapnel. 'With me!'

His surviving Coterie brothers rose from cover and charged after him. Bolters pumped shots towards the Chapter Master and his entourage, then Sabtec broke into a run, brandishing his humming power sword.

He saw one of the enemy, an Apothecary, lose an arm, and a dozen holes were shot through the banner that was unfurled as its bearer stepped from within the Land Raider. The banner bearer was felled a moment later, his faceplate shattered by a concentrated burst of fire. The standard of the Chapter teetered and started to fall.

Everything seemed to be happening in slow motion.

Bolts screamed past Sabtec's head, missing him by centimetres, and he registered one of his 13th brothers' dying roar as he fell beneath a melta gun blast. Another brother fell as the twin-linked assault cannons of the Land Raider tore him in half at the waist. Sabtec heard the warrior still shouting litanies of Lorgar as he crawled towards the enemy before a bolt silenced him.

A warrior armed with power sword and buckler, his blue crusade-era helmet adorned with a red crest of stiffened hair, stepped in front of the Chapter Master, his voice ringing with challenge.

Sabtec rolled beneath the enemy's attack and smashed his power sword into the enemy champion's head as he came to his feet. The warrior fell silently, leaving the path to the White Consuls Chapter Master clear.

With a snarl, Sabtec leapt forwards. His first blow was smashed aside by his enemy's heavy storm shield. His second was cut short as the White Consul's immense thunder hammer smashed down on his forearm, shattering his bones. His power sword, that revered weapon that had been gifted him by Erebus himself, dropped from fingers that no longer worked, and Sabtec stared up into the face of the White Consuls Chapter Master.

'Emperor damn you, heretic,' said the White Consul.

'We're all damned,' Sabtec breathed, 'You, me, all of us. This whole galaxy will burn.'

'That time is not yet upon us,' growled the White Consuls Chapter Master, and hefted his thunder hammer to deliver the killing blow.

A plasma blast struck the Chapter Master's hammer-arm, distracting him just long enough for Sabtec to roll away. He rose to see the arrival of First Acolyte Ashkanez, firing a plasma pistol. Two-score warriors charged behind him, and now outnumbered, the enemy began to fall back.

'Your timing is impeccable, First Acolyte,' said Sabtec.

MARDUK CURSED AS he slammed his last sickle clip into his MkII bolt pistol.

Almost half the warrior brothers that had accompanied him in taking the enemy defence tower had fallen. He and the last survivors were holed up in the lower levels, guarding the way down to the defence laser's controls, ensuring that the potent weapon did not come back online.

Another of his brothers fell, a crater in his chest, splattering Marduk with blood.

'Kol Badar,' snarled Marduk as he leant around a corner and fired. He ducked back as White Consuls returned fire. 'How long until those damned transports are down?'

'Five minutes more,' came the reply.

'Five minutes,' said Marduk. 'And how long until I get some support?'

'Entering the compound now,' said Kol Badar. 'Two other towers have fallen. It's just minutes before their defence lasers are back online.'

'Perfect,' said Marduk.

The sound of distant gunfire and shouting came to Marduk's ears.

'You are in?' said Marduk.

'Affirmative. Perimeter breached,' said Kol Badar.

'Come brothers,' snarled Marduk. 'Let us drive these loyalist filth before us like dogs.'

'We go to kill the Emperor?' said the hulking Warmonger, standing before the defence laser's control panels, clenching his power talons in eagerness.

'His minions,' said Marduk. He motioned towards the corner. 'After you, revered one.'

The Dreadnought growled and broke into a run that made the ground shake. He rounded the corner, smashing loose marble slabs from the walls, and hundreds of bolt rounds pinged off his armour.

'Kill them all!' roared Marduk, right behind the Warmonger.

\* \* \*

A HUNDRED SOLDIERS of the Boros Imperial Guard surrounded Coadjutor Aquilius as he pushed on the enemy position. He could feel the pride of the soldiers to be fighting alongside Astartes, and he smiled grimly. He towered over them, like an adult amongst a sea of children. One of the defence lasers that the Guardsmen, *his* Guardsmen, had retaken fired suddenly with a crackling boom that made his ears ache.

One of the huge, cylindrical mass transports descending planetward was struck, shearing a devastating wound up its side and destroying one of its mass stabilisers in an explosion of fire and sparks. They were the largest drop-ships he had ever seen, and he felt some consternation as he looked upon them, knowing the terrible machines they contained. Consternation was about as close to fear as he had ever come since his indoctrination into the Chapter. He vaguely remembered the emotion from childhood, but it meant nothing to him now.

With some satisfaction, he saw the mass transport begin to accelerate towards the ground, tipping to one side as it came down, its stabilisers unbalanced. It accelerated past the other transports, its velocity increasing rapidly. In satisfaction, he saw another defence laser strike a second of the descending transport cylinders.

'Brace yourselves,' said Aquilius.

The container struck the surface of Boros Prime fifteen kilometres away. A section of the city five hundred metres in diameter was crushed beneath its weight. An obscuring cloud of dust and smoke spread in all directions like a widening ripple in a pond, shaking the city to its foundations. The ground shuddered and a rising mushroom cloud of dust erupted hundreds of metres into the air. The deafening boom of the impact reached them a moment later, so loud it was as if the planet were splitting in two.

As the sound of the collapsing city section subsided, there came the horrible death cry of something unnameable. Images of the warp, of tentacles flailing from the void, filled Aquilius's mind.

'What do they contain, sir?' said the recently promoted trooper, Verenus. The soldier's superior, the regiment's ageing Legatus, had died just minutes earlier, his torso torn apart in a bloody explosion as a bolt detonated within his chest. Aquilius had promoted Verenus to the position as acting regimental commander of the Boros 232nd.

'Corrupted engines of the Adeptus Mechanicus,' said Aquilius.

He regarded the trooper. Verenus was still in shock at his sudden rise to power, but was handling it well. The poster child for the ideal Boros Prime Guardsman, Verenus was strong and self-assured, his eyes an icy blue and his hair bleached pale from sun and radiation. Aquilius had been impressed by the 3rd Prime Cohort's combat record, but it had been because of Verenus that Aquilius had chosen them to accompany him on this mission. The man had impressed him on the parade grounds of Boros Prime months earlier.

Throne, he thought. Had it been only months? It seemed like a lifetime. There were few regiments on Boros Prime that had as much combat experience as these men, and they had not disappointed. Aquilius could see the effect that fighting alongside Astartes was having on them – the Guardsmen stood taller, their chests puffed out proudly, despite having recently lost their commanding officer.

A great cheer went up from the Guardsmen as the mass transport crashed to earth, but Aquilius's mood was still grim. One had been destroyed and another was plummeting to the ground, but that still left three untouched.

They descended to the ground seemingly in violation of the laws of gravity, coming down slowly and steadily, grav-motors, stabilisers and thrusters bearing them sedately towards the surface of Boros Prime. They were hateful, vile things, with giant, mechanical tentacles beneath them that waved lazily in the air like sea-fronds in a current.

The first of the massive transports touched down in the middle of a distant square, causing another violent earth tremor. Instantly, giant tentacles flailed, ripping at the armoured sides of the cylinder, tearing the armoured sheath away like it was sloughed off skin.

Until now, the reality of the situation had not been fully driven home to Aquilius. The enemy had a foothold on his beloved home world. Worse, they had unleashed terrors of such power entire cities would be razed to the ground.

A ululating roar echoed across the city, followed by another. Aquilius glimpsed two of the terrible engines as they loped from their cylindrical cages. They stood as tall as a five-storey building, and though he knew these were but the smallest of the enemy Titans – corrupted Warhounds – he felt again a stab of consternation.

'Titans,' hissed Verenus, his eyes widening.

'They are the remnants of one of the cursed Legios that sided against the Emperor in ages past,' Aquilius told him.

The White Consul felt the resolve of the soldiers around him waver in the face of the daemonic Titans.

'By the grace of the Emperor,' breathed one soldier.

'Titans?' muttered another. 'What hope have–'

'There is always hope,' Aquilius said forcefully, cutting the soldier off. '*Always*. I am a son of Boros, as are you. As are we all. Our bloodline is a bloodline of heroes, and this is our world. The enemy thinks they can take it from us, but we will show them their error. We will punish them for every metre of ground they take, striking hard and without fear, for we are sons of Boros, and we shall not falter. The Emperor is with us, my brothers, and mark my words: Boros Prime *will not fall.*'

MARDUK'S EYES BURNED with zealous fury as he picked his way through the sea of bodies left in the wake of the Warmonger. Belagosa and Ankh-Heloth were inbound, leading their warriors against the other prime targets. He smiled grimly, exposing serrated, shark-like teeth. It had been costly, but Marduk had gained their foothold on the planet.

Now its corruption would begin.

# BOOK FOUR:
# THE TAINT

*'A man can be convinced to do anything,
no matter how abhorrent, with the right
motivation.'*

– First Chaplain Erebus

# CHAPTER ELEVEN

THE CLEAR BLUE skies of Boros Prime were long gone. In their place, the atmosphere was thick with rust-coloured haze, choking pollutants and vile toxins. The twin suns, bright and clear before the arrival of the Word Bearers, were now barely discernible, hidden behind the festering cloud. The temperature and humidity of Boros soared. An ever-thickening pall of smoke hung low over the war-torn cities of the Imperial world, heavy with cinders and ash that caught in the throat and made breathing for the unaugmented difficult and painful.

Tens of millions had already perished, and the corruption of the planet and its occupants was well underway.

Legatus Verenus, acting regimental commander of the Boros 232nd, slammed the butt of his lasgun into the face of the cultist, splintering the traitor's nose across his face. The man refused to go down, growling and hissing like an animal, hands like claws scrabbling for Verenus's eyes.

The traitor's face was so twisted with hatred that it was barely human at all. Fire-blackened hooks pinned the man's eyelids open, and an eight-pointed star had been cut into his forehead, leaking blood. He was a vision of depravity, but what sickened Verenus most of all was that the man wore a breastplate of the Boros Guard; once, mere weeks or days past perhaps, this man had given praise to the Emperor of Mankind and fought alongside him. What had the enemy done to him to make him fall so low?

Verenus smashed away the man's clutching hands and again slammed the butt of his lasgun into the man's face. The savage cultist staggered back a step, giving Verenus the space he needed. He reversed his grip on his weapon and shot the man in the chest. The traitor collapsed with a gargled sigh, a searing black hole burnt through his chest. The stink of melting plastek and charred flesh stung Verenus's nostrils.

More cultists were rushing his position, a veritable flood of heretics that bayed for blood like wild dogs.

'Back!' roared Verenus, snapping off shots into the mob as he walked steadily backwards. 'Move to the fallback position!'

The Guardsmen of the 2nd Cohort fell back along the war-torn street, gunning down scores of screaming heretics as they moved. Explosions from grenades and rockets rocked the ground beneath Verenus's feet, and aircraft screamed overhead through the smoke and fire. Heavy stubbers positioned behind shuttered windows above opened up, providing covering fire for the retreating soldiers.

Muzzle flare spat from barrels of the clattering weapons, and empty shells fell down to the street below in a deluge, the sound of them hitting the ground like the jingling of wind-chimes. In the distance, the heavy thump of siege mortars and Whirlwinds could be heard, followed a few seconds later by the shriek of incoming artillery.

The street was a shattered ruin, lined by the skeletal shells of buildings. Rubble was piled high, and the dead littered the ground, piled in gutters and at the base of crumbling walls. An all-pervading stink hung in the humid air, rancid and foul, like rotting meat. Verenus blinked soot and sweat out of his eyes as he backed away, snapping off shots with his lasgun, too busy just trying to keep his soldiers alive another day, another hour to allow the direness of his situation to press upon him.

It had been two months since the enemy had first descended upon Boros Prime, and the beautiful cities of Verenus's home world were almost unrecognisable. They had been turned into a living hell, once majestic tree-lined boulevards reduced to scorched rubble, the clear blue skies thick with black smoke and wheeling creatures that defied description.

The once proud citizens of Boros Prime – or at least those that had not yet been slaughtered or taken – now bore haunted, hunted expressions. Every citizen of Boros Prime of eligible age, no matter his or her standing or profession, underwent years of military training. Every able man, woman and child had been issued with a lasgun and formed into auxiliary units to support the PDF and Guard units.

Nevertheless, it was one thing to know how to arm and fire a lasgun, another to face an enemy such as they faced, day in day out, and to see one's home world torn apart by warfare. The enemy's corrupt presence could be felt everywhere, a vile, malignant touch that plagued the minds of every one of the Imperial world's defenders.

Verenus had not had a decent night's sleep since the enemy's arrival, plagued with violent nightmares filled with blood and malevolent, skinless daemons that had him awake and screaming minutes after closing his eyes. It was the same with everyone and Verenus knew that these were no normal dreams – they were an insidious weapon of the enemy, designed to sow terror and despair amongst the regiments. And damn them, but it was working, Verenus thought.

It had become so bad that Verenus was starting to see those skinless daemons while he was awake. He saw them leering at him from the corner of his eye, but whenever he turned towards them there was nothing there. Sleep deprivation, he told himself. You are imagining things. And if he, a veteran with decades of fighting against the minions of the Ruinous Powers under his belt, was becoming unnerved by the dreams, then he could only imagine what it would be doing to the minds of those not trained for war. Indeed, suicides had already accounted for one man in twenty within the Guard units, a staggering total when one considered how many soldiers were fighting here on Boros.

Tens of millions had been killed in battle. Millions more, the unlucky ones, had been taken by the enemy. Verenus grimaced to think of their fate. He'd put a lasround in his head before he allowed such a fate to claim him.

He could hear the enemy chanting as they approached. It was a deep, mournful sound, filled with hatred. An even worse sound accompanied them – a hellish blare of insanity that made Verenus's flesh crawl. It felt as though something was scratching painfully behind his eardrums, penetrating his head and reverberating within his mind. It made him feel sick, and his gorge rose.

The infernal chanting was deeply unnerving, and he had already seen more than a dozen soldiers succumb to its madness, men that the commissars were forced to put down as insanity claimed them.

It sounded like a faulty vox-unit, amplified a hundred times louder, deafening static overlaid with screams, whispers, roars, the sound of children crying. The pounding industrial clamour was overlaid with the sound of women screaming in unwholesome pleasure, of bones breaking, of animals howling in pain and terror.

Verenus had come to associate it with Chaos itself, the sound of bedlam and despair. He heard it when he slept, insinuating itself into his dreams, and it was always there in the back of his head, even when the hideous floating machines that projected the discordant sound were nowhere nearby.

Verenus ducked around the corner of a building and pressed himself back against the wall. Weapon lifted to his shoulder, he glanced around the corner. Most of the cultists his cohort had ambushed were dead, but it was not them that drew his attention. Through the fire and smoke he saw first one, then more of the hellish, red-armoured enemy, their faces obscured behind horned helmets fashioned into the horrific visage of beasts and daemons. The huge figures moved forward steadily, bellowing their hateful catechisms as they came.

'Move it, soldiers! Move,' Verenus bellowed. Then the enemy Astartes began to fire, and his words were drowned out by the noise.

A dozen soldiers of the 232nd were gunned down before Verenus's eyes as they raced for cover, their bodies ripped apart as bolter fire raked across their backs. One of his men stumbled only metres from the corner as a ricochet clipped the back of his knee; the soldier fell with a cry.

Verenus swore and ducked back around the corner, snapping off a pair of shots as he moved to the soldier's aid. He saw one of his shots strike an enemy square in the forehead, but it did not even slow the warrior. The wall behind Verenus collapsed as a bolt struck it, showering him with dust and rock. Verenus kept moving, and dropped to one knee before the fallen soldier. He fired off another hastily aimed shot, and gripped the soldier by the scruff of his uniform, hauling him back into cover.

Heavy stubbers ripped across the advancing enemy, buying the retreating soldiers precious moments, but the traitors kept advancing steadily, gunning down more Boros Guardsmen with every burst of fire. One of the Word Bearers fired up at a window, almost casually taking out one of the heavy weapon operators. His head exploded, spraying blood and brain matter across the face of his shocked comrade, reams of ammunition still held in his hands.

There was only a handful of the traitor Space Marines, Verenus saw. Even so, it was enough. He had learnt the hard way that each of those cursed giants was easily the equivalent of thirty or forty of his own battle-hardened veteran Guardsmen, or more than a hundred auxiliary draftees. More, perhaps. Each one of the bastards that his regiment took down was cause for celebration.

He had been engaged with the enemy in constant battle for the past two months, and though the war had devolved into a horrid, bloody grind, he knew that they were winning.

Tank companies and hundreds of millions of soldiers fought the enemy toe-to-toe, day in day out, and it had become an exercise of military logistics, a constant rotation of regiments to and from the front in order to maintain pressure. The Word Bearers could not keep up this pace forever, and would eventually be ground down, or at least Verenus prayed that this would be so, but how many Imperial citizens would be lost in the meanwhile? And what would be left of Boros Prime once the dust settled? Nothing worth salvaging, he thought darkly.

'Thank you, sir,' said the soldier that he had just hauled to safety, and he nodded to him. A pair of Guardsmen lifted the man from the ground, and hurried him away from danger.

Verenus signalled, and broke into a run, his soldiers scattering into the ruins at his order. He threw himself over a smashed low wall into what had once been a beautiful garden, and propped himself behind it, keeping his head down. Blackened skeletons of trees stood sentinel above him. With curt hand signals, he moved his troops into position. Soldiers hefted heavy tripod-mounted autocannons into cover, slamming them down behind low walls and piles of rubble and hurriedly loading them with fresh spools of ammunition.

'Come on, you bastards,' said Verenus.

He was lathered in sweat and grime, the unbearable Boros Prime heat only emphasised by the oppressive black smoke filling the sky. There was a horrible stink in the air, something akin to burnt flesh and bones. Verenus thought again of the men and women that the enemy had forced into servitude, slaving away upon the horrific construction works that were sprouting up all across the continent, corrupting them into base creatures that spurned the light of the Emperor.

There seemed to be some form of pattern to the location of the enemy's construction, but Verenus was damned if he knew what it was. He snorted without humour as he realised he probably *would* be damned if he understood.

A corrupted Guardsman was the first around the corner, diabolical symbols of the Ruinous Powers smeared in blood and faeces across his helmet and breastplate. He held a standard-issue lasgun in his hands, but was gunned down before he could raise it. Another heretic appeared, his face contorted with hatred and loathing, his blackened cheeks streaked with tears. He too was shot down, smoking burns riddling his chest and face.

The first of the Word Bearers rounded the corner, a hulking traitor encased in gore-splattered plate. Curving horns of obsidian rose from his helmet, which had been fashioned to resemble a snarling beast. Verenus fired. His lasgun beam struck the immense warrior in the chest, to little effect. From all around, dozens of blue lasbeams were fired as more of the hated traitors appeared. The heavy thump of autocannons joined the fusillade, spraying bullets across power-armoured foes.

One of the enemy went down, peppered with bullet craters and covered in lasburns. Verenus grinned savagely. That grin turned into a grimace as he saw the enemy warrior push himself back to his feet, blood and oil leaking from his wounds.

A handful of the Boros infantrymen were cut down with short bursts of enemy fire. The man next to Verenus was struck as he raised his lasgun to fire, the shot tearing his arm off and creating a gaping hole in his chest. He gaped up at Verenus in the second before he died, a look of shock on his blood-drenched face.

The enemy were moving steadily forwards, conserving ammunition as they took their shots with robotic precision. Few of their bolts did not find their mark, and any of his warriors that were hit suffered horrendous injuries. He fired another shot then ducked into cover as one of the enemy swung a bolter in his direction. Verenus dropped flat and began to crawl arm over arm to a new position as bolter fire smashed into his cover, blowing it away in explosive detonations.

'Armour in position, sir!' shouted one of his sergeants, a heavy vox-caster unit strapped to his back.

'Finally,' said Verenus. He turned and shouted, 'Back! Fall back!'

His soldiers responded instantly, slipping back into the rubble of the shattered buildings, snapping off occasional shots as they scrambled into heavier cover. Verenus pushed himself to his feet, and began running, keeping his profile low. A man further along the street turned and shouted something, but Verenus couldn't make it out. Then the man was killed, his torso becoming one huge, bloodied crater, and he fell without a sound. Glancing back, he saw the enemy perhaps halfway along the street. Verenus hurled himself over a fallen statue and dropped in behind it, his heart pounding, and gunfire zipped past him.

He heard the grind of engines nearby, followed closely by a crash that shook the ground. There was a whoop of joy from one of his soldiers, and he peered over the top of the fallen statue. His fire-blackened face broke into a smile as he saw a wall collapse, brought down by the dozer blades of three tracked armoured vehicles.

The tanks, a support division of the 53rd armoured company, were Hellhounds, close support vehicles based on the Chimera STC chassis. Armed with their flame-throwing Inferno cannons, they had proven themselves invaluable in the brutal, close quarter fighting on Boros Prime in the last months. While some battle tanks had proved unwieldy within the tight confines of the cityfight, the Hellhounds had excelled.

They rumbled through the dust and smoke, crunching over the rubble of the fallen wall. A half-cohort of the 232nd swarmed in their wake, scrambling to take position amongst the debris. Inferno cannons spewed liquid fire across the Word Bearers, who stoically refused to back away, bolters roaring even as they were consumed in flame.

Their armour cracked and blistered, but still they gunned down almost a score of Guardsmen before they fell. Their resilience and their absolute refusal to back down even in the face of certain death never ceased to stagger Verenus. One of the Hellhounds exploded in an incandescent plume of fire as krak grenades ignited its fuel reserve.

Only two of the enemy Astartes were still standing, bolters blazing in their hands when there came a hideous screeching sound from overhead.

'The sky!' shouted one of his men.

Verenus panned his weapon across the smoke-filled heavens. For a moment he saw nothing, then a blood-red flock of skinless, winged horrors swept over the rooftops, screaming towards the Boros soldiers.

'In the name of the Throne,' breathed Verenus, seeing his nightmares come to life.

The daemons, for they could have been nothing else, descended in a screeching rush, leathery wings tightly furled as they dropped towards the ground. They were horrific creatures, their glistening exposed musculature a perverted mockery of humanity. Lipless mouths were twisted into feral grins, exposing needle-like fangs, and barbed, serpentine tails of wet muscle trailed behind them as they hurtled towards the horrified soldiers below. Their forms shimmered like a mirage, as if they were at once there but not there, or perhaps existed simultaneously in more than one realm.

Cold fear gripping him, Verenus began to fire wildly up at the incoming daemons. His soldiers began to run.

The monsters swooped down low over the Boros 232nd, unfurling blade-like talons to slash at their prey. The face of one soldier was ripped off as claws hooked into his flesh. Several soldiers were lifted off their feet, talons locking around their necks and shoulders, and others fell screaming as daemons dropped upon them, bearing them to the ground under their weight, biting and ripping.

A wild shot from Verenus hit one of the creatures in its skinless head. Its flesh, the colour of raw liver, turned grey and black as it cooked, and it crashed to the ground, the bones of its wings snapping as it impacted and rolled, bowling one of his soldiers over in the process. The man screamed horribly as the creature tore at him, slashing with its talons and biting with its needle fangs.

All semblance of order was lost. The Guardsmen of the Boros 232nd scattered blindly, and the daemons continued to sow their terror, ripping the soldiers apart in a gory frenzy.

Verenus was shouting orders, but no one heard him. Hot blood splashed across his face as the man at his side was slain, his throat torn out. Talons raked his shoulder, and Verenus screamed in pain, dropping his weapon. Wild with panic, one of his own soldiers ran into him blindly, desperate to escape, and Verenus was knocked to the ground. All hope was lost. Death had finally come for him.

A shadow descended on Verenus and he dropped to one knee, raising an arm protectively as a hideous, screeching fury hurtled overhead, talons slashing. He gasped as the daemon's claws locked shut around his forearm, digging deep into his flesh. His shoulder was almost torn from its socket as he was dragged to his feet. Leathery wings covered in a spider web of red and blue veins flapped heavily, and Verenus felt a sudden panic as his feet lost contact with the ground.

The fury looked down at him, snarling. Its eyes were yellow and catlike and oozed steaming, milky tears. It opened its mouth wide – too wide – and strings of saliva dripped from its needle-teeth. A dozen worm-like tongues squirmed in its throat, and Verenus felt its hot breath upon his face. It smelt like sulphur, rotting meat and electricity.

A heavy weight suddenly pulled the fury back down towards the earth, and it screeched in anger. It released Verenus, who fell to the ground heavily, and coiled around to slash at the figure that had a solid grip upon its tail.

From the ground, Verenus looked up to see an imposing figure surrounded in a halo of light, a holy aura that made his breath catch in his throat. For a moment it was as if time stood still. Verenus was not alone in witnessing this divine vision; all the soldiers of Boros Prime nearby saw it, this holy figure bathed in seraphic light.

The glowing nimbus lasted just a fraction of a second, and while the rational part of Verenus's mind insisted it was nothing but a momentary trick of the light reflecting off alabaster armour plates, the impression was indelible.

The halo bathing the figure dissipated, and the immense figure of a White Consul stood there, defiant and unwavering. Brother Aquilius, Coadjutor of Boros Prime, held the daemon by one of its hind legs. As it turned to swipe at him, spitting in hatred, he slammed his bolter into the side of its head. The force of the blow smashed it to the ground, crushing its skull.

Still alive, it landed heavily upon its back, and in one swift, violent movement it flipped itself over, snarling, crouched on all fours. Its tail cracked like a whip as it readied to spring, but before it could, Aquilius planted his foot upon its back and pinned it to the ground.

The White Consul pressed the barrel of his bolter against the back of its skinless head. It thrashed wildly but could not escape the crushing weight of the Space Marine.

'Begone daemon-spawn!' said Aquilius. The infernal beast's movements ceased as he planted a bolt in its head. Within seconds, the creature had rotted away, its flesh ridden with maggots and worms before liquefying, leaving just a foetid pool of foulness upon the ground.

'Be strong, men of Boros!' shouted the White Consul. 'The Emperor is with us!'

Verenus snatched up a lasgun from a fallen Guardsman and began firing on full auto, all fear evaporated. Other soldiers of the Boros 232nd fell in around Aquilius and Verenus, forming a tight knot of defiance anchored around the holy Astartes warrior.

One by one the screaming daemons were cut down, hissing ichor bursting from their Chaotic bodies, and Verenus felt savage joy to see the deviant, unholy beasts banished back to the warp.

In the aftermath of battle he felt exultant, invigorated and inspired. He had felt the presence of the Emperor in that battle, and he saw the same glow of belief reflected in the eyes of his soldiers.

'We are going to win this war, aren't we?' said one of his men.

'We are,' said Verenus, for the first time actually believing it. He turned his gaze towards Aquilius, talking softly with some of his soldiers. 'The White Angel is with us.'

\* \* \*

To the Word Bearers, the battlefield was their most sacred church, and Boros Prime had become one immense battlefield. The full Hosts of three Dark Apostles had descended upon it, hatred in their hearts. Every death was a sacrifice, and Marduk could feel the gluttonous pleasure of his infernal deities. Yet he could also sense their impatience, mirroring his own, and those of his captains.

Marduk's chainsword was glutted with blood, but it still hungered for more. He was crouched low, moving towards the enemy position. He saw the enemy gathering for another assault, he knew that the daemon within his weapon, Borgh'ash, would not have long to wait.

'It offends me that we have not yet won this war,' came Kol Badar's voice in Marduk's ear. 'This wretched planet resists us with every step!'

Marduk and Kol Badar were communing over a closed vox-channel, their words heard by none but each other. The Coryphaus was located over a hundred kilometres away, in the north-east of the sprawling city known as Sirenus Principal, fighting to hold a key landing-zone from Imperial counter-attack. The Imperial Guard, bolstered by White Consuls, had been battling for six solid days to retake the location.

'Their resistance is frustrating,' said Marduk. 'But it cannot last.'

He rose to his full height and dropped two Guardsmen with carefully aimed shots from his bolt pistol. Shouts and gunfire erupted all around him, and Marduk broke cover, closing the distance with the enemy swiftly.

'They threaten to overrun us at a score of key locations, through sheer numbers,' continued Kol Badar.

'The other Hosts too are struggling to maintain their footholds.'

'Our faith is our armour,' growled Marduk as he killed, tearing apart the chest of a Guardsman with his chainsword. He stepped forward and gunned down two more Guardsmen who were backing away from him, horror written across their faces. 'With true faith, nothing can harm us.'

'Empty rhetoric,' came Kol Badar's crackling reply. 'It means nothing.'

'Speak not such heresy, Kol Badar,' said Marduk, breaking the arm of a Guardsman with a backhand swipe, before clubbing him to the ground with his bolt pistol. He slammed his boot down upon the warrior's neck, breaking it with an audible crack. 'Armoured with true faith, nothing can defeat us.'

'All your praying will not stop their Bombards and Basilisks from ripping the Host to pieces, little by little.'

'We will break them,' said Marduk. 'Their world is falling around them. It will be only a matter of time before their will is broken.'

The Dark Apostle lowered his smoking bolt pistol as the enemy routed before him.

'Casualties?' he said over his shoulder.

'Two,' replied Sabtec, champion of the exalted 13th. 'Shulgar of 19th Coterie, and Erish-Bhor of the 52nd.'

'The enemy?' said Marduk, surveying the carnage before him. Bodies were strewn across the open square that the Imperials had been trying to retake.

Sabtec shrugged, the servo-motors of his power armour whining as they tried to replicate the movement.

'Two hundred, give or take.'

'A goodly sacrifice,' said Marduk.

Sabtec grunted in response, and the Dark Apostle could feel what his champion was thinking.

'Every one of their deaths brings us closer to victory,' he said. His words sounded hollow, even to his own ears.

Sabtec saluted and spun away, barking orders.

A hot wind clawed at Marduk's blood-matted cloak, bringing with it the redolence of butchery and oil, industry and suffering, and the insidious electric tang of Chaos itself.

The world was changing, and it would never again be the same. Like a worm wriggling its way through the core of an apple, the taint of Chaos was now rooted in the very substance of Boros Prime. Even if the Word Bearers were to leave, the Imperium would be forced to abandon it.

Even so, Marduk's face was grim. Victory was a certainty, he was sure of this, and yet with every passing day it seemed further from their grasp. The acidic taste of defeat was in his mouth, no matter how he tried to deny it.

His warriors were genetically enhanced killers armoured in the finest power armour. Each was more than a match for fifty or a hundred lesser mortals. Their weapons slew tens of thousands with every passing day, and their war engines sowed terror and destruction across the length and breadth of the world. A demi-Legion of Titans marched behind them, laying waste to entire cities.

Nevertheless, the number of XVII Legion warrior brothers fighting upon the surface of Boros Prime numbered less than seven thousand all told, whereas Imperial vermin infested this world.

Boros Prime was home to more than twelve billion, and almost another two billion had been evacuated to the relative safety of the planet from its surrounding planets and moons. More than half of that number served in its armed forces, or had been drafted into service. Every citizen of eligible age served a tenure in the Guard – even the bureaucrats and public servants knew their way around a lasgun and basic small-unit tactics. By Marduk's reckoning, the five thousand warriors of Lorgar faced off against nigh on ten billion soldiers. Added to the mix were the White Consuls, and while there were no more than three companies engaged here on Boros – three hundred loyalist Astartes – their mere presence bolstered the resolve of the Guardsmen, and they were always to be found in the thickest fighting. In these battles, neither side gave any quarter, their fury and hatred fuelled by ten thousand years of mutual loathing and bitterness. It was glorious.

Industrious forge-hives located towards the poles spewed out a constant stream of weapons and armour, and the smoking plains outside the world's sprawling cities were dominated by massive tank formations. The Titans of Legio Vulturus had stalked out to meet one of these grand tank companies, and had notched up a kill-tally numbering in the thousands. Nevertheless, these confirmed kills were rendered insignificant against the sheer number of tanks taking the field. Four Titans, ancient war engines that had stalked across battlefields for ten thousand years, were brought down and three others suffered crippling damage as their void shields and armoured carapaces were hammered by ordnance and focused battle cannon fire. One of the Titans, one hulking

Warlord-class engine, now a daemonically infested monster, was laid low by a devastating barrage from super-heavy Shadowswords. Suffering these losses, the Legio had been forced from the plains back into the relative safety of Boros's cities.

Far to the north, in the frozen wastes, the Dark Apostle Belagosa, the ranks of his host swollen with the warriors of Sarabdal's Host, fought a bloody siege against the largest of the world's industrial forge-hives. Five thousand kilometres southward, Ankh-Heloth's 11th Host ranged eastward, occupying and destroying the equatorial city-bastions in turn.

Every day tens of thousands of enemy soldiers perished, but every day scores of Word Bearers fell, and their loss was felt keenly. On all three fronts, the Word Bearers suffered.

Marduk's gaze lifted. Though he could see past the choking fumes engulfing the lower atmosphere, he knew that beyond, hanging in orbit like a malevolent sentinel, was the Kronos star fort. It too still held out, fighting Ekodas and his Host to a standstill. Like clockwork, every hour the star fort would unleash its barrage upon the world below, decimating everything within a three-kilometre radius of its target. The constant need for Marduk's Host to shift its battlefront to avoid annihilation was growing tiresome, and while on one hand he wished that Ekodas would hurry up and take the orbital bastion, there was a part of him that relished the Apostle's failure.

Nevertheless, Marduk felt his anger rise as he gazed heavenward. If the star fort had fallen, then the Chaos fleet would have been able to move into high orbit and commence a devastating bombardment upon the planet below that would have quickly changed the tide of the war. As it was, no Chaos warship was able to move into position without coming under fire from the Imperial star fort. For the thousandth time, Marduk cursed Ekodas's name for his weakness.

Like rolling thunder, artillery batteries in the distance began to roar.

'They attack again, Dark Apostle,' called Sabtec.

'Let them come,' said Marduk.

ASHKANEZ STALKED BACK and forth within the centre of the gathering of hooded Astartes of the 34th Host, the strength of his faith and conviction obvious in every inflection, in every movement.

The clandestine meeting was taking place in the dead of night within the burnt-out shell of a bunker complex. The ground shook with intermittent artillery shelling in the distance, and flashes lit the night sky. Aircraft could be heard roaring overhead. It was a small group, numbering less than twenty of the cult members. With the war raging, it was difficult for Coterie members to slip away from their warrior brothers unobserved, yet even so, the Brotherhood met in dozens of small congregations like this whenever it could.

Burias draw his hood up over his face as he ghosted in to join the gathering.

'In the aftermath of the cleansing, the Legion shall be stronger,' Ashkanez was saying. 'The Legion shall be unified once more.'

Ashkanez stopped stalking back and forth and lowered his voice.

'But more than this,' he said, 'it is prophesied that the Urizen shall once more walk among us.'

Burias's eyes widened, and there were gasps and muttering from amongst the gather warrior brothers.

'Yes, my brothers,' said Ashkanez after a moment. 'Once the cleansing has been achieved, our lord and Primarch Lorgar shall rejoin the Legion. Once more he shall lead us in glorified battle, striding at our forefront and setting the universe aflame with faith and death.'

'Then let us begin!' growled a voice in the crowd, which was greeted with murmurs and foot-stamping in agreement. Burias found himself nodding and lending his own voice to the proclamation. Ashkanez lifted a hand for silence.

'I understand your eagerness, my brothers, for I feel it too. But no, we must not act yet. We must gather our strength, for the reach and cunning of our enemy is great.'

'Who *is* the enemy of the Brotherhood, lord?' said a voice from nearby.

Burias smiled, for he recognized that voice – it belonged to the brutal champion Khalaxis, a mighty warrior. He was pleased that Khalaxis too had been embraced into this noble fraternity.

'I cannot say,' said Ashkanez. 'Not yet, at least. The enemy has ears everywhere. Perhaps even amongst us here.'

A heavy silence descended on the gathering. Ashkanez's gaze fell upon Burias, noticing him for the first time. Even hooded as he was, Burias felt the First Acolyte's eyes burrowing into his own.

'But know that the day draws near, my brothers. And when it comes, we will all have our part to play.'

Ashkanez's eyes lingered on Burias as he spoke these last words, and the Icon Bearer knew that they were spoken for him in particular. He would be ready, he swore to himself.

'Return to your Coteries, my brothers,' said Ashkanez. 'All will be revealed soon.'

As the hooded warriors began to filter out of the shattered bunker-complex, Burias almost bumped into a towering warrior. Burias had noted his presence at several other Brotherhood conclaves, and though the warrior had always been careful to keep his identity concealed, as did all the brethren, from his size he was clearly garbed in Terminator armour – one of the Anointed.

'My pardon, brother,' said Burias.

The warrior did not respond, but as he looked up into the dark shadow of the warrior's hood his eyes widened. The hulking warrior turned away, pulling his cowl down lower, and moved off.

'It surprised me as well,' said Ashkanez in a low voice, suddenly at the Icon Bearer's side. Burias had not heard the First Acolyte's approach. 'But he has been with us since the beginning.'

'But…' said Burias. 'You promised me–'

'This changes nothing,' said Ashkanez.

Burias's face split in a daemonic grin, though hidden within the darkness of his cowl, it was all but invisible.

# CHAPTER TWELVE

Proconsul Ostorius's humming power blade was a blur as he cut through the melee. Wave after wave of boarding parties were assaulting the Kronos star fort in this, the latest attack by the Word Bearers, and as ever Ostorius was in the thick of it.

Ostorius fought with astonishing economy of movement, expending no more energy than was required. For all his skill, there was no flourish or showmanship in his combat style; he merely killed, effectively and efficiently, again and again.

He slashed his sword across the faceplate of a Word Bearer, cutting deep into flesh and bone, before spinning and driving his blade into the throat of another enemy. Blood bubbled up from the wound, spitting off the super-heated power sword's blade.

Ostorius whipped his sword free, and before the Word Bearer had even hit the ground he was already away and moving, engaging a new foe. With his combat shield he turned aside a blade stabbing for him and cut down the Word Bearer with a stroke that sliced the enemy open from right shoulder blade to left hip.

Another Word Bearer leapt at Ostorius, animalistic growls emitting from the vox-amps set into his helmet. He hefted a massive chainaxe in both hands, and brought the screaming weapon down towards Ostorius's head.

The Proconsul of Boros Prime swayed aside at the last moment, the roaring teeth of the chainaxe missing him by centimetres. He ducked beneath a second blow and severed one of the traitor's legs above the knee, his power sword shearing through armour, flesh and bone. The Word Bearer fell with a snarl, blood pumping from the terrible wound, and Ostorius moved on.

The next minute passed in a blur of motion and blood, until Ostorius came to a halt. Blood splattered his armour, and he was breathing heavily, his heart beating fast. Dimly he felt pain receptors flaring, and glanced down to see the rerebrace protecting his left upper arm shorn completely through, the flesh beneath a bloody ruin. He could see the white of bone, but could not even remember being struck.

He glanced around the deck as pain nullifiers flooded his system. A dozen White Consuls, all splattered with blood and carrying injuries, moved amongst the fallen, dispatching those Word Bearers that still lived without mercy.

Twenty-five Word Bearers lay strewn across the deck floor, all dead. Eighteen White Consuls had fallen. Nine of those would recover, given time – Astartes did not die easily. Nevertheless, only one, perhaps two, of the fallen White Consuls would be able to fight again within the next few days or weeks, and time was not a luxury that Ostorius could afford.

Kronos had held out for two months now – an astonishing feat given the force besieging it – yet the Proconsul knew that it would be but days now before it was overrun. He prayed that Librarian Epistolary Liventius would uncover the source that shrouded the Boros Gate soon. If he did not, then Boros would fall, it was as simple as that.

His gaze was drawn to the enemy Thunderhawk, sitting idle on the deck. A carefully aimed shot had taken out its pilot as it had attempted to pull away. A foul reek emerged from within its gaping assault ramp pods, along with a growling sound of static that made Ostorius feel faintly sick.

The enemy was growing bolder. Previously, all attacks had been launched via Deathclaw, corrupted drop-pods that burrowed through the thick armour plating of Kronos like flesh-eating maggots. However, with Kronos's shields failing, they were now able to launch attacks directly into its launch bays, with Word Bearers delivered right into the heart of the star fort via Thunderhawk and Stormbird.

'Shall we set explosives to destroy it, Proconsul?' said a battle-brother.

'Not just yet,' said Ostorius, eyeing the Thunderhawk thoughtfully. Apart from some exterior damage it had sustained in the assault, it was mostly intact. With minor repairs, it would again be spaceworthy.

An Apothecary was kneeling beside the bodies of dead White Consuls, extracting their precious geneseed, the lifeblood of the Chapter. His narthecium whirred and crunched as he cut through plate and flesh.

Vox-chatter from elsewhere upon the star fort crackled in his ear; the latest assault had been underway for perhaps fifteen minutes, and already the enemy had breached the star fort's defences in more than a dozen places.

'Not today,' said Ostorius under his breath.

Never in his life had Ostorius felt this weary, and his mind was hazy with exhaustion. He had not slept – not truly slept – since the start of the siege. He had snatched moments of rest here and there, in between attacks, and during those lapses in battle he allowed isolated sections of his brain to shut down, but it was not real, healing rest. Plenty of time to rest when he was dead, though, he thought, morbidly. He was sure that time would come soon enough.

Frantic calls for reinforcements were broadcast suddenly from a deck location eighty floors below his current position, and Ostorius snapped back to full alertness. He responded curtly, and was moving purposefully a moment later.

'Come brothers,' he called. 'We are needed. Deck 53b-E91.'

MARDUK'S SPIRIT RIPPED away from the prison of his flesh, soaring free.

The release had been more difficult than usual to attain, and this caused him a moment of disquiet. It was forgotten when he was overwhelmed with stimuli.

The material world around him was now nothing more than a shadowy presence rendered in shades of grey, yet his witch-sight afforded him a vision richer and more alive with colour and movement than mortal eyes could ever realise.

His aural senses too were overwhelmed. Billions of voices screamed out in terror and fear, joining the sublime cacophony of the Discords, which could be heard in both this plane and the real. Theirs was an unholy, rapturous din.

He could hear the leathery flap of wings as kathartes circled around him, brushing his soaring soul affectionately. A hundred kilometres away, a corrupted Titan of the Legio Vulturus let out a cry, the reverberant bass note shaking the doomed planet to its core.

Invisible to mortal sight, daemons in their tens of millions had descended upon Boros Prime, and Marduk saw them now in their full glory, a dizzying panoply of radiance and majesty, of horror and despair. Like a swarming tide they had come here, attracted by the sheer scale of the savagery being enacted in the name of the gods of Chaos, summoned by the powerful emotions being unleashed across its continents.

Invisible to all but those with the witch-sight and will to see them, these daemon spirits swarmed across the skies like a hellish, ethereal living soup, and waited in great, menacing groups around the living. Even those pathetic mortals unable to perceive them felt their presence, perhaps as nothing more than a shiver or a breath of ice across the back of their necks. They suffered the nightmares that the daemons brought with them, their minds giving voice to their doubts and their fears.

The scale of fear, revulsion, hatred, terror and panic of the system's inhabitants had drawn the daemons to this world, like flies to a corpse. They fed off these raw emotions, gluttonously supping at them, but more delectable still were the souls of those dying in torment and fear.

The daemons licked their ethereal lips in hunger, clustered in eager packs around the glowing soul-flames of those about to die. As the mortal soldiers of Boros Prime perished, the hellspawn descended upon them in a whirlwind of hunger and savagery, rending, tearing and feeding. Whether they fell on the field of battle, killed beneath the blades of the faithful or merely took their own lives, all were consumed to feed the insatiable hunger of the true gods, for these lesser daemons were but aspects of the greater powers. In the depths of the warp, the gods rumbled their pleasure.

But Marduk was not spirit-journeying merely to witness the majesty of Chaos, as glorious and inspirational as it was.

Turning his attention away from the beauteous carnage, he streaked across the heavens, the monochromatic war-torn planet blurring beneath him. He hurtled invisibly across the ravaged planet's continents, rising up higher and higher into the airless upper atmosphere, drawn towards a dark nimbus of power that called to him like a siren. He could see it from afar, a malignant blot upon reality, oozing potency.

At last, he slowed his ascent, and hovered in the air before this powerful warp-presence.

*Greetings, Apostle of the 34th Host,* boomed the shadow-soul, making Marduk's spirit waver.

*My lord Ekodas,* answered Marduk.

The amorphous, insubstantial shape of Ekodas's soaring shadow-soul coalesced into a shape more recognisable, an anthropomorphised form projected from his mind. He appeared before Marduk in the guise of a giant, robed figure hanging effortlessly in the sky, his head that of a snarling beast. Flames surrounded him, and the sheer brutality and force of the power Ekodas radiated buffeted Marduk's spirit like a gale.

Two other soul-spirits coalesced in view alongside Marduk.

Belagosa's presence was hazy and flickering. He took the form of an archaic warrior-knight, his body encased in ancient plate armour. Ankh-Heloth's presence revealed itself as a coiled serpent, eyes glinting with malign light.

*This war threatens to slip from our grasp,* boomed Ekodas into the minds of the gathered Apostles.

*If there is any failure it is yours alone,* shot back Marduk.

Ankh-Heloth's avatar bared its fangs, hissing and spitting, but Marduk ignored him.

*We are making progress,* said Belagosa. *So long as the Nexus holds and the warp gate is kept shut, there is no hope of salvation for the followers of the Corpse-God. This world's corruption is assured.*

*I want this world to burn,* roared Ekodas. *Its continued defiance offends me. The spirit of the Imperials is not yet broken. There is one amongst them who is their talisman; their so-called White Angel. Find him, my Apostles. Find him, and bring him to me.*

*We are not alone,* said Belagosa suddenly.

Marduk looked around him, probing with his mind's eye. An insubstantial flicker played at the edge of his vision.

*There,* he said.

Ekodas spun, ghostly arms extended and flames of the spirit roared. Amidst the inferno, a glowing figure armoured in silver plate appeared. A shining tabard of white was worn over his armour. The flames licked at this newly revealed presence, but they could not touch him, for a glowing bubble of light surrounded him.

*Spying on us, Librarian?* said Ekodas. *It will avail you little.*

*This world shall never belong to you, traitors,* pulsed the White Consul.

*It already does,* boomed Ekodas. *And now, you die.*

*I think not, heretic,* replied the Librarian.

Ekodas grew in stature, his bestial face twisted in hatred. His arms sprouted insubstantial claws and he flew at the Librarian's soul-presence, flames flaring all around him.

There was an explosion of blinding light that made Marduk and the other Apostles shrink back. When it cleared, the Librarian's presence had disappeared.

*He is gone,* said Belagosa.

*How much did he hear?* pulsed Ankh-Heloth.

*It matters not,* boomed Ekodas.

*Go now, my Apostles. Find their White Angel. We destroy him, and we destroy their hope.*

With his dictate conveyed, the blaze surrounding Ekodas burst outwards, slamming into Marduk and the other two Apostles with the force of a psychic hurricane. Marduk fell, spinning out of control, and slammed involuntarily back into the cage of his earthly flesh.

He collapsed to his knees, blood dripping from his nostrils.

'My lord?' said Ashkanez, kneeling beside him. Marduk waved him back.

'Get Burias,' he said hoarsely. 'I have a job for him.'

THE SOUND OF the battle was loud even kilometres from the nearest of the ever-shifting front lines, dull explosions that shook the planet to its core. Thunderbolts and Marauders roared overhead, heading towards the warzones with full payloads, while others chugged back towards the scattered airbases, trailing smoke, their ammunition spent. The screams of the wounded and dying echoed from makeshift medicae facilities, and corpses were strewn throughout the streets.

Aquilius gazed around him as he marched. The sky was filled with smoke and cinders. The once pristine, gleaming white marble of Sirenus Principal, his birth-city, was now pocked and chipped from small-arms fire, scarred by ordnance and covered in soot and blood. The beautiful gardens and arboretums were now little more than charred wastelands of scorched earth. The blackened skeletons of trees protruded mournfully from the ash, like headstones, and lakes and fountains were now cesspools of foulness, choked with scum and unnatural algae blooms. Corpses floated face down in the waters.

Boros Prime was changing. Aquilius could feel the change in the air itself, and it had nothing to do with anything as mundane as pollutants, ash and death. The taint of Chaos had taken hold of Boros Prime, and he despaired as to what would be left here, even if they were victorious. A week ago, one in ten thousand had been identified as exhibiting some unnatural taint, planetwide – tens of millions of citizens and soldiers. All had been removed from their units and habs and transported under guard to the quarantine sanitation camps – death camps by any other name.

The number of the afflicted had risen sharply in the last days, and it was judged that the taint was now affecting one in five thousand, and rising daily. Paranoia was rife within the ranks of the Imperial Guard and the citizenry, for no detectable pattern to determine who would be affected was apparent. Where would it end? *Would* it end?

So far no warrior brother of the White Consuls had suffered any visible or detectible taint, but not even Astartes were immune to the perverting effects of Chaos if exposed to it for long enough.

It was like a plague that the invaders brought with them, an insidious creeping sickness that had infiltrated Boros Prime. It was worse than the Word Bearers themselves, perhaps, for it was an enemy that could not be fought with bolter or chainsword.

Rebreathers had been issued, but already the supply of filter plugs was running short. In truth, the insidious, corrupting effect of Chaos was not transferred through the air – it was far more insidious than that – but it had been deemed an appropriate calming measure.

In consultation with the Chapter's Apothecaries and the Guard's senior medicae officers, Aquilius had rolled out daily screening and purity testing for all soldiers, to be conducted in the presence of a superior officer. Any individual exhibiting any taint was removed from their unit. Commissars prowled the ranks, and each day Aquilius read depressing communiqués tallying the numbers of soldiers executed for exhibiting hostile effects of taint, or for concealing and avoiding screens.

Coadjutor Aquilius moved through the press of soldiers. He towered head and shoulders above them, and conversations died as he passed.

His armour was battle worn, his cloak was tattered and burnt, yet he walked with his head held high, his blue-crested helmet tucked under one arm. A melta burn scarred the left side of his face, and his short-cropped blond hair was blackened from fire.

Aquilius saw the soldiers' expressions lifting as they moved reverently from his path. He nodded to them. Hands blackened with grime and ash touched his armour plates. Murmurs spread like ripples on a lake as he made his way through the press of stinking, battle-weary soldiers. They spoke in hushed tones, but Aquilius could hear them all. The White Angel, they whispered. That was what the men were calling him now. He had tried to stop them, but it had done no good.

He did not feel worthy of their adoration, but it didn't matter. It was Chapter Master Valens who had made him realise that, and his respect for the warrior had grown immeasurably.

'This is not about you,' Chapter Master Valens had said. 'This is not about what you need, or what you deserve. This is about what those soldiers need. They need hope, Aquilius. The *White Angel* is that hope. The men must hold until the veil over the Boros Gate is lifted.'

He had not understood the Chapter Master's words at first but as weeks passed he slowly came to.

Amidst the horror and darkness of this escalating, planet-wide war, the White Angel had become a beacon of hope.

In the months since the enemy had attacked, Aquilius had fought fearlessly alongside the regiments of the Boros Imperial Guard, fighting as one of them. He faced the dangers they faced, and was ever at the forefront of the most intense battles, and he – or rather the fiction that was the White Angel – had become a legend.

The Imperial propaganda machine was in full swing. Printed leaflets were distributed amongst the ranks speaking of the White Angel's exploits, all highly exaggerated, and how the enemy was being slowly repelled. It made him intensely uncomfortable, but he could see the positive effect it was having on the men. Spirits lifted wherever he went, and soldiers that had been about to break redoubled their resolve in his presence.

He understood his role here now, and had come to accept its burden. It was his job to ensure that the Guard and the PDF, the tank companies and the auxiliary regiments were operating at their peak, that their morale held, and that their will to fight was not eroded by the insidious tools of the enemy. If that meant that he must become their talisman, their *White Angel*, then so be it.

The soldiers and citizenry of Boros Prime saw the White Angel as their saviour, their divine protector. While Aquilius stood, there was hope. And despite everything, that ray of hope was burning brighter with every day that passed, with every day that victory was denied the enemy.

As he moved through the regiments, making himself seen, he could not shake the feeling that hostile eyes were watching him. He stopped and scanned the rooftops and damaged battlements. He told himself he was being foolish, but the nagging impression would not budge.

The vox-bead in his ear clicked.

'Coadjutor Aquilius,' came a voice as he accepted the incoming communication. It was Chapter Master Titus Valens, located halfway around the world, engaged in the frozen north.

'Yes, my lord?'

'We are close to unearthing the secret that locks down the Boros Gate. Librarian Epistolary Liventius believes it is a device, something called the Nexus. Our brother Librarian is launching an attack upon it as we speak.'

'This is auspicious news, my lord!'

'Hope is at hand, Coadjutor. Pray that the Librarian is successful. But there is more.'

'Yes, my lord?'

'The enemy have learnt of the White Angel. The enemy is coming for you, Aquilius. Be vigilant.'

The Coadjutor's gaze never left the rooftops. Something *was* watching then.

'Let them come,' he said.

'I myself am returning to Sirenus Principal,' said Chapter Master Valens. 'My Thunderhawk should reach you in six hours. You will rendezvous with me, Aquilius. I cannot allow you to fall. You are too important.'

'I am a Space Marine, my lord,' said Aquilius. 'I need no protection.'

Hidden in the shadows of a high alcove, Burias-Drak'shal crouched like a malignant gargoyle. A bestial snarl issued from his lips and his daemonic eyes narrowed as he focussed on his prey.

THE CLOISTERED ANTECHAMBER of the Temple of the Gloriatus had been sealed with psychic wards, and incense billowed from censers. The only light came from hundreds of brightly burning candles. Wax pooled beneath them.

Thirteen psykers of various abilities and specialities knelt in a circle, as if in prayer, their minds linked. They had been gathered from all across Boros Prime as the embattled fleet still fought to protect the Kronos star fort. Their number was made up of four blind astropaths, three haughty navigators from the Imperial Navy, three sanctioned psykers of the Boros Guard command, and three young inductees of the schola progenium who showed marked psychic abilities. All of them had been vetted by Librarian Epistolary Liventius, and judged worthy. The White Consul himself sat cross-legged in the centre of the circle, like a shaman of the old times.

*It is time*, said Liventius.

Those arrayed around him readied themselves, conducting their own rituals in preparation of the coming conflict, lending Liventius their strength. Each of them knew that the chances of them surviving this encounter were slim. Maddening glimpses of their thoughts and fears flashed through the Librarian's mind.

*Focus*, he said, gently nudging the psykers' minds with his own.

As their united trance deepened, the temperature in the room dropped markedly. Hoarfrost began to crystallise upon the blue plates of Liventius's armour. Deeper he drew the psykers into him, focussing their power and uniting them, until he was no longer a single entity, but rather all of them bound together as one.

For two hours, the trance continued before Liventius judged them ready to proceed. He surged from his body and passed on up through the ceiling, striking heavenward.

Up and up and up he soared, cutting through the atmosphere of the tortured planet, passing effortlessly through its gravity and out into the airless vacuum beyond.

He saw the beleaguered Kronos star fort, and could see the glowing souls of every individual on board. Even as he watched, he saw scores of the glowing soul-flames snuffed out, blinking out of existence as they perished.

Liventius turned his attention towards the Chaos fleet. For weeks and months he had been probing their defences, attempting to locate the origin of whatever it was locking down the Boros Gate's wormholes. At last, he had narrowed his focus down onto one ship, the hulking Infernus-class battleship, the *Crucius Maledictus*. And from what he had garnered from overhearing the gathering of the enemy Apostles, he now had a name for whatever it was – the Nexus.

With a thought, Liventius closed the distance to the immense warship. Immediately he came up against a wall of psychic force, an almost impenetrable barrier that actively resisted his presence. However, bolstered with the strength of the thirteen minds linked to his own, he began pushing through the defences, focusing all his will on worming his way through its intricate layers of protection.

Stabbing pain erupted in his mind, and he heard the psychic scream of one of the astropaths linked to him as he perished. Shielding himself and the other minds linked to his own from the trauma of the dying man, Liventius pushed on. It was like swimming though a viscous pool of acid, and agony rippled across his spirit-form.

He was less than halfway through the potent wall of psychic force when he felt a malignant presence swell into being around him. This was the psyker who had erected the barrier, and Liventius siphoned off a portion of his prodigious power to hide himself from its soul-eyes; for all his strength, he was as a child next to this being.

*You cannot hide forever*, boomed the presence. *I will find you.*

Liventius continued burrowing through the force wall, but even as he did, he felt the resistance against him redouble. He began losing ground, the wall repelling him, and he screamed out soundlessly as psychic shockwaves of pain flowed through him.

Another of the astropaths perished under the strain, further weakening Liventius. Knowing that he would never penetrate the ever-strengthening barrier while still trying to conceal his presence, he dropped his shielding completely, focussing all his will into cutting through the barrier before him.

*There you are, little man*, boomed the voice, and Liventius screamed in torment as his spirit was bathed in incandescent flames. Two of the minds linked with his own were instantly fried, blood exploding from their eyeballs.

Nevertheless, with all his strength now focused, Liventius was making headway once more, and with a final surge, he penetrated the psychic barrier surrounding the *Crucius Maledictus*.

Suddenly free, he surged through the corridors of the battleship, touching every mind that he passed, seeking answers. Roaring in fury, the spirit of the apostate dogged him, surging behind him like a tidal wave, threatening to drown him.

From what Liventius gleaned from the repulsive minds that he touched, there was something unnatural aboard the vessel. As he got closer to its source, he felt its touch, and he was at once repelled and attracted to it. It was anathema to a psychic's mind, and yet he was drawn towards it, like flotsam pulled inexorably into a whirlpool. Rather than resisting its pull, Liventius went along with it, hurtling towards the source at a speed far beyond anything capable of physical matter. He burst into a high-ceilinged room located centrally within the *Crucius Maledictus's* bloated belly, and came to an abrupt halt, desperately pulling up short before he was consumed.

Here was the source that had locked down the Boros Gate, he knew that instantly. It appeared to him as a pulsing sphere of utter darkness, drawing all psychic energy into itself. It was all Liventius could do to hold himself back from being sucked into that emptiness. Two of the minds linked with his own were not so strong. Their souls were dragged into the darkness screaming and snuffed out, as though they had never been. The blackness shuddered, growing stronger.

A number of souls burned fiercely in the room, one so bright it caused him pain just to look upon it. Word Bearers.

With a thought, Liventius slammed into the mind of one of the traitors. It was vile and repellent, and the Word Bearer struggled against him, but he drove into him with all the focus of an assassin's knife, overcoming his will completely.

He blinked and turned his meat-puppet towards the psychic black hole, so as to see it with physical eyes.

It appeared before him: a spinning orb of silver held captive within a series of rotating arcs.

Seven other Word Bearers stood in a circle around the device, but if they realised an impostor was within their midst, they did not show it. There was another being within the room, reclined as if in a trance upon a high-backed throne, and Liventius knew instantly that this was the psyker who had erected the defences around the Word Bearers fleet, the one who was hunting him now. He dared not let his gaze linger, lest the monstrously powerful psyker feel his touch.

Not yet fully in command of this borrowed flesh, Liventius's movements were sluggish and awkward. He took one ponderous step forwards, breaking the circle of Word Bearers. He felt the attention of the others turn towards him. In his hands he held a corrupted bolter, and this he lifted towards the spinning silver device, the source that held the Boros Gate in its thrall. His finger tightened upon the trigger of the borrowed weapon.

The awesomely powerful mind of the Word Bearers apostate caught up with him, slamming into him with staggering force. He was almost dislodged from the flesh of the Word Bearer, but he clung on, ignoring the searing pain. He was desperate to finish his task, knowing the fate of the Boros Gate rested with the destruction of this infernal device.

The Word Bearers puppet was fighting him once more, attempting to regain control of his own movements, and he began to lower his weapon. Redoubling his efforts, Liventius dragged the bolter back up towards the spinning device.

Bolt rounds struck him as the other Word Bearers turned their guns on their brother, and he staggered. Again, the Apostle struck him psychically, this time with even more force, and he was knocked out of the borrowed flesh.

*Now you are mine,* thundered the voice of the Apostle.

Liventius roared in agony as his spirit was wracked with soul-fire. Agonising psychic shackles closed around him, but he thrashed and struggled against them, until with a final surge he tore himself free.

WITH A GASP, Librarian Epistolary Liventius opened his eyes. Agony crashed in upon him, and his vision wavered. Steadying himself, wiping blood from his nose, he looked around him. All the candles in the antechamber were out, but even in the near pitch darkness, Liventius could see the thirteen psykers that had aided him were dead.

He had failed.

# CHAPTER THIRTEEN

OSTORIUS KNELT BEFORE the holo-images of Chapter Master Titus Valens and his Captain, Marcus Decimus of 5th Company. His head was bowed, and he held his power sword flat in his hands as he waited for an answer.

'If I allow this,' said the ghostly image of the White Consuls Chapter Master, 'it will leave Kronos critically undermanned.'

'If you do not allow it, we stand no chance of ending this war,' said Captain Decimus. 'Liventius failed in his attempt. A direct assault upon the device is the logical next step.'

'If it fails, Kronos will belong to the Word Bearers.'

'If it fails, then none of this matters anyway,' said Decimus.

'Were it practical, I'd lead the attack myself,' said Valens. Ostorius could hear frustration in the Chapter Master's voice. 'But I believe you two are right. This is our best chance to end this war. Do it.'

'Assemble your kill-team, Ostorius,' said Captain Decimus.

'Thank you, my lords,' said Ostorius.

'May the Emperor guide your sword, Proconsul.'

BURIAS-DRAK'SHAL RACED ACROSS the battlements in bounding leaps, his claws gouging deep rents in the marble. Like a shadow chased by the sun, he moved across the rooftops in a blur.

Bunching his powerful leg muscles, he exploded off the top of a bastion, his leap carrying him clear over the wide-laned street far below. Chimeras and front-line Leman Russ battle tanks were advancing along that boulevard, completely unaware that their movement was being shadowed by the possessed warrior high overhead.

Arms bulging with daemonic muscle, Burias-Drak'shal came down hard, clearing the thirty-metre expanse with ease. He turned in the air, landing on the rooftop of the lower bastion. He rolled and came to his feet smoothly, and again was off, bounding and leaping on all fours.

He launched himself off another vertigo-inducing drop-off and landed halfway up the side of a vertical antennae-pylon, clinging to the sheer surface like a spider. With swift movements, barely pausing to find handholds, he scurried up the vertical incline, pulling himself hand over hand to its peak. There he paused, tasting the air and cocking his head to one side, listening. All his daemon-enhanced senses were utterly focussed on the hunt.

The sound of battle was loud; a major confrontation was playing out less than ten kilometres away. It was a battle that the Chimeras were angling towards.

He was ahead of the armoured column now, and as it rounded a corner, it was forced into single file to navigate past a fallen building.

Burias-Drak'shal's eyes focussed on the third Chimera in the line. The APC had a cluster of communication arrays rising from its hull, like the spines of an insect, differentiating it from the others. This was the one that Burias-Drak'shal had seen the White Consul enter, several hours earlier.

The possessed Icon Bearer dropped off the pylon, falling like a stone. He landed thirty metres below, crouched on all fours. His bestial head turned from side to side, sniffing. Then he set off once more, closing inexorably with his prey.

THE FULL EXTENT of the 34th Host had come together, and the warrior brothers of the Host fought shoulder-to-shoulder, laying waste to all that dared oppose them.

The turrets of corrupted Predator battle tanks rotated, spewing torrents of high-calibre shells down boulevards and byways, killing hundreds. The air crackled as Land Raiders unleashed the power of their lascannons, targeting armoured columns and tank formations.

The heavy, bipedal forms of Dreadnoughts ranged out in front, roaring with mechanised insanity as they killed, gunning down scores of Guardsmen with heavy gauge weapon systems and ripping them apart with power talons and electro-flails. The Warmonger stalked amongst them, bellowing catechisms and holy scripture, reliving the days when he was a warrior of flesh and blood, fighting upon the walls of the Emperor's Palace and exhorting his Host to kill and kill again in the name of Lorgar and the Warmaster Horus, ten millennia earlier.

Daemons numbering in their thousands had been summoned forth from bleeding rents ripped in the fabric of reality, and they brayed in fury and bloodlust as they charged into the densely packed ranks of Guardsmen. Kathartes descended upon the Imperial soldiers in flocks a hundred-strong, dragging their victims high into the air before ripping them limb from limb and dropping them into the streets below.

Titans as tall as buildings stalked in the distance, their bestial howls reverberating across the city. Their princeps and moderati had long been subsumed into the substance of the Titans, and powerful daemonic entities bound and infused with them, making the mighty engines more living, breathing beasts than mechanised constructs.

Heavily armed Warlord- and Reaver-class engines laid waste to entire city blocks with the power of their ordnance. Their armoured hulls were pitted from ten thousand years of warfare, and kill-pennants hung from their weapons.

Comparatively smaller Warhound-class Titans loped through the streets, hunting. Unnervingly stealthy for engines four storeys high, they stalked through the mayhem of battle, annihilating colonnades of battle tanks, and butchering entire brigades of Guardsmen with salvoes of their Inferno cannons.

Their bestial howls ululated across the city as they claimed another kill.

Somewhere out there was the enemy that had come to be known as the White Angel. That individual was the lynchpin of the enemy's resolve. Kill him, and the world would soon falter.

'Come on, Burias,' Marduk hissed.

THE TAINTED STENCH within the Word Bearers Thunderhawk was vile, yet Ostorius repressed his revulsion. He had claimed the assault shuttle a week earlier, and although he could not have said why at the time, he had not ordered its immediate destruction.

Now, as it carried him and his carefully chosen kill-team of White Consuls across the gulf of space between Kronos and the largest of the enemy battleships, he hoped that his decision had proved a wise one.

Priests of the Ecclesiarchy had cleansed the shuttle of the worst of its taint, yet Ostorius could still feel its corrupting touch all around him. It made his skin crawl, and he repressed a shudder of disgust. He wore his helmet so as not to breathe the foetid air within the Thunderhawk, yet even so he could taste the poison of Chaos in his throat. He was not alone in his discomfort. The White Consuls of his kill-team murmured prayers of purification, and several of them held holy icons tightly in their hands.

At any moment Ostorius expected the Thunderhawk to be gunned down. Even as the shuttle entered the shadow of the monstrous enemy flagship, the *Crucius Maledictus*, and began to angle down towards one of its gaping launch bays, he still expected the enemy to see through the ruse and obliterate them.

His fears proved to be unfounded, and after what seemed like an eternity, the Thunderhawk's landing gear touched down. They were onboard the enemy vessel.

'Move out,' he said grimly.

THERE WAS AN almighty crash that shook the occupants of the Chimera, and it ground to a halt. Voices were raised.

'What was that?' said Aquilius. It had not sounded like ordnance.

Gears ground together, and the Chimera began slowly backing up.

'Apologies, my lord,' said one of the other occupants, Versus of the Boros 232nd. 'There is a blockage ahead. This area has suffered heavy shelling, and is structurally unsound. We are being forced to re-route in order to rejoin the column.'

'Casualties?'

'None, my lord.'

Aquilius shifted his weight in discomfort, and cursed as his head hit the roof with a dull thud. The APC had not been designed to hold the bulk of a Space Marine.

'I'm going up,' he said, and began clambering awkwardly across the tight enclosed space within the Chimera towards its cupola.

Climbing the slender ladder, his shoulders only barely fitting through its aperture, Aquilius popped the cupola hatch and pulled himself up. He breathed in deeply, pleased to be out of the enclosed space. A pintle-mounted heavy stubber lay at rest within arm's reach.

A massive statue lay smashed across the boulevard twenty metres in front of the Chimera. Dust filled the air. Shielding his eyes, Aquilius looked up to see from where it had fallen.

There was a heavy thump behind him, and the Chimera rocked. Aquilius's first thought was that more falling masonry had struck the APC, but then the tainted smell of Chaos reached his nostrils.

'Enemy!' he shouted, reaching for his bolt pistol.

There was a blur of movement behind him and he caught a glimpse of a horrific, daemonic creature crouched upon the back of the Chimera's hull. He lifted his bolt pistol as the thing snarled and leapt towards him, but the weapon was smashed out of his hand. A taloned claw grabbed him around the neck and he was hauled out of the Chimera and hurled aside.

Aquilius hit the ground hard, crashing down onto a pile of rubble that had been pushed up against a shattered building wall. He heard frantic shouting above the growl of the Chimera's engines.

He came to his feet quickly, reaching for his blade, but his daemonic foe was faster. It leapt from on top of the Chimera and tackled him to the ground again, snarling and spitting. The Astartes was hauled back to his feet and slammed face-first into the side of his turning Chimera, denting its armoured plates and shattering Aquilius's nose.

The Chimera's rear hatch was thrown open, and he heard boots hitting the ground as the APC's occupants leapt out to aid their Coadjutor.

A lasgun burn seared across the back of the possessed warrior's head, and he snarled in anger. It drove Aquilius's head into the Chimera once more before releasing him and leaping towards these new enemies, its jaw opening wider than should have been possible.

Screams and the sickly sound of meat being hacked apart reached Aquilius's ears as he steadied himself. He drew his thick-bladed combat knife and rounded on his foe.

Four men were down, screaming as blood poured from their horrific wounds. One was missing his left arm, the limb having been ripped from its socket, while another was clutching vainly at his savaged throat. The daemon's maw closed around the head of another, helmet and all. It popped like an overripe fruit, and blood splattered across the beast's face and chest.

Aquilius bellowed a challenge and leapt towards the unholy creature that was butchering his men. It turned towards him as it heard his cry, eyes narrowed to blood-red slits.

The butt of a lasgun slammed into the side of the monster's head. It was a powerful blow, delivered with all of Verenus's strength, but for all his size and strength, he was but a man. The daemon grabbed him around the neck and hurled him away, throwing him deep into the ruins. Still, Verenus had distracted the creature long enough for Aquilius to close the distance.

He lowered his shoulder and slammed into the possessed Word Bearer, throwing him back into the Chimera. He knew that his combat knife would have no chance of penetrating his enemy's power armour, so he wielded it like a dagger, driving it down towards his foe's exposed neck.

The blade bit deep, sinking to the hilt, and hot blood spilt over Aquilius's gauntlet. The beast roared in pain and fury, and one of its curving horns slashed across Aquilius's face as it bucked and struggled in his grasp. He ignored the pain and stabbed again but the daemon spun him around, slamming him up against the Chimera, and the knife missed its target, glancing off the Word Bearer's shoulder plate.

Using all of its infernal strength, the Word Bearer slammed its knee up into Aquilius's mid-section, cracking ceramite. The White Consul gasped as the wind was driven from him, and sank to his knees. The possessed warrior dropped his elbow into the back of his neck as he went down, slamming him to the ground.

The beast bent over him, and Aquilius felt a warm rivulet of drool upon his cheek. He strained to fight on, but he was helpless. The beast drew back one of its hands, thick talons poised to kill.

'Their hope will die with you,' snarled the beast, in a guttural voice.

'Hope never dies,' managed Aquilius.

The beast's lips curled in a sneer. Then a blue-hot las-gun burst took the beast in the side of the head, and it was thrown off Aquilius.

He struggled to his feet to see Verenus advancing, lasgun raised to his shoulder. The beast was crouched low, snarling.

Dust rose as a deafening gale roared around them, and Aquilius glanced up, shielding his eyes, to see a Thunderhawk dropping in on his position. It came down, its pilot carefully navigating its way between the steep sides of the ruins.

When he looked back, the possessed Word Bearer had gone.

His vox-bead clicked in his ear.

'Go ahead,' he said, shouting to be heard over the roar of the Thunderhawk's engines as it touched down.

'The enemy have your position surrounded,' came the voice of Chapter Master Titus Valens as the assault shuttle's main ramp slammed open. 'Get your men inside.'

THE BLASTDOOR EXPLODED inwards as melta charges detonated, and Ostorius was through them in a heartbeat, humming power sword in hand.

The directions that Liventius had given him were perfect, and he and his kill-team had made steady progress through the repulsive hallways of the *Crucius Maledictus*. They had encountered less opposition than the Proconsul had envisaged, for which he was thankful. The vast majority of the Word Bearers were evidently fighting on the planet below, or intent on taking Kronos. It seemed that the last thing the Word Bearers were expecting was a direct attack upon their flagship.

Even so, only five of Ostorius's kill-team still lived. Moving warily, the Proconsul led them into a wide, circular room, taking in its details in a quick glance.

The roof was high and domed, and it was ringed with huge stone pillars. One wall was dominated by an immense view portal that looked out across the exterior of the ship. Beyond its armoured prow lay Boros Prime.

A tracked crawler unit was positioned centrally within the room, at the bottom of a stepped dais, and it was to this that Ostorius's gaze was drawn. Humming arcs of black metal revolved around each other with the hum of displaced air. Within these spinning rings was the device that he had been tasked with disabling, even though Liventius wasn't certain that nullifying the Nexus would reopen the

Boros Gate. To not make an attempt to destroy the device, no matter how futile, would have been akin to conceding defeat. For a moment he was lost in its form, mesmerised by its rotating silver rings, but he dragged his attention away as he registered that there were other beings in the room.

A massive robed figure plugged into the crawler unit turned towards the intruders, tentacled mechadendrites rising threateningly. He was a corrupted mirror image of the tech-adepts that served on Kronos. Ostorius's gaze flicked towards a circle of Word Bearers standing sentinel around the device, bolters held across their chest.

Finally, Ostorius's eyes darted up the steps of the dais, and he looked upon what must have been the corrupted Chaplain leading the Word Bearers fleet.

The Apostle sat upon a high-backed throne crafted from the bones of some immense, draconic beast. His eyes were closed, as if he were in some form of trance.

Ostorius took in all this information in the space of single heartbeat, and before any of the Word Bearers could lift their bolters, he was sprinting forwards, power sword singing in his hands.

Burias-Drak'shal roared his frustration as the Thunderhawk lifted off. His scowl turned to a vicious grin as he saw the immense shape of a Reaver Titan rear up from within the shell of a ruined building one street down.

The monstrous war-engine's weapons fired, glancing the Thunderhawk and shearing off one of its stabiliser wings. The shuttle began veering sharply in an uncontrolled nose-dive.

Burias-Drak'shal roared again, this time in triumph, and set off once more through the ruins.

'MASTER,' SAID ASHKANEZ, pointing.

Marduk followed his First Acolyte's gaze, and saw a White Consuls Thunderhawk in the distance. It was spewing smoke and going down fast.

'Let's go,' said the Dark Apostle.

OSTORIUS WAS BLEEDING from a dozen wounds, but he felt no pain. He knew he was not going to live beyond this fight, but it didn't matter. All he cared about was that he completed his mission.

The bodies of three Word Bearers lay upon the floor behind the Proconsul. He spun gracefully, and killed another of the enemy warriors, impaling his head on the blade of his humming power sword. The sword penetrated the Word Bearer's skull and burst through the back of his helmet. Ostorius slid the blade clear and the warrior crashed to the deck floor.

Two more of the White Consuls battle-brothers that made up his kill-team were down, but there was only a handful of Word Bearers now standing between Ostorius and his goal. The Apostle was still seated motionless in his high-backed throne atop the dais, apparently lost in a trance.

A bolter came up and Ostorius threw himself into a roll, the bolt pistol clasped behind his combat shield booming. His shot hit the Word Bearer in the arm, throwing his aim off, and Ostorius felt the passage of displaced air as a bolt round accelerated past his ear. He came up to his feet in front of the Word Bearer, spinning his power sword up as he came, hacking into the Traitor's groin. The blade cleaved through power armour and flesh, lodging itself halfway up the Word Bearer's abdomen. Kicking the body away with the flat of his boot, Ostorius freed his weapon and spun ever closer towards the device.

A power axe sliced in for his neck, but he turned it aside with his combat shield and beheaded his opponent with a powerful sweeping blow.

'Cover my back!' he roared, seeing a gap appear through the melee. His battle-brothers closed in behind him as he darted towards the spinning device atop the tracked crawler unit.

The corrupted tech-magos heaved itself between Ostorius and his goal. As wary as he was of this one now, having seen it tear one of his battle-brothers apart, he needed to end this fight quickly.

Servo-arms snapped towards him, but Ostorius was already moving at speed. He ducked the first of them and leapt over the second, his sword carving an arc through the air.

He took the tech-magos in the throat, his power blade shearing through altered flesh and arterial cabling. Milky blood and oil spurted, and Ostorius swept past the hulking robed adept as he reeled.

The Proconsul hauled himself onto the back of the crawler. He could feel the rush of displaced air over him, and he drew back his sword, preparing to thrust it between the spinning arcs and impale the silver device at its centre.

'For Boros,' he said.

At that moment, the Apostle seated upon the skeletal throne atop the dais rose to his feet.

'Enough!'

An invisible force struck Ostorius, lifting him off the crawler unit and slamming him to the deck floor.

The Apostle was descending the steps of the dais now, throwing off his robe.

Ostorius struggled to rise, but there was a numbing pain in the back of his mind and his vision was wavering.

The other White Consuls were down, their precious lifeblood leaking out across the deck.

The Apostle descended to the floor of his inner sanctum. He approached Ostorius as he struggled to his knees.

'Lower your weapon, Kol Harekh,' the Apostle said to a Word Bearer aiming a bolter at the White Consul.

Ostorius understood his words, though the Traitor's guttural accent was thick and archaic.

Like a blade of fire, a piercing pain jabbed into his mind and he clutched at his temples in agony.

'I could kill you with a thought,' said the Dark Apostle, twisting the invisible psychic needle inside the Proconsul's head, 'but that would not placate my rage. Get up.'

The pain suddenly left Ostorius, and he rose to his feet, holding out his power sword. The unarmed Apostle marched on him. With a gesture, the Word Bearer ordered his minions back. A space developed between him and the White Consul.

Without ceremony, Ostorius leapt forwards to cut down the apostate.

The Word Bearer caught the humming power sword between the flat of his hands, halting its descent centimetres from his face. Ostorius had not even seen him move.

The blade was pushed to the side and released, and the Word Bearer slammed the palm of a hand into the grille of Ostorius's helmet, which cracked and crumpled inwards.

The White Consul tore his helmet free and tossed it aside, eyeing his foe with newfound respect.

'I'm going to enjoy this,' said the Word Bearer, closing in on Ostorius.

# CHAPTER FOURTEEN

Upon the steps of the Temple of the Gloriatus, Titus Valens made his final stand.

The temple-fortress was one of the largest and most impressive structures in the south-eastern quadrant of Sirenus Principal, and it dominated the landscape. The expansive victory square before it was almost five kilometres across, and titanic columns lined its approach. Not a single one of the mighty marble pillars still stood intact, however, and the defiant statues of Astartes heroes that had stood atop them were in ruin.

It seemed like a lifetime ago that Aquilius had stood on this square inspecting the ranks of the Boros 232nd.

The smoking carcass of the Thunderhawk lay in the middle of the square behind them. It had been brought down by a glancing blow from a gatling

blaster, fired from a feral Reaver-class Titan lurking in
the streets. Nine battle-brothers, including its pilot,
had perished as the devastating fire ripped through
the assault shuttle as if it were made of tinfoil. More
had died as it had fallen from the sky like a bird with
its wings clipped and ploughed into the square,
smashing through colonnades in its spiralling descent.

Nevertheless, there had been only a handful of survivors. Chapter Master Titus Valens, Librarian
Epistolary Liventius and six Sternguard veterans had
crawled from the wreckage, along with Coadjutor
Aquilius. Against all odds, Verenus of the Boros 232nd
had also survived along with three of his soldiers. 'Status report,' growled the Chapter Master as he stomped
up the steps of the temple.

'We are cut off and completely surrounded,' said one
of the Sternguard veterans, accessing an auspex built
into his bionic left arm. 'Captain Decimus of 5th
Company is moving on our position, coordinating
Guard platoons and armoured companies. A Thunderhawk is inbound to pick us up.'

'We move into the temple and hold out for reinforcements,' said the Chapter Master. 'Now.'

Supporting their injured, the cluster of Space
Marines and Guardsmen began hurrying across the
open square towards the steps leading up to the Temple of the Gloriatus.

'Any word of Proconsul Ostorius yet?' said Titus
Valens.

'Not yet,' came the reply.

'The enemy,' warned Librarian Epistolary Liventius.

Aquilius lifted his gaze towards the top of the stairs
to see Word Bearers marching into view, blocking their
access to the Temple of the Gloriatus.

Chapter Master Titus Valens called a halt, and the cluster of Space Marines readied themselves, slamming fresh clips into bolters and unsheathing chainblades. The Chapter Master activated his thunder hammer, and the sharp odour of ozone reached Aquilius's nostrils.

'Aquilius, you must not fall,' said Chapter Master Valens. 'The White Angel is all that is holding Boros together. We have to buy Ostorius the time to finish his mission. All else is of secondary concern.'

'My lord,' said Aquilius. 'What are you saying?'

'Liventius, get him to safety,' said the Chapter Master.

At the top of the stairs, the Word Bearers gave way deferentially, bowing their heads and stepping aside. A savage-looking warrior-priest appeared atop the stairs. The Word Bearer wore a skull-faced helmet and bore a profane mockery of a Chaplain's crozius arcanum in one of his armoured fists. The Traitor's plate was bedecked in unholy oath papers and insane scratchings. Aquilius felt a surge of hatred and revulsion. This foul warrior must have been who they were waiting for.

'A Dark Apostle,' Aquilius spat.

'Listen to me,' said Chapter Master Valens. 'There is a fortified landing pad within the golden dome of the Temple of the Gloriatus. It is accessible via subterranean tunnels. There are service elevators less than two kilometres south-south-east of here.'

Librarian Epistolary Liventius raised an eyebrow.

'I trained here as a novitiate,' the Chapter Master said in answer to the unspoken question. 'I am target-marking the location for you now.'

'My lord, you are coming with us?' said Liventius, frowning.

'It has been an honour to lead you, my brothers,' said the Chapter Master.

'My lord,' said Liventius. 'Titus! You cannot be considering this!'

'I am giving you an order, Epistolary,' growled the Chapter Master. 'All of you. I will hold them here. Keep Aquilius alive.'

Aquilius's eyes were wide. He looked between the Chapter Master and Librarian Epistolary Liventius.

'I cannot–' said Liventius.

'I am giving you an order!' barked the Chapter Master, beginning to climb the stairs towards the waiting Dark Apostle. 'Go!'

Aquilius and the other battle-brothers stood in silence, indecision clawing at them.

'Go!' boomed their Chapter Master. 'Liventius! I am ordering you to lead these men to safety.'

MARDUK SMILED BEHIND his skull helm as he watched the Chapter Master of the White Consuls climbing the stairs to meet him. The Space Marine was garbed in gold-edged Terminator armour and rivalled Kol Badar in size.

He wore no helmet, and his face was broad. As he drew closer, Marduk could see the shadow of the primarch Guilliman within the Chapter Master's features, and hatred swelled within him.

The Chapter Master carried a thunder hammer and storm shield, and his ornate armour was hung with a blue, battle-scorched tabard. Several of his pathetically small retinue of veterans moved to interpose themselves between their lord and Marduk, but they were ordered curtly back by their Terminator-armoured commander.

'Do we shoot him?' asked Kol Badar, at Marduk's shoulder.

'No,' the Dark Apostle said. 'Let him approach.'

At Marduk's urging, the Word Bearers backed away, forming a wide semi-circle at the top of the stairs. Warily, the White Consuls stepped into the circle, gaze locked on Marduk's.

'Burias!' barked Marduk, not taking his eyes off the White Consuls. The slender Icon Bearer, having recently regrouped with the Host, stepped forward instantly. 'You want him?'

Burias smiled broadly in response, and handed the Host's icon to Khalaxis. He allowed the change to come upon him and became one with the daemon within.

THE CIRCLE OF Word Bearers stood in silence as Burias-Drak'shal and the White Consul circled each other. Daemons looped overhead.

The White Consul was easily three times the Icon Bearer's weight, and he stomped around heavily, keeping his storm shield between them. Burias-Drak'shal stalked around him, moving in a low crouch. He bore no weapon. He needed none. His fingers had fused into elongated talons easily capable of punching through ceramite, and his distended jaw erupted in a savage display of tusks.

He loped left and right, bestial head low, seeking a weakness in his enemy's defence. The White Consul kept his storm shield up, his thunder hammer held at the ready.

When the possessed warrior struck, it was with all his preternatural speed and strength. With a roar, he flew at the White Consul, little more than a blur. The storm shield sparked, and the Icon Bearer was thrown backwards, landing heavily. He was on his feet again in an instant, leaping at the Chapter Master with talons extended.

He landed on the White Consul Terminator's storm shield clawed feet first, and clutched at the top of it with the talons of his left hand. Barbed claws hooked around the edge of the storm shield, dragging it low even as the stink of scorched flesh filled the air. With his free hand, the Icon Bearer slashed at the Chapter Master, thirty-centimetre talons raking across his gorget.

The White Consul slammed the haft of his thunder hammer into Burias-Drak'shal's face with staggering force, dislodging him from his shield. The Icon Bearer dropped to the ground, landing on all fours. The Chapter Master moved after him, hammer crackling with arcs of electricity.

Burias-Drak'shal leapt backwards, talons scratching deeply into the marble slabs beneath him as he scrambled to avoid the hammer blow. The head of the White Consul's weapon slammed into the marble slab with a sharp crack of discharging power. Stone splintered beneath the strike.

Burias-Drak'shal caught the next blow with a taloned hand, halting it mid-swing, his warp-spawned musculature straining to keep the weapon at bay. The Chapter Master smashed his storm shield into him, knocking him backwards.

Moving with surprising swiftness, the White Consul followed up on the momentarily stunned possessed warrior and struck a brutal blow towards his chest. Burias-Drak'shal tried to sway aside, but the hammer caught him on the shoulder. There was an explosive, percussive shock, and he was thrown to the ground. When he came back to his feet, his left arm was hanging uselessly at his side. His shoulder pad had been torn loose, and his plate armour underneath was sundered and leaking red-black ichor that hissed as it dripped onto the marble underfoot.

Within seconds the possessed warrior's arm was healing, but he was in considerable pain.

When it came, the end of the fight was brutal and abrupt. A hammer blow ripped one of Burias-Drak'shal curving horns from his head, and hot daemon-blood sprayed from the wound. A droplet struck the Chapter Master in his left eye, burning into the retina, and for a fraction of a second the White Consul turned his head away, eyes closing reflexively. That was all the opening that Burias-Drak'shal needed.

Ducking beneath the Chapter Master's backhand swipe he leapt in close, talons ramming into the warrior's side. He could not penetrate the thick armour, but using the momentum of the blows, he swung his mutated body up around the heavier Marine's back like an ape, coming to rest in a crouch atop the White Consul's broad shoulders, the claws of his feet digging deep.

Stabbing downwards with all his might, he punched the talons of his left hand through the top of the Chapter Master's skull, killing him instantly. With a tremendous crash, the warrior fell.

Burias-Drak'shal mounted the Chapter Master's chest in an instant, pounding at the already dead warrior's face over and over. The White Consul's skull collapsed beneath his blows, even super-hardened Astartes bone unable to withstand the sheer brutality Burias-Drak'shal unleashed upon it.

'Enough,' said Marduk, finally.

Breathing heavily, the Icon Bearer rose to his full height. The blood liberally coating his face matched the colour of his armour. He lifted both arms high into the air and threw his head back, howling his victory to the heavens, that the gods might witness his triumph.

AQUILIUS AND THE other White Consuls heard that cry as they reached the bottom of the temple stairs. The young Coadjutor made the sign of the aquila. Atop the stairs, the hateful silhouette of the Dark Apostle could be seen. More than one of the veterans seemed ready to run back, but Librarian Epistolary Liventius forestalled any such rash move.

'More Traitors moving in,' warned one of the veterans. Rhinos and Predators were rolling up the boulevards and causeways leading into the square, threatening to box the White Consuls in.

The Librarian held for a moment and put his hand to his face. He pulled it away to find splashes of crimson coating the fingertips of his gauntlets. Trickles of blood flowed from his nostrils.

'Liventius…?' said Aquilius.

'I sense something.'

'More of the enemy?'

'No. This is something… new. I've never felt a presence like this before. Let's move. Now, brothers,' said Liventius.

Aquilius cast one last glance up towards the top of the stairs.

'Let him not have died in vain,' he said. 'Everything rests with Proconsul Ostorius now.'

\* \* \*

ANY LESSER MAN would already have been dead.

Ostorius was a bloody ruin, his body broken and his face unrecognisable. One eye was swollen shut, and his nose had been broken in three places. His left cheekbone was fractured and splinters of bone pressed through his flesh. His skull was cracked and leaking. Blood and spit dribbled from his mouth, and he spat a handful of teeth out onto the deck floor as he pushed himself unsteadily back to his feet once more.

His left arm was broken and hanging useless at his side. Nevertheless, he still clasped his power sword in his right hand. He lunged at his foe, the tip of his sword stabbing for the Word Bearer's heart.

With a dismissive backhand slap, his attack was knocked aside. A thunderous open hand strike hit Ostorius square in the face. A chopping blow to the side of the White Consul's neck sent him crashing back to the floor.

Grand Apostle Ekodas was completely unscathed, though his hands were covered in blood. He stalked back and forth as he waited for Ostorius to pick himself up.

Again and again, Ostorius got up, attacked and was knocked down. The circle of Word Bearers watched impassively as their lord dismantled the White Consul piece by piece, breaking bones and rupturing organs at will.

At last, Ekodas tired of his sport. He caught Ostorius's arm as he launched a weak overhead strike. Spinning in behind his opponent, Ekodas wrapped an arm around his neck.

'All over now,' said Ekodas in Ostorius's ear. The brutalised White Consul's unfocussed gaze lingered on the Nexus Arrangement.

With a violent twist, Ekodas broke the Proconsul's neck.

MARDUK'S EYES WERE narrowed as he watched the pitiful cluster of White Consuls and Guardsmen scurrying across the square below.

'Take them,' he said, and the warriors of the 34th Host broke into a charge, leaping down the steps in pursuit.

They were halfway down when the heavens exploded.

Like a star going supernova, the Kronos star fort detonated in an almighty explosion that lit up the planet below in blinding, harsh white light.

'What in the name of the gods?' breathed Ashkanez.

Something changed in the quality of the air. Marduk could feel it even within his hermetically sealed armour. It was as if the air were suddenly charged with electricity, making the thick, matted hairs of his cloak stand on end.

A hot wind blew down from above, sending eddies of dust and ash spinning across the square. The heavens had began to roil like an angry whirlpool, clouds of ash, smoke and toxic pollutants swirling madly. Directly overhead, they began to spiral in an anticlockwise direction, as if a cyclone of tremendous proportions were brewing. It looked like a giant maelstrom, a vortex that began to rotate with increasing volatility. Marduk felt unease begin to form within his gut. His natural response to such an unfamiliar emotion was aggression and violence, and fresh combat drugs were pumped through his veins, flooding his system.

'Are *we* doing that?' growled Burias, once again holding his revered icon in his hands, the daemon pushed back below the surface.

'No,' said Marduk. 'I feel no touch of the warp here. None at all. It is… something else.'

Whatever it was, it began descending into the atmosphere.

And it was *huge*.

# BOOK FIVE: RETRIBUTION

*'We are all eternal, my brothers. All this
pain is but an illusion.'*

– Dark Apostle Mah'keenen,
scrawled in blood on the eve of his sacrifice

# CHAPTER FIFTEEN

AT FIRST IT was nothing more than a shadow in the heavens, obscured by the crimson miasma hanging in the atmosphere of Boros Prime. It blotted out the twin suns, casting darkness as deep as night across the city below. It loomed large, seeming to spread from horizon to horizon, and it was got nearer.

At first, Marduk thought perhaps it was a battle-cruiser crashing down to earth, a casualty of the ongoing war in orbit above Boros, but he saw that this shape was bigger than that, larger even than Ekodas's flagship, the immense *Crucius Maledictus*. The star fort itself?

The spiralling downwind intensified and a gap in the centre of the maelstrom appeared. This break in the cloud cover should have afforded those upon the surface of Boros Prime their first unobscured glimpse of the sky since the arrival of the Word

Bearers. The angry welt of the Eye of Terror should have been visible across the heavens, but something blotted out the view. Blue skies should have been visible within that growing gap, but all that could be seen through it was darkness, an enveloping emptiness that seemed to swallow all light.

It was the underside of a vessel so vast as to put the largest battlecruiser to shame, yet Marduk knew instantly that this was not the falling Kronos star fort. Whatever this vessel was, it had destroyed the orbital bastion, utterly and completely. The rotating clouds continued to part before it. As it descended ever closer, eerie glowing green lights lit up along its black underside. Marduk felt a spike of trepidation.

The last of the clouds were sent fleeing over the horizon, and the xenos vessel was finally fully revealed. It must have been easily fifteen kilometres across, and it cast its shadow over the entire city. The dull glow of the obscured suns framed it like an eclipse, giving all those below a sense of the vessel's shape.

It was an immense, perfectly geometric crescent, curving like a sickle-blade, and it hung in low atmosphere, an executioner's axe ready to fall. Something so large should not have been able to descend so close to the planet's surface without being dragged down by the planet's gravity, no matter how powerful its engines were. Yet still it descended.

The energy it must have been exerting to resist the pull of gravity and keep its immense bulk from crashing to earth was beyond imagining, far in excess of anything that could be fathomed by a human mind. Nevertheless, while the fierce down-wind continued to buffet the city below, they were hardly of the scale that Marduk would have imagined necessary to keep such a structure aloft. Indeed, there appeared to be no blazing engines burning with the heat of a thousand suns upon the vessel's underside at all.

How it was controlling its descent was beyond his understanding, and yet in defiance of all natural law and rational thought it continued to penetrate the low atmosphere, drawing steadily nearer the surface of Boros Prime.

The immense xenos vessel was so utterly black that it seemed to absorb the light, and this darkness made the glowing green lines that spread across its underside in alien, geometric patterns all the brighter. Tens of thousands of glowing hieroglyphs could be discerned upon its sheer underside, symbols that might have been some form of inhuman picture writing consisting of lines, circles and crescents. One symbol was larger than the others – a circle with lines of differing lengths projecting from it, like the stylised beams of a sun.

Marduk had seen this symbol before on an Imperial backwater planet called Tanakreg. There, it had appeared upon the sheer obsidian flanks of an alien structure deeply embedded in the rock of an evaporated ocean floor. He knew what manner of beings resided within: undying constructs of living metal, devoid of fear, compassion or mercy, unfettered by mortal concerns. They were a deadly foe, nigh unstoppable, and his blood ran cold as he realised for what purpose they had surely come here.

'Call in our Stormbirds,' ordered Marduk as he reached the bottom of the Imperial temple's stairs. His voice was tense. 'Have the *Infidus Diabolus* readied. I want full and immediate extraction. *Now*.'

'WHAT NEW HORROR is this?' breathed Coadjutor Aquilius, eyes wide, pausing just before he dropped down into the sub-tunnels that would lead into the lower levels of the Temple of the Gloriatus.

Librarian Epistolary Liventius too was looking up. His face was grave.

'Come, brothers,' said the Librarian at last.

Moving warily, weapons at the ready, the cluster of wounded White Consuls and Guardsmen ducked their heads and moved into the tunnels. The heavy blast-doors slammed behind them with grim finality.

KOL BADAR'S EYES were locked on the immense shape hovering low in the atmosphere overhead. He had offered no argument to the Dark Apostle's order to abandon this world. Marduk knew that he too recognised the nature of this vessel hovering oppressively over the city. Marduk heard the crackle of vox-traffic as the Coryphaus began ordering the evacuation.

'Master?' said Ashkanez, scowling darkly. 'What is this? We are going to abandon all we have fought for?'

Ignoring his First Acolyte, the only member of the 34th Host who had not fought on Tanakreg, Marduk began barking orders, commanding his forces to pull back and regroup, ready for extraction.

'Master!' said Ashkanez more forcefully. 'We must finish what we started! The sons of Guilliman cannot be allowed to live!'

Marduk continued to ignore him.

'This world is not yet ours,' growled Ashkanez. 'We cannot make extraction before Grand Apostle Ekodas gives us leave to commence the–'

The First Acolyte was silenced as Marduk spun around suddenly and clamped a hand around his throat, snarling. The broad features of Ashkanez flared with anger and for a moment Marduk thought – even hoped – that his First Apostle would strike out at him, but the stony mask of composure fell across Ashkanez's features once more, and the First Acolyte lowered his gaze.

'No, this world is not yet ours, and nor will it be, not now. You have no comprehension of what that is,' said Marduk, gesturing up at the immense shape looming ever larger in the heavens, 'nor of what its appearance portends. We leave *now*. Ekodas be damned.'

'So the Imperials have unexpected reinforcements,' said Ashkanez. 'What does it matter? We must finish the Consuls while they are weak and vulnerable.'

'Ignorant fool,' said Marduk. 'These are no Imperial allies.'

He released his First Acolyte with a shove, sneering.

He saw Ashkanez glance over Marduk's shoulder, and only then did he register the hulking presence of someone standing threateningly close behind him. With a glance he saw it was the berserker Khalaxis, exalted champion of 17th Coterie. The big warrior's chest was rising and falling heavily, and his ritualistically scarred face, framed by matted dreadlocks, was contorted in a bestial snarl.

'Is there a problem, Khalaxis?' growled Marduk, glaring up into the champion's red-tinged, frenzied eyes. He was amongst the tallest warriors of the Host, and Marduk came barely to his chin.

Out of corner of his eye, Marduk saw Ashkanez glance skyward, then back at Khalaxis. The First Acolyte seemed indecisive for a moment, then gave a brief shake of his head – reluctantly, it seemed to Marduk.

'Move away now, brother,' said Sabtec, stepping protectively in front of Marduk. The champion of the hallowed 13th had his hand on the hilt of his sword.

The massive exalted champion refused to back down, still glaring over Sabtec's head at Marduk, violence written in his gaze. Marduk was very aware of the immense chainaxe clasped in the towering warrior's hands and blood-rage that Khalaxis clearly held only barely in check.

'Khalaxis,' snapped Ashkanez.

With a last threatening glare, the berserker swung away, stamping off to rejoin his Coterie.

'Do not be too hard on Khalaxis, my lord,' said Ashkanez. 'His choler was in the ascendant. He meant no disrespect.'

'When we get out of this, you and I are going to have… words, First Acolyte,' said Marduk.

Ashkanez bowed his head in supplication.

'As it pleases you, my master,' he said, his tone neutral.

Marduk saw Burias smirk.

'Assault shuttles inbound,' confirmed Kol Badar.

Marduk glanced across the expanse of the square. The White Consuls were long gone now. Ever since Calth, the desire to kill and maim the sons of Guilliman, to destroy all that they stood for, had consumed him. Now he was allowing these gene-descendants of the Ultramarines to escape him, but he swallowed back his hatred, for there were issues of more pressing importance that demanded his attention. Namely, keeping himself alive. His gaze ventured skywards once more.

On Tanakreg, a xenos pyramid of ancient, inhuman design had sat deep within an abyssal trench located far beneath the acidic oceans of that backwater planet. There it had resided for countless millennia, dormant and lifeless. Its location had been revealed after the oceans had been boiled away by the actions of the 34th Host, under the leadership of Marduk's predecessor, the Dark Apostle Jarulek. Marduk, Jarulek's First Acolyte, had been amongst those that had penetrated the alien pyramid, descending into its claustrophobic interior. It was a tomb, Marduk had realised, and by penetrating into its dark heart, the Word Bearers had awakened its guardians from their eternal slumber.

It had been there, deep within the alien crypts of the xenos pyramid, that he had entered the inner sanctum of a being the ancient apocrypha of the Word Bearers named the Undying One. This being was unimaginably ancient, a thing that Marduk suspected was as old as the heavens themselves. There in the Undying One's insane realm, a place far beyond his understanding where distance and time seemed as malleable as living flesh, Marduk had discovered the Nexus Arrangement, the potent piece of alien technology that had made this attack on the Boros Gate sector possible. There too, Marduk had left his master, Jarulek. The Dark Apostle had turned on him once his usefulness had passed, but it had been Marduk that had emerged triumphant.

Marduk had long plotted Jarulek's downfall. It might not have happened the way he had planned, but it mattered little. Jarulek had perished, and Marduk had escaped from the Undying One's maddening realm, taking with him his prize, the Nexus.

A niggling doubt remained, buried deep within his consciousness, that the malevolent sentient being had *allowed* him to leave its realm. Always, Marduk had refused to entertain the errant thought, but now, seeing this immense vessel descending down towards the city, the whisper of doubt returned. Instinctively, he knew the malign intelligence that commanded this vessel was the same as that he had encountered beneath the alien pyramid. Doubtless it came to reclaim what had been stolen from it.

The immense xenos vessel was now so close that Marduk imagined he could almost touch its obsidian underside, yet it was still at least a kilometre above the city.

It is not my fate to die here, Marduk thought, defiantly. Nothing in the portents had spoken of his death.

The immense alien vessel had come to rest some two hundred metres above the city, looming claustrophobically low overhead. No hint of the sky beyond it could be glimpsed now. It felt as if the planet had an unsupported low roof that might drop to crush those beneath it at any moment.

Green-tinged lightning arced across its underside, dancing across its obsidian surfaces. Geometric designs throbbed, growing brighter and then dimming, like a heartbeat, and thousands of alien hieroglyphs flared into glowing, green life.

'Where are the Stormbirds?' hissed Marduk.

'Incoming, one minute,' said Kol Badar. He pointed into the distance. A flock of dark craft could be seen hurtling in their direction, flying low over the city. 'There.'

A high frequency electronic whine that made Marduk's skin crawl sounded in the distance. Its pitch ascended sharply, and as it moved beyond the range of Astartes hearing, a column of ghostly light as wide as a city block stabbed downwards from the alien vessel, perhaps two kilometres away to the north. Arcs of electricity danced along the shaft's ethereal edges. The light of the column did not dissipate, but stayed firmly targeted on the city, like some immense, motionless spotlight.

'What in the hells of Sicarus is that?' said Ashkanez.

A second whine sounded and another spotlight stabbed downwards, this time appearing perhaps five kilometres south of their position. Further whines heralded more columns of ghostly light, until there were a dozen of them projected blindingly downwards, linking the alien craft to the city below. They shone like divine pillars in the darkness, as if holding the xenos vessel aloft.

A further electronic whine began to sound, piercing in its intensity, louder than any other so far. Gazing upwards Marduk saw a ring of light burning brightly on the underside of the xenos vessel, directly overhead. It grew steadily more intense, and while the auto-reactive lenses of his helmet compensated for the sudden, white-hot light, dulling it back to a manageable level, he nevertheless raised an arm to shield his eyes. If it were some form of weapon, a lance-beam of monstrous scale, Marduk realised that he and his brothers would be directly beneath the blast.

Setting his feet firmly, Marduk roared his fury at the heavens. If he were to die, then he would do so defiant and unrepentant to the last.

Blinding, diffuse light surrounded Marduk and his brethren, and the air crackled with a powerful electrical charge. It took Marduk half a second to realise that he lived still, that the column of light was not destructive in nature, and he gave a short prayer of thanks to the gods of the æther.

The moment's respite did not last.

The air around him shimmered and crackled with intensity, as if the particles of the air were vibrating violently, and sparks of bright light danced across the armour plates of the uneasy Word Bearers.

'Energy readings are off the scale,' said Sabtec, his brows furrowed, looking at the daemonically-infused auspex in his hands.

'Something is making transference,' hissed Kol Badar, the bladed lengths of his power talons clenching and unclenching reflexively. 'I can feel it in my bones.'

'Stand ready!' said Marduk, hefting his crozius.

'Something is coming through,' shouted Sabtec, turning around on the spot, eyes locked on the throbbing red blister-display of his auspex. He stopped abruptly, and his eyes lifted. 'There! Three hundred and twenty metres! Elevation 3.46!'

Marduk looked where his champion pointed. At first he saw nothing. Then a ball of crackling energy

blinked into existence, hanging perhaps twenty
metres above the city. It was positioned in the centre
of a wide boulevard that led up towards the square.
The Word Bearers began to back away, weapons
raised. The air around the sphere of flickering energy
wavered, and sparking electricity stabbed outwards
from its centre.

'What–' began Ashkanez, but he never finished.

With a deep whoosh, the crackling ball of light
expanded suddenly to a hundred times its former
size. Coronas of lightning sparked madly within it,
and the Word Bearers fell back a step defensively as
the blast overtook them. It lasted only a fraction of a
second before it contracted sharply once more,
accompanied by a deep sucking sound like air being
vented into a vacuum. It shrank in upon itself, collapsing to something the size of a pea before
exploding.

With a deafening crack, blinding white light burst
out in all directions, and the sphere of energy was
gone. In its place was a slowly spinning flat-topped
pyramid roughly the size of a super-heavy tank, hovering ten metres above the ground. It was formed of
light-absorbing black stone, and green electricity
played along its blank, sheer surfaces.

It hung there in the air, turning lazily, and then its
form began to alter. Glowing green lines appeared
upon its smooth surfaces, and four oblong pillars of
black stone rose from the corners of its top, rising
like battlements atop a fortress. Rib-like sections of
the prism's sides slid upwards, forming a hollow cage
atop it. A single wider arc, like an architectural buttress of unearthly design, glided smoothly upwards
to position itself over the hollow cage.

A massive dark green crystal, easily three metres in height, rose up from within the prism until it was hanging unsupported within this hollow cage-like formation. This crystal was perfect in its angular symmetry, and flickered with inner light. Sparking green electrical impulses darted between it and the rib-like buttresses enclosing it, tentatively at first, then building in frequency and power. The light within the crystal intensified, until it was glowing brightly, and the shower of sparks coalescing around it crackled like sheet lightning.

Hieroglyphs and pictograms pulsed into life upon the sheer sides of the prism, and weapon-turrets emerged from crenellations that appeared upon the four corners of the pyramid. They began to rotate mechanically, and green lightning flickered along the length of their barrels. Targeting reticules within Marduk's helmet flashed, locking onto these weapons.

'Take it down!' he roared.

COADJUTOR AQUILIUS EMERGED with his brethren from the service elevator. They stood upon the high crenulated battlements of the designated landing pad the incoming Thunderhawk was aiming for, high atop of the Temple of the Gloriatus. A golden dome rose behind them, topped with a gleaming statue of the Emperor. How it still remained intact among the destruction was a minor miracle in itself, Aquilius thought.

Standing nearly thirty metres tall, it was to view this that so many of the devout made the pilgrimage to Boros Prime. It was said that to look upon the statue was to look upon the divine. So skilled had its artisans been that the sublime expression upon the statue's face brought tears to the eyes of all who looked upon it. Aquilius felt some comfort to be standing beneath its gaze.

One of the injured Sternguard veterans was lowered to the ground. The battle-brother propped himself up with his back to the crenulations and Aquilius stood, looking out over the battlements across the square below. What he saw made his breath catch in his throat.

The Word Bearers below firing upon a slowly revolving black pyramid hovering above the ground. Where the xenos thing had come from, Aquilius knew not.

Missiles detonated ineffectively upon the structure's sheer, black surfaces, and he watched as autocannon rounds stitched across its sides. The heavy-calibre shells ricocheted harmlessly off the dark stone, causing not so much as a crack in its surface. Lascannon beams struck its angled sides, yet the energy was merely absorbed into the alien structure, making its hieroglyphs momentarily glow brighter.

A widening circle was cleared before the alien prism as the Word Bearers spread out into cover as it descended towards the ground. It came to rest a metre above the marble square, and began to return fire.

An arc of lightning erupted from one of its rotating armatures, striking a cluster of Word Bearers who had taken cover behind a low balustrade. There was a blinding explosion of light and half a dozen of the traitor Space Marines were sent flying, their bodies blackened and smoking. They hit the ground hard, their bodies twitching as remnants of green electricity flickered across their armour. The marble balustrade was completely obliterated, and a circle of smoking ash marked where the potent arc had hit.

The other rotating armatures fired, causing destruction to all and sundry, striking anything within a thirty metres radius. A Predator battle tank, a crucified White Consul nailed to the front of its armoured chassis, was reversing away from the deadly xenos prism, its turret-mounted twin lascannons firing desperately and ineffectually. A lightning arc whipped out and struck the Predator, sending it flipping backwards, end over end, a blackened shell flickering with sparks.

A doorway of shimmering light appeared within one side of the black prism, and Aquilius watched in horrified fascination as a pair of deathly, robotic skeletons marched from within, stepping down onto the marble surface of Victory Square, their movements in perfect synchronicity.

Their gaunt, skeletal bodies appeared to be formed of dark metal, and glowing green light oozed from their empty eye sockets. They held long-barrelled weapons across their hollow chests, and the light of gunfire and electricity reflected sharply off their silver craniums and bones.

In pairs, skeletal soldiers marched from within the prism in a steady stream, and they began to form a phalanx. Several of them were felled by concentrated Word Bearers fire, but many of the undead warriors simply rose back to their feet seconds later, the damage they had sustained repairing itself seamlessly. Severed limbs reattached themselves and craters caused by detonating bolt rounds in heads and chests disappeared as if they had never been.

Still more skeletal warriors stepped through the doorway of flickering light, far more than could have possibly fitted within the prism, moving steadily, their pace unhurried and relentless. Aquilius realised the prism must be acting as a form of gateway, linking to the immense ship hanging in low orbit overhead. His mind boggled as he imagined the number of humanoid sentinels that a vessel of such size might contain.

More of the black-sided prisms blinked into existence above Victory Square, spinning lazily as they descended slowly towards the ground. Each began undergoing the same transformation that the first had, glowing crystals rising from their centres and rib-like buttresses sliding up their sheer sides as they powered up.

A krak missile struck the crystal emerging from the inside of one of the xenos prisms before it had come fully to life, and it exploded into a million shards. Like a marionette with its strings cut, the prism dropped like a stone, its glowing hieroglyphs fading to darkness. By the time it hit the square below, it was nothing more than an inert, lifeless hunk of stone.

Smaller spheres of light glimmered in the air, like a host of sparking fireflies, before contracting sharply, and other shapes blinked into reality.

Spider-like robotic constructs the size of Dreadnoughts appeared, looming above the Word Bearers, their arachnid, metal legs clicking beneath them. Clusters of glowing green eyes blinked and locked onto the milling traitors below. Binaric clicks issued from their silver mandibles, and they descended upon the enemy's ranks, huge metal pincers snapping Traitor Astartes in two.

Other xenos beings materialised, resembling some kind of bizarre, mechanised centaur. From the waist up they were the manifestation of horrific skeletal humanoids, while their lower bodies were some form of anti-grav skiff. Their right arms had been replaced with multi-barrelled cannons, pulsing with intense, green electrical currents. Moving with unhurried grace, their movements conducted in perfect unison, these new arrivals hovered several metres above the heads of the Word Bearers. They began to unleash the power of their alien weaponry, and Aquilius felt a mixture of horror and awe as he witnessed the beams of light passing right through the bodies of the Traitors, leaving gaping holes in ceramite armour and flesh alike.

Victory Square was now a chaotic warzone, with traitors battling furiously with the xenos constructs.

A flight of traitor Stormbirds and Thunderhawks, their gore-splashed hulls hung with chains and daemonic symbology, came screaming in low over the rooftops, engines spewing orange flame. One of them was instantly struck by a whiplash of discharging electricity, sending it into a spiralling death spin. It came down hard, one wing ripping off as it struck a soaring buttress of the Temple of the Gloriatus. The fifty-tonne piece of masonry came crashing down in a shower of marble, and the Stormbird ploughed into the square, killing dozens of traitors and skeletal xenos warriors as it exploded into a towering fireball.

The other shuttles dropped down through the mayhem, weapon systems firing, and the Word Bearers began streaming towards them as their assault ramps slammed down onto the square.

'Thunderhawk inbound,' said one of the blue-helmed Sternguard veterans, his white crest shivering from the amount of electricity pulsing through the air. 'Three minutes.'

Aquilius wondered briefly what the point was anymore. Ostorius had failed. There was no hope of salvation.

He felt a hand on his arm, and looked down into the strong face of the Imperial officer, Verenus of the Boros 232nd.

'As long as the White Angel is with us, there is always hope,' said the solder, with a smile.

Aquilius shook his head, smiling despite himself.

Then Verenus's head disintegrated, ripped apart molecule by molecule as an arc of green energy struck it.

Aquilius swore and fell back, scrabbling for his bolter.

A TRIO OF skeletal constructs hove into view, flying along at the same level as the temple's battlements. Aquilius was dragged backwards as the xenos constructs fired again, and a head-sized chunk of the battlements disintegrated, right where he had been standing a fraction of a second earlier. One of the Sternguard veterans fell, a gaping hole torn through his body.

The veteran that had pulled Aquilius back fired his plasma pistol, taking one of the mechanoids in the head. Its leering skull face was replaced with a molten crater as the white hot burst of plasma struck it, and it dropped out of sight, falling to the ground thirty metres below the wall.

Bolts pattered off the chests of the other two, and the Imperials fled before them, retreating inside the temple precinct. Aquilius glanced back over his shoulder to see the fallen construct rising from the ground, its skull reforming before his eyes.

'Emperor above,' breathed Aquilius.

'How long till that Thunderhawk arrives?' barked Liventius.

'One minute, Epistolary!' came the reply.

It seemed like a lifetime.

'HURRY, REVERED ONE!' bellowed Marduk, urging the Warmonger up the ramp of the Stormbird. The Dreadnought clomped its way into the shuttle's assault bay, even as more warrior brothers bolted up the ramp to take their seats.

'Full!' shouted Sabtec, and Marduk nodded.

'Go!' roared Marduk.

He was standing in the doorway of the Stormbird, firing his bolt pistol. He slammed his fist onto a panel on inner wall, and the embarkation ramp began to close. Retro thrusters roared, and the heavy assault craft lifted off.

He could see First Acolyte Ashkanez and his Icon Bearer, Burias, some distance away, boarding another Stormbird. He raised his hand as Burias looked in his direction, but the Icon Bearer turned away.

All the Word Bearers within the square were streaming towards the assault shuttles that were touching down. Rhinos accelerated up embarkation ramps, tracks skidding, and Land Raiders and Predators were grasped by coupling claws beneath Thunderhawks, ready for transportation

Before Marduk's Stormbird could pull away, a giant mechanical pincer tore into the closing assault ramp, punching through the reinforced plasteel. In one violent motion the entire hatch was ripped off its pneumatic hinges, and Marduk came face to face with one of the immense, robotic spider-constructs, hovering outside. Its cluster of green eyes glimmered with malign intelligence. Its mandibles quivered and it emitted an indecipherable torrent of electronic clicks and whistles. It lifted its other slender fore-claw, which ended in a long barrel flickering with energy.

Marduk swore and threw himself sidewards as the mechanised construct fired into the cramped inte-rior of the Stormbird. Three Word Bearers were consumed in the blast, and they roared in pain. The searing beam took apart their power armour mole-cule by molecule, before setting to work on the flesh, flaying skin and muscle exposing the skeleton beneath. In turn, even the warrior brothers' bones were atomised. It was a deeply unsettling sight, even to one such as Marduk.

Kol Badar planted his feet wide and unleashed a burst of fire into the spider's head, and a dozen of its glowing eyes darkened. It twitched, gliding back-wards in the face of the fusillade, and then the Stormbird's engines fired at full power, lifting the assault craft away from the corpse-strewn square, which was still bathed in cold diffuse light projected from above.

As the Stormbird rose, it passed through a thick cloud of dust that manifested out of nowhere amid a million tiny flashes of light.

No, not dust, Marduk realised. The particles were too large, and shone with reflective light. It was a cloud of tiny metallic insects, he realised, a million buzzing, robotic scarabs.

They swarmed in a tight-knit cloud that obscured his vision as the Stormbird rose through it.

Hundreds of them swarmed through the gaping rent left in the side of the Stormbird where the assault ramp had been torn loose, tiny metal wings buzzing and thoraxes vibrating. Marduk staggered back away from the opening, keeping his centre of gravity low and swatting at the massed insects.

The scarabs, most no larger than the palm of a hand, some so small as to be almost invisible, skittered across every surface of the Stormbird's interior, their tiny silver legs and mandibles clicking. They flowed like a tide up the legs of the Word Bearers locked into the harnesses nearest the doorway and burrowed into their thick ceramite plates. One warrior screamed as he was covered from head to toe, the mechanical insects crawling up over the lip of his breastplate and down the inside of his armour, tunnelling into his flesh. The Word Bearer threw his restraint harness clear and rose to his feet, slapping and scratching at his armour. Marduk saw a bulge of scarabs beneath the skin of the warrior's face. He saw one of the tiny creatures emerge, its silver carapace slick with blood, burrowing out through his left eye socket.

The warrior turned around on the spot, grimacing, slapping and tearing at his own skin. As the Stormbird's angle of ascent steepened, he lost his footing and was sucked out of the gaping hole in the shuttle's hull.

'Flamers!' roared Kol Badar, and controlled bursts of promethium bathed the interior of the Stormbird. Scarabs squealed as they were consumed, and within a minute, the majority of the tiny constructs were gone.

The Stormbird continued to rise, leaving the chittering cloud behind.

Gripping onto guide rails tightly, Marduk moved to the gaping hole where the assault ramp had been torn away and leant out into the deafening wind, studying the lay of the land below. The full spectacle of the xenos' arrival could be seen as the Stormbird rose above the city.

Thousands of skeletal warriors were marching through the streets below, moving in perfect pha-lanxes. Tens of thousands of Guardsmen flooded the streets, fleeing before them. As the Stormbird pulled higher, Marduk could see hundreds of the black-sided prisms dotted all over the city, and even more xenos constructs were marching from them onto the streets with every passing minute.

As the Stormbird gained altitude, he saw a Reaver Titan of Legio Vulturus surrounded by six of the mono-liths. The fire-blackened forms of two Warhounds lay twitching in smoking heaps nearby, buildings crushed beneath their carcasses. Arcs of energy struck the Reaver repeatedly. It brought one of the pyramids down with a concentrated burst of missiles launched from the pod upon its shoulders. Another was swatted aside by the Reaver's immense chainfist, the blow tearing the alien prism in half and sending it smashing into a fortified tower, bringing it crashing down. But even the mighty Reaver could not last against the monoliths, and one by one its flickering void shields were brought down by the relentless barrage it was sustaining from all sides. Like a cornered beast, it turned one way and another, seeking escape. It howled its fury as it came under direct assault again, arcs of green electricity ripping one arm away and tearing into its black carapace. It was finally brought down, and its ululating death cry rang out across the city.

Marduk whistled through his teeth as he witnessed the death of the ancient engine.

Reports flooded in. All across Boros Prime, the xenos were making their presence known. Ekodas's order came through, ordering all Hosts to evacuate immediately.

The planet belonged to the xenos.

IN THE CENTRE of the square below, unseen by mortal eyes, the thick cloud of metal scarabs was swarming into an ever denser, impenetrable cloud, hovering just metres above the scorched stonework. Robotic warriors formed up in precise ranks around this violently writhing shoal of mechanised insects. These warriors were larger and more heavily armoured than the other deathly automatons, and they clutched glaive-like weapons in their skeletal hands, their blades formed of flickering green light

The scarabs started to latch onto each other, barbed legs and mandibles locking together, and a vaguely humanoid shape began to take form. Insectoid bodies seemed to melt as if under an intense heat, their bodies turning to molten metal as they blurred together, sacrificing their individual forms to create something altogether more terrible.

Ghostly green light began to burn within hollow eyes sockets. Coldly, the ancient being known as the Undying One turned to watch the Word Bearers retreat before it.

# CHAPTER SIXTEEN

'Look at the size of it,' exclaimed Sabtec. The champion of the exalted 13th Coterie stood next to Marduk, peering out of the port-side window of the Stormbird's cockpit.

The surface of Boros Prime was receding away below them as the heavy assault shuttle hurtled up through the tortured planet's atmosphere, angling towards the *Infidus Diabolus*, which was on an intercept path with them in orbit above. They were three thousand kilometres from the ground and rising steadily, and from their vantage point they were afforded a view across the immense, crescent-shaped vessel of the enemy xenos-constructs.

It was truly massive, larger than any ship that Marduk had ever laid eyes on. It rivalled the bulk of a Darkstar fortress. Having witnessed the effectiveness of the enemy's weapons upon the ground, the thought of what this titanic vessel might be capable of was horrifying. Marduk prayed to the Weaver of the Fates that they were out of range of whatever weapon systems it might have at its disposal.

Blinding pillars of light beamed from the ship's underside down onto the city below, deploying its inhuman armies across the city in a spread of more than fifteen kilometres. Marduk shook his head in wonder. Less than ten minutes after first appearing in the upper atmosphere, the enemy had deployed tens of thousands of its troops and established complete dominion within the city below. Not even Astartes were able to deploy in such force at a speed to match that feat.

'How did they make translocation?' growled Kol Badar, removing his heavy, quad-tusked helmet. 'Has your precious Nexus Arrangement failed? Are the gates to the warp open?'

Marduk's eyelids flickered as he reached out with his soul-spirit. His entire body jolted a moment later as he slammed back into his body.

'No,' he said. 'The device remains effective. Nothing could have entered the system through the æther.'

'Well, it came from *somewhere*,' said Kol Badar.

'Perhaps it does not need the warp at all,' commented Sabtec.

Marduk shrugged.

The Word Bearers continued to study the enemy ship, their silence broken only by the crackling hiss of scanners, and the guttural growls and mechanical wheezing of the piloting servitors hardwired into the controls of the shuttle.

They were almost on a level with the xenos vessel, separated now by the three hundred kilometres of curved space. From this angle they could see three black-sided pyramids rising from the rear of the ship's crescent shape. Marduk judged them to be its command decks, and it was the largest of these that attracted his interest. He narrowed his eyes, and nodded his head slowly.

'I have seen this ship before,' said Marduk.

'What? Where?' said Kol Badar.

'On Tanakreg,' said Marduk.

'I do not recall seeing any such thing,' said the Coryphaus.

'That pyramid,' said Marduk, stabbing a finger onto the transparent, ice-cold surface of the port window. 'We have been inside it, Kol Badar.'

The Coryphaus nodded slowly, realisation dawning.

'Only its tip was exposed,' said Kol Badar. 'The rest of the ship was hidden beneath the ocean floor.'

'The gods alone know how long it was buried there,' said Marduk. The roar of the main drive engines subsided marginally, and stabilising jets kicked in, adjusting the Stormbird's angle of ascent.

'We've broken atmosphere,' confirmed Sabtec with a glance at the hissing display screens. As the shuttle came to a new heading, and the crescent shape of the xenos ship disappeared from view behind them. Ahead of them, just appearing over the red-tinged curvature of the world, they could make out the dark shape of the *Infidus Diabolus*, ploughing to meet them.

A veined blister in the ceiling began to blink.

'Transmission,' said Kol Badar, keying a sequence of buttons with the bladed tips of his power talons, his touch surprisingly delicate. 'It is from the *Crucius Maledictus*.'

'Ekodas,' said Marduk. 'Ignore it.'

'How many of our brothers made it off the ground?' asked Sabtec.

'Not enough,' said Marduk.

HALF A DOZEN assault shuttles had already docked as Marduk's Stormbird passed through the shimmering integrity field and entered one of the lower launch bays of the *Infidus Diabolus*. The deck was a hive of activity, with black-clad overseers and slave-gangs hurrying to attend to the newly arrived craft. Tracked crawlers ground across the floor, loaded high with fresh ammunition and fuel cells. Limping mecha-organics shrouded in black robes wafted incense, and hunched chirumeks attended to the wounded.

As the landing gear of the Stormbird touched down, Marduk marched from the shuttle, attended by his Coryphaus and a bodyguard of Anointed. He saw the burly figure of First Acolyte Ashkanez emerging from a nearby smoking Thunderhawk, Burias and Khalaxis flanking him. Marduk sneered, shaking his head.

Seeing him, the First Acolyte angled his march to meet him.

'I have had contact from Grand Apostle Ekodas,' said the First Acolyte by way of greeting. Marduk did not slow his pace, forcing Ashkanez to fall into step beside him. 'Fresh orders. We are to form up with the rest of the fleet and fall back out of range of the xenos ship. If it is Boros Prime that they want, then let them have it.'

'It is not the planet they want,' said Marduk. 'It is the Nexus.'

SIX SLAB-SIDED NECRON monoliths had formed a perfectly equidistant perimeter around Victory Square.

Thousands of gleaming, skeletal warriors stood in serried, outward-facing ranks between these structures, silent sentinels that guarded all routes leading to the square. They stood in perfect, deathly stillness. If it was their master's wish, they would stand there for all eternity. They existed solely to serve, any semblance of will long having eroded to nothingness within the cold, lifeless shell of their bodies. Formations of destroyers patrolled the area, gliding soundlessly in perfectly coordinated patterns over the heads of the phalanxes below.

The being referred to in the ancient texts of the Word Bearers as the Undying One was positioned centrally within the square, the beaming light from its tomb ship overhead reflecting sharply off its gleaming, silver skeleton. Alone amongst its undying legions, it moved with grace and suppleness as it stretched its long, slender limbs. Alone amongst its kind, it retained some semblance of its former self, from a time long past, before the rise of man or eldar, when it had been a creature of flesh and blood.

From the waist up the ancient, hate-filled being was humanoid, a deathly parody of what it had resembled in life. From the waist down, however, its body was akin to one of the great tomb spyders that tended the undying legion across the emptiness of passing millennia. The Undying One's curving spine ran along the top of its insectoid lower body, which was covered in a series of protective armour plates of gleaming black, their smooth surfaces inscribed with intricate geometry. A dozen slender, arachnoid legs hung beneath its bulky dark silver abdomen, the long, multi-jointed limbs narrowing to slender blade-points.

A reflective obsidian breastplate had formed across the Undying One's thin, cadaverous chest. Upon this lustrous plate were fine, golden lines representing a sun and its life-giving rays. It wore a circlet of gold upon its silver skull, a regal crown of rulership that seemed to burn with the contained power of an enslaved sun. A death shroud billowed lazily around it, as if waving gently in an undersea current, the sheer material glistening with iridescence.

The ancient being's limbs were inscribed with arcane geometry and hieroglyphs, and it stretched its arms upwards, long, skeletal fingers unfurling. In response, the Undying One's immortal guardians began to emit a deep, reverberant note, a sound at once mournful and hollow.

A swirling wind picked up, and dust and ash eddied around the Undying One. Its death shroud was unaffected, wafting languidly in the air around it.

As the low bass note continued unabated, darkness descended over the square. The glowing eyes of the Undying One and its minions burned more fiercely in the deepening shadow. Green light spilled from the Undying One's underbelly, throwing the ancient being's body into silhouette.

Rolling its deathly head back, the terrifying being began to emit an unnatural shriek, making the air visibly vibrate. A shiver seemed to ripple out across the shadowed square, and filled with diabolic impulse, the wailing cry lifted up into the heavens, reaching out in all directions. Subtle vibrations were sent out like a fine mesh, and deep within the bow-els of the *Crucius Maledictus*, the Nexus Arrangement responded to its master's summons.

GRAND APOSTLE EKODAS stood at the view portal, his expression unreadable.

'Grand Apostle,' said Kol Harekh, his Coryphaus.

'What is it?' Ekodas said over his shoulder, not taking his eyes off the xenos ship in the distance. Despite the distance, it still loomed impossibly large.

'I think we may have a further problem.'

Ekodas turned towards his Coryphaus, who gestured at the Nexus Arrangement, positioned centrally within his circular throne room. The corrupted magos worked feverishly, babbling nonsensically in his monotone drone.

The Grand Apostle stepped over the brutalised body of the White Consuls fool that had somehow managed to penetrate his inner sanctum and moved towards the magos, frowning. There was something happening, but he was not immediately sure what it was.

'The device, it looks unstable,' said Kol Harekh.

It was barely perceptible at first, but as he narrowed his eyes, Ekodas could see what his Coryphaus meant. The Nexus Arrangement was vibrating, and that movement was becoming more violent with every passing second, as if it were fighting to free itself from the contraption the magos had used to ensnare and control it.

Ekodas felt an uncomfortable pressure tugging at his soul, and he redoubled his potent psychic defences.

The kathartes daemons crouching in the alcoves high overhead clearly felt something too, and they began screeching.

'Are you doing this, magos?' said Ekodas.

Darioq-Grendh'al was hissing in agitation, his mechanised limbs shuddering and his mechadendrites a blur of motion as they danced across keypads and control dials. Bloody organic data-spikes were thrust into the cognifiers. A torrent of data, both spoken and clicking binaric cant, spilled from the corrupted magos's dead lips, a ceaseless flow of noise that Marduk found for the most part indecipherable.

'Previously inert beta power levels surging beyond charted magnifiers, peaking at 99.224952 gamma-parsecs, expanding exponentially, outside source unknown, controlling mechanisms failing to compensate, capacitors levelling out, gone, failure, dead,' blurted the magos, his agitated voice interspersed with frantic clicks and beeps.

'Do something!' Ekodas said. 'You are losing it!'

Abruptly, one of the spinning rings that surrounded the Nexus seemed to wilt, the integrity of its shape compromised. Its rotation was thrown out as the ring became ovular in shape, and it began to list around unevenly. The light spilling from the Nexus Arrangement surged, becoming painfully bright, forcing Marduk to turn away.

A keening wail echoed through the room, making the walls and workbenches shudder and vibrate.

'What in the gods?' said Kol Harekh, backing away.

The rings spinning around the Nexus exploded, riven into a thousand shards that burst outwards, embedding themselves deep into the room's walls, and into ceramite armour plates. Darioq-Grendh'al was thrown backwards, mechadendrites flailing. Two of his tentacles, still attached to control panels with umbilical data-spikes, were ripped from his spine as he was knocked backwards.

Ekodas hissed in pain as one of the shards impaled his thigh, the sliver of metal passing clean through his armour and flesh to protrude out the other side.

The housing that had been constructed to control and temper the alien device was a shattered ruin, electrical sparks leaping across its broken rings.

The Nexus Arrangement hung in mid-air. It was still for a moment. It had reverted back to its seamless orb form, and its violent vibrations had died down, leaving it utterly motionless.

Then, moving at a speed that not even an Astartes could follow, it began to accelerate.

THE SILVER ORB punched its way clear of the *Crucius Maledictus*, moving at tremendous speed, tearing clean through metre-thick bulkheads and countless levels of decking. It ripped straight through everything in its path, causing untold damage. It rent a gaping hole through the engine decks, coming within scant centimetres of penetrating the plasma core. It cut straight through the cavernous expanse of the ship's cavaedium, instantly killing a warrior brother of the 64th Coterie as he knelt in prayer. It ripped through the lower slave pens, killing dozens, before passing on through the sepulchres, filled with the raging screams of shackled daemon-engines. Down it plunged, until finally it tore out through the thick armour plates of the immense ship's underhull. Over a hundred slave-proselytes were slain as they were sucked out the fist-sized hole before bulkheads slammed shut, isolating the integrity breach.

With a streaking tail of fire arcing out behind it, the silver sphere hurtled down through the atmosphere of Boros Prime like a shooting star.

Moving at such velocity, were it to strike the surface of Boros Prime it would cause a crater tens of kilometres wide, but before it struck it came to a sudden halt, its velocity arrested instantly.

Glowing with pale light, it hovered between the Undying One's outstretched hands.

DARIOQ-GRENDH'AL WENT BERSERK, his body mutating wildly as his stress-levels increased exponentially.

'It is mine!' he bellowed. 'Mine! Bring it back to me!'

New tentacles burst from his flesh, barbed and fleshy and dripping with blood. They flailed around him wildly as the corrupted magos railed against the loss of the Nexus Arrangement. Effortlessly, he flipped one of the workbenches bolted to the ground, tearing up sheets of the metal flooring in the process. He hurled it into a far wall, which collapsed beneath the sheer force.

Snarling in anger Ekodas ducked beneath a scything, toothed tentacle that would have taken his head off had it connected.

'Restrain him,' Ekodas barked.

Kol Harekh stepped in close and backhanded the magos across the head, using all of his strength. There was a heavy metallic clunk, but Darioq-Grendh'al was not felled. With surprising swiftness, the two servo-arms that extended over the magos's shoulders darted down and forwards, taking hold of the Coryphaus by the shoulders. Ceramite armour groaned beneath the pressure, and Kol Harekh was lifted off of his feet.

Kol Harekh's bolt pistol came up, levelling at the corrupted magos's head, even as a dozen tentacles altered their form, their tips becoming elongated, barbed prongs, poised to impale.

'*Enough!*' barked Ekodas, his intonation carefully weighted to convey a portion of his gods-given power.

The magos froze, though he strained to finish his the killing blow.

'*Put him down,*' he ordered, and the magos gently lowered Kol Harekh to the ground. The Coryphaus lashed out, fingers encircling the magos's scrawny neck. Ekodas knew that it would take little effort for Kol Harekh to tear the magos's head loose.

'Don't do it,' he growled. 'We may need him yet.'

The Coryphaus released Darioq-Grendh'al with a snarl.

Ekodas gritted his teeth as he used his psychic powers to drag the length of metal impaling his leg clear of his flesh. His armour squealed in protest. Telekinetically, he lifted the razor-sharp spike up before him. It was slick with blood. Carefully, he ran his tongue along its length before he hurled it aside with a flick of his mind, sending it clattering to the deck.

'My, my,' said Ekodas. 'That *was* quite a tantrum, wasn't it?'

He walked slowly around the now motionless figure of Darioq-Grendh'al. The magos's mechadendrites quivered with suppressed rage as he struggled against Ekodas's will, straining to break loose and unleash their fury.

'Locate the device,' said Ekodas. His Coryphaus nodded and opened a vox-channel to the bridge, barking orders.

Still maintaining his hold over the magos, Ekodas walked to the view portal staring out into the void of space.

'I have a lock on it,' said Kol Harekh, finally.

'Well?' said Ekodas.

'The device is on the planet's surface.'

'Without the device, we are not going anywhere,' said Ekodas. 'Get a hold of Marduk. Perhaps it is time for him to prove himself useful.'

THE BRILLIANT LIGHT of the Nexus Arrangement reflected sharply off the metallic body-shell of the Undying One. The silver sphere spun impossibly fast, hovering steadily between the ancient being's elongated fingertips, which tapered to curving needle-like nails. It caressed the air around the device, fingers moving like the legs of some metallic arachnid, and it tilted its head to one side, as if captivated by the device.

For untold millennia, the Undying One had been trapped within the prison of its crypt. So long had it been confined that the heavens it now looked upon were strange and unfamiliar. A billion new suns had been born since the time of its imprisonment, and tens of thousands had burnt out, becoming lifeless, wasted husks or light-sucking black holes. Everywhere, it saw the taint of the Old Ones. Their engineered Young Races were spread across the universe in a verminous tide. Hatred, cold and ancient, burnt within its cavernous heart.

Now released, it would take up the old fight, and finish what had been started millions of years earlier.

With a slow, deliberate movement, the Undying One drew the Nexus Arrangement in towards its chest. The centre of the sun-disc emblazoned upon its breastplate sunk inwards, forming a half-moon depression, and the spinning device slotted neatly into place.

The Undying One's body was jolted with the force of the connection, its metal spine curving backwards violently, and its head thrown back. A patina of shimmering iridescence rippled across its metallic limbs, and a web of intricate, golden lines burning with hot light crept across its every surface, delicate labyrinthine veins forming shifting, geometric patterns across its living-metal skin.

The solid, silver orb embedded within its chest seemed to blur, its seamless surface melting and reforming to become a series of delicate rings arrayed around a miniature, green-hued sun. Those rings began to spin around each other, liquid metal rotating faster and faster.

The glowing sun at its centre seemed to swell, spilling light outwards in a blinding wave, and as the Undying One threw out its hands, the Nexus Arrangement began to operate as its creator had intended... and a psychic black hole was torn open.

ACROSS THE CONTINENTS of Boros Prime, unaugmented men and Astartes reeled as the effects of the Nexus Arrangement washed over them. Many of them fell to their knees, gasping, as a terrible, aching pain clutched at the very fibres of their being. It felt as though their souls were being wrenched from their bodies and cast into the abyss, leaving them empty and hollow, mere shells.

A terrible, all-pervading pall of utter futility descended upon Boros Prime, affecting even the most fervent and strong-willed individuals. Millions of soldiers and civilians simply gave up, their will to fight fading, their will to even *live* deserting them. Some, men who moments before had been fighting for their lives, dropped their weapons and sank to the ground, a fugue of hopelessness overcoming them. With haunted, unfocussed eyes they stared into the distance, oblivious or simply not caring about what was occurring around them. Others turned their weapons on themselves, unable to live with this gut-wrenching emptiness in their souls.

Tens of thousands were slaughtered by the merciless necron warriors marching steadily through the streets, gunning down every living creature that they encountered, whether they resisted or not. It was a harvest of sickening proportions. The streets were awash with blood, and mutilated corpses and severed limbs were scattered about like discarded toys.

Those with the strongest warp presence suffered the worst. Blood clots blossomed within the minds of Imperial astropaths and the sanctioned psykers attached to the command sections of the Boros Guard, and they collapsed to the ground, their bodies wracked with violent convulsions, screaming incoherently as their souls were torn from their fragile bodies.

'What in the Emperor's name has happened?' breathed Aquilius, clutching at a marble railing for balance.

Librarian Epistolary Liventius's eyes were clenched tightly shut, and his teeth were bared in a grimace of pain. A droplet of blood ran from his left nostril.

'My lord?' said Aquilius in concern. The Librarian was leaning heavily upon his force staff, and after a moment he opened his eyes. They were bloodshot and sunken. He placed a hand to his temple, a shadow passing across his face.

'My powers,' breathed the Librarian. 'They are gone.'

In orbit above Boros Prime, the *Infidus Diabolus* shuddered as if it had been struck with cyclonic torpedoes. It listed heavily to one side, its hull groaning in protest as the daemons that had infused its essence since before the outbreak of the Horus Heresy were banished. The strike cruiser's central processing cogitator units sputtered and died. Reliant on the daemon essences bound into its mainframe, the ship's thinking computers and hard-wired servitors were unable to function as the malicious spirits were driven out. The ship threatened to come apart at the seams, so intrinsic was the warp to its very existence.

Marduk dropped to his knees, a terrible empty pain clutching at his hearts as he felt his connection to the warp stripped away.

Aboard the *Crucius Maledictus*, the corrupted magos, Darioq-Grendh'al, seemed to shrink, his fleshy, daemonic appendages withering and beginning to rot at an accelerated rate as the daemon within him was sent screaming back to its plane of origin. Cancers and tumours long kept at bay by the infernal spirit that had become a part of the tech-magos began to bloom, and his life-support system began to bleat plaintively.

Skinless kathartes daemons took flight, but they had barely stretched out their flayed-flesh wings before they blinked out of existence, dragged back to their own turbulent realm of Chaos.

Arachnid-legged daemon-engines fell lifelessly to the floor, rendered utterly inert, their hulls nothing more than empty shells, the daemons bound into their iron skins dragged into darkness by the power of the Nexus Arrangement.

There was not a warrior brother within any of the Word Bearers ships that did not suffer as the link between the material universe and the empyrean was severed. Isolated from their gods, they were utterly and terribly alone.

Marduk regained his balance, steadying himself. Pain throbbed through his mind, but he forcibly pushed it away. Twice before he had experienced this emptiness, this complete isolation from the blessed warp.

'The æther is being blocked,' growled First Acolyte Ashkanez, massaging his temples. 'We are cut off, adrift. It is… It is an abomination! Such a thing should not be.'

Burias was pale and drawn, and he stared at his shaking hands, the expression upon his face one of rising panic. Marduk could only imagine the horror of separation that the possessed warrior was experiencing.

Kol Badar was down on one knee, steadying himself with a hand to the floor. Never one to have been strongly attuned to the warp at the best of times, the Coryphaus was nonetheless shaken, his face waxy and an even more deathly shade than usual.

Marduk unsheathed his chainsword and studied it closely, turning it over in his hands. There was no familiar daemonic presence within the weapon; the daemon Borhg'ash was gone.

A blister light throbbed weakly on one of the few still functioning command consoles of the bridge. Kol Badar pushed himself to his feet and moved to it.

'A message from the *Crucius Maledictus*,' he said.

'And what does the Grand Apostle have to say?'

'Gods,' swore the Coryphaus. 'He has lost the device.'

'What?' said Marduk. 'How?'

'It does not say. He has identified its location, however. He is ordering us to retrieve it.'

'Of course,' he said. 'Where is it?'

'On the surface.'

Marduk scoffed, shaking his head.

'He wants us to go back and get it, cut off from the warp completely, as we are? It would be suicide.'

'It is suicide if we do not,' said Kol Badar.

'Explain yourself.'

'The *Crucius Maledictus* has us in her sight. The message says that it will fire unless an attempt is made with the next fifteen minutes.'

'He's bluffing. His systems will be offline, just as ours are.'

'Perhaps,' said Kol Badar.

'Gods!' swore Marduk. 'Fine. How do we do this?'

'The daemon-infused guidance systems of the Dreadclaws will be non-operational,' said Kol Badar, shaking his head. 'We cannot use them.'

'Damnation!' growled Marduk, seething. 'Assault shuttles, then.'

'Five Thunderhawks and three Stormbirds were destroyed attempting to get us *off*-world,' said Kol Badar. 'None of those that made it out are undamaged. It will be weeks before they are ready to be redeployed. It would be futile to launch an assault using them. We will be annihilated.'

'Then what do you propose, Coryphaus? Tell me! We must reclaim the device! Failure is not an option!'

The deck shook as the towering shape of the War-monger stepped forwards from the shadows.

'There is another way...' the ancient Dreadnought boomed.

WITHIN THE DARKENED expanse of the Temple of the Gloriatus, Aquilius and the handful of Sternguard veterans of 1st Company were fighting back to back, desperately seeking to keep the necrons at bay. They had abandoned their location atop the temple half an hour earlier, when they had seen the Thunderhawk that had been closing on their position blasted out of the sky. It had crashed into the city below in a blossoming explosion of fire, killing all the battle-brothers on board.

They fired their bolters in short, concentrated bursts to conserve ammunition, but all were running perilously low. The inhuman automatons came on relentlessly, their movements unhurried and in perfect unison. In the darkness of the temple, their soulless eyes glowed brightly, and the flickering energy of their infernal weapons was reflected upon their silver skeletons.

Aquilius held the scrimshawed pole of the unfurled Chapter banner tightly in his left hand. Only in death would he relinquish his hold on it, and even then, the enemy would be forced to pry his fingers open before he dropped the holy standard. The young Coadjutor felt both fierce pride and an awed humility even to be in the presence of the holy relic, let alone to be holding it aloft in battle.

Were the situation not so dire, he would have been overawed to be surrounded by such vaunted heroes as now fought at his side. He could not imagine a better death than to fall fighting alongside these 1st Company Veterans, and death seemed a certainty.

The huge, gold-plated doors of the Temple of the Gloriatus had been obliterated, exploding inwards as arcs of green energy struck them, and the ranks of the deathly xenos had marched inside. Their mere presence was an affront, and the White Consuls had met them with bolter and chainsword, yet they were but a handful, and arrayed against them was a numberless tide of evil.

The White Consuls had been pushed further and further back. They had chosen to make their stand upon the stairs of the central dais, and it was here that Aquilius had planted the Chapter banner, swearing that while he drew breath, it would not fall.

The temple was immense, the largest cathedral in the Boros system, and tens of thousands of men and women made the pilgrimage to its hallowed halls every month, many using their entire life savings to make the passage. The arched ceilings soared impossibly high overhead, before disappearing into darkness. Each of the four expansive wings of the cathedral had their own pulpits, chapels and choirs, but it was within the central nave that Aquilius and the battle-brothers of 1st Company now stood. The sound of the enemy's metal-boned feet upon the marble flooring echoed loudly through the cavernous temple.

Seven levels of tiered seating looked down upon them, and hundreds of low benches were arrayed upon the floor of the temple below the steps. All told, more than two hundred thousand worshippers could be accommodated comfortably within the temple walls. On holy days, a hundred times that number packed into Victory Square to hear the choirs of the Gloriatus and witness the sermons on flickering holo-screens. Now the floor was seething with deathly abominations, marching resolutely upon the White Consuls, death spitting from their ancient weapons.

'Out!' shouted one of the White Consuls as the chambers of his weapon emptied. The veteran battle-brother swung his ornate bolter over his shoulder and drew his power sword, itself a holy relic of the Chapter. Coruscating arcs of green energy took down two of the blue-helmeted veterans, stripping them to the bone.

Scores of the skeletal automatons were felled by the disciplined fire of the Sternguard, but more were advancing into the cathedral, their numbers beyond counting. The twisted wreckage of destroyed necrons was piled at the base of the broad stairs, which soon resembled an island amidst a sea of skeletal, metallic corpses.

The necrons were incredibly difficult to put down, each one soaking up enough fire to drop an Astartes before their implacable advance was halted. Even then, many simply rose back to their feet moments later, all evidence of the damage they had sustained gone.

Aquilius saw one of the necron warriors stoop and pick up its own arm, which had been blown off with a melta gun blast. Sparks spat from the robotic xenos's shattered shoulder, but as the severed limb was placed back against the joint the sparks stopped. Metal ran like quicksilver as the joint reformed. Within the space of a heartbeat the limb was reattached, and the necron continued its relentless advance, climbing the stairs towards them.

The front ranks of the enemy were only metres away now, each heavy step bringing them ever closer.

Apart from the echoing stamp of their metal feet striking the marble in perfect unison and the crackling discharge of their weapons, the necrons made no other sound as they advanced. The lack of battle cries, the absence of screams of pain and cries of victory was, to Aquilius's way of thinking, more ominous and unnerving even than the frenzied ranting of the traitor Word Bearers.

Step by step, the necrons closed the distance, until they reached the cluster of White Consuls at the feet of the golden statue of the God-Emperor. They hefted their weapons over their heads, intent on bringing them crashing down upon the blue helms of the Astartes. Aquilius saw that curving axe-blades of alien design jutted from beneath their deadly guns, and while the xenos were neither particularly swift nor skilled, they wielded them with deadly intent, their blows heavy and powerful.

Power swords hummed as they carved through skulls and alien ribcages, melting easily through living metal. Chainswords tore chunks out of skeletal limbs, and bolters fired at point-blank range sent obliterated necrons tumbling back down the stairs into their comrades.

Aquilius fired his bolt pistol, blowing out the back of the skull of one enemy before switching targets and gunning down another necron with a burst of fire. The mass reactive explosive rounds detonated within the xenos's skeletal chest, ripping it apart. It fell without a sound but was replaced by another, stepping mechanically forward to take its place.

The ammunition counter on the back of his pistol was counting down steadily, and he was on his last sickle-clip. His last few shots were measured and deliberate, careful to ensure that every last bolt took down an enemy. With his final bolt, he gunned down a necron as it hefted its heavy weapon back over its head to strike him down. The shot struck it in one of its baleful, glowing eyes, and its head was split in two as it exploded, the ruin of its skull hanging from its spinal column. Still, it did not fall.

Aquilius gave a grunt of frustration as the two halves of the necron's skull came back together, the damage self-repairing seamlessly. Tossing aside his bolt pistol, the Coadjutor grasped the pole of the Chapter banner in both hands, wielding it like a spear. The base of the pole was spiked, and with a grunt of effort, he drove it into the necron's chest, smashing it backwards.

Something clutched at Aquilius's leg, and he looked down into the inhuman, emotionless face of a necron. Its slender, skeletal hands scrabbled at his armour, seeking purchase. The wretched thing was missing its entire lower body and had only one arm, but its eyes still burnt with cold, alien fury. Even rent limb from limb, the inhuman imperative to kill drove the creature on. The Coadjutor kicked it away from him in disgust, and drew his chainsword.

Looking out across the nave, Aquilius saw a sea of glowing witchfire eyes in the gloom, closing in around them inexorably. There seemed to be thousands of the alien warrior-constructs closing in around them, far too many for them to have any hope of survival.

It would only be minutes at best before it was over, Aquilius realised.

As if to emphasise the hopelessness of the situation, the Coadjutor heard a gasp of pain and, as he kicked the body of a necron off the wildly revving blade of his chainsword, he glanced over his shoulder to see Librarian Epistolary Liventius fall to his knees, blood pumping from his chest. A gaping hole ran completely through the aged Librarian, and a necron warrior stood over him, its weapon raised. Aquilius cried out and tried to turn, to interpose himself between them, but he was too slow.

With a devastating force, the necron warrior brought the heavy axe-blade of its weapon down upon the Librarian's skull with a sickening, wet crack. The dark blade was embedded down to the teeth, and while the automaton struggled to pull it free, Aquilius stepped forward and smashed his chainsword across its face. It reeled backwards, but the damage had been done, and Liventius fell face forwards to the ground, the weapon that had slain him still embedded in his head.

There were only four White Consuls left alive now. So many of his brothers had died, so many warriors that were far more important than he – Chapter Master Valens, Librarian Epistolary Liventius, Captain Decimus, Proconsul Ostorius. It seemed perverse that such mighty warriors had been slain while he yet lived.

Aquilius gritted his teeth. If he were to die this day, and it seemed a certainty that such would be his fate, he swore that he would take as many of the enemy down with him as he could. He swore that he would make his ancestors proud.

'For the Emperor!' he roared, before hurling himself into the fray.

\* \* \*

THE UNDYING ONE's head snapped around sharply. The baleful pinpricks of its soulless eyes glowed brightly, and they roamed across the square, searching. Hovering a metre above the ground, the ancient being rotated smoothly on the spot, head turning to and fro as it sought the origin of the energy build-up that it detected nearby.

With an elegant movement it extended one of its slender limbs, and a cloud of tiny scarabs burst from the darkness beneath its shroud. The tiny, robotic insects flew up to the Undying One's hand as its long, needle-like fingers unfurled. They began to latch onto each other, each scarab grasping its neighbour with barbed leg and mandible. The tiny creatures locked into place and become motionless, forming a two-metre-long staff. Its shape completed, the scarabs melted together to create a smooth, seamless implement. At either end of the weapon, green light flared, creating a pair of energy blades that crackled with barely contained potency.

With a grace far beyond that of its servants, the Undying One swung the twin-bladed staff around it in a glittering arc and waited for its enemy to appear.

Responding to the unspoken orders of their master, the Undying One's bodyguard stood to attention, energy surging through their long-bladed warscythes.

SURROUNDED ON ALL sides by endless phalanxes of motionless necron warriors, a shimmering light began to materialise within the centre of the square, swiftly followed by a hundred others. They gleamed and flickered, like dense clusters of fireflies, and within a fraction of a second they began to solidify into ghostly figures. With a sharp crack of displacing air, a hundred Terminator-armoured warriors of the cult Anointed teleported in from the *Infidus Diabolus*.

The immense shape of the Warmonger appeared amongst them, the immense killing machine one of the few remaining Dreadnoughts capable of such deployment. At the Word Bearer's fore materialised the Host's war leader and Coryphaus, Kol Badar, Dark Apostle Marduk at his side.

The Dark Apostle was encased within an ancient suit of Terminator armour, its deep red plates lustrous and gleaming. The armour was edged with barbed dark metal, and thousands of holy passages from the *Book of Lorgar* had been painstakingly engraved across its plates in tiny Colchisite cuneiform script. His own matted fur cloak was thrown over the immense shoulders of his new armour, and in his right hand he held his staff of office, his deadly crozius arcanum, its bladed tip crackling with energy. In his left he held an archaic, daemon-mawed combi-bolter, a weapon last wielded by the Warmonger himself during the battle for the Emperor's Palace on Terra.

The Terminator armour had not been worn for over nine thousand years, not since the Warmonger – then the 34th Host's Dark Apostle – was fatally wounded and had been peeled from it before being interred within his eternal sarcophagus prison. The revered suit of armour had been dutifully repaired, yet no one had ever been bold enough to have donned it since. For millennia it had remained dormant, empty and unused, locked away in the sepulchre of the great hero. Now, at the urging of the

Warmonger, it tasted battle once more. Within his skull-faced helm, Marduk grinned savagely, rejoicing in the feeling of power that the suit conveyed. He felt like a god.

His eyes fell upon the Undying One, less than one hundred metres distant. He had faced the creature once before, and recognised it instantly. Even from this distance, he could make out the spinning orb of the Nexus Arrangement set into its chest plate.

'There!' roared Marduk, levelling his crozius in the direction of the enemy xenos lord.

'Target acquired,' confirmed Kol Badar, his combi-bolter roaring in his hand. 'Come, my Anointed brothers! Kill for the living, kill for the dead!'

More than three hundred necron warriors separated the Terminators and the Dreadnought from their target. Thousands more surrounded them. As if being suddenly awoken from their slumber, the necrons turned as one to face the Anointed, and in an instant, battle was joined.

'Death to the betrayer of the crusade!' boomed the Warmonger, reliving once more battle of days past.

Kol Badar snarled as he gunned down necrons, ripping dozens of them to pieces with each concentrated burst of fire.

'Close formation! Keep moving!' he bellowed. Deeper into the enemy formation the Anointed strode, destroying dozens of the xenos machines for each step of ground they gained.

Hot blood pumped through Kol Badar's veins, his twin hearts hammering in his chest. He closed his power talons around one of the necron's heads, and with a savage twisting motion ripped it clear. He backhanded another of the xenos automatons, smashing it heavily to the ground. As it struggled to rise, he placed the twin barrels of his combi-bolter against its head and squeezed the trigger.

One of the necrons was lifted off its feet as an Anointed warrior rammed his chainfist into the hapless robotic being's chest, sending shards of metal spitting out in all directions before it was torn in two. Another was liquefied as combi-melta fire turned its body molten.

Half a dozen of the Anointed were down, felled by the brutally effective gauss weapon fire of the necrons. None of their brethren made any move to aid them. Kol Badar saw more of his battle-brothers, warriors he had fought alongside through countless campaigns spanning the galaxy, fall under the devastating weapons of the necrons. It was horrifyingly effective, even Terminator armour proving to be little protection against their touch. Under each searing volley of crackling energy, armour was stripped away layer by layer, until pallid flesh was exposed and stripped to the bone; a fraction of a second later, and bone too was torn apart at a sub-atomic level.

A beam of energy sliced across his shoulder, cleaving through his armour plating. Kol Badar turned and gunned down his attacker, driving it backwards, only for it to be finished by one of his brethren, who smashed its head from its shoulders with a blow of a power maul.

The Warmonger barrelled through the orderly ranks of the enemy, smashing dozens of the skeletal warriors aside with each sweep of its massive talons. Dozens more were ripped apart as the Warmonger's heavy bolters tore a swathe through their ranks.

Emotionless and seemingly oblivious to the danger they faced, more necrons moved forward to fill the gaps left by their fallen comrades, stepping into the path of the rampaging Dreadnought. Arcing green beams stabbed at the Warmonger's armoured hull, ripping gaping holes in his carapace that exposed the Dreadnought's inner workings, but it was not slowed.

A necron warrior before Kol Badar raised its weapon over its head, bringing the axe-head underslung beneath its barrel down towards his shoulder. The Coryphaus caught the blow in his power talons. He clenched his hand into a fist and the weapon crumpled, ghostly green energy leaping in all direction. He smashed the necron across the side of the head with the barrel of his combi-bolter with a sharp, metallic clang, and then stabbed his bladed talons into its chest.

Crackling with energy, his fingertips passed through the gaps of the necron's ribcage, and with a flick of his hand he sent the corpse-machine flying.

Death was assured. There was virtually no chance that any of them would make it out alive.

Kol Badar began to laugh. He had not felt this alive in centuries.

MARDUK SMASHED HIS crozius into the head of a necron, exposing sparking wiring and circuitry as it was sundered by the force of the blow. As the robotic corpse collapsed to the ground, a space was momentarily cleared before him, affording him a glimpse towards his target.

The ancient being of living metal was gliding smoothly towards him and the Anointed and Marduk saw that there was only a thin line of enemy constructs that separated him from his immortal foe.

The warriors that marched before the Undying One were unlike any that he had faced thus far. Their bodies seemed to be an armoured mockery of the living, rather than reflections of death as were the other necrons. They moved differently as well, their movements smooth and natural, more like those a living foe, rather than the stilted movements of the lesser warriors. They were tall and slender, easily matching the height of the Terminator-armoured Anointed, though they were a fraction of their bulk, and in their hands they wielded halberd-like warscythes, their blades flickering with green energy.

The Anointed and the elite bodyguard of the Undying One came together with a crash, energised warscythes meeting power mauls and chainfists. The enemy moved with supple grace, their weapons leaving gleaming contrails in their wake as they were whipped around in blinding arcs.

Those weapons proved utterly deadly, shearing through Terminator armour with ease. Marduk glimpsed one of the Anointed raising a barbed power sword to parry a blow scything in towards its neck, only to see the blade of the power sword neatly sheared away. The energised necron weapon continued on into the body of the veteran Word Bearer, slicing him open from neck to sternum.

Having witnessed the shocking power of the warscythes, Marduk swayed backwards out of the way of a hissing blade rather than attempt to block it. His movement was slowed by the sheer bulk of his newly donned Terminator armour, though not as much as he had initially expected.

Marduk turned aside the next blow aimed at him, careful only to allow his crozius to touch the metal haft of the warscythe rather than its energised blade. His return blow all but tore the necron's head from its shoulders, and the Dark Apostle grinned savagely. What he had lost in speed was more than made up for by the boost in sheer brute strength that the tightly bound servo-muscles of his Terminator armour gifted him.

Battering another enemy aside, his combi-bolter scoring deep wounds across its armoured chest, Marduk surged forward, desperate to close the distance with the Undying One.

The dull ache in his chest, the pain of separation from the warp, seemed all the worse in close proximity to these deadly warriors. He wanted to end this battle swiftly. He did not know how long he could endure the gaping void that seemed to fill him.

The Undying One glided smoothly into the brutal melee, double-bladed staff spinning in its hands. With consummate ease, two of the Anointed were instantly cut down. Both of the warriors were sliced neatly in two with a contemptuous lack of effort. The spinning Nexus Arrangement embedded in the ancient being's chest spilt its ethereal light before it, taunting Marduk.

Another Anointed warrior was slain, the Undying One's bladed staff slicing neatly from shoulder to hip, and the two parts of the warrior slid to the ground. The necron lord spun the staff around in a blinding arc, levelling one of its tips at another Chaos Terminator, and a searing blast of energy slammed into the unfortunate warrior. The Anointed warrior reeled backwards, a head-sized hole punched clear through his chest.

Marduk snarled and launched himself forward, coming at the Undying One from the side. He saw the hulking form of Kol Badar moving to attack the ancient being from its other flank, combi-bolter roaring in his hand, and he felt a surge of rage at the thought of his Coryphaus stealing his kill.

The Undying One's head was turned away from him, focussed on Kol Badar. He stepped in close, lifting his crozius arcanum with all his might, aiming his strike at the fell being's delicate-looking, slender skull. The blow never landed, for without so much as turning its head, the necron lord parried the blow with one of the energy-bladed tips of its staff, even as the other blade sliced across Kol Badar's torso, almost eviscerating him.

Turning with a deceptively languid, smooth movement, still hovering a metre above the ground, the Undying One fended off the attacks of both Marduk and Kol Badar with ease. A third warrior entered the fray, power maul striking out. The Anointed brother was instantly slain, an energy blade plunged through his head.

Blood welling from the deep wound slashed across his torso, Kol Badar lifted his combi-bolter, spraying bolts from its twin-barrels. The Undying One's shroud billowed out around it as it turned, and a dense cloud of scarabs was unleashed upon the Coryphaus, biting and clawing at him. Though the miniscule, robotic insects could do little real damage to him, encased as he was within his Terminator armour, they soaked up the fury of his weapon fire, the bolts detonating well before striking their intended target.

Marduk aimed another strike at his enemy. But again the double-bladed staff came around in a blinding arc, turning his weapon aside. Marduk had prepared for this reaction, and swiftly altered his angle of attack, but this too was blocked, a deft circular parry disarming him neatly, sending his crozius arcanum spinning away, landing several metres away.

Still turning, the Undying One cut another Anointed brother in two as he stepped forward to attack the ancient being, before neatly ramming one of the energy-blades straight through Kol Badar, impaling him on its length.

Marduk lifted his combi-bolter towards his enemy, squeezing the trigger. Before the first bolt was launched from the chamber, the Undying One slid its blade clear of Kol Badar and swung it around. Marduk was knocked back a step, and it was only when he saw blood spraying out in a geyser that he realised something was wrong.

The pain kicked in a heartbeat later, and the Dark Apostle gazed down in disbelief at his severed arm lying on the ground. His combi-bolter was still clutched in his hand.

On the other side of the Undying One, Kol Badar dropped to one knee, blood pumping from his chest wound. The ancient being twirled its staff around in a deft display of skill. A ring of bodies surrounded it.

Necrons closed in on all sides, gauss flayers spitting death, and Marduk, refusing to accept defeat, felt his anger build.

'Face me, betrayer!' came a booming cry and the immense figure of the Warmonger burst through a cluster of necrons, smashing them out of its path with a sweep of one massive, mechanised arm. Heavy bolters spewed a torrent of fire before it as it charged.

\* \* \*

THE WARMONGER'S VOICE was hoarse from leading the Host in their battle psalms, yet it still carried great power and authority. His eyes were locked on the hated figure of his foe, bedecked in fluted, golden armour.

His crozius dripped blood from its barbed tips, and his armour was pitted with battle damage. He was exhausted, for this battle had been raging for weeks. He could not recall when he had last rested. But none of that mattered, not now that the being that was the focus of all his hatred and bitterness was within his reach.

The bodies of his defeated foes lay strewn about him, their yellow armour splattered with blood. None of them stood in his way now.

As far as the eye could see, the battle raged on, brother fighting brother. It was glorious, and yet it filled him with a deep burning hatred for the one who had, in his arrogance, been the cause of it all.

He licked his blood-flecked lips and clenched his hand tightly around the haft of his crozius as he looked upon the one whose hands were stained with the blood of every noble brother Astartes that had fallen.

Once he had called this man Emperor. Once he had even worshipped him. He spat, as if his mouth were suddenly filled with a vile poison.

Liar. Betrayer of the Crusade. Betrayer of the War-master.

He had deceived them all.

'Now, it is over,' he said. 'Your lies shall lead no more brother Astartes to their deaths, false one.'

And on the walls of the largest palace ever constructed, he hurled himself at his mortal enemy,

determined to be the one that killed the False
Emperor.

'Now, IT IS over,' the Warmonger boomed. 'Your lies
shall lead no more brother Astartes to their deaths,
false one.'

The Undying One turned smoothly to face the
Dreadnought rampaging towards it, and with inhuman speed and suppleness, it contorted its body like
a dancer's. Bolts sprayed around it, tearing holes
through its billowing shroud, but failing to strike its
body.

On the Warmonger came, roaring incoherently as it
pounded forward, a ten-tonne behemoth of metal
and brutality.

The Undying One ducked neatly beneath the
Dreadnought's swinging talons, its double-bladed
staff slicing out, striking across the Warmonger's
armoured chassis amid an explosion of sparks and
the agonising scream of rending metal.

The Warmonger struggled to arrest its forward
momentum, which took it past the Undying One.
The Dreadnought's damaged chassis was rotating
before it had yet ground to a halt, dragging its heavy
bolters around. The heavy weapons roared, belching
an impenetrable curtain of high-calibre shells around
in a wide arc, chasing its elusive foe. The Undying
One was too swift, always a fraction of a second in
front of the devastating salvo.

Hefting its double-bladed staff like a spear, the
Undying One glided forward, heavy bolter rounds
ripping at its shadow-cloak. With inhuman strength
and speed, the Undying One rammed its weapon into
the heart of the Dreadnought's chassis. The glowing

energy blade slid effortlessly through the Warmonger's thick armour plates, impaling it.

Marduk roared in outrage and denial but was helpless as the Undying One ripped the glowing energy blade free, tearing it out sideways in a disembowelling stroke that ripped open the Dreadnought's sarcophagus. Stinking amniotic fluids gushed from this fatal wound, and Marduk caught a glimpse of the Warmonger's corpse within, shrunken, pallid and foetal.

It was hard to believe that once this had been one of the Legion's proudest warriors, a Dark Apostle no less. It now looked like an exhumed cadaver, a half-rotten corpse cruelly kept lingering in some horrific unlife. Wires, cables and tubes connected this lifeless, drowned thing to the Dreadnought's nervous system. It was only this spider web tangle that kept it from flopping out onto the ground. It was little more than a wasted torso, upon which a skeletal head hung loosely.

Most of its skull was gone, either from the extent of the injuries that had seen it interred or surgically removed, and the exposed brain matter – a horrible colour, like rotten fruit – was pierced with dozens of needle-tipped wires. It was missing its lower jaw. Only its visible fused ribcage and the gigantism of its skeleton revealed that this had once been a proud Astartes warrior.

The Warmonger's mechanised Dreadnought body shuddered and twitched, sparks bursting from damaged wiring and cabling.

Marduk hooked his sacred crozius at his waist and dropped to one knee, prying the archaic combi-bolter from his own dead hand. He fired at the back of the Undying One's head as he rose, snarling in hatred.

Displaying unnatural prescience, the Undying One swayed aside from the burst of bolter fire, twirling its energy scythe around its hands as it turned.

It was unable to avoid the Warmonger, however.

The Dreadnought was not yet finished and as the Undying One turned away, the Warmonger lashed out, clamping its immense power talons around the body of its adversary. The necron lord struggled, its double-bladed staff flailing, but it could not escape. It was completely enclosed within the Warmonger's grasp.

'Death to the False Emperor!' the Dreadnought roared, clenching its fist.

The Undying One's humanoid form splintered, exploding into a million scarabs. In the centre of the buzzing cloud of metallic insects hovered the Nexus Arrangement.

Sparks and sickly black smoke rose from the Warmonger as the Dreadnought twitched spasmodically. The Undying One's bodyguard stepped forward, warscythes flashing as they tore into the Warmonger's armoured flanks.

Marduk roared in anger, stamping forwards, combibolter roaring in his hand. Kol Badar smashed a pair of Immortals and stepped into the midst of the scarab swarm, swatting at the robotic insects.

He only registered the Coryphaus when his power talons closed around the Nexus Arrangement, plucking it out of the air. As the hulking warlord's bladed fingers closed around the spinning orb the device once more took on its prior form, that of an inert, solid sphere.

Reality shuddered, and Marduk gasped as he felt the blessed touch of the æther crash in upon him once more. The Dark Apostle whispered a prayer of thanks to the gods that he sensed around him.

Kol Badar held the Nexus Arrangement within his power talons, gunning down a pair of necrons with his combi-bolter. The blood around the hole in his chest was already scabbed and dry, the Larraman cells in his bloodstream having sealed the wound.

The angry buzzing of the scarab cloud became more insistent, and Marduk saw it begin to coalesce into a tight, dense swarm once more, forming the unmistakeable outline of the Undying One.

'We need to leave. Now,' said Marduk, firing his combi-bolter on full auto, blasting holes in the reforming necron lord. Even as he did so, he knew it was futile – the Undying One was reforming, and no matter what he did, nothing would halt its progress.

'Ashkanez,' said Kol Badar. 'Initiate teleport return. Now!'

'Do it,' said First Acolyte Ashkanez, nodding his head towards Burias. All around them, the ship was repowering, coming back to unholy life as the daemons that had for so long been infused with it returned.

'Why not just leave them?' growled the hulking figure of the champion Khalaxis. 'Let the xenos finish this for us?'

Burias's hand hovered over the activation rune upon the teleporter's control panel, waiting for the First Acolyte's response.

'Don't be a fool,' snapped Ashkanez. 'They have the device. And besides, the Anointed are ours. Do it.'

Burias slammed his fist down onto the glowing rune.

\* \* \*

LIKE DROPLETS OF molten metal coming together, a million tiny scarabs gave up their individual form as they combined, until once more the Undying One hovered in the air before Marduk, gleaming, untarnished, perfect. Pinpricks of light began to glow malevolently within darkened eye sockets. The necron lord turned its head from side to side, as if stretching its neck, before its inscrutable gaze locked onto Marduk. The air shimmered as the immortal being spun its deadly, twin-bladed staff, and it began to glide towards the Dark Apostle.

'Any time now, Ashkanez,' hissed Marduk, backing away, still firing with his archaic combi-bolter. His twin-sickle clip ran dry and he holstered the revered old weapon, drawing his crozius once more.

Then there was a sudden feeling of vertigo, and a bright light obscured his vision.

When it cleared, Marduk was standing upon a dimly lit sub deck of the *Infidus Diabolus*, staring down the barrel of a melta gun.

'Welcome back, Apostle,' growled First Acolyte Ashkanez.

# CHAPTER SEVENTEEN

First Acolyte Ashkanez stood five metres away, the melta gun in his hands levelled squarely at Marduk. The weapon was designed as an anti-tank weapon. At such range, even Terminator armour would offer little protection.

Without making any threatening or sudden move, Marduk turned his head to glance around him, careful to keep the First Acolyte within his frame of vision. Kol Badar stood at his shoulder, but of the other brethren of the Anointed there was no sign. The five of them were alone.

'You *dare* draw a weapon against your Dark Apostle?' snarled Marduk, his voice quivering with barely contained fury. 'What is this?'

'This is your hour of judgement, Apostle,' replied Ashkanez.

The First Acolyte's face was hidden in the shadow of his hood. In the gloom behind Ashkanez stood Burias and Khalaxis. Both were hooded, but easily recognisable.

'*You* seek to pass judgement upon *me*? You arrogant whoreson. Look at you,' said Marduk, his voice thick with scorn, 'unwilling even to show your faces. You are cowards, worthless cowards who bring nothing but shame upon XVII Legion.'

The towering form of Khalaxis stiffened, his hands clenching tightly around the haft of his huge chainaxe. Burias pulled away his hood angrily.

'You brought this upon yourself, *master*,' the Icon Bearer snarled.

'You have always been a treacherous dog, Burias,' retorted Marduk. 'I should have put you down long ago.'

'Enough,' growled Ashkanez. 'Where is the device?'

'I have it,' said Kol Badar.

'Good,' said Ashkanez. 'Remove your helmet, Apostle. I want to see your eyes as you die.'

Marduk glanced down at the stump of his left arm, then at his sacred crozius still clasped in his right hand, then back up at Ashkanez.

'I might need a little help. Would you care to step closer and take my crozius from me, Acolyte?' he said. 'It is clear that you intend to claim it anyway, why not now?'

'I think not,' said Ashkanez, clearly having no intention on closing the distance between himself and the huge figure of the Dark Apostle, ensconced in the Warmonger's ancient Terminator armour.

'Coward,' mocked Marduk.

'Prudent,' corrected Ashkanez. 'Your helmet, Apostle.'

Marduk hooked his crozius onto his barbed chain belt and reached up to remove his skull-faced helmet. It came loose with a hiss of pressurised air. The malignant red glow of his helmet's lenses faded as he hooked his helm at his waist. The Dark Apostle's eyes simmered with hatred.

'Happy?' he snarled.

The First Acolyte nodded.

'Where are my Anointed brothers?' growled Kol Badar.

'Does their blood stain your hands as well, Acolyte?' said Marduk.

'Their deaths would serve no purpose. They have been teleported back safely,' said Ashkanez. 'I did not feel it necessary for them to witness any of this.'

Marduk licked his lips, and glanced between the three warriors ranged against him.

Ashkanez still had the melta gun levelled squarely at Marduk.

'You rate yourself rather highly, First Acolyte,' he said. 'Do you really think that the three of you can take us both?'

'No,' said Ashkanez. 'I do not.'

Marduk opened his mouth to speak, then shut it as Kol Badar stepped away from him.

'You bastard,' he snarled as the Coryphaus bowed his head in deference to the First Acolyte. His eyes were murderous as he watched Kol Badar take a position alongside the others, a step behind the treacherous First Acolyte.

'This day has been a long time coming, Marduk,' said Kol Badar.

'They have all turned against you, Apostle,' said Ashkanez, unable to keep the smirk from his voice. 'All your most trusted captains.'

'Not all. Sabtec would never turn,' said Marduk.

'True,' said Ashkanez. 'I believe the fool would maintain his deluded loyalty to you to the end. A shame. He is a fine warrior. But in this war, sacrifices must be made. He will die soon enough. You are all alone, Apostle.'

'No,' said Marduk. 'The gods of Chaos are with me. And hell's torments shall be as paradise to the pains that I shall unleash upon you. I'll see you all burn for this outrage.'

'No,' said Ashkanez, 'you won't.'

'You are a traitor and a whoreson, Ashkanez. How long will it be before he turns on you, Burias? Or you, Khalaxis?' said Marduk. 'Once he has control over the Host, your usefulness will be over.'

'I've heard enough,' growled Khalaxis. 'Let's kill him now and finish this.'

'The Council will see through this petty mutiny,' said Marduk. 'They will never endorse you as Dark Apostle of the Host, Ashkanez.'

'Traitors?' said Ashkanez. 'No, you are mistaken, Apostle. We are not traitors; we represent the future. The Legion has stagnated under the Council's rulership, its ideals have corrupted. Only a fool could fail to see how Erebus has twisted the Legion's ideals to his own end, corrupting the Council to his will. We represent a new order, one that will cast down Erebus's grip upon the Council.'

'Ekodas has been filling your head with lies,' said Marduk. 'His little uprising will go nowhere. You will be hunted down like the traitorous dogs you are.'

'You are wrong, Marduk. This is no petty uprising. We are the Brotherhood. The time of the Third Cleansing draws in.'

'The Brotherhood?' said Marduk, in surprise. 'The Brotherhood is a relic of the past. It died out ten millennia ago.'

'And now it is reborn, under a new High Priest.'

Marduk laughed.

'You are more deluded that I had thought,' he said. 'Ekodas thinks he can rebuild the Brotherhood in some petty grab for power? Does he truly think he could ever pose any sort of risk to the Council? That he could ever be a threat to Erebus and Kor Phaeron?'

'It is you who is deluded,' said Ashkanez, grinning. 'This goes far beyond Ekodas.'

'I find that hard to believe.'

'That is of no consequence to me. But before you die, know that the Keeper of the Faith, Kor Phaeron himself, is the one that has raised the Brotherhood once more.'

'Impossible,' hissed Marduk, though his blood ran cold at his First Acoylte's words.

'More than twenty Hosts have sworn their allegiance to the Brotherhood,' said Ashkanez. 'Dozens more will join before Erebus has any idea of the danger he is in.'

'It will never work,' said Marduk.

'Erebus's perversion of the Council draws to an end. Under Kor Phaeron's leadership, the Legion shall be guided back to Lorgar's true teachings.'

'The Keeper of the Faith would drag the Legion into civil war?' said Marduk. 'He would cause a schism within our ranks merely to overthrow his brother? Such a path is madness!'

Ashkanez smiled.

'Too long has Erebus manipulated our Legion from the shadows. His time has come to an end.'

'Enough of your poison, traitor,' snapped Marduk, lifting his head high. Without fear, he stared into Ashkanez's eyes. 'It is as Khalaxis says: it is time to finish this. Would you not agree, Kol Badar?'

'Yes,' said the hulking warlord, standing at Ashkanez's back. 'I would.'

Before anyone could react, the Coryphaus stepped forward and rammed the electrified lengths of his power talons into Ashkanez's back.

Ashkanez was lifted up into the air. The tips of Kol Badar's power talons burst from his chest, hot blood dancing off the blades. The melta gun in Ashkanez's hand fired, and Marduk hurled himself to the side to avoid its searing blast. Curse papers affixed to his shoulder plate burst into flame as the shot glanced him, melting a furrow across his armour as if it were butter.

Dark energy flickered across the barbed spikes at the head of Marduk's holy crozius as his hand closed around its hilt, thumbing its activation rune.

Burias was the first of Ashkanez's conspirators to react. The change came over him instantly, his features blurring with those of the daemon within. With a dismissive flick, Kol Badar sent Ashkanez crashing into the Icon Bearer, momentarily taking him out of the fight. The melta gun in the First Acolyte's hand went flying.

The dimly lit chamber suddenly resounded with the deafening roar of Khalaxis's chainaxe. The towering champion launched himself at Marduk, his face twisted in berserk fury.

Marduk met the murderous, double-handed blow with one of his own, dark crozius and chainaxe coming together with awesome force. Marduk's strength was augmented by the tightly knit servo-bundles of his newly donned Terminator armour, yet even so his arm was forced back as Khalaxis exerted his strength. The teeth of the chainaxe tore at the crozius, and sparks flew.

Khalaxis's face was close to Marduk's, flushed with hatred and battle fury. His teeth were bared.

'I'm going to rip you apart, *master*,' growled the towering, dreadlocked aspiring champion, spittle and foam glistening at the edges of his mouth.

'In your dreams,' spat Marduk, stepping forward and slamming his forehead into Khalaxis's face, breaking his nose with a sharp crack and splatter of blood.

The berserker snarled in fury and reeled backwards, letting go of the haft of his axe with one hand. Marduk stepped forward to crush his skull, but walked straight into a thundering backhand. Khalaxis's spiked gauntlet hammered into the side of his face, snapping his head around, and he tasted blood in his mouth.

Stepping backwards, Marduk brought his crozius up instinctively, blocking the madly whirring chainaxe slashing towards his neck. With impressive speed, Khalaxis turned, spinning on his heel and bringing the axe cutting around to strike from a different angle. Still recovering from the previous blow, Marduk had no hope of getting his weapon in the path of the new attack, and so turned his shoulder into the chainaxe. It hacked deep into his armour plating, ripping and tearing furiously, but did not penetrate to the skin.

Marduk slammed his crozius into Khalaxis's side, the bladed points punching through his armour with a sharp discharge of energy that hurled him backwards. The stink of burnt flesh rose from the wound, but the champion leapt forwards once more, pain merely adding fuel to his rage.

As the chainaxe roared, scything through the air towards Marduk, the Dark Apostle brought his crozius down hard, smashing it down onto one of Khalaxis's arms. Bone and armour were splintered, knocking his strike aside, and stepping back to give himself more space, Marduk swung his weapon around in a brutal arc that connected solidly with the side of Khalaxis's head.

The bladed spikes penetrated the champion's skull, which crumpled inwards as the heavy head of the mace slammed home. Blood splattered across Marduk's face and Khalaxis staggered drunkenly. He looked strange, his features caved inwards, like wax melting under a hot sun. The dreadlocked champion swayed on his feet for a second, then fell in a crumpled heap at Marduk's feet, dead.

Ashkanez's power maul smashed into Marduk from behind, battering him to his knees. A second blow, delivered with malice, crashed down onto his arm and he lost his grip on his sacred crozius. Moving faster than Marduk, bedecked as he was in hulking Terminator armour, the First Acolyte stepped swiftly forward and kicked the holy weapon across the floor.

Marduk regained his feet and rounded on Ashkanez, his expression furious.

'You don't know when to stay down, do you?' he hissed.

The First Acolyte's face was pale from blood loss, and red foam bubbled at the corners of his mouth. The four terrible bloody wounds in his chest were leaking his lifeblood, but they would close soon enough. Still, Marduk was surprised that the Icon Bearer was still alive, let alone fighting on.

With a roar, bloody spittle spraying from his mouth, the First Acolyte stepped forward and brought his power maul crashing down towards Marduk's crown.

The Dark Apostle caught the blow in his gauntleted hand, holding the crackling weapon at bay. Electricity ran up and down the length of his arm, but still he held on. The veins in the First Acolyte's neck bulged as he exerted all his considerable force to bring the maul down upon Marduk's, but his strength was fading, and they both knew it.

Marduk slammed a heavy kick into the side of one of Ashkanez's knees, snapping tendons and ligaments, and the First Acolyte fell to the ground, snarling in agony. The Dark Apostle stepped forward and kicked him hard in the side, lifting him off the floor. The First Acolyte crashed into a nearby control panel, which crumpled beneath his weight.

The melta gun that Ashkanez had been holding was lying on the ground nearby, and Marduk stooped to retrieve the deadly anti-tank weapon. Ashkanez pulled himself from the crumpled wreckage of the control panel, struggling to rise. His shattered knee would not support his weight, however, and he was forced to cling to the control panel merely to keep upright. Marduk grinned evilly as he hefted the melta gun one in his hand and stalked towards him. He came to a halt within a few steps of the First Acolyte.

'Whether I live or die, it won't affect the days to come,' Ashkanez snarled up at him, blood foaming from his lips. 'The Brotherhood is already moving. You cannot do anything to stop it.'

Marduk levelled the melta gun at Ashkanez's intact knee and squeezed the trigger. The heat from the weapon was staggering, making the air shimmer with haze. Marduk kept his finger depressed on the trigger for a good two seconds, cutting his First Acolyte's leg off neatly above the joint and searing the wound shut. Marduk chuckled in good humour.

Ashkanez refused to scream out, even as the searing blast turned his armour and flesh molten, his bones to ash. He collapsed, gritting his teeth in pain.

'With or without the 34th Host, the Brotherhood will cleanse the ranks of our Legion,' hissed Ashkanez from the deck floor. The stink of burnt flesh was heavy in the air. 'This changes nothing.'

Marduk snorted, and turned away to witness the outcome of the conflict between Burias and Kol Badar. Ever since Burias's rise to the station of Icon Bearer, so long ago, the pair had been needling each other. Now they let a millennia of hatred spill out.

Burias-Drak'shal was crouched on all fours, his shoulders and arms swollen out of proportion with his body. Ridged horns curved backwards from his forehead, and his needle-like teeth were bared in an animalistic snarl. His armour was hanging off him in bloody tatters. Deep gouges were carved across his chest, but even as Marduk watched, they began to heal, his flesh closing up as his warp-spawned flesh regenerated itself.

With a snarl, the Icon Bearer leapt sideways as Kol Badar brought his combi-bolter up, twin barrels roaring. Burias-Drak'shal leapt onto the nearby wall, his neck bent at an unnatural angle to keep his hellish, altered eyes locked on the Coryphaus. His claws had hardly touched the wall before he had sprung off again, leaping directly at the Coryphaus. Kol Badar tried to follow the possessed warrior's movement with his combi-bolter, tearing chunks out of the metal walls and smashing delicate display screens, but he was too slow.

The three middle fingers of each of Burias-Drak'shal's hands had fused into thick talons, and with his arms at full extension he struck the Coryphaus in his wounded chest, punching the daemonic claws deep. The force of his attack knocked Kol Badar back a step, but the Terminator-armoured warlord did not fall. Burias's clawed feet sank into Kol Badar's chest, and he squatted there like a hellish primate. With one clawed hand holding him in place, he punched several holes in the Coryphaus's chest with his free hand before Kol Badar sent him flying, swatting him off with a backhand blow of his power talons.

Burias-Drak'shal spun in the air then landed hard, snarling, his powerful leg muscles bunched beneath him. With an explosive movement, he sprang back at the Coryphaus, but Kol Badar's combi-bolter was raised, and he was slammed back down into the floor as a heavy burst of fire impacted with his chest and face.

Bloody craters were blown in his armour and flesh, exposing muscle and bone, and Burias-Drak'shal shook his head in anger and pain. Part of his jaw was ripped away, exposing shark-like teeth and glistening flesh. As he tried to rise to his feet, another burst of fire sent him reeling back again, mass reactive-tipped bolts ripping into him. The Coryphaus's weapon jammed suddenly, falling silent in his hands, smoke seeping from its twin barrels.

A vicious grin split Burias-Drak'shal's brutally damaged face, and his flesh began to reform. He spat a gobbet of flesh and blood to the ground as Kol Badar hurled aside his daemon-mawed combi-bolter in disgust.

'Now you're in some trouble,' said Burias-Drak'shal, forming the words with difficulty as thick tusks began to emerge from his lower jaw.

Kol Badar scoffed derisively. 'I've waited a long time for this,' he said, flexing his power talons.

Both warriors were bloody, their armour compromised in a dozen places, yet while Burias's wounds continued to heal even as he sustained them, the Coryphaus was starting to slow.

With a sigh, Marduk turned the melta gun in his hand on Burias-Drak'shal. Without ceremony, he fired a searing blast that hit the Icon Bearer in the lower back.

The shot melted through his plate armour and deep into his flesh. It knocked the Icon Bearer forwards a step, and off-balance, he stumbled straight into Kol Badar's power talons. The half-metre blades impaled Burias-Drak'shal through the throat. They sank in deep, almost to Kol Badar's fist, and their tips emerged from the back of his neck.

'Who's in trouble now?' snarled Kol Badar.

Blood bubbled up around the energised lengths of his talon, and Burias-Drak'shal stood there transfixed upon them. Kol Badar's combi-bolter barked deafeningly, and Burias-Drak'shal was hurled backwards, his chest cavity exploding from within.

'The Council *will* be overthrown,' gasped Ashkanez through clenched teeth, and Marduk turned to regard the pitiful creature once more. 'It is just a matter of time. Erebus will be brought to justice.'

'You fool,' said Marduk. 'Do you really think that Erebus could be so duped? He knows all about this pathetic uprising within our Legion's ranks. All he needed was for it to expose itself, and learn how deep it ran. All the Hosts will unite against the Keeper of the Faith once the full extent of his treachery is known.'

Ashkanez's eyes narrowed, and Marduk laughed.

'Did you never question why the Council appointed me to accompany this crusade? It was to draw out the serpents within the Legion, to bring their treachery to light. I knew what you were doing from the start.'

'You'll never get word back to Sicarus,' he said.

'Enough talk. I grow weary of your presence. Goodbye, First Acolyte.'

Marduk fired the meltagun, killing Ashkanez instantly. The stink of burnt flesh rose from his corpse.

KOL BADAR HAD Burias-Drak'shal pinned to the ground beneath one knee, and had encircled the Icon Bearer's skull with his power talons. With one squeeze, Burias would be no more – not even his prodigious regenerative qualities could save him from such an injury. As if knowing that its host body was about to perish, the daemon Drak'shal abandoned the Icon Bearer, and his flesh seemed to shrink as he took on his natural form. His injuries were many, and blood pooled beneath him. His chest was splayed open, and while his primary heart was nothing but a pulp, his secondary heart still beat weakly.

'You… you used me,' snarled Burias, looking up at Marduk. Blood was leaking from his swollen lips, and one of his eyes was filled with blood and rolling blindly in its socket. 'You knew about the Brotherhood all along.'

'I knew about the Brotherhood, yes,' said Marduk, kneeling down besides the broken Icon Bearer. 'But I did not drive you into its arms. You made your decision. Nevertheless, you have done me a great service, brother. For that, I thank you. You played your role to perfection.'

'I was your… blood-brother,' spat Burias. 'I would have followed you… anywhere.'

'But instead you chose to stand against me, all because you could not stand to accept your limitations,' said Marduk.

'Kill me then,' snarled Burias. 'Finish it.'

'Oh no, my dear Icon Bearer,' said Marduk, grinning evilly. 'Your pain is only just beginning. An eternity of suffering awaits you for this treachery, have no fear of that.'

Burias spat into Marduk's face, his eyes blazing.

Marduk smiled, wiping the bloody, stinging sputum from his cheek, and rose to his feet.

'You know, for a moment there,' he said to Kol Badar, 'I thought you were going to forget our little pact.'

'For a moment there, I almost did,' said Kol Badar, heaving himself to his full height with a groan.

For the first time, Marduk thought the warlord looked old. He kept Burias pinned to the ground beneath one heavy foot, but he needn't have bothered. The Icon Bearer was a broken figure, exposed and ruptured organs pulsing within his blasted chest cavity.

'What stopped you?' said Marduk.

'You are a devious whoreson, Dark Apostle,' said Kol Badar. 'And one day I *will* kill you.'

Marduk snorted.

'That does not answer my question.'

'Let me just say that I'd rather follow a devious bastard than a dog like *that*,' he said, gesturing towards the body of Ashkanez, sprawled upon the floor. 'At least *you* are of the 34th.'

'We must get word to Erebus of Kor Phaeron's place in this rebellion,' said Marduk. 'This runs deeper than even the First Chaplain could have expected. Contact the bridge. Ekodas will soon know that Ashkanez is dead. I want to put as much distance between us and the *Crucius Maledictus* as possible.'

'We will have a reckoning one day, you and I,' growled Kol Badar as he rose to his feet, dragging the broken body of Burias up with him. Hatred simmered in his eyes as he stared down at Marduk.

'We will,' said Marduk. 'And that will be an interesting day indeed.'

# CHAPTER EIGHTEEN

THE *Infidus Diabolus* ploughed through the vastness of space away from Boros Prime, plasma engines burning with hellish white-hot ferocity as every iota of power was eked out of them.

'We are being hailed,' said Sabtec. The champion was standing to the fore of the Chaos strike cruiser's darkly shadowed bridge. 'It is the *Crucius Maledictus*.'

'Bring it up on screen,' growled Marduk.

The glowering visage of Dark Apostle Ekodas appeared, filling the curved vid-screen. Intermittent static and blaring white noise interrupted the visual feed before it came into full focus.

'Apostle Marduk,' said Ekodas. He covered it well, but Marduk could tell that Ekodas was surprised to see him.

'You expected someone else, Apostle?' said Marduk, mildly.

'The retribution is not yet complete,' snarled the broad-faced Grand Apostle, ignoring Marduk's question. 'Our job is yet not done. Once we bring the xenos down, the pacification of the Boros Gate shall be re-commenced. Move the *Infidus Diabolus* back into formation, now, or I will not hesitate to target you.'

'It cannot be destroyed,' said Marduk. 'Stay and fight if you will. It will be the death of you all.'

'Coward!' hissed Ekodas. 'You would flee before foul xenos?'

Marduk cast his gaze towards the slowly spinning three-dimensional display showing the relative positions of the Chaos battlefleet. He paid particular attention to the blinking icon that represented the massive xenos vessel. For now, at least, it remained stationary. Already, the Chaos battleships had begun pummelling its sheer hide with torpedoes and ordnance, but they had thus far elicited no response; nor had they caused any noticeable effect.

Marduk returned his focus back onto the glowering face filling the vid-screen before him.

'It's over, Ekodas,' he snarled. 'The attack on Boros has failed. You have failed. And your worm, Ashkanez, has failed.'

Marduk lifted his First Acolyte's head aloft for Ekodas to see.

'Where do you think you can run, Marduk?' said Ekodas, his face looming threateningly upon the vid-screen. 'The wormholes remain inactive. This system is still cut-off. You cannot escape.'

'You and all of your conspirators will burn,' hissed Marduk. The Dark Apostle of the 34th could already feel Ekodas worming his way into his mind, breaking down his defences. 'Once the Council learns of your treachery, the Brotherhood will burn.'

'And how, may I ask, will the Council learn of its existence? From you? I think not.'

The psychic pressure that Ekodas exerted was building, and Marduk could feel dark tendrils plundering the depths of his mind, writhing like razor-worms.

'Enough,' said Marduk, struggling to maintain his control. 'Good-bye, Ekodas. See you in hell.'

Marduk cut visual feed and stood clutching at his command podium as the barbed claws of Ekodas's mind were forced to retract. He breathed deeply as he recovered his composure, wiping a bead of blood from his nostrils.

'The *Crucius Maledictus* is coming around,' warned Sabtec. 'Correction: the entire fleet is redeploying to take up the pursuit. I think you might have displeased him, my lord.'

'Good,' said Marduk. 'We continue as planned. All power to the rearward thrusters. I don't want them overtaking us before I am ready.'

Kol Badar stood stock-still, his eyes clouded.

'What?' snapped Marduk.

'If this does not work, then you have damned us all,' said the Coryphaus.

'Wondering if you made the right decision after all?' said Marduk.

'Too late now,' said Kol Badar.

'Keep a watch on the xenos vessel,' said Marduk as he swung away. 'Inform me the moment it moves.'

'What now?' said Kol Badar.

'I want the names of every damned warrior brother that is part of the Brotherhood. Now is the time of their reckoning.'

'OUT,' SAID COADJUTOR Aquilius, hurling his spent bolt pistol aside and drawing his broad-bladed combat knife, determined to fight to the very end.

The young White Consul was bleeding from a score of wounds that even the blessed Larraman cells within his bloodstream could not seal. He knew that death was coming for him, yet still he held the Chapter banner tightly in his grasp.

Only two other battle-brothers remained alive at his side, Brother Severus Naevius and Brother Lucius Castus. Both were Sternguard veterans of 1st Company, and figures that Aquilius held in awe. Together, the trio fought back to back, facing out in all directions. The number of necrons assailing them was beyond counting, and it was only a matter of seconds before they were overwhelmed.

The darkness within the Temple of the Gloriatus was alleviated in sudden flashes as weapons discharged, sending shadows fleeing to the hidden corners of the temple. Brother Castus blasted a necron warrior to liquid with his plasma gun, before hurling the weapon aside, its core emptied.

The 1st Company veteran unsheathed a humming power sword smoothly from its scabbard at his waist.

'Ammunition one per cent,' said Naevius. His ornate bolter kicked in his hands, and after two final short bursts of fire, he too discarded the sacred weapon in favour of a revving chainsword that he clasped in both hands.

The three White Consuls stood together facing outwards as the circle of deathless robotic constructs closed in around them.

The necrons closest to the trio lowered the barrels of their weapons as they stepped forward. Green lightning flickered along their lengths, reflected across the xenos's gleaming skeletons.

'It has been an honour, brothers,' said Aquilius, lifting his head high. A dry wind rasped through the open doorway of the temple, ruffling the banner clasped tightly in his left hand.

'The honour has been ours, Coadjutor,' replied Brother Severus Naevius. 'You have done the Chapter proud.'

Aquilius stood a little taller for the praise.

Abruptly, every necron warrior halted mid-step. Aquilius tensed, eyes darting between the array of enemies before him, and his fingers flexed on the hilt of his knife, waiting for the necrons to unleash the barrage of destruction that would flay the White Consuls apart molecule by molecule.

It never came.

As one, the necrons lifted the barrels of their weapons skyward, the movement performed by every one of them simultaneously.

They turned in an abrupt about face, and commenced marching uniformly from the temple, filing out in ordered ranks.

'What is this?' said Brother Castus.

Veteran Brother Naevius shook his head in wonder. 'The Emperor protects,' he breathed.

Moving warily, unwilling yet to allow hope to lodge itself within them, the three White Consuls followed the departing necron warriors out of the grand golden doors of the temple, keeping their distance.

As they ventured out onto the mighty stairs leading to the temple's face, they could see the ordered echelons of necron warriors in the square below filing back into the black-slabbed monoliths, marching in unhurried, ordered lines. One by one, the monoliths began to fade, and Aquilius had to blink his eyes several times to make sure that he was not imagining it. But no, the monoliths *were* fading out, each in turn, until they had all disappeared, like mirages fading into nothingness. Nothing but corpses remained on the square. Even the skeletal warriors that had fallen had now faded, disappearing without a trace.

Silence descended over the city like a shroud.

Unmoving and exhausted, the trio of White Consuls stood and watched the xenos depart Sirenus Principal. Only when the immense crescent-shaped vessel hanging threateningly overhead began to lift away did it sink in to Aquilius that he had survived. His sudden euphoria was short lived as he reflected on the full horror of the war; almost five full companies of the Chapter had fallen, along with one of its hallowed Chapter Masters. It would be centuries before the Chapter recovered.

'By the blood of Guilliman,' breathed Aquilius. 'Is it over?'

'It will never be over,' said Veteran Brother Severus Naevius.

'THE XENOS VESSEL is moving,' came Sabtec's voice from the bridge. 'Accelerating fast. It will be upon us within minutes.'

'Understood,' said Marduk.

The Dark Apostle was caked in blood, and his chest was rising and falling heavily, his breath ragged. Accompanied by Kol Badar and twenty of the Anointed, he had spent the last two hours isolating each warrior that had been identified as Brotherhood. Already, he had killed over a hundred and eighty of his own brothers, and his *khantanka* blade was not yet done.

'I hope this plan of yours works,' said Kol Badar.

It had been a close-run thing, and at full burn the *Infidus Diabolus* had only barely managed to keep out of range of the Chaos fleet's weapons.

'Have faith, my Coryphaus,' said Marduk.

THE *Infidus Diabolus* speared inexorably towards the Trajan Belt, the thick ring of asteroids that divided the Boros Gate system into inner and outer worlds. Only as the mighty Chaos ship approached the detritus of the previous battle with the Imperials did it slow its progress. The carcasses of dozens of ships hung here, a veritable graveyard of devastated vessels. Slowing, the *Infidus Diabolus* slipped amongst the wreckage like a grave robber, an unwelcome intruder into the silent realm.

Immense sections of destroyed battleships and twisted hunks of scrap spun lazily in the vacuum, and as the *Infidus Diabolus* glided into the midst of the flotsam, Marduk ordered all systems, primary and secondary, to be shut down. Shimmering void shields flickered and dissolved one after another, and all internal lights, air-recycling units and weapon systems went offline. Deep within the slave pens, thousands gasped as they rose from the floor as the ship's inertial antigravity inhibiters powered down and their oxygen supply was cut.

Within minutes, the ever-present hum of the engines subsided into silence as the beating warp-drive heart of the vessel was silenced. All that was left behind was the sound of the ship's hull contracting and expanding alarmingly. Dull echoes boomed through the silent hallways of the ship as debris stuck the *Infidus Diabolus.*

'Unshielded, we'll be crushed if we are hit by anything of considerable size,' growled Kol Badar. Marduk could see the shape of the Coryphaus clearly, despite the darkness.

'Silence,' said Marduk.

And in the darkness, they waited.

'THEY SEEK TO hide from our scans,' said Dark Apostle Ankh-Heloth from the bridge of the *Anarchus.*

'It buys them a few minutes, nothing more,' replied Belagosa, from his own flagship, the *Dies Mortis.*

'Commence the bombardment,' transmitted Ekodas.

EXPLOSIONS DETONATED WITHIN the field of space wreckage as the Chaos fleet's weaponry was brought to bear, firing indiscriminately into its midst.

The *Infidus Diabolus* was jolted as a detonation nearby peppered its hull with debris.

Marduk and his captains stood upon one of the ship's assault decks, a dozen Deathclaw drop-pods waiting patiently for the order to launch.

'We won't last long in this barrage,' said Kol Badar.

'They are in position, my lord,' said Sabtec.

'Give me the device,' said Marduk.

Kol Badar produced the Nexus Arrangement and Marduk took it from him. It looked so insignificant now, just a simple silver orb. He had been through so much to attain the device and unlock its secrets...

It had surprised him that, even still, the device was holding back the warp, disallowing transference. He prayed fervently that what he had planned would work, though in truth he had no idea whether it would or not. Still, in a few minutes it would not matter either way.

'Are you sure about this?' said Kol Badar.

'It is the only way,' said Marduk, his voice tinged with bitterness. 'We must get word to Erebus about Kor Phaeron's treachery. He must learn how deep the Brotherhood runs. Nothing else matters. Not even this,' he said, holding aloft the Nexus Arrangement.

'How many brothers have we lost because of that device?' said Kol Badar. He snorted, shaking his head. 'And it comes to this?'

'There is no other way,' said Marduk. 'Gods damn it!'

Marduk looked down at the violently shaking device in his hand. His search for the Nexus and unlocking its secrets had seen him battle all manner of foe, entire worlds burn, and thousands of loyal warrior brothers perish. He had been through so much to claim the device. So much had been prophesised of the power it contained within its inscrutable form. And for what?

What was he thinking? How could he even contemplate going through with this?

The device began to vibrate in his hand, almost imperceptiibly at first, but it was getting stronger.

'The xenos approach,' hissed Marduk. 'They are calling it to them.'

'If we are going to do this, we need to do it now,' said Kol Badar.

Another explosion shook the *Infidus Diabolus*.

'We cannot take much more of this,' said Kol Badar.

Marduk came to a decision.

'Do it,' he said.

Sabtec held the vortex grenade that Marduk had claimed from magos Darioq-Grendh'al, the most potent man-portable weapon that the Imperium had ever produced. He prayed that this was going to work. Sabtec readied the device, thumbing its activation code and timer, his movements precise and careful. It began to blink with a repetitive red beacon.

'Armed!' said Sabtec.

Marduk muttered a prayer to the gods and tossed the Nexus Arrangement through the gaping, spherical aperture of one of the Deathclaw assault pods.

Sabtec lobbed the vortex grenade in behind it, and Kol Badar slammed his fist onto the launch press-switch.

The Deathclaw's hatch slid closed with a metallic screech.

'Now, we pray,' breathed Marduk.

Half a second later, the assault pod fired, shooting down the launch tube at high speed. Spiralling like a bullet, the drop-pod screamed down the fifty metres of tube before launching out into space, engines roaring.

Marduk held his breath as he watched the Death-claw blasting out away from the *Infidus Diabolus*.

Three seconds later, the vortex grenade detonated.

A sphere of absolute darkness appeared, swallowing all light as the vortex grenade created a miniature black hole three hundred metres off the starboard bow. Its hemisphere touched a twisted mess of space debris half the length of the *Infidus Diabolus*, and it was instantly consumed. Marduk shuddered to think what would have happened had the device detonated prematurely.

The Deathclaw was swallowed instantly, crumpling to the size of an atom and blinking out of existence.

The Nexus Arrangement was destroyed along with it, and with it gone, its hold over the Boros Gate was lifted.

'WE HAVE MULTIPLE contacts!' bellowed Ankh-Heloth. 'Mass transference is underway!'

'Gods above!' swore Belagosa. 'The gateways are open!'

'No!' roared Ekodas as his scanners lit up with dozens of flashing icons. Gazing out of the curved portal before him, he saw the first of the Imperial ships materialise on his starboard bow, the Astartes battle-barge emerging from the rent that had been ripped in realspace, its hull blackened and the iconography of a bared sword plastered across its prow. Its hull was bathed in warp-light and it lurched towards the *Crucius Maledictus* as its weapons powered up.

'We must fight clear! We cannot win here!' yelled Ankh-Heloth.

'No!' spat Ekodas. 'I will not flee the enemy like a coward! Target them! Take them down!'

Ignoring his order, Ekodas saw the flickering icon of the *Anarchus* begin to turn away, desperately attempting to extricate itself from the soon to erupt firestorm. Ekodas knew that it would be too slow. They were all dead.

'Nova-cannon ready to fire,' drawled a servitor hardwired into the battle control systems of the bridge.

'Target the battle-barge,' Ekodas bellowed, gesturing frantically. With painful reluctance, the *Crucius Maledictus* began to swing around, even as the first shots began to pound at her shields.

Dozens of enemy ships were making transference now, materialising all around the *Crucius Maledictus* and its beleaguered fleet. He saw a massive starship, a Darkstar fortress, emerge directly in front of his own hulking flagship.

'New target!' roared Ekodas.

Cross-hair reticules upon vid-screens blinked as they locked onto the massive battle station.

'Fire!' ordered Ekodas.

The *Crucius Maledictus* shook as her mighty nova cannon was unleashed, and the Darkstar was momentarily hidden within its blast. Then it emerged, unscathed, though more than half its shields had been stripped. He saw the *Anarchus* explode in a billowing corona, targeted by the combined fire of two newly arrived Astartes battle-barges and four Imperial battle cruisers. The battle would be over in seconds.

'Ready the cannon for another shot!' bellowed Ekodas. He did not see the silver strike cruiser blink into existence on his flank, nor see it turn and begin angling towards his vessel.

The first he knew of the Grey Knights' attack was when twenty Terminator-armoured battle-brothers of the Chamber Militant appeared on his bridge, teleporting across the empty gulf between their own vessel and the hulking Chaos flagship in the blink of an eye.

Garbed in their archaic armour and with Nemesis force weapons clutched in their gauntleted hands, the

Terminators of the Ordo Malleus obliterated everyone on the command deck in a devastating salvo.

Alone, Ekodas rose from the hail of fire.

'A curse upon your name, Marduk,' snarled Ekodas. He stepped forward to meet the Grey Knights. He did not even make it two metres before he was cut down.

MARDUK LAUGHED OUT loud as he witnessed the destruction of his brethren. The spectacle was awe-inspiring.

'The xenos?' said Kol Badar as the lights began blinking back into life upon the bridge's control dais.

'Gone,' said Sabtec, studying the vid-screens. 'They disappeared as soon as the Nexus was destroyed.'

'Power up the warp drive,' Marduk ordered, not taking his eyes off the scene of glorious destruction occurring beyond the curving view-deck. 'Set co-ordinates for Sicarus. We are going home.'

# EPILOGUE

MARDUK MARCHED BESIDE First Chaplain Erebus through the high vaulted halls of the Basilica of Torment. The sound of their footsteps echoed hollowly in the high vaulted space. Immense vertebrae-like pillars towered above them. Robed adepts skulked in the shadows, prostrating themselves as the holy duo passed them by.

'The loss of the device is disappointing,' Erebus was saying. 'But it served its purpose. The enemies of the XVII Legion have been exposed.'

'Will the Council declare war upon Kor Phaeron?' said Marduk in a low voice. Bedecked in his ancient suit of Terminator armour, he loomed over the compact figure of Erebus.

The First Chaplain's head was shaven smooth and oiled. Every inch of exposed skin was covered in intricate cuneiform.

'The Brotherhood and all who gave them succour shall burn, have no doubt of that,' said Erebus. 'But my brother shall not be touched. He has already distanced himself from the Brotherhood, severing all links that tied it back to him. He has left them to the wolves, and there shall be no reparations against him. And if I ever hear you refer to the Keeper of the Faith by name again, Marduk, I will see you flayed alive.'

The First Chaplain had not raised his voice, and spoke in a calm, matter-of-fact voice, yet Marduk paled.

'I do not understand, master,' said Marduk.

Erebus smiled.

'The Keeper of the Faith and I have known each other for a very long time,' he said. Every Word Bearer knew that Erebus and Kor Phaeron were the first and closest comrades of their lord primarch, Lorgar. 'It has always been like this between us. Our little struggles against each other mean nothing.'

Marduk walked in silence, baffled. For long minutes the pair marched through the basilica. The immense, carved bone doors of the Council chambers loomed up ahead of them.

'The death of the Black Legion sorcerer displeases me, however,' said Erebus finally, and Marduk's blood ran cold. 'It will have consequences. But no matter. What's done is done.'

'Will the Black Legion seek amends?'

Glancing sideways, he saw that Erebus was smiling. It was a mocking and sinister sight, and Marduk's unease redoubled.

'Abaddon seek amends against us? No,' said Erebus. 'But he will not be pleased. It will raise his suspicion.

We will have to be more... circumspect in the coming days.'

Marduk felt like a child, not understanding a half of what Erebus implied.

'There are some who feel that Abaddon is not worthy of bearing the title Warmaster any longer,' said Erebus. 'Some feel the time approaches for him to be... relieved of the position.'

Marduk's eyes widened in shock.

'Ekodas's death leaves a gap on the Council,' said Erebus, and Marduk looked at him in surprise. Erebus's face gave away nothing. His eyes were as cold and dead as those of a corpse. 'I want someone that I know I can trust to take his place.'

Marduk's heart was beating hard in his chest.

'I can trust you, can't I, Marduk?' said Erebus, coming to an abrupt halt and turning towards the Dark Apostle. His voice was silken with threat and promise.

'Implicitly, my lord,' said Marduk, dropping to one knee. 'My life is yours.'

'Good,' said Erebus, laying his hand upon Marduk's crown in a casual benediction. 'There is much work to be done.'

## ABOUT THE AUTHOR

After finishing university **Anthony Reynolds**
set sail from his homeland Australia and
ventured forth to foreign climes. He ended
up settling in the UK, and managed to blag
his way into Games Workshop's hallowed
Design Studio, where he worked for four
years as a games developer. He now resides
back in his hometown of Sydney,
overlooking the beach and enjoying the sun
and the surf, though he finds that to capture
the true darkness and horror of Warhammer
and Warhammer 40,000 he has taken to
writing in what could be described
as a darkened cave.

# SONS
## OF DORN

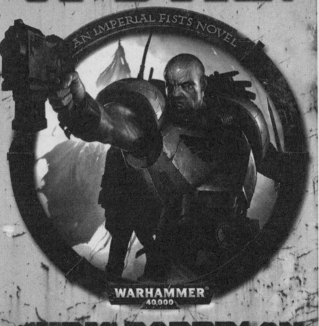

AN IMPERIAL FISTS NOVEL

**WARHAMMER**
40,000

## CHRIS ROBERSON

UK ISBN 978-1-84416-788-3   US ISBN 978-1-84416-789-0

# WARHAMMER 40,000™

# Dark Creed

*Blistering SF action set in the nightmare
future of the 41st millennium*

DARK APOSTLE MARDUK faces challenges from
within his own Legion as he wages war with the
White Consuls Space Marine Chapter.
Harnessing the power of the Nexus
Arrangement, a powerful necron device, Marduk
can turn the tide in the Word Bearers' favour. But
just as the White Consuls are on the verge of
defeat, an old enemy returns to throw the entire
dark crusade into ruin. If Marduk is to survive
and fulfil his ambition, he must defy an
onslaught from the ~~...~~ Consuls
and his own L~~...~~

In the same series

## DARK APOSTLE • DARK DISCIPLE

ISBN-13: 978-1-84416-787-6
ISBN-10: 1-84416-787-9

50799

9 781844 167876

EAN

A BLACK LIBRARY
PUBLICATION

US $7.99 CAN $9.50

SCIENCE FICTION

Printed in the US

www.blacklibrary.~~...~~

P9-CEW-074